P9-DVO-433

Dear Reader

ALSO BY MARY O'CONNELL

Living with Saints
The Sharp Time

Dear Reader

MARY O'CONNELL

FLATIRON
BOOKS
NEW YORK

DEAR READER. Copyright © 2017 by Mary O'Connell. All rights reserved.
Printed in the United States of America. For information, address Flatiron Books,
175 Fifth Avenue, New York, N.Y. 10010.

www.flatironbooks.com

Designed by Anna Gorovoy

The Library of Congress Cataloging-in-Publication Data is available upon request.

ISBN 978-1-250-07708-0 (hardcover)
ISBN 978-1-250-07710-3 (e-book)

Our books may be purchased in bulk for promotional, educational,
or business use. Please contact your local bookseller or the Macmillan Corporate
and Premium Sales Department at 1-800-221-7945, extension 5442, or by
e-mail at MacmillanSpecialMarkets@macmillan.com.

First Edition: May 2017

10 9 8 7 6 5 4 3 2 1

This is dedicated to the ones I love:
Steve, Juliana, Zach, and Veronica.

Dear Reader

One

Miss Sweeney disappeared on the first day of March, an icy Thursday morning of gloves and boots and veneers of diamondy frost on the windows of Sacred Heart High School. Her classroom was not bathed in the stark yellow glow of school-issued lightbulbs; the only light came from the windows, and it was morning-soft gray and gave the classroom a surprising bedroom coziness. When Flannery Fields walked into the room, she took the start of this Thursday as a gift. Yesterday she had been mocked for her enthusiasm about *Wuthering Heights,* but she remained eager to defend her favorite novel. Still, what could trump a free hour? Did anyone want to flip the light switch and start a new school day?

There were already a few girls sitting at their desks, playing games on their phones or listening to music or texting or spacing out entirely. Somebody greeted the dim, teacher-free room with an exuberant "Sweet!" and somebody else snickered before complete quiet descended. It was as if all the girls had taken an implicit vow of silence; they didn't want to draw the attention of a random teacher roaming the halls during her planning period. Flannery put in her earbuds but didn't turn on her music. She cocooned herself in the filtered silence and wondered when Miss Sweeney would show up.

But soon, the peaceful scene was shattered by the Calculus teacher's voice droning up through the heat vents. Flannery dug her book from her backpack, figuring she'd better study for her third hour test. But she heard a few giggling snorts from the girls who sat behind her, a friendly reminder that only a geek of Flannery's towering stature would be studying when one was basically free to do anything at all. And so Flannery gave in to the strange languor of the morning and played Boggle on her phone until it vibrated: It was Megan Swenson-Saenz texting her from the next desk. *This is awkward. Also great. Where do u think she is?*

Flannery looked out the window at the teacher's parking lot, thinking that she might see Miss Sweeney frantically getting out of her car and running into Sacred Heart High.

Maybe she's sleeping in? She texted a smiley face emoji and a series of *z*'s after that, as if Miss Sweeney were not merely sleeping in, but had morphed into a dozy, cheerful cartoon character. Most teachers arrived at school by 7:30, but occasionally Miss Sweeney raced in from the teacher's parking lot at five till eight with her green eyes looking smaller and sleepier without their usual plum liner and fringe of mascara, and her long light brown hair not flat-ironed smooth, but wavy and wet at the tips.

It didn't occur to Flannery that anything was truly wrong, her intuition felled, perhaps, by drowsy inertia. But 8:00 became 8:15, and then 8:20, and Flannery started to worry: Miss

Sweeney's behavior in class yesterday had been beyond erratic. But maybe she was just sick? Miss Sweeney had been out for a few days in February—strep throat—and had returned to the substitute teacher's stained coffee cup on her desk.

"Really?" she'd said, holding the coffee cup away from her body, her arm locked straight. She looped her finger and thumb gingerly around the handle, as if holding a tarantula by the leg. A cough drop clacked against Miss Sweeney's teeth when she sighed. "Really and truly?" The mug was painted tart apple green with black lettering: KISS ME I'M IRISH. Flannery wasn't sure if Miss Sweeney was referring to the general pig-gishness of the substitute—a pleasant old man in taped glasses and a linty black sweater vest who wanted to go off-syllabus (and off-planet) and discuss random scenes from *The Martian Chronicles*—or if her AP English teacher was offended by the corndog leprechaun sentiment.

At 8:30 Megan Swenson-Saenz pulled her headphones off and walked to the front of the classroom. She stood in front of Miss Sweeney's desk and waved her hands over her head, largely, ironically, as if she were landing planes, until everyone stared at her.

"Does anyone know where Miss Sweeney lives? Should I drive to her house?" She spoke with the officious confidence of a student council president, which she was, and had to endure exaggerated sighs from the popular girls. But Flannery could sense a growing worry, the mood in the room changing at-mospherically.

Changing atmospherically. Flannery was pretty sure that if she wrote that phrase in an essay, Miss Sweeney would circle it in red pen and write in the margin: *How does a mood change atmospherically? Does a mood coyly sprinkle a few raindrops before said mood swings and burns you with a noonday sun?*

She could be a little snarky like that; she was a detailed, precise grader. On days Miss Sweeney handed back their essays, most girls glowered and muttered until the bell rang and they were free to flip through their pages and openly complain in the hall: *"What's with her hatred of extraneous adjectives? Why does she get so bent out of shape by clichés? She probably gets her panties in such a twist because Miss Sweeney herself is a cliché— the teacher who thinks she's so special, SO different from the other teachers. And how pathetic is her obsessive love for meaning, sense, and clarity?"*

Meaning, sense, and clarity were the guiding principles upon which Miss Sweeney judged student writing. Because Flannery's first impulse was to make her sentences obliquely profound and/or jazzy, she was certainly not immune to Miss Sweeney's sharp red pen. But Flannery loved getting her essays back from Miss Sweeney. Not that her comments didn't sometimes sting; they did. But Flannery appreciated the time and effort Miss Sweeney put into grading. (Last year's Lit teacher had just crossed out a few typos or at most wrote a quick, perfunctory "nice simile" or "cool adjective" comment on her students' essays. She had four children in elementary school and drank coffee from a squat, rocket-shaped mug that said FUEL.) And Miss Sweeney had written Flannery an encouraging note on the first essay she'd turned in, back in September. *F: I hope you are not discouraged by my many suggestions. I am only trying to help you take a closer look at your writing. You are talented: observant and empathetic. I do think you could be a writer.* Flannery kept the paper buried in her socks and underwear drawer. When she was having a bad day, she would dig it out and read that last sentence over and over.

Now Megan wagged her finger at the clock. "Seriously, Miss Sweeney should *so* be here by now. If now was thirty minutes ago."

The meanest of the mean girls rang in, lightening things up: "Sweeney's probably gone *completely* Sylvia Plath on us and now we'll get stuck with another moronic sub for the rest of the year." The nervous laughter of her half dozen acolytes even sounded like the bleating of sheep: *Behh heh heh. Beh heh heh.*

Flannery didn't have time to mull over their vapid cruelty because there was the thudding of slow footfalls in the hall, not the skittering click-click of high-heeled boots that would belong to Miss Sweeney, had she been running to her classroom, her adrenaline jackrabbiting ever since that heart-stopping moment she'd opened her eyes and looked at the alarm clock. Flannery imagined Miss Sweeney jolting out of bed and screeching: *It's after eight? Students are walking into my classroom and I am still IN MY BED?*

Doom arrived, tartan-bright and petite and smelling of lily of the valley: Mrs. Piccone, the freshman English teacher. She stepped into the classroom like a polite, curious neighbor, but her smile slackened as she stood there in the soft light in her pinned kilt and red turtleneck. It had been three years since Flannery had heard Mrs. Piccone recite the Robert Burns poem "To a Mouse" but the memory remained cringingly fresh. Mrs. Piccone was from Atlanta, but her soft Southern accent had disappeared into a sudden and aggressive Scottish burr, and she'd wrung her hands and made eye contact with each girl in the class, one by one—each and every wee mousie!—as

she tortured out the lines. Normally Flannery would empa-
thize with anyone who had given an impromptu and brave—if
poorly considered—reading, but poetry lovin' Mrs. Piccone
sucked up to the smirking popular girls, which anyone could
see was futile.

Now Mrs. Piccone squinted hard at Miss Sweeney's desk, at
the pale green tissue billowing up out of a Kleenex box patterned with gold and green falling leaves. Everyone waited for
Mrs. Piccone to speak, but her eyes stayed locked on the
Kleenex box, as if she were mining for autumnal metaphor, for
symbolic meaning. But Flannery had seen the fall-themed tis-
sues in the red-stickered sale aisle at Target: Miss Sweeney's
box of Kleenex was really just a box of Kleenex.

Mrs. Piccone finally turned to the class and said: "What,
pray tell, is goin' on *in here*?"

Silence. No one wanted Miss Sweeney to get in any trouble.
Plus, nobody knew what was going on. And so Mrs. Piccone
crossed her arms over her chest and smiled triumphantly, as if
she'd just stumbled onto a secret bunker of party girls swirling around the room in sparkly disco dresses, not a class of
morning-dazed girls sitting quietly at their desks. She hustled
off to the office and returned with the principal, who walked
into the room flushed, his commanding forehead glazed with
sweat. His eyes were the eerie iced blue of martyred Scandina-
vians and he was skinny and nearly seven feet tall. To compen-
sate for his serial killer ambience, he was always aggressively
cheery.

He cleared his throat dramatically. "Morning, ladies!" The
principal flung out his lanky arms, a weird air-embrace for the
class. He occasionally appeared in local commercials for car

dealers or real estate firms, and in fact had directed the Sacred Heart fall musical, an all-girl (of course) version of *Oklahoma!* But, fearing blowback from the conservative Sacred Heart parents, he'd taken a little artistic license with the key romantic scene. Instead of kissing, Will (Emily Wolfe) and Annie (Alysa Lockheart) had exchanged exuberant smiles and the heartiest, hand-stinging high-five.

"Cold one today, right?" He fake-shivered and gave himself a little hug. "I rolled out of bed this morning and told my wife: Time to salt the sidewalks, honey."

Flannery dearly wished he hadn't used *wife* and *bed* in the same sentence, let alone a phrase overripe with euphemism. From the back of the class, some valiant girl whisper-sang: *Chick-a-bow-wow!*

The principal (who was never called Mr. Miller; he was solely referred to as the principal as he was both a *prince* and a *pal!*) ignored the not-quite-suppressed laughter and asked if Miss Sweeney had been in the classroom that morning. The head-shaking chorus of *no, no, no, no, no* made his shoulders slump. He clucked out a series of annoyed tongue sounds—*deh deh deh*—and fussed with his broadly striped necktie before he rallied with a pleasant: "So . . . you haven't seen her?"

So you haven't seen her?

The principal's verbal style certainly lacked meaning, sense, and clarity, but so did everything else that had happened that morning. He floundered on with small talk: The magazine sales fund-raiser had been a laudable success, and he was looking forward to Friday's volleyball tournament! He just loved volleyball! He loved seeing everybody having a blast on the court! Flannery blanched at his next sentence, knowing that his words would linger forever, knowing that even when she was a ninety-year-old draped in a pink afghan, clutching prayer cards and trying to discern the terrifying mystery of the afterlife, she would still remember the principal saying: "*Holy Toledo, ladies, I love to see those balls really get spiked.*"

Still, Flannery felt sorry for him, because everything he said was so stupid and so hilarious, but mostly because his gaze kept straying to the windows, as if willing Miss Sweeney to appear. But everyone was a little off their game by that point and not a single girl snickered or texted a hastily composed sonnet entitled "The Prince and the Pal of the Double Entendre: Ode to His Spiked Balls."

The bell rang, and the principal looked as startled as if he'd heard the fire alarm, and that was the end of the Awkward Fest. He took a deep breath, and as if absolutely determined to try to impose normalcy, offered up his trademark cheese-ball grin. "Move on to second hour, ladies! Orchestra and band! I want to hear some beautiful music ringing through the hallways." But a hairline fracture of annoyance cracked his buoyant voice—a teacher not showing up for school was not going to make his day any easier: "You can turn in any homework tomorrow when Miss Sweeney returns."

Flannery had zippo musical talent and took a second hour study hall, so she loitered, loading her backpack with precision. She wound her earbud cords into a neat bundle, like thin licorice, and pulled the pens and pencils from the dark cavity of her backpack and rearranged them in the outer zippered pouch. She wanted to be the last person left in the room, and when she was, Flannery took a careful look around. Everything appeared unchanged. The framed black-and-white photographs of Miss Sweeney's favorite writers lined the walls: Sylvia Plath and Langston Hughes and Emily and Charlotte Brontë and J. D. Salinger and Flannery O'Connor and Anne Frank stared down at her, along with Jesus, who convalesced on a small metal crucifix by the door. (Miss Sweeney was a big fan of the Christ figure in literature, but Flannery couldn't quite decipher how she felt about Jesus Himself: savior or mere quotable and compelling biblical character?)

From the hall came the excited speculation about her whereabouts—Sweeney had slept in!—and the chattering energy of Miss Sweeney's absence crashed onto Flannery like a wave. Even as she thought that, the critical portion of her gray brain mass simultaneously noted how Miss Sweeney would not care for the wave description. And so Miss Sweeney's imagined words scrolled through Flannery's brain in vivid red ink: *Flannery, can you think of a less pedestrian description for your sudden despair? Perhaps something non-oceanic? Okay,* Flannery? As if she were contrasting Flannery's embarrassing literary name with her embarrassingly non-lofty efforts. But the wave crashed anyway, the creamy gray-green water roared like a lion. Flannery knew that Miss Sweeney had not overslept, that she was not enjoying some midweek *carpe diem,* eating scrambled eggs and cinnamon toast with a foxy new boyfriend. Flannery knew something was really wrong, and she had the accompanying queasy feeling that it was a wrong that might not be easily fixed.

She picked up her backpack and paused, staring at the green board; she hoped for some kind of Hogwarts Magic, for Miss Sweeney's whereabouts to be written on the board by an invisible hand skilled in calligraphy, for an exact location to be spelled out in an ominous, jagged font. Flannery cut behind Miss Sweeney's desk, which felt like a social violation, traipsing through the kitchen area of a restaurant or using the upstairs bathroom of a house when the party was happening in the basement. She rested her hand on the back of Miss Sweeney's chair for a quick moment and then, as if unbidden, her hand reached to open the top desk drawer. But before she touched the metal handle, she noticed a quarter-inch strap of red leather sticking out of the bottom drawer: Flannery jerked back as if it were a swaying coral snake and then looked at the door before she casually pulled open the drawer as if in search of Scotch tape or a manila folder.

Flannery offered up an aggrieved sigh to the empty room—I am so, so BUSY—acting as if rooting through a teacher's desk was just one of a multitude of thankless, monotonous tasks she had to perform before day turned to night and she could pull on her comfiest sweatpants and watch *Downton Abbey* with a big old glass of chardonnay. In short, Flannery acted like one of the teachers. She had studied their tedious delights (along with their whimsical, flattering selfies) via their Facebook updates, until the archdiocese had ruled that students and teachers could not correspond via social networks. Flannery did not particularly miss the sad subtext of adults curating their online lives, and anyway, the one teacher she was interested in had never friended a student. At Sacred Heart High, Miss Sweeney was a stoic Beyoncé in the frothy Kardashian Sea.

Flannery took Miss Sweeney's purse out of the drawer, slung it over her own shoulder, and walked briskly into the hallway as if pursuing important errands. The loudspeaker crackled, and the principal's amplified breathing—a fine bouquet of hay fever and mucous—filled the hallway. She flinched but did not hear: *Flannery Fields, do not steal Miss Sweeney's purse.*

With the cheery cadence of a sports announcer the principal said: "Attention please. Students in Miss Sweeney's second hour English Lit class, *pleeeeeeaaase* report to the gym."

A few stragglers lingered, covertly texting by their lockers, but by the time Flannery had cut into the bathroom, there was just one other person in a stall, a lone pair of black Converses showing beneath the partition wall. Flannery took the farthest stall and stood waiting, hugging Miss Sweeney's purse to her chest. When the girl finally flushed and exited her stall, she primped at the mirror for an eternity but never bothered to wash her hands. Normally Flannery would have peered through the crack in the door to see the guilty girl; she would have made a mental note to keep an eye on her in the lunch line, as she was undoubtedly one who would bypass the tongs and plunge her fecalicious hand into the communal breadbasket. Finally there came the *sah-woosh sah-whoosh* of the bathroom door sweeping open and shut, and Flannery took a seat on the closed toilet and unzipped Miss Sweeney's purse.

The contents made her heart sink.

Of course she imagined Miss Sweeney standing on the toilet seat of the next stall, her hands gripping the partition wall, her face a perfect smirk as she looked down at Flannery. *Did your heart really sink? Are you in possession of a sunken heart? Sunken, as in treasure, or ships? Ahoy there, Matey!*

But Flannery really could feel her heart sinking through

her chest cavity. Because everything in that purse was useful. She believed there was not a single item Miss Sweeney would willingly leave behind.

An asthma inhaler.

Her keys—four of them—on a cheap, touristy Lady Liberty key ring.

Three tampons.

Stila eyeliner in morning plum.

Her cell phone.

Crest Whitestrips.

Concealer.

Her paperback edition of *Wuthering Heights*. (An older edition with a pulpy, Harlequin-looking cover. The pages were stiff and ruffled at the edges, as if it had been dropped into the bathtub.)

Her wallet, containing a ten and four ones, a library card, her driver's license, her insurance card, a blurred photo of—was it a rat with a fluffy pink *wig*? . . . and her frequent-customer punch card at Java Joe's.

Flannery ran her fingers over the fragmented paper and counted out the punches: Miss Sweeney was two espresso drinks away from a free beverage of her choice. Flannery wasted a long moment in the bathroom, oddly comforted by the smell of Clorox and the incessant swirl of the running toilet, wondering if Miss Sweeney would choose a standard latte or beat the system with a four-shot caramel Freebird, which, with tip, was usually seven dollars.

She was putting the wallet back into the purse when she thought to unzip the change compartment. It had felt flat, empty, but contained a folded-up piece of paper:

LCPL Brandon J. Marzetti-Corcoran, Kansas City, MO, was killed in action in the Helmand Province of Afghanistan on Sunday, March 11. Born in Kansas City, he graduated from Holy Angels High School in May 2005 and entered the Marines on November 19, 2005. He was devoted and loyal, to a fault, to family and friends. An accomplished athlete, Brandon was the starting quarterback for the Holy Angels 2004–2005 championship team. He was an avid sports fan, devoted to the Kansas City Chiefs and Kansas City Royals. He is survived by his loving parents, Lisa Marzetti (Liesel Charles) and Ray Corcoran; his fiancée Megan Reynolds and grandmother Helen Marzetti. He is also survived by his future in-laws, Suzanne and Phillip Reynolds, and many friends all over the world. Mass of Christian burial will be at 10:00 am Thursday morning at Saint Thomas More Catholic Church. Burial with full military honors will follow at Oak Hill Cemetery. A rosary will be said at 6:30 pm Wednesday evening and family will receive friends until 9:00. In lieu of flowers, the family suggests memorials to the Holy Angels Athletic Department in care of Holy Angels High School.

Flannery thought obituaries were always tragic, even when the person was elderly, because whether they were ascending to nothingness or Neverland, to Heaven or a fiery, multi-pitchforked Hell (fingers crossed, for many denizens of Sacred Heart!) their time on earth was over and how could you imagine or train for nonexistence? But Brandon Marzetti-Corcoran wasn't old; he was twenty-five and had died violently. He also had the symmetrical features of a Hollywood hero, which shouldn't have mattered in the least, but Flannery found herself running her finger over the photo and rereading the obituary . . . Brandon Marzetti-Corcoran's funeral was happening in an hour. No, two hours, she thought, with the time difference in the Midwest. Could Miss Sweeney have gone out of town for the funeral and not told anyone? Flannery folded up the obituary and put it back in the change compartment, realizing that Miss Sweeney's erratic classroom behavior was not mimicking the violent emotions in *Wuthering Heights*— she was not reenacting the Mood Swings of the Moors. Her grief was purely personal, nonliterary. But, oh, the eternal tenderness of the world, the random ravaged sadness! It all made Flannery want to become a bedroomed hermit keeping the world at bay with books and blankets, with YouTube and cherry Pop-Tarts, because any old day was pure *Wuthering Heights* for someone.

Flannery took Miss Sweeney's *Wuthering Heights* out of her purse and studied the cover: A generically dashing Heathcliff stood behind busty, black-haired Cathy, who wore a daffodil yellow gown tied with a scarlet sash. Her face in profile was the carved jewel of a Fifties starlet, and Heathcliff was standing behind her, holding her by the elbows. Flannery couldn't decide whether this was sadistic or merely manly, but with her eyes-and-mouth-half-open expression of ecstasy, Cathy herself seemed pretty okay with his grip. Flannery thought back to Monday morning when Miss Sweeney had introduced the book, claiming that *Wuthering Heights* got a bad rap about being a mere literary bodice-ripper, the madcap antics of Heathcliff and crazy Cathy. For the reader with an open heart and an open mind, *Wuthering Heights* was more than an entertaining read about doomed lovers roaming ravaged estates and postcard-lush moors.

"Every single thing you need to know about life can be found in the pages of this book." Miss Sweeney had raised her hands, palms up, a bossy priest bullying her congregation with a personal truth. "Depression and heartache and joy and love and loss? Integrating the dark and the light, the calm and the storm? Ladies! It's all there." But she had lost her condescending composure when she'd sighed and said: "God. It's just such a good book."

Now the door swooshed open, and Flannery quickly flushed the toilet, as if she'd needed a legitimate reason to be in the bathroom. There were three stalls, and Flannery was in the one farthest from the door. Instead of taking the other end stall, the girl who had just entered the bathroom chose the middle one, as if in some grotesque game of toilet tic-tac-toe. Vexed, Flannery started to stick Miss Sweeney's book back into her purse, but then found she couldn't quite part with it; she held it to her face and breathed in the dusty, papered sweetness of secondhand bookstores. Flannery always loved to see what was written in the margins of old books, those random penciled words that added up to a cryptic love letter to both the author and the next reader: *OH YES! Ughh creepy shades of Uncle Joe here; Just like the kitchen smell of celery + loneliness.*

The chance to read Miss Sweeney's marginalia about a book they both loved? Flannery, perched on the closed toilet, opened *Wuthering Heights.* She fanned quickly though the pages, looking for any red-inked comments in the margins. But Emily

Brontë had apparently fared better than Flannery. Miss Sweeney had circled no extraneous words, there were no mocking
exclamation points, and she had not advised *YOU MIGHT
WANT TO WATCH THE HYPERBOLE METER*, as if casually endorsing a new indie film. She turned to page one, and
she read:

Manhattan! My old Alpha and Omega!

Flannery thought just one thing, just one word: "*WHAT?*"
    She flipped back to the title page: *Caitlin Sweeney* was writ-
ten in red ink in the left-hand corner, and then in the middle
page, in flourished black typeface, was the standard "*Wuthering Heights* by Emily Brontë," nothing unusual, all was well,
and then she turned to the next page, a genealogy chart to help
the reader keep track of the names and dates of birth of the
characters in *Wuthering Heights*; okay, sure. But when Flannery turned to the first page of text, she read:

Manhattan! My old Alpha and Omega! I was in the backseat of a cab!
I was back! Back to the towering rents and the naturally beautiful and
brilliant and the strivers trying to become beautiful or brilliant, and
the hipster douchebags and the fatigued-looking women in their
Dunkin' Donuts polo shirts and always a lonesome summertime
voice calling out, *Delicioso coco helado! Delicioso coco helado!* Or
there's the winterbliss dream of ice-glazed Central Park, the buses
lumbering up Central Park West in the violet-blue hour, and of course
the seasonless surprise of seeing the shockingly miniscule Madonna
jogging with her two bodyguards, of seeing Lady Gaga nee Stefani
Germanotta at Duane Reade with her four bodyguards, and the old

men playing chess on the stoops, and the rich moms laughing into their cell phones while the nannies trail with the toddlers, and all the other celebrities and stereotypes I am neglecting! I was back! I had no purse, no ID! I was fluid! I was free!

I was not following my bliss, not even the memory of bliss, nor was I deluged with melancholy, trying to escape into the sepia-toned past. Dear Reader, I was all about the future! I was Ray Bradbury's pin-up girl! I was following the angel of my life, the one and only Brandon Marzetti-Corcoran, and when I found him, I wanted New York City to swallow us whole, to take us into its glittering and gritty manic jaws and hold us close.

Flannery was not only thinking "*WHAT*" but saying the word over and over, drawing out the vowel and sounding so gasping and questioning and, apparently, grating, that the girl in the next stall sighed with lavish aggravation. Flannery didn't blame her, because who wouldn't be annoyed to be in the bathroom with an odd girl talking to herself, a girl whose heartbeat was thundering into what felt like a sternum-cracking crescendo?

Flannery certainly knew the beginning of her favorite book by heart, and the setting was not New York City: "*I have just returned from a visit to my landlord—the solitary neighbor that I shall be troubled with. This is certainly a beautiful country! In all England, I do not believe that I could have fixed on a situation so completely removed from the stir of society. A perfect misanthropist's heaven: and Mr. Heathcliff and I are such a suitable pair to divide the desolation between us.*"

Where had *that* page gone?

She peered at the book spine to see if pages had been added;

she ran her thumb along the space where the pages met the spine and found it smooth. Flannery touched the cool beige metal of the partition wall—just for the sudden comfort of a stable, physical object—and read the good-hearted bathroom graffiti. *Peace to all who read this! Jesus loves YOU!* (Along with the less sanguine: *Maribeth K is a total whorebag.*)

She opened *Wuthering Heights* again.

As soon as I'd arrived at my classroom this morning I'd seen Brandon at the window. I put my trembling hands on my desk and watched him from my peripheral vision. *"You're back,"* I whispered to the empty room, wanting to confirm the itinerant miracle of it by saying the words aloud. Brandon had appeared at the window the previous day when class had already started, but I'd found it difficult to simultaneously process a miracle and lead a class discussion on Heathcliff's going rogue from *Wuthering Heights* as my own personal narrative arc was careening so wildly. But I had prayed for Brandon to return—throughout the night, while taking breaks to watch infomercials and seeing his face on every body selling acne wash and exercise machines—and there he was at the windows of Sacred Heart, again: my miracle man, my personal Huck Finn, coatless and wearing an I HEART NYC shirt. O, he was his sweet younger self, my way-back boy. Except for his super-short hair—sexy, sure, but I missed his foppish bangs of yesteryear—he looked just as he had looked seven years ago when we had moved to New York City together, a couple of kooky eighteen-year-olds in sweet, sweet love.

Flannery snapped the book shut and closed her eyes. She took a deep breath in, which was not particularly cleansing, and counted . . . 1, 2, 3, 4 . . . and then opened her eyes as she exhaled . . . 5, 6, 7, 8, 9. She looked at the bathroom floor, the white tile that had yellowed around the base of the toilet, hopefully from age, and reached down and touched her short, flowered combat boots, which looked and felt real, but perhaps were dream replicas of actual boots? Had the trip to T.J.Maxx where she'd bought them with her birthday money been a dream too?

But a comforting thought stemmed Flannery's existential crisis, if not her panic, because when you read in a dream the words appeared scattershot, changed. A traffic sign might say: WARNING! CARAMEL APPLES FOR THE NEXT 10 MILES, or if you opened *On the Road* while dreaming, the paragraphs might contain kitten emojis and Roman numerals, and who knew why a brain might churn out candied fruit instead of road construction, or muddled code instead of manly adventures. But it made perfect sense that Flannery's adoration of *Wuthering Heights* and her concern for Miss Sweeney had comingled into this lucid dream of a changed narration. Flannery nodded vehemently—yes! Yes! She tapped the book on her leg, warming to her dream theory, which formulated as she sat there on the closed toilet. Emily Brontë herself had considered the power and sway of dreams with a vivid curiosity that had inspired some of her best dialogue, the meme-friendly lamentations of Cathy: "I've dreamt in my life dreams that have stayed with me ever after and changed my ideas; they've gone through and through me, like wine through water, and altered the color of my mind."

That Flannery was in the midst of a dream was a bit more appealing than the other option, that she was going insane. And so she read a little more, hoping: *dream, dream, dream.*

Standing in my empty classroom seven years later (Dear Reader, cue the bad luck!) and seeing Brandon as he once was, whole and free and beautiful, filled me with a distilled nostalgia that veered into nausea; my stomach roiled and the room was a sudden sauna. It was the morning of his funeral, but I was remembering another ending, the first ending, the exalted one: the last summer night Brandon and I spent in Kansas before we moved to Manhattan.

We had driven out to the Flint Hills, to the Tallgrass Prairie National Preserve. He parked his truck by the locked Park Service gates, which were low and inviting and seemed a mere formality. We scrambled over them easily, and then it was just the bison and deer and the owls and the eagles, and Brandon, and me. Throughout our school years we had learned from many a dull speaker on Kansas History Days that the soil in the Flint Hills was never used for farming because it was laced with flint and limestone: All those miles of rocky ground had never known the sharp mouth of machinery, and so the native prairie grasses flourished. The sun-blanched bluestem glowed orange in the darkness, halving the world into dark sky and bright ground, and beneath that was the rock, the flaw that would save the prairie.

It was almost midnight, and the air was still thickly warm, weighted with Kansas humidity. Brandon and I held hands as we walked along the winding trail cut by the Park Service. We were quiet. We had talked nonstop on the drive out to the Flint Hills, an hour of marveling over the fact that we had a direct flight to NYC in the morning and we weren't merely visiting—no tourism for us, baby! How lucky I felt to have Brandon give up everything he knew to move to NYC with me, to have a person support me so fully. My journey was his journey.

Unburdened by the zest for irony and oh-so-quirky originality that

I would find in boyfriends of the future, Brandon, my one true love, my soul mate, looked at me in the passenger seat and simply said: "I love you so much. We're starting the next phase of our lives together. Columbia, Caitlin."

When the college brochures had started piling up, it was Brandon himself who had pulled Columbia from the wicker basket on my nightstand. Instead of the ubiquitous campus photography of students listening attentively in lecture halls or peering through microscopes, the Columbia brochure had featured a street scene of students walking through the gates at 116th and Broadway, and photos of the great city itself, so vast and heralded with promise that it seemed anyone could land there and succeed.

Brandon was squinting, moving his finger along the fine print: "Columbia alum Herman W-Wouk?" He struggled with dyslexia. I believe this was the first time I'd heard him read aloud.

I shrugged. "Whoever that is."

He was sitting on the edge of my twin bed, and I was on the floor, painting my toenails the color of Brandon's eyes: a dreamy aquamarine. I held my breath as he finished the sentence: "Herman Wouk said Columbia was a world of . . . doubled magic, where the best things of the moment were outside the . . . rectangle of Columbia and the best things of all history and human thought were inside the rectangle of Columbia."

"Doubled magic," I said. "Abracadabra times two." I flicked my nail polish brush like a magician's wand, and a dot of aquamarine landed on the carpet, an iridescent moon I rubbed away. "They sound a little in love with themselves at Columbia. And, please, I could *never* get into a school like that." But truthfully I knew I probably could get into a school like that: I was a National Merit Scholar from an underserved state.

"You should try to go there," he said. "You're brilliant. And it sounds *great*."

Brandon's *brilliant* was so flattering, his *great* so winsome, that his words made me feel, not for the first time, that I couldn't live without him.

"And people move to New York City for all sorts of reasons," Brandon said quietly. He ran his hand through his lion-colored hair. "Not just for college."

I joined him on my twin bed—quietly, as my parents were in the kitchen cooking dinner—trashed my pedicure, and we made a plan. More importantly, Dear Reader, we executed that plan. I was going to go to Columbia and live in the dorm, and Brandon was moving to NYC too, where he would find a cool apartment and a job. And now it was all coming true. The day had finally come.

But not quite yet; we were still in the heart of the Kansas night. Brandon led me off the trail, and with the bluestem scraping at our calves, we walked deeper into the prairie. We might have been the only souls on earth that night—it did feel like that—except for the migrant cicada chorus singing us their buzzy migraine of a love song and the occasional truck rumbling down the two-lane highway in the distance.

We made an impromptu bed out of a flat plane of limestone rising out of the soil. Fear not, Dear Reader, I am not about to go all Harlequin on you. I will move onto the safe terrain of "afterward" when we were naked (sorry!) on our backs on the cool rock, watching a fast bloom of storm clouds move through the endless lava lamp sky: bruised purple melting into navy blue, then charcoal. The sky, the swirling sky. The parched rattle of the prairie grass. The lonely birdsong of an Eastern Phoebe: *Fee-bee. Fee-bee.* The spent, ragged breath of someone who loves you.

Flannery startled at the sound of gagging and splashing. And then came the familiar odor. In dreams, she knew, one could not smell. She pressed Miss Sweeney's copy of *Wuthering Heights* to her chest and hissed: "Oh my *God*."

"*Sorry,*" the girl in the next stall gasped out.

"Oh, no. It's not you." Flannery turned the book over and held it close to her face, squinting as if she were a Quik Shop clerk checking the authenticity of a fifty-dollar bill. To double-check her fading dream theory, Flannery gave the soft ridge of fat bordering her thumbnail a vicious little pinch. It hurt. In dreams, one did not feel physical pain. *That leaves crazy,* she thought. *That leaves exceedingly super-crazy.*

She heard another splash and looked over and saw that the girl's chestnut brown boots were pointed toward the toilet so that the UGG tags faced the front. All the beautiful Sacred Heart girls had long moved on from the ubiquitous Uggs that middle-aged women wore to the grocery store, so aside from the rosary of potential torments beading though Flannery's mind—*extreme anxiety, the flu, bulimia, pregnancy, extreme anxiety, the flu, bulimia, pregnancy*—the girl was barfing in mom boots.

Flannery church-whispered: "Are you okay?" Her trembling hands made the pages of *Wuthering Heights* quiver as she re-read the sentence: "The spent, ragged breath of someone who loves you."

"I have food poisoning," the girl said, her voice high and hoarse.

"Oh, I'm so sorry." Whenever someone vomited on the school grounds, the janitor covered the puddle with colorful, absorbent rock poured from a fifty-pound bag, so as Flannery sat on the closed toilet reading, her mind's eye envisioned not only the deep colors of Miss Sweeney's Kansas prairie reverie but also the chemical pastels of aquarium gravel: blue and yellow, lavender and green. Flannery tried not to breathe through her nose as she attempted to both puzzle out how the beginning narrative of *Wuthering Heights*—Mr. Lockwood meeting the adult, embittered Heathcliff—had been seemingly replaced by Miss Sweeney's first-person account, and to comfort the girl in the next stall.

"Um. Do you want me to call someone?"

"God! *Seriously?*" Flannery marveled at how quickly the girl's vulnerable sick-voice reverted to snark: "Just leave me alone, obviously."

"Sorry!" Of course—what was she thinking?—of course she should give the girl her privacy. Flannery stood and unlocked the stall door; she grabbed up her backpack and Miss Sweeney's purse, but kept the copy of *Wuthering Heights* splayed open, her thumb and pinkie stretched wide. She walked to the sink, turned on the tap, and looked down at the page.

Dear Reader,

Flannery paused, pressing her finger to the typeface. Addressing the reader belonged to the world of *Jane Eyre* (Charlotte Brontë taking an epistolary pause to remind the Dear Reader, the Gentle Reader: I'm talking to *you*). Emily Brontë hadn't used this coaxing convention in *Wuthering Heights,* and she wondered why Miss Sweeney was, apparently, using it to tell her tale now. She flipped the book over and looked at the cover—as if the lushly illustrated Cathy and Heathcliff could answer that question—before she started reading again:

So there I was at the Tallgrass Prairie National Preserve—the Kansas sky evidence of God's Glory, his gorgeous nighttime aesthetic—having a religious experience in reverse. My hand was on Brandon's heart; his hand was on my rib cage. I stared up at the sky with zero curiosity about the Kingdom of Heaven because the physical world was plenty. Brandon and I would love each other while we were on earth, and when we returned to stardust, another girl and boy would take our place—that was the deal. I had never felt more connected to the earth, to all of the people who had ever walked the Flint Hills. I believed in the innate goodness of everyone: even the piggish family who had visited that very day, as evidenced by a Capri Sun wrapper glinting in the prairie grass, and the starving pioneers who longed for home, and the Pawnee, who would have original sin forced upon them by priests and preachers in love with a book whose varied inter-pretations would cause so much cruelty. But even those warriors for Christ must have felt so confused when they raised their eyes to the prairie heavens, because how could a person ever really believe in anything but the big sky, in anything but love?

When the sky opened up, Brandon pulled me closer, his hands moving down the length of my back, and said *Caitlin*, as if he were naming the rain itself, the Word made flesh.

Yes, Dear Reader, back in the day I had no use for religion yet I was—conveniently!—my very own Christ figure! Alas, I was certainly no longer the Word made flesh, or if I were, the Word would be *RE-GRET. Wuthering Heights* ribboned through my thoughts, Cathy mourning the moors, and Heathcliff: *I wish I were a girl again, half-savage and hardy, and free . . . why am I so changed?*

O, sing it, sister.

I did not especially want to be a clinically depressed twenty-five-year-old schoolteacher. I wanted to be that love-dazed eighteen-year-old at the Tallgrass preserve and afterward, on the dark drive home, watching raindrops quivering on the windshield before the *whisk whisk* of the wipers, rubbing my kiss-chapped lips and listening to Neil Young sing "After the Gold Rush": *Well, I dreamed I saw the silver spaceships flying in the yellow haze of the sun.* Oh, and now I wanted to erase my mistakes, to escape from the harsh world of the living and the unknowable world of the dead and join Brandon in that silver spaceship.

When Brandon put his palm on my classroom window, I walked away from my desk and put my hand to his. In my peripheral vision he closed his eyes, as if in bliss or merely relieved. I had closed out Brandon before and I would not do so again; I would not let Brandon stay on the other side of the glass. And so I walked out of my classroom. I walked right out of my life. By the time I was outside Sacred Heart High and taking a quick lap around the perimeter of the building, Brandon had disappeared, but I knew where to find him: in the city where you could get lost, where you could drop the mask. Say goodbye to the vibrant young teacher from that wonderful Catholic girls school in suburban Connecticut! While I searched for Brandon I could blend in with all the other lost souls, my people. Because though I fancied myself as a kind of postmodern prairie girl, I hearted NYC, too.

And so I became a deluded pioneer on Metro North at 8:17 without my iPhone or lip gloss. I was *so* saintly in my lack of possessions! My purse was in my desk drawer at Sacred Heart High, my hands were empty. I could not be weighed down by the minutia of my regular life. Pilgrimage ahoy! No keys or ID for me! Without my ties to my old life, I imagined I was freer to find Brandon, to meet him on his own terms. I'd stopped for gas on my way to Sacred Heart that morning and had left my credit card in my coat pocket—Providence!—so I was able to buy my train ticket and a coffee.

How wonderful it was to be without my phone, to be unreachable, and if Sacred Heart tried to track me down via my emergency contacts, it would be impossible: My emergency contacts were, sadly, my parents. They were at a yoga retreat in Wisconsin while their kitchen was being remodeled, a journey of comingled hopes: curing middle-age malaise and the unfettered installation of quartz countertops and a Wolf gas range. Namaste!

As I stepped off the train at Grand Central Station—It was Grand! And Central!—I kept my gaze straight; I didn't gaze up at the ornate ceilings or whip my head around, touristy and indiscreet. I searched for him, discerning all the rushing people and images in my peripheral vision—*not him, not him, not him, not him.* Despite all that had happened between us, his boyish voice of optimism was still in my heart: *Columbia, Caitlin!* I decided to splurge on a cab and go uptown to Columbia, in search of doubled magic.

"Look who can't get enough *Wuthering Heights!*" Flannery looked up to see Jordan King giving her a big Disneyland smile as she walked into the bathroom, holding the door open for— great—Callie Martin. They were her past tormenters, though this year they hadn't been quite as evil; perhaps they were discovering empathy or at least they were giving their raging stupidity a break. Still, Flannery would normally be horrified at a chance encounter with the bitchiest girls at Sacred Heart, but just now they seemed a respite—life resuming its familiar natural pattern—from what she had just read in Miss Sweeney's copy of *Wuthering Heights.*

"Hey," Flannery said. She turned off the water and protectively

tucked Miss Sweeney's book under her arm, and, never wanting to invite torment, picked up her backpack and Miss Sweeney's purse and headed for the door.

Jordan elbowed Callie: "Hey, look who has Sweeney's
purse."

Flannery looked down at her shoulder and grimaced at
the purse strap as if it were a leathery red growth, a cancerous
lash she had just now discovered. "Oh, yeah, this is her purse.
I found it in the hall, so . . . I'm going to go turn it in to the
office."

"You do your thing, Nancy Drew," Callie said, accompanying her laugh with an air horn blast, short and harsh.
Flannery pressed the book closer to her body. She almost
felt sorry for her, for all stupid Callie didn't know about
Miss Sweeney, about the malleable parameters of the known
world.

"God, it smells *terrible* in here," Jordan said.

Callie glanced over at the stalls. She pointed at the backward-
facing Uggs and made a gagging motion, her index finger
pointing to her open mouth.

"I don't smell anything," Flannery said, feeling great com-
passion for the barfing girl, for she considered herself a sort of
millennial, suburban Dalai Lama, not only wise and calm in
the face of her own detractors, but also leading the Sacred
Heart girls by example. So she immediately regretted her next
cowardly, caving sentences: "But my sense of smell isn't all that
great. I have asthma. And pretty bad allergies."

Callie nodded. "Of *course* you do. But, hey! I'm having a
party on Saturday, and I'd love it if you could come."

Getting in early decision to Columbia had been a game-changer for Flannery, and though the girls still made fun of her—she knew Callie's invitation wasn't sincere—they no longer took such sport in mocking her. At her last teacher-student conference Miss Sweeney had told Flannery that once she was away from Sacred Heart, the world would crack wide open. Flannery had thought of cracked-open geodes, jagged and ugly on the outside, glowing and colorful on the inside. Like a decayed tooth in reverse, you had to drill through the dull gray granite of your days to reach the inside, the new world, which might be creamy opalescent blue, royal purple, garnet, or emerald, and threaded with gold. In Flannery's mind came Miss Sweeney's red pen: *This dental simile seems a bit slobbery . . . consider your co-pay before further treatment.* But in real life, Miss Sweeney had been kind: "The trick is just to hold on until you make it to Manhattan, to Columbia. Once you get there, you'll find your people."

And now it was Miss Sweeney who was going to find her people, her *person,* Brandon Marzetti-Corcoran, if what Flannery had just read was true. But how could it be? Flannery tried to think of what to say to Callie—the invitation was surely encoded with a mean joke—but her brain was in pure fun-house mode: all undulating words and images and facts and fonts.

Callie flipped her hair. "It's just super-casual, my parents are out of town, so . . . you can bring a date if you want, Flannery."

"I'll think about it," Flannery said lightly.

Jordan gave a hearty nod and smiled, the bitchy curve of it showing a quarter-inch of carnation-pink gums. "Thinking is *good.*"

Flannery muttered *Um* and *Oh* and thus created a new

word that braided dread, knowledge, and fear of the up-close future: It was *Ummoh* time to be sure. She ran her hand through her hair, as if breezy, confident, and the book slipped from under her arm.

"Smooth," Callie said.

Jordan promptly gave her a suck-up affirmation: "Right? *Soooo* smooth."

Flannery picked up *Wuthering Heights,* unzipped her backpack, and quickly sandwiched it between her bulky Econ book and pencil bag, but Callie had already noticed the distinctive, romantic cover of Miss Sweeney's vintage edition. "Stalker alert," she stage-whispered to Jordan. "Flannery has Miss Sweeney's purse *and* her book."

"I do," Flannery agreed.

Flannery hadn't needed to explain anything to Miss Sweeney about her experience at Sacred Heart. And in this way Miss Sweeney was so different from the other teachers, not just the ones that blatantly sucked up to the rich, popular girls, but from the teachers who didn't care enough to notice. Once, after class when Flannery was feeling particularly run-down, Miss Sweeney had looked her in the eye with great solemnity and said, "Flannery, Jesus himself said it best: The mean girls you will always have with you, but you will not always have me."

Flannery had laughed, delighted with Miss Sweeney's quick revision of the New American Standard Bible. "I thought it was the poor that we will always have with us."

"No, Flannery. That kind of error, so endemic to biblical translations, clouds our vision of the true heart of Jesus, who wanted us to know that the mean girls would be a never-ending problem for humanity, a feminist conundrum, which, though documented in popular films and literature, would never be truly untangled."

"It's really hard to be a feminist if you go to a girl's school," Flannery had replied.

Miss Sweeney nodded. "Or if you live in the world."

"I don't mean, like, that I don't believe in equal pay or anything crazy like that."

"Flannery! I know exactly what you mean."

Now Callie and Jordan were practically blocking the door, but Flannery scooched past them, her body turned to the side. She reached for the steel door handle, which would be so smooth and reassuring, nirvana on the palm. She thought of Miss Sweeney on the streets of New York City, mourning and grief-dazzled on her pilgrimage to reunite with a dead boyfriend. But Flannery also felt a sting of shameful jealousy: Miss Sweeney was free of Sacred Heart for the day.

Callie's smile was neutral, polite. But Flannery could see her eyes shining with predatory excitement as she raised her brows at Jordan, conveying the ancient code: *Here it is, here is how one becomes the Alpha Doggett: Listen, dear underling, and you shall learn my evil and triumphant ways.*

And then Callie pounced. "Flannery? I'm dying for you to come to my party. And maybe you could bring Heathcliff as your date?"

Secreted away in her stall, the barfing girl laughed.

Flannery looked through the square of glass in the door of the school office. A police officer was already there, forming a somber semicircle with the principal, the school secretary, and the ever-creepy guidance counselor, Mrs. Howell, who grinned when she saw Flannery's face at the glass, but also flapped her hand, trying to shoo, shoo, shoo her away. But Flannery fixed her face in a mask of triumphant innocence—as if she hadn't just rifled through Miss Sweeney's purse and discovered her transformed copy of *Wuthering Heights*, now safely zipped in Flannery's own backpack—and opened the door.

"Excuse me," she said. "I found Miss Sweeney's purse. It was behind her desk." She used an officious tone and then inflated it further as she overexplained with a hearty: "It was just there, just *right* behind her desk."

Behind, inside . . . for Flannery, this was not a time to be picky about prepositions.

The police officer, who looked about her dad's age, offered up his polite, crestfallen thanks. "Much appreciated. That will help us immensely." Flannery's own father was in Florida with her mother, not at the beach or wandering awkwardly through amusement parks, the childfree couple at Disney World. No, they were at a conference on Irish Literature. And they weren't professors; this was something they did for *fun*.

She handed the officer Miss Sweeney's purse, and he held it at an awkward angle away from his body. Flannery's hands were still trembling, and when she balled them up at her sides, he gave her a kind smile. The lipstick-red leather of Miss Sweeney's bag really made his navy blue uniform pop, but he looked so melancholy standing there holding Miss Sweeney's bag, as if he knew that wherever she was at that moment, she probably needed her purse. Flannery wanted to whisper to him, and only to him: *Miss Sweeney's in Manhattan. Her old Alpha and Omega.*

"Better hustle to class, Flannery," the principal said. He gave her a hearty, crinkly-eyed smile, as if he found her dear or amusing, before he stole a quick glance at the clock. "Miss Sweeney probably just had to leave for an appointment and forgot to get a substitute. So no worries, Flannery! Don't you fret about Miss Sweeney's whereabouts. Joe saw her this morning when he was out shoveling the walkway. She parked her car and walked into school, same as always, and according to Joe, Miss Sweeney seemed just fine."

The counselor grimaced, perhaps only worried about the principal blabbing details to a student. And the police officer shot him a look, but to Flannery, the officer's disapproval seemed a bit more nuanced. Joe was the custodian and the only adult at Sacred Heart that students addressed by his first name, and Miss Sweeney was the only adult to ever correct them: "Hey, girls, I have a *really* super idea! Let's not call the janitor by his first name, okey-dokey? You should all at least pretend that you think people are equal, and thus, equally deserving of your respect. Say it with me, now: Mr. Ferguson. Mr. Ferguson!" She had started off mocking the Sacred Heart girls, using the singsong cadence of a sweet kindergarten teacher, but in her disgust Miss Sweeney had resumed her regular voice: "Oh my God, it's such stereotypical Catholic elitism—what is this, Galway, 1957?—that it makes me laugh. Almost."

As Flannery turned to leave, perhaps too slowly, she received a jolting shriek of encouragement from Mrs. Howell: "March!" She broke into an ironic march as she said the word, her knees high and arms swinging, and she hooked her thumb toward the office door before she let loose with some high-pitched, hysterical laughter and said, "Keep on truckin', Flannery!" To make everything that much worse, she had on a burnt-orange turtleneck underneath a sweater vest patterned with tabby cats.

Flannery did not march down the hall to her second hour study hall; she walked out of Sacred Heart High without her coat and looked up at the meaningless gray clouds, expecting . . . what?

She hoisted her backpack over both shoulders and took a little walk, feeling like she could run for miles and miles, and wondered why no one had created a fruit-flavored energy drink based on turmoil, anxiety, and excitement. She had no fear of being caught, as no one would think a thing of it if Little Miss 4.00 GPA Flannery Fields were not in study hall.

Well, she had never skipped class before, and doubted that she would ever skip it again. But Miss Sweeney's copy of *Wuthering Heights* stowed in her backpack changed the rules for the day, even though she was terrified to open it again and find that the pages had reverted back to their original text, her reading a mere bathroom dreamscape. Flannery was also terrified that it was somehow true, that Miss Sweeney's dead boyfriend was ghosting around the Sacred Heart campus, and that Miss Sweeney was unraveling.

Shivering, Flannery gingerly stepped over the slick spots and marveled at the litter—the clogged earth mosaic of Starbucks cups and Luna wrappers and cigarette butts, and a lipstick palette that must have dropped out of a purse and flipped open: The palette now bled a slushy stream of rose and fig and pink. Yes, Miss Sweeney was there with her, saying: *Flannery, the lipsticks are bleeding? Are they in a sort of cosmetic critical condition? A Lancôme coma?*

She walked through the rows of cars, the occasional beat-up Escort among the Mercedes, the BMWs, and all the shimmering SUVs, until she arrived at the mouth of the long, winding lane that would lead her off the Sacred Heart campus. In the distance was the roar of the highway, which could have been anything at all, lions or typhoons or machete-twirling pirates crooning: *Come here, my pretty, I have some lovely candies for you.*

But Flannery had the unwelcome premonition—butterflies in her stomach, circling her sunken heart—that the danger was entirely real, and not for her, but for Miss Sweeney. Yesterday she had seemed pretty animated during class, though contrasted with the dullardly instructional style of the other teachers at Sacred Heart, Miss Sweeney's literary flamboyance was a delight. But, no, yesterday *was* really different: Flannery recalled Miss Sweeney chewing her lower lip during class, not pensively, but with alarming enthusiasm. Was her behavior a manifestation of grief, or was she already seguing into something worse? When Miss Sweeney started crying during class, well, sure, it was shocking—later, the words *freak show* floated down the hallway along with the faux-adult complaints: *"God, she's so unprofessional . . ." "Somebody missed their therapy appointment this week"*—but the blood rosettes staining Miss Sweeney's chewed lips looked far more jarring than her tears. And of course Flannery thought of *Wuthering Heights*, of Edgar Linton finding Cathy in a frenzy after he issued an ultimatum about giving up Heathcliff: *"She stretched herself out stiff, and turned up her eyes, while her cheeks, at once blanched and livid, assumed the aspect of death . . . 'She has blood on her lips' he said, shuddering."*

Still, Flannery adored the day's assignment, a short essay about where Heathcliff might have gone when he dropped out of the narrative of *Wuthering Heights,* brokenhearted and furious that his beloved Cathy had decided to marry her rich neighbor, the iconic milquetoast blonde guy, Edgar Linton. Flannery's essay, spell- and grammar-checked to perfection, was sheathed in a manila folder in her backpack, and Flannery was already daydreaming of her modest gaze and slight shrug—Oh, it's nothing, nothing at all, really—as she handed it to Miss Sweeney, of Miss Sweeney reading and rereading and chuckling in droll admiration at the lyrical sentences Flannery had crafted with no help from a mystical wood sprite muse or a perky helicopter mom cooking up adverbs. Flannery's only tools were Frappuccinos and M&M's. She imagined Miss Sweeney giving an impromptu reading of her Heathcliff essay in the teacher's lounge, before push-pinning her paper to the corkboard above the hot chocolate packets and coffee machine and offering a pro tip to her fellow educators. "Peruse it at your leisure, people. You might learn a little something. This kind of work is the reason Flannery Fields got into Columbia."

Flannery walked faster, faster still, accelerating to the optimistic mall walk of a senior citizen before she broke out in a full-on run, her backpack pounding her back as she considered the likelihood of her teacher's lounge dream-sequence. Probably Flannery's sentences would receive Miss Sweeney's standard cutting comments flourished with mocking question marks, which were especially mortifying in triplicate: *Is*

Heathcliff really a "sardonic shepherd" trying to herd Cathy's eternal love??? Even her ellipses were terrifying: *Flannery you might want to reconsider this entire paragraph . . .*

Still, always there was the brightness of *I think you could be a writer.* And she had Miss Sweeney to thank for getting her into Columbia, her alma mater; she had written a beautiful recommendation letter for Flannery. The day her acceptance letter had arrived, Flannery had sat at her desk, her index finger on the track pad of her computer, already crestfallen. She knew what she would read when she opened the Columbia University e-mail: *We sincerely thank you for your application, and regret to inform you that you are a loser who will not be invited to attend our esteemed institution. Alas!* But when she had clicked on the e-mail that glorious random Saturday, Flannery had discovered she had no gift for prophecy.

She kept her thoughts trained on the future, but in her head was the depressing sound of the present: *"Flannery, maybe you could bring Heathcliff as your date?"* And so a mean girl's voice kept her moving when she reached the end of Sacred Heart Lane and made her way, breathless, down the sloped embankment next to the highway. Flannery walked sideways on the slippery earth, descending in careful goat steps. She thought about how happy Miss Sweeney had been when she'd been accepted to Columbia, and how she'd said that Flannery would love going to school in Manhattan, which was the best city in the world to get lost in. It had seemed fairly weird at the time— had she mistaken Flannery for someone so definitely *found*? And yesterday's proclamation, straight from Miss Sweeney's blood-bitten lips: *I would go to New York City and I would never, ever come back.*

And today's words: *Manhattan! My old Alpha and Omega!*

Flannery thought of the obituary in Miss Sweeney's purse: the good-looking Marine, Brandon Marzetti-Corcoran, his sonorous, hyphenated last name elevating his first name, his ghost-self at the window staring in at his Caitlin, at Flannery's Miss Sweeney.

She stood next to the highway and took a quick look back at Sacred Heart.

I'll do it. I will find you. And I'll help you.

She would repay Miss Sweeney for the incredible gift of giving Flannery a future to think about beyond the world of Sacred Heart High, a future wherein she would find her people. And so, bravely, foolishly, and with the laughter of the barfing girl ringing in her mind, Flannery made her way across six lanes of highway traffic, cautious as a drunken squirrel darting back twice—Holy crap, that eighteen-wheeler is *flying!*—no, three times before racing victoriously to the other side, keeping her head down as she crunched along in the frosty gravel, lest a passing car mistake her for a hitchhiker on the exit ramp.

Maybe she was just stoned on the sudden adventure of finding herself on the other side of the highway, the world of quotidian miracles: a Metro North ticket to NYC and a cruller and a large white coffee from Dunkin' Donuts, purchased with the crisp twenties her parents had given her before they went on vacation. Because Flannery wasn't puzzling out why she had decided to ditch school to look for Miss Sweeney in Manhattan, she was wondering why she'd never before given in to the unfurling magic of any old weekday, all the truant adventures that had passed her by while she learned how to detect hyperbole and dissect a fetal pig and try, try, try, to hover beneath the radar of the popular girls. If AP English via Miss Sweeney had taught Flannery anything, it was that life was brimming with various traumas and tragedies—the great novels didn't lie—and that there was no need to court sorrow by writing Goth poetry in a black spiral notebook or listening to death-rock because sorrow was always, always looming, sorrow would be thrust upon you, and, as the foot-stomping song from the junior year musical went—everyone was a girl who couldn't say no, everyone was in a terrible fix.

But sorrow's wacky twin was on the Metro North train from Nowheresville, Connecticut, to Manhattan: Euphoria rode along with Flannery, even as she worried about Miss Sweeney, even as Flannery texted her friends (*Went home. CRAMPS. Awesome.*) and her parents in Florida (*Got sick of school, went home. Oops, AT not OF*). And even if she was the kind of girl to skip class, the teachers at Sacred Heart would be too busy concentrating on Miss Sweeney's absence to worry about an errant girl, and no one and nobody knew that Flannery was lighting out for the territory. How she knew the hard-core thrill of carpe diem, as she sipped her coffee and looked out the window, the ice-glazed world spilling past. Miss Sweeney's copy of *Wuthering Heights* stayed safely zipped in her backpack—she didn't have the courage to open it again, not quite yet, but the original text was there in her mind as she rode to Manhattan, Emily Brontë's winter words: *"One could hardly imagine that there had been three weeks of summer: the primroses and crocuses were hidden under wintry drifts; the larks were silent, the young leaves of the early trees smitten and blackened."* Flannery looked out at the smitten trees of

Connecticut, their branch ends like bony bark hands poking out of their snow shroud to wave good-bye.

Miss Sweeney's red ink wrote the next thought in Flannery's mind: *Maybe reconsider your waving winter trees? Seems a bit too "Farewell from Ye Olde Cold Hickory Tree" or "Au Revoir, Exclaimed the Weeping Cherry," if you see what I mean.*

The Day Before

The universe was offering up a miracle.

If I stared right at Brandon, if I turned my face even an inch to look more directly out the window, he would vanish. This knowledge was purely instinctual: I needed only to relax my peripheral vision in order to take in a gauzy view of him out in the snowy parking lot of Sacred Heart High School. His arms hung relaxed at his sides. He wore no coat over his fatigues but didn't seem to feel the cold. I tried to be calm: I couldn't feast on the vision of him, couldn't let my rods and cones fire away—It's Brandon! O, Brandon!—or he would leave me again.

But I had to remain steady while I stood in front of my classroom of AP English students. I endured severe feast-or-famine corporeal problems: Sweat drenched my hairline and slicked my palms, but my mouth had dried to turtle shell. I had to bite my bottom lip to keep it from trembling, which I hoped would make me appear intensely, lip-quakingly interested in the comments of the girl geniuses who were shredding *Wuthering Heights*. Heathcliff, especially, was the victim of their reductive wrath.

"So Heathcliff is supposed to be this great romantic male character, but, come on, he's just a bitter, obsessive freak and the whole
my love burns eternal theme of the book is just so massively lame."
This dour critique was juxtaposed with a smile that gleamed chemically bright, radiant; the Sacred Heart girls overbleached their
teeth.

The second most popular girl in the senior class rang in after the
top dog: "Right? He needs to get over Cathy and get a prescription
for Zoloft. You can't be a Byronic hero *24-7.*"

I tasted blood. I was biting my lip too hard. In my peripheral
window-vision, snow fell, soft and silver-white, and Brandon raised
his face to it. I silently mouthed his name, my tongue striking the roof
of my mouth at the *d* sound, the melancholy of the second syllable.
Bran-*duhn*. It was the most beautiful name in any language, and the
loneliest. He had folded his hands into the prayer position over his
heart as if at yoga or mass. They were large-knuckled, and I remembered the chapped coolness of them on my back, in summer. Brandon.

Meanwhile, haters kept hating:

"And when Heathcliff drops out of the novel, *of course* he returns
and has oh so *conveniently* made his fortune, and the reader never
finds out where he went, nor do we care. We only know that with
Heathcliff back in the house, more misogynistic romance may be on
deck. O, joy."

Typical Sacred Heart girls! They equated snark and mockery with
intelligence; they thought to really love a novel was pure weakness,
foolishness perhaps. Except for my favorite brainiac, Flannery Fields:
A stripe of muscle in her jawline twitched, and she repeatedly tucked
her bobbed, dark hair behind her ear, as if this gesture might ready
her for class combat. I recalled her August excitement when she saw
Wuthering Heights on the syllabus. It was her favorite novel. My
young soul mate!

Like Flannery, I was growing increasingly vexed by the girls' trashing of Emily Brontë's genius, so I was delighted to hear her lone voice of dissent. Flannery defended Heathcliff with supreme nerd-girl righteousness: "But the reader does care! Heathcliff's disappearance is not some gigantic authorial misstep on the part of Emily Brontë. She's inviting us to use our imagination, to be part of the narrative. She's breaking open the story for us."

I blinked purposefully, trying to relax my eye muscles so that my peripheral vision would expand: I longed for the sharp, shaded vision of a bubble-eyed squirrel, for the sudden gift of super-powered side eyes. Of course I knew I couldn't achieve a truly enhanced corneal performance via my simple eye exercises. But it seemed that I possessed sharpened optical clarity as I watched Brandon cut across the student parking lot. He lost his footing on an icy patch but quickly steadied himself, one hand on a blue Toyota to his left, one hand on a white SUV to his right. I flinched when he slipped, but kept my eyes trained on my class—the straight-up dullardly world of uniformed girls wearing white Polo shirts and the knee-length Black Watch plaid skirts that made it seem like bagpipes should be playing in the foggy distance. Cue the crumbling country estates! Ah, the heather, mist, and moors!

Flannery kept on talking; Flannery was on fire. "And *Wuthering Heights* is *not* some rabid, retro romance. It's a feminist love story, since Heathcliff and Cathy are equals in their obsessiveness. And when he leaves, he's not just running off to forget about Cathy and make his stereotypical fortune. He wants to get *lost*; he wants to change, and he does." Flannery held up one finger, imploring us to wait, wait, while she flipped through the pages. When she found the page she wanted, Flannery gently fist-bumped the air—yes!—and then read aloud: "*Now, fully revealed by the fire and candlelight, I was amazed, more than ever, to behold the transformation of Heathcliff. He had grown a tall, athletic, well-formed man; beside whom my master seemed quite slender and youth-like . . . His countenance was much older in expression and decision of feature than Mr. Linton's; it looked intelligent, and retained no marks of former degradation.*"

Flannery flipped her book shut, but she kept one thumb inside, marking the page. "In the three years he was away from Wuthering Heights, Heathcliff transformed himself. He wanted to escape from his physical self, to change his entire narrative, and he *did*."

The two requisite awful girls sitting behind Flannery Fields cracked up, their shoulders bobbing with silent laughter. Not being super-pretty or super-smart, they were going with super-mean, and these BFFs were owning it. They were strivers and suck-ups, with long, flat-ironed curtains of hair highlighted in expensive earth tones—oak, walnut, sunshine—and their families donated the big bucks to Sacred Heart High School. But unlike most of the teachers, I didn't favor these types. I was all in for the geeks; I hearted the downtrodden. Granted, Flannery was way over the top: *Rabid retro romance* was some awfully audacious alliteration and *To Escape from His Physical Self* sounded like a Very Special *Lifetime* movie. But I had the power to penalize nastiness, and I would. My thoughts formed in ye olde 5-7-5 syllabic form.

Giggle on, mean ones.

Guess who has just lost their A's?

Mom and Dad will weep!

Dear Reader, I present this craptacular haiku—Fear not! There will be only one—as evidence of my straying, jangled thoughts. Because I could see the briefest snowflakes in Brandon's hair before his body heat turned them to water and my brain turned giddy, biblical, and out floated the word *transubstantiation*. He was the loaves and the fishes, the water and wine; he was a Marine who had shaved his head, but now his hair was just growing back, maybe an eighth of an inch, and I wondered how the velvet prickles would feel on my lips. He held his palm out, the sweetest beckoning, and with one slow curl of his hand—*O, come back to me*—I felt my stomach hollow and drop as the harsh yellow fluorescence of the room turned golden, incandescent. Brandon was not any kind of Christ figure, not really, but he had certainly gone full-on archangel.

I cleared my cottonmouth throat. Swallowing was like gurgling sand, a Saharan Listerine of broken glass. Though Flannery was racing ahead to Heathcliff's return, I stuck to my original lesson plan. "When Heathcliff is brokenhearted over Cathy, when he drops out of the narrative of *Wuthering Heights,* where do you think he goes?"

Flannery flipped her book open, literary excitement trumping all shyness. She zigzagged her index finger down the page: "His 'upright carriage' suggests him being in the army."

Brandon offered me a sardonic smile before he arranged his face into a bodybuilder's grimace, flexed his arms, and gave his right bicep a quick kiss. I willed myself not to turn to him as the girls duked it out. One-third of their grade was based on classroom participation, so it was a regular Greek chorus of grade grubbers:

"Wouldn't Heathcliff just go back to Liverpool, where he was born?"

"*Right.* For that matter, he could time-travel to the early 1960s and join a band with the city's other celebrities: George, John, Paul, and Ringo."

"Heathcliff would SO be the Goth guy in back playing cowbell!"

"Seriously, why would he go back to Liverpool, where he'd been a homeless orphan? He'd make his fortune in a new city, Paris, maybe, or Rome."

"No, there's the language problem. Heathcliff isn't formally

educated, so he's not going to be able to speak French or Italian.
Maybe London . . ."

After each comment, a girl would look at me with expectant eyes:
*Miss Sweeney, are you noting my cleverness, which clearly shows I have
read the text and highlighted pertinent passages? For God's sake, woman,
flip open your laptop and put a check next to my name in the class participation column!*

I couldn't be bothered, but they kept going.

"When Heathcliff moves to any city, he's bound to meet a new
girl. For him to still be weirdly obsessing over Cathy when he returns?
What is he, a girl? Guys move on—I don't know how, but they do.
He'd have to be more isolated to keep his obsession so pure. Maybe
Heathcliff went to, like, a monastery?"

"The text is sprinkled with religious allegory, but it doesn't indicate his beliefs, so, though it would probably be pretty sweet for
Heathcliff to live at a monastery and brew beer or decorate cakes
after life with crazy Cathy, how would he make his fortune?"

Wuthering Heights in cupcake motif—with sprinkles!

And oh, how those girls loved the word *text*. Yes, they were hyper
for the text. They thought *text* sounded smarter than *novel*, or God
forbid, *book*. But they were dear, in their annoying way, and I would
miss them. Not all of them, but really, quite a few. There was some
kindness in the mix; there was unironic enthusiasm. Flannery was taking in a deep breath, gearing up for her next comment.

Dear Reader, I couldn't wait forever. Brandon had his hands on
the window, the mystery of his whorled fingertips pressed against the
cold glass. Even if I had to crash through the window like a sunblind
pigeon, I would go to him. I would find him. I would tell him: *You have
always been in my thoughts.* I would leave my little world and meet
him in his new one. Love was the map, and I would have to draw it

myself; I would be the most repentant cartographer, verve and passion making up for skill, for basic understanding.

"I've done a little research on this," Flannery said. "Some *lit theorists* think he sailed to the New World." (She said "lit theorists" like an ethereal, dreamy candy, the briefest spun sugar on your tongue.) "And that Heathcliff made his fortune in New York City before returning to Wuthering Heights."

When I opened my mouth to speak, my top lip stuck to my gum, giving me a weird dog smile. Also, I was panting, but just a bit.

"New York City, that's the place, right? For adventure, reinvention, to become someone new, it's the place: the city of dreams. Flannery, I agree: I think that's where Heathcliff went to lose himself when he was so full of anguish. Well, that's where *I'd* go if I wanted to get lost. By myself, or even with someone else."

Brandon tipped his head so that it was touching the window, and I felt a quick bliss of chilled glass on my own warm forehead.

"I would go to New York City and I would never, ever come back." My words were coming so quickly, a row of falling dominos I could not stop or even predict, so I bit my lip again, to quiet myself. There.

The girls all looked a little wide-eyed, except for Flannery. A slight frown gripped the skin between her eyebrows, but she was smiling, too, the very picture of concerned radiance.

"But, Miss Sweeney, I think for Heathcliff, the whole point in leaving *is* coming back. He wants to return a changed person; he wants to impress everyone who has shunned him and underestimated him his whole life. But mostly, he wants to show Cathy, who chose the wealthy, safe person, what she could have had—Heathcliff himself—if not for her reprehensible social-climbing."

Brandon lifted his face. Was he smirking?

"Right. Hmm." I gave Flannery the weakest smile. I rolled my tongue around the sides of my dry mouth, trying to dredge up moisture. "Cathy and Heathcliff are teenagers, of course, and as such, given to impulsive decision-making—no offense, ladies. Clearly, Cathy shows some pretty substantial regret about choosing Edgar Linton over Heathcliff. And of course Cathy and Heathcliff are both such complicated characters. And, probably, mirrors of each other, as we know from *Wuthering Heights's* most famous line of dialogue, Cathy's dramatic announcement: I *am* Heathcliff."

Flannery smiled, obviously besotted with the tragic romance of *Wuthering Heights*. "Actually, Cathy and Heathcliff seem pretty different to me throughout the book. And when Heathcliff does return, he's somewhat recognizable, but *entirely* different, as anyone is after a long, deep journey." Flannery was stuck on the idea of Heathcliff's return! She cleared her throat and ran her finger down the page: *"It was a deep voice, and foreign in tone; yet there was something in the manner of pronouncing my name which made it sound familiar."*

Flannery had employed a slight British accent while reading, and the eye-rolling from the super-mean girls was so intense it seemed that their irises might disappear entirely, that not even a crescent of color would survive their scorn. How I wished that I possessed a cartoon freeze-ray gun, so that they would be stuck with their boiled-egg eyes. But Flannery powered on, holding one finger in the air as she flipped through the book with her other hand, imploring us to wait, wait. When she found the passage she wanted, she read it softly, and with an injured poignancy, if she were talking to Heathcliff himself. *"What! You come back? Is it really you? Is it?"*

I clapped my hands together. "Great! Thanks for reading that aloud, Flannery. That really freshened my memory." I nodded in vigorous appreciation, as if I were being filmed for a public TV documentary about inspirational English teachers. But there was the sudden smell of Brandon's fragrant deodorant, which I used to tease him about: *'Tis a bouquet of zesty spearmint intermingled with burning rubber tires, a veritable ode to zingy manliness!* Dear Reader, he was everywhere.

Flannery clamped her hands to the edge of her desk as if she were worried she might levitate: "I've always wondered what the book would be like if the plotline switched from the masculine to the feminine, if Heathcliff had died first, and Cathy had gone mad, chasing his spirit."

"Good! That's good!" I couldn't disguise a harsh little laugh. "Do you think Cathy would go mad or would she mourn Heathcliff properly—with socially acceptable amounts of nostalgia and regret? Would she succumb to the provincial coziness of her life at Thrushcross Grange? The bland husband, motherhood, her sewing circle. The rewards . . . or the restraints, perhaps, of her brief fling with—and I am quoting you here, Flannery—'reprehensible social-climbing'?"

Dear Reader, I had paid quite a price myself: Somehow—how? How?—my academic promise and wild-hearted romantic inclinations had devolved into my current, narrow life as a single schoolteacher who perused grad school catalogs and Match.com with equal fatigue. "Do you think she would always regret being shallow and traditional and disloyal to Heathcliff, who was clearly no prince, ladies? Still, would Cathy always regret dumping him so cruelly?" I looked at each girl's face before continuing: Boredom, revulsion, and mild curiosity were the day's emotional themes, but I had one disciple leaning forward, her mouth parted. "Yes, I do believe she would regret her short-sighted cruelty. I think it would cut her as deeply as it had cut him. Deeper."

Not only had I weirdly answered my own questions, but I had also started to weep in my classroom. Not a full-blown ugly cry, but the precursor to that, welled tears breaking free of my lower eyelids and drizzling down my cheeks. My antics produced a sudden and unfamiliar emotion in my Sacred Heart girls: uncertainty.

As they looked around at one another, trying to gauge the correct response, their smiles were, just for these few fast seconds, merely nervous, stripped of all cruelty and slyness. Later I would find that my waterproof mascara—a bargain brand suited to a teacher's salary and tested on rabbits—had drizzled down my cheekbones, heightening my crazy-lady visage into a sad tableau: *Cottontail's Revenge.*

Brandon took one hand off the window glass and touched his heart. His mouth formed my name, a cold cloud: *Caitlin.*

I grabbed a tissue from the box on my desk and turned toward the green board while I blew my nose. Then I rallied with a bright, professional smile. It seemed as good a time as any for a break via a creative writing exercise! I stuck to my original lesson plan. "Okay, ladies! Use the rest of the hour to write a one-page response: Where do you think Heathcliff goes when he drops out of the narrative of *Wuthering Heights?*"

I sat at my desk and I ruined everything by looking directly out the window. Brandon disappeared; I had killed him with my lack of concentration. When I blinked, a splotch of his fatigues cometed through the blackness of my closed eyelids. I snapped my head to the left and looked out the window. Again. Still gone.

My AP girls already had their earbuds in, rocking out while writing or studiously gazing up at the water-stained ceiling or the roses and crosses carved in the crown molding. Except for Flannery, who was chewing the end of her pen and watching me. I tapped my imaginary wristwatch, whereupon she looked down, put pen to paper, and wrote with the confidence of a National Merit Scholar.

My breath was coming in tight, asthmatic bursts. I was cradling my chin with my hand to keep myself from turning to the window. Once upon a time, it's true, I'd wasted my chance—O, my miraculous chance!—to be with Brandon.

Dear Reader, I would never waste another.

Two

Stepping off the train in Grand Central Station was pure Shakespeare, pure *O brave new world that hath such people in it* . . . in extremis. Flannery had the thrilling, terrifying realization that no one knew who she was and no one knew where she was, and though Miss Sweeney always chided her students to move from the general to the specific in their writing, Flannery felt the joy of doing the opposite. Because on the island of Manhattan on this particular winter morning, Flannery was nobody; but she was anybody and everybody, too.

Her thoughts zoomed, addressing all the people at Grand Central Station: *Um . . . hey! Who are you and you and you? And what, exactly, is this shared experience we are all having?* She wanted to ask the elderly businessman death-gripping his iPhone: *Why am I me and not you?* She wanted to look into the mascara-ed eyes of the masked and gowned Muslim woman and ask: *Why are you wearing that, or why am I not wearing that?* She watched a group of dazzled Midwestern tourists with their ill-fitting jeans and marshmallow white tennis shoes, catcalling: "Let's all stay together, m'kay? Let's just all stay to-gether. M'kay?" Flannery longed to tell them not to rue their cheerful ski jackets, which probably seemed awfully bright right about now. She wanted to deliver a bolstering message to the Heartland folk, not from Flannery Fields, but from the teeming city itself: *Do not feel inferior, for we are all so terribly random!*

And the staying together was pretty solid advice, because when Flannery raised her head and looked at the ceiling of Grand Central Station—the heavens painted a soft, cerulean blue and glammed up with white constellations—she felt so tiny, so all alone, like one specific twinkling star in the vast night sky or an individual grain of sand on an endless beach.

Miss Sweeney smirked in her mind: *Twinkle, twinkle, little Flannery! Also? You might want to uh, beach that beach metaphor.*

She wished Miss Sweeney had gone to the airport instead of the train station, that she'd chosen not to revisit the stormy past, but to zoom off to a tropical island—a bikini and a beach book and a coconut ice. But Flannery realized the frothy beach fantasy resulted from her waning courage, because being in NYC without her parents was a little scary. She scolded her-self for being such a big baby—one exasperated, whispered *REALLY?*—as she walked out of Grand Central Station and into the mouth of the wide, wide world—the rushes of people, the sirens and pigeons and screeching taxis, the shops selling mini-cupcakes or cologne and bright rayon dresses. Flannery looked up at the sky—a stripe of mottled blue-gray between the buildings—and brought her hand to her chest to feel her heart beat out the two-syllable joy of it all:

I'm here.

I'm here.

I'm here.

But she was there to find Miss Sweeney, to help Miss Sweeney! That was the journey, she reminded herself, not personal delight and/or fear and freedom. Flannery cradled her elbows against the cold wind and wished she'd gone to her locker for her coat before leaving Sacred Heart. She looked at the buses barreling up the street. Which way was north? She needed to get moving, to get up to the Columbia neighborhood. Well, it would be *Flannery's* neighborhood in the fall, and that seemed nothing short of miraculous. So Flannery, emboldened, walked to the curb and held up her hand—a cinematic gesture that at first felt awkward and staged, and then sexy and commanding—*Hello, you big bad world!*—and a cab slowed to a stop next to her.

She opened the door and slid into the backseat, her backpack jutting her forward up to the plastic partition.

"Yes?" The cabdriver peered in the rearview mirror at her.

"Oh, hi!" On the TV screen in the backseat, Beyoncé was modeling bikinis for H&M. Flannery reflexively sucked in her stomach. "Thank you for stopping." He sighed and turned his head to the side, and Flannery smiled at his whorled ear and took a deep breath of the rose-scented air freshener.

"Where are you going?"

"Um, sorry, Columbia University? Do you know where that is? Sorry, I don't have the exact address, which is crazy because . . . but . . . I can get it, hold on." Flannery pulled her phone out of her backpack to Google the address, but the cabdriver was already roaring down the street and turning the corner, heading uptown. She slung her backpack onto the floor

next to her and heard cellophane crinkling. She wasn't smelling rose-scented air freshener but the real thing, a bouquet of
red roses there on the floor of the backseat. Flannery picked up
the roses—luckily, she'd only crushed the stems, the blooms
looked perfect—and breathed in the chilled, chemical sweetness of a winter greenhouse.

"Excuse me? Um, someone must have left their flowers back
here." Flannery held up the bouquet so the driver could see it.

The driver frowned into the rearview window. "Flowers?
Okay. They're yours now. You keep them." His heavily accented
English sounded a bit accusatory, though, as if Flannery were
being treated to an unfair beneficence. "You're the one who
found them."

As the cab zoomed up Broadway, Flannery delivered her
awkward thanks, a confused chirp of a sentence spliced with
nervous laughter and delivered coquettishly to the back of the
cabdriver's head: "Oh, these are so pretty, *heh heh,* are you, *heh
heh* . . . sure?"

"I'm very sure." He sighed. "It's *your* lucky day." He clicked
on the radio to a star shower of flutes playing "Clair de Lune."
Flannery rested her head on the seat back and looked out the
window.

She knew that true good luck would be meeting a person
who cared about you enough to give you roses. Still, finding a
bouquet in the backseat of a cab was pretty fortunate, and she
enjoyed clutching it to her chest like a homecoming queen cab-
bing it through Manhattan. The ribbon of news bannering
along the bottom of the TV screen let her know that it was 38
degrees; it was 11:37. Flannery smiled down at her bouquet,
thrilled with herself. On any other March Thursday at this

exact moment she would be back in AP World History right now, with lunch on deck, the cafeteria smells comingling up through the heat vents: warm chocolate chip cookies, reheated soy burgers, and woodsy pine cleanser. Flannery looked out the taxi window, the narrowed sky and sunlight shimmering across the top floors of the buildings. There was a window cleaner on skyscraper scaffolding, a stern reminder that the world was actually full of duty and potential peril, and that Flannery should concentrate on Miss Sweeney, who surely would not be Spider-Manning around midtown Manhattan. She would already be at Columbia, where Flannery was heading, too fast it seemed. Would Miss Sweeney even be glad to see her? Would their potential meeting be irrevocably weird?

The light turned red, and Flannery lowered her eyes to the crosswalk, to the blonde woman in a winter-white coat and tall, toffee-colored boots, the leash of her corgi in one hand, a plastic poop bag in the other. From the opposite direction two tiny old men walked with their arms linked, as if they were French girls in the movies. In her mind's eye Flannery Photoshopped Miss Sweeney into the crosswalk, her hands in the pockets of her dark coat, her gait loose and carefree until she saw Flannery's face in the cab and stopped cold, her mouth forming the words: *Flannery? What the . . .*

Flannery knew she needed to open Miss Sweeney's book again; she needed to check what she'd read in the Sacred Heart bathroom to make sure she hadn't hallucinated the pages.

But then the light turned green; the clouds shifted. The cab-driver revved the engine and flipped down the sun visor, and Flannery became distracted by the clipped-on photo of a smiling dark-eyed baby with chubby cheeks, striped footie pajamas, and two lines of oxygen snaking into his nose, two thin tubes that would stop anyone's heart, the saddest spagh . . . But even before Flannery's thought had formed the last syllable, she envisioned Miss Sweeney's red pen writing away, the soft thud of pen striking paper when she dotted the *i* in *spaghetti*: *Really? The oxygen tubes are not merely "like spaghetti"? They are in fact the saddest spaghetti? The most despondent of all pasta . . . ?*

Oh, if only Miss Sweeney hadn't left her purse, Flannery thought, for the idea of free hands made it all seem so final—no money, no wallet, no tampons, no lip gloss. But maybe she was doing a bare-bones adventure, going off the grid?

In Miss Sweeney's classroom there was a black-and-white photograph of a sheet of paper in a Royal typewriter with one sentence: *"He explored the island, although he created it."* Flannery stuck a mental *S* in front of the He, and in her mind's eye she sent Miss Sweeney off on lighthearted adventures on the island of Manhattan: Taking the mic for some impromptu scat singing at a jazz club, reading a few profanity-laced lines at a poetry slam, walking through Central Park with a boyfriend on a starry night. You could probably do all those things with a purse, though.

As the cabdriver pulled up to the ice-spiked iron gates of Columbia University on 116th and Broadway, Flannery felt the familiar panic of entering a new room, and the campus was no mere room, it was a *GoodbyeToAllThat*MagicKingdomMoorsUtopianHogwartsOz mash-up of potentialities. And yes, Flannery had already earned the Golden Ticket of admission, but in the stereotypical lingo of high school guidance counselors: *It would be up to her to make the most of her experience!* Seventeen long years on earth had taught Flannery that it was always better to think or daydream or read about experiences than to actually live them out, and while she didn't wish to be back at Sacred Heart, she also didn't want to step out of the cab, not ever. She wondered if she could pay the driver to just let her cozy up in the backseat and read Miss Sweeney's copy of *Wuthering Heights,* for the cab was so safe and rosescented, not just Flannery's private chapel of contemplation but her window to the world.

Wherever Miss Sweeney was on the Columbia campus, her mocking spirit swirled in Flannery's mind. *Window to the World! Well, now! Why not a porthole to a planet? O, brave pilgrim, are you standing in a doorway to a dream?*

"Okay?" The cabdriver looked at her in the rearview mirror. Flannery marveled at his economy of word choice: two syllables that conveyed that she needed to pay—the meter flashed fourteen dollars—and hustle out of his cab. The sun visor was flipped back up so the tethered baby was out of view, but Flannery envisioned a late-night family tableau: the cabdriver sitting with his head in his hands at a grim kitchen table—a bowl of bruised clementines and a stack of medical bills on the speckled gray Formica—and his wife next to him on a folding chair, snuggling their sick baby.

Flannery unzipped her backpack and handed the driver an ATM-fresh twenty. "I don't need any change. Thanks for letting me keep the bouquet." She manically jammed her hand in her backpack to do a quick touch of her essential items: Phone! *Wuthering Heights!* Wallet! The driver told Flannery to have a good day and raised one hand, not quite a wave, but a few inches of kindness that levitated there above the steering wheel. She needed that gesture, because as she stepped out of the cab to the falling snow and iced asphalt and car exhaust, to the throngs of hazardously cool-looking people on the sidewalk, Flannery's Grand Central Station zeal was entirely replaced by Morningside Heights apprehension.

An oncoming car honked and seemed to just miss brushing her arm as it revved past, so Flannery hopped up on the sidewalk. As she struggled her backpack to a more secure spot on her shoulder, the cellophane bouquet crackled; she pressed it to her chest and lowered her face to breathe in the calming sweetness. Flannery tried to puzzle out why she was now holding a dozen red roses. Yes, she had found them in a cab, but what was the origin of the roses? Had a hopeful romantic felled by ADD left them behind? Had arguing lovers—*"You can take back your goddamn roses"*; *"No, you keep the stupid roses!"*— left the bouquet in the cab to spite one another? Well, Flannery *knew* the roses were a symbol—the muted red muscle of her heart thudding along—and naturally she loved literary symbolism and was eager to deconstruct the meaning of her found bouquet, but the words scrolling along in her brain were accompanied by Miss Sweeney's laughter: *Audacious Alliteration Alert! Flummoxed Flannery Finds Floral Foreshadowing!*

Flannery looked up at the statues flanking the Columbia gates: a male statue holding a globe, and a female statue holding an open book over her chest as if shielding her heart. *Of course,* thought Flannery, the man was going to see the whole world and the woman would stay home and read all about his big adventure! Yippee! She smiled at her own observation and gazed up at the female statue's hair—carved Marcel waves— and flowing granite robe. As Flannery entered the gates she took a last sideways look at the statue and offered up a reverential nod, as if she were gazing at a primary apostle, as if sucking up to a stone spirit guide could help her find Miss Sweeney.

And then she was just another girl walking on campus, and if Flannery were not wearing her school uniform—which she severely, severely regretted—she could have been mistaken for an actual college student. This would be her daily routine by autumn, and Sacred Heart would recede into kitschy heartache and emo anecdotes, because she would find her people, and life would be gorgeous, interesting, magical: the book thrown open. Flannery thought of Miss Sweeney, not of her current peril, but of an eighteen-year-old Caitlin Sweeney, fresh from the plains. Surely arriving at the Columbia campus from Kansas would be no less exotic than a lunar landing! But, no, Flannery remembered saying as much during one of their college talks, and Miss Sweeney had given her a piqued sigh and a droll lecture on the ubiquity of the suburbs, how Kansas was not so different from Connecticut, and that she'd misspent her youth in the same bland manner as any old girl from Darien or Roxbury: listening to Fleet Foxes and the Arctic Monkeys and drinking Frappuccinos and dodging the Starbucks manager who enforced the inane rule about not smoking within thirty feet of the building. Flannery thought Miss Sweeney's response was shaded with a bit of *Thou Doth Protest Too Much*, and in any case, it was better to imagine the campus seen through the thrilled gaze of someone who had only known sunflowers and pick-up trucks, the big sky and Friday night lights.

A girl brushed past close enough for Flannery to smell her almond-scented leave-in conditioner and then turned and gave her a quick, polite *"Sorry!"* She wore a pomegranate red leather coat that made Flannery think of Miss Sweeney's purse, a quick punch to Flannery's heart. The girl took a second glance back at Flannery's bouquet and offered up the briefest nod of recognition to convey: *Good for you! And FYI: I, too, am a girl who is given flowers.* Flannery was delighted to be thought rose-worthy, to pass for a girl with a boyfriend who would shyly present her with a dozen roses—along with a bit of arched eyebrow to acknowledge that floral expressions of love were goofy and stereotypical, but that he loved her anyway and so . . . here you go! Miss Sweeney would probably vomit at the imagined scenario of insipid romance. Oh, Miss Sweeney! Flannery thought about the solemn eyes of the police officer when she'd given him Miss Sweeney's purse, of how he'd put his hand out slowly, as if reluctant to take it, and Flannery's own hands trembled from the cold, and even on the Columbia campus the scenario from the bathroom at Sacred Heart popped up in Flannery's thoughts like a Whack-a-Mole carnival game she could never win: Is your sorrow here? No, it's here! Now look: It's your humiliation! Over here: It's your injured indignation! Ha! Can't quite win, can you? Time's up!

But happiness trumped her standard self-pity. Though sure, she certainly felt deep concern that bordered on dread for Miss Sweeney, off on her addled adventure to locate her old, dead, boyfriend, Flannery's adrenaline raced just from the delight of being on campus—I'm here, I'm here! I'm here! And the world was bursting with possibility, all those dream-laden bumper stickers were factually correct! Flannery wanted to COEXIST *and* COMMIT RANDOM ACTS OF KINDNESS *and* BE THE CHANGE SHE WANTED TO SEE. She imagined future friends among the students passing by: the aggressively freckled girl with the red curly hair and lotus flowers tattooed on the backs of her hands, two boys in athletic wear joyfully discussing last night's episode of *Game of Thrones,* the girl in a gray-and-green hijab looking down at her phone and then raising her face and giving Flannery a polite smile before she went back to texting. It was thrilling, but perhaps not unusual, because everyone on campus looked pretty friendly; no one moved with the predatorial grace of the Sacred Heart girls, eyes scanning the distance for any perceived weakness. And she would soon be away from Sacred Heart! The girls who had ignored her or tormented her would fall away; they would be nothing but haunting marionettes that she could easily snip away with the beauty of her NYC life. Because Flannery was choosing to believe what Miss Sweeney had told her. When she was at Columbia, she would find her people.

Miss Sweeney's cursive words scrolled along in Flannery's brain: *Oh, Flannery . . . haunting marionettes? Do not string me along with your putrid puppetry prose!*

Still, Flannery tried to hold on to her empowered feeling because, looking around the quad, the handsome square of buildings that created the walled campus, she started to feel a little discouraged, as well as being coatless and cold. If Miss Sweeney were on campus, where might she be? She stepped out of the throng of people walking along the main sidewalk bisecting the campus and cut across the dead lawn. Flannery slowly spun around—there was Butler Library, and Carman Hall, where she would live in the autumn, and the statue of Alma Mater—but wasn't so preoccupied with finding Miss Sweeney not to notice a dark-haired boy on a bench by himself, reading. In his skinny jeans, ratty black leather jacket and stocking cap he was every inch the stereotype of the self-involved hipster; he was even reading his newspaper with a disaffected scowl. He sat very straight, not even a centimeter of slouch, so of course Flannery's mind churned out the line from *Wuthering Heights*: *"He is . . . rather slovenly, perhaps, yet not looking amiss with his negligence, because he has an"*—cue the unstifled giggles of AP English Lit!—*"erect and handsome figure."* She felt a blast of contextual joy that came from the intersection of books and life: It was the best thing ever! But of course not everyone felt that way. All the Sacred Heart mothers were in book clubs, and liked to discuss narrative arcs while enjoying coffee and dessert, but this hadn't filtered down to their daughters.

"Reading too much makes you a freak," Maeve McKenzie had once whispered to Flannery in the Sacred Heart library. Flannery had been kneeling down, looking at the spines of books on the bottom shelf, and Maeve's words had literally put her off balance: She'd had to grip the dusty metal shelving for support. Flannery recognized Maeve's revolting faux-stupidity, but she also pitied herself: *I am just kneeling here trying to decide between* Bleak House *and* Dubliners. *I'm not hurting anyone.* In the movie version of Flannery's life, Maeve McKenzie would have to be a dyslexic girl living in a subsidized apartment and bullied by her alcoholic stepfather. But in vexing real life, Maeve had already been accepted to Brown, her grandmother's name on a dorm.

Uggh! Flannery tried to shake off all her bad memories with a bold gesture: She walked over and sat right down on the opposite end of the concrete bench, only five feet away from the boy. Well, Flannery needed to read too, and so she'd have a little company. They sat peaceably together, but cold concrete radiated up from her legs to her spine, and Flannery wished she'd worn thicker tights with her school skirt, and of course, if she were wishing, she'd wish for an entirely different outfit, and to be an entirely different person altogether, etc.

An icy breeze made Flannery draw her flowers to her chest, and the boy winced at the crush and rattle of the roses, the crackling cellophane cone. He gave Flannery a glancing frown and returned to his paper.

She apologized, but immediately felt annoyed by her own mousey behavior. The bouquet was not an air horn, and anyway, who was he to be so delicate, so very perturbed by the sound of *cellophane* in a public square? But his jerky behavior gave Flannery courage: "*Um,* excuse me. But I was wondering if there was some sort of, like—I don't know—like, an alumni club around here?"

When he looked up, Flannery saw that he had smiling brown eyes. Unbidden, Miss Sweeney snarked about in Flannery's brain: *Do his "smiling" eyes have a dimple smack in the middle of his irises? That is just precious! That is just Precious Moments!*

"I am *not* aware of any alumni club." He went back to his newspaper. He put the emphasis on *not;* the first definitive consonant was a harsh starburst that made her feel a little swoony, and while the *o* was straightforward, the *t* was the lightest touch of tongue to upper palate, a mere suggestion before it evanesced into its own sexiness: Oh, baby. He had a British accent!

Miss Sweeney's voice was so close, a red pen on the bench between Flannery and the boy, her voice tight with choked-back laughter. *The letter* t *is evanescing into its own sexiness? Alrighty.*

Well, the letter F *is for* Flannery *and you, my dear letter girl, are the bomb. The* F *bomb! Just take it down a notch, lest you evanesce into your own freakiness.*

Flannery cleared her throat. "Okay, thanks."

He raised one hand from his newspaper and dismissed Flannery with a half-wave. "'S alright."

Well then. She was apparently a very taxing person to talk with. The boy couldn't have been more bored. Flannery unzipped her backpack and checked her cell phone: no missed calls, no texts. Did no one care about her fake cramps? Did no one miss her? It was best to be pined for when you went missing. And the handsome boy sitting on the bench with her—reading his paper and ignoring her—had just given Flannery a big old dose of Manhattan reality. She was just herself, and she would be herself in the fall, too. She wouldn't morph into a desirable or mysterious girl. It was as if the boy himself had just stage-whispered: *Newsflash! Your future does not sparkle with possibility.*

Flannery watched a trio of girls race past, laughing a lot—possibly high?—with scarves looped around their necks in that carefree fashion impossible to replicate. Two wore high ponytails shined and straightened into glossy whips, minimal makeup, and dark, lint-free pea coats. But the most beautiful one was waifed out: A pixie cut and Cleopatra eyeliner, skinny legs in skinny jeans, and silver spaceman boots. She was as towering and precisely beautiful as any girl in a magazine.

But, wait! Oh, crap, the pixie-cut girl WAS a model: Flannery remembered her from a mascara commercial. Maybe going to college in Manhattan, land of college student/fashion models, was the worst idea *ever*; maybe she should have been

Miss Sweeney in reverse, and gone off to college in the Midwest. But when the college rep from Notre Dame had visited Sacred Heart, Miss Sweeney had steered Flannery clear of the session, telling her that, with the world being so vast and gorgeous, why spend four years at a Disneyland for Catholics? Flannery must have looked startled by her teacher's smackdown of the venerable college, because Miss Sweeney had laughed and said: *"I say this both as a Catholic and as a fan of Disneyland."* She'd also advised against Grinnell—*"People want to get* out *of Iowa!"*—though it was an excellent school, sure. But Flannery was reluctant to let these options go: The Midwestern schools seemed like they would be so much less intimidating. Miss Sweeney admitted (with pleasure) that though she had been the homecoming queen in high school, it wasn't, beauty-wise, a major accomplishment because Midwesterners were generally pretty regular-looking: Even the beauties, even the beauty *queens,* were quite often short and looked like they would eventually morph into moms who drove minivans and gorged on snack cakes. "So, Flannery, aside from the fact that you are a beautiful girl in the first place, you would also have that exotic East Coast thing going for you and drive all the boys crazy and get yourself in over your head with all variety of romantic drama. Just go to Columbia! Why not start your adult life in the City of Dreams?"

Flannery knew she was not a beautiful girl, though not a homely one either, and so her problem was not even fixable with a magazine makeover. She just *was the way she was.* But Miss Sweeney had said the words "you are a beautiful girl" without any sugared inflection, as if Flannery's beauty was an inarguable fact, but also no big deal: *Yep, beautiful. Fine.*

Whatever. And so sometimes at home, when she looked into the bathroom mirror—her face freshly powdered, her lips glossed—Flannery would tilt her head to the side, a sweep of brown-black hair framing her face, the sides of her mouth sucked in to carve her cheekbones, and think: *She's . . . right?* Mostly, though, Flannery examined herself harshly, and despaired: Was it just dry scalp flaking along her part or full-on dandruff so hideously visible in her dark hair? The antibiotic that she took every morning—a festive capsule of neon pink and white granules—had slowed her acne, but pinpricks of infection still swelled the pores on her nose. So. Very. Gross.

But no matter where she fell on the beauty gradient, Flannery was heartened to see that the boy on the bench kept reading; he didn't glance up at the Manhattan beauties, no slack-jawed gawking for Mr. Coolio, not even a furtive once-over as the three girls receded from his field of vision. Flannery looked around the campus—the passing break must be over, the quad was quieter, and Miss Sweeney would be easily visible now if she were strolling along, hoping to meet up with her deceased boyfriend. Flannery was cold; she was also stumped, and so it was time to open the book and see if she would find direction for the day.

"Okay," she said aloud, agreeing with herself, and then took a quick look at the boy, but he read on, impervious to her weirdness. Flannery reached her hand into her backpack for Miss Sweeney's copy of *Wuthering Heights.* But she didn't feel the soft cover of the paperback, so she put her roses on the bench, and with both hands she pawed through her things, her heart racing. No, it had to be here, she just wasn't finding it, she was panicking for nothing—Kleenex, pencil bag, candy wrappers, a tube of lip stain, a compact, an unwrapped piece of gum—she knew she'd had *Wuthering Heights* when she'd gotten out of the cab . . . she'd had it, she had to have it.

But she didn't. And—*"Shit!"*—a loose lead from a mechanical pencil jammed beneath her fingernail. Her breath was coming in ragged puffs, and when she looked up, she had gotten the boy's attention. He had his chin tucked toward his neck, and his shoulder curled forward, as if protecting himself from her manic search.

Flannery slapped at the bench behind her. "I can't find my book!"

The boy nodded. "I see."

Flannery searched in her backpack again, She scanned the ground; she lifted her roses off the bench and put them back. "I can't find it anywhere."

The boy tuned back to his paper, so it looked as if he were reading a news story aloud: "This very morning I heard a large, scrabbling-about sound in trash cans in front of my apartment. Soon enough, a raccoon roughly the size of a well-loved house cat emerged with a cantaloupe rind. So. Victory for one wild thing in the city."

"What?" What was he talking about? One wild thing? There was a joke embedded in his story, probably a mean one, and directed at her, of course. Did raccoons prowl around Manhattan? Flannery thought not; she thought NYC wildlife consisted of rats and pigeons and clichéd cockroaches scurrying from the kitchen light. But oh, dear God, where was the book?

Flannery zipped up her backpack, picked up her roses, and began backtracking her steps, her eyes trained on the ground. She took one long last look back at the boy at the bench, who was now looking back at her, the tamped-down thrill of that, as she scolded herself for being so careless with Miss Sweeney's book—stupid, stupid, stupid—and for her cowardice. Yes, she'd enjoyed a brief renegade moment when she'd crossed the highway and taken the train to Manhattan to look for Miss Sweeney, but she'd had *Wuthering Heights* at her disposal since then and had been too afraid to open it, afraid that whatever enchantment had occurred in the Sacred Heart bathroom had vanished, and equally afraid that it was real, that Miss Sweeney's words would remain, that Miss Sweeney was in fact delusional and roaming the streets of Manhattan.

Oh, she was the mousiest of explorers, too nervous to check the map and now desperate to find it. Had the book perhaps dropped out of her backpack when she paid the driver—was it in the cab, whisked off forever, and Flannery an unwitting barterer, now holding a dozen roses in exchange?

At the gates of Columbia Flannery searched the sidewalk—no book—and the street . . . but saw only bits of paper and crushed coffee cups in the snow sludge by the curb. She looked up at the statue of the woman holding the open book: How odd it was to see a female statue holding something other than the baby Jesus. Flannery thought of her grandmother's wedding photo, where she had paused in the Mass to lay a bouquet of red roses at the marble feet of the Virgin Mary. Her grandmother had been a true believer, while Flannery's parents were merely sarcastic, and Flannery herself was just unsure. But she knew her grandmother's gesture had been meant to honor what she believed in: a fullness of heart that made space for the miraculous, motherhood, and the promise of Heaven. Because Flannery believed in the relief and comfort of books, of ideas, she propped her roses at the pedestal of the goddess of the open book, reverent. She bowed her head, as if being dramatic and freaky might help her find Miss Sweeney's book, might help her divine Miss Sweeney's precise whereabouts, and she looked up at the blank, iris-free eyes of the statue and said aloud: *"I will find her!"*

Miss Sweeney answered back, her voice smooth carmine ink on creamy cardstock paper: *And you will do it with the skill set of the self-aggrandizing high school narrator, you dear icon whisperer.*

Three

"Caitlin! Caitlin!"

Flannery looked away from the statue and saw the boy from the bench, walking quickly, waving at her. Oh, how her heart pounded at his thrilling mistake. He'd shouted the name so beautifully—the hard *C* and the lush *l* of it!—that she wished it were her own. As he came closer, and Flannery saw what was in his hand, relief—*ahhhh*—made her weirdly place her own hand to her heart, as if she were perched on a Tuscan veranda in a low-cut ball gown. He was holding Miss Sweeney's copy of *Wuthering Heights* like a choirboy with a missalette, the open book placed in his palms.

"Hey! You dropped your book." His fingerless gloves revealed his bitten-down fingernails, his mashed nail beds. He pointed to Miss Sweeney's name on the title page. Once upon a time, not so very long ago, really, Caitlin Sweeney must have sat on a flowery canopy bed in Kansas and written her name in this copy of *Wuthering Heights*: the *C* had a curlicue, the *Y* had a swirling, baroque tail. Now a boy was pointing to her name, thinking Caitlin Sweeney was the girl standing in front of him in Manhattan. Flannery considered the unpredictable migration of physical objects, and she wondered if Miss Sweeney was safe—she did!—but the boy was standing so close she could smell his breath mint.

"Your book dropped out of your backpack. It was under the bench."

"Oh, okay," Flannery said officiously, as if this were a profitable business deal she was closing with confidence. *Ah, yes, the inevitable return of the missing book.* "Thanks so much."

But she was so happy to have the book back in her possession that she began to giggle with a nervous enthusiasm that suggested the return of a lost paperback book was pure comedy gold. "How embarrassing! I guess I did drop my book." It wasn't much of a conversational gem, but the boy rallied.

"I'm always dropping books myself. It's *quite* the hobby." He flashed the peace sign and in the stoned cadence of an ancient American hippie, he said, "Drop, like, you know, *books,* not bombs, people."

Cold clouds shooting from his mouth and books and bombs and low winter clouds and a dog walker brushing past, being pulled along by three dogs: a schnauzer and an apricot poodle wearing a fuchsia diamanté collar, and another dog, the breed the Obamas owned—oh, what was it called? As Flannery looked into the boy's eyes she envisioned the First Dog bounding across the White House lawn and she dearly wished she were not the sort of person to conjure presidential dogs when something exciting happened, which was never, except for right now, the world cracking open.

He put *Wuthering Heights* into her hands. "Right. There's your book, Caitlin Sweeney." He pointed vaguely at Flannery, raising his fingers up and down. "What's with the look, Caitlin? Going for the school-girl look or are you an actual schoolgirl?"

Her stupid uniform! "Actual schoolgirl. And my name's actually not Caitlin."

"Well, then. What's your name, actual schoolgirl?"

"Flannery Fields."

He cocked his head to the left. "Flannery Fields? Is that *really* your name?"

"It really is."

His first moment of interest! Squinting, he smiled, as if delighted by what he had stumbled upon: Flannery Fields. Even if he was about to make fun of her name, he was suddenly interested in her because of it. Flannery floated back to an impossible memory. She sensed her neonatal self opening her mouth, amniotic fluid bubbling in her throat as her parents stared at the sonogram that revealed her gender, and debated the name *Flannery*: *I really want to! You sure? I think so! Should we . . . ?* Even with her organs still forming, tethered to her mother by a length of umbilical cord, the fetus that would be Flannery could divine this moment, could offer up a gurgling, ghosty, *Do it, people!*

Miss Sweeney chortled in her brain: *Though it would be the best band name ever, let's not dwell too much on The Fetus that Would Be Flannery.*

"Flannery's really *quite* a fantastic name."

And there it was, from the boy's lips to God's ears, forever and ever, amen. The belated yet definitive victory of her name, for having to endure the eye rolling—even from the flipping *teachers*—at roll call, and the inane nickname that revealed the dullardly meanness of her tormenters. (Was *Flannel Sheets* really the best they could cook up?) And of course the grand-daddy of all horrors: studying her namesake's classic short story, "A Good Man Is Hard to Find," in freshman English class and the accompanying jokes about mixing up the adjectives in the title, of having Mrs. Piccone announce, her voice an octave too high for sincerity: *"Aren't we lucky to have our very own Flannery at Sacred Heart!"* Of having Callie Martin lean in close and whisper, her breath Trident fresh, her voice syruped with faux kindness: "And wow—weird!—you look just like Flannery O'Connor too!"

Flannery had studied the black-and-white photo on the book jacket, and while it was true that Flannery O'Connor was The Very Worst Thing A Girl Could Be (not pretty), she had rather liked her cat-eye glasses and sleeveless plaid dress; she thought that Flannery O'Connor looked polite and intelligent, fully cognizant that the God she adored had not only had graced her with the famed lupus but with an underdeveloped jawline, so that boys, who were apparently enslaved to visual symmetry—regular madmen for the quotidian!—might pass her over for the generically pretty, thus leaving Flannery O'Connor free to develop her formidable talent. Flannery Fields, to her dismay, could imagine no worse fate.

"If you like people to mock your name," Flannery told the boy matter-of-factly, "you can't do much better than mine. What's *your* name?" Oh, God, wait! Stop! Do-over! Had she put too much emphasis, weirdly, on the *your*? Draped that one syllable with nonsensical innuendo? There were so many potential ways to embarrass oneself, millions of replicating snow-flakes of humiliation, each uniquely cut.

"I'm afraid my name's not quite as good as yours, Flannery. It's Heath. It's Heath Smith."

Flannery laughed out loud, but felt the burn of his mean joke. Must everyone taunt her with her love for her favorite book?

"Very clever." She held up *Wuthering Heights*. "Rhymes with?"

"I imagine I'm not quite as taken with rhymes as you are, Flannery. And is that really your given name? Flannery Fields? You're not actually Caitlin Sweeney?"

"It's a long story." Flannery stretched her social skills by attempting some jokey small talk: "But chances are good that I'm not Caitlin Sweeney."

"Well, chances are good that you're going to say no to this; I shouldn't even bother asking." He sighed, as if he were no stranger to the myriad disappointments a day might put forth. Flannery looked up at his dark eyes and the curved planes of his face, wondering how *that* could ever be true. She thought of Cathy contemplating her deep, spiritual love for Heathcliff. *"He shall never know how I love him: and that, not because he's handsome, but because he's more myself than I am."* The handsome part probably didn't hurt, though.

"If you're not in a terrible hurry, maybe you'd have a bit of lunch with me?" He was not charmingly tentative; he sounded confident that Flannery would indeed like to join him for lunch. And she needed to read—not go to lunch—she needed to find Miss Sweeney on the Columbia campus. Yet the whereabouts of Miss Sweeney slipped into a category marked SEC-ONDARY and happiness came as a trapped bird in her chest, bashing his soft wings inside her rib cage, and she wondered if she might be levitating. At this rate Flannery would have to work hard to keep Miss Sweeney in her birdbrain thoughts at all.

"Actually, even if you're in a hurry, I guess I'd still like for you to have lunch with me." Now his voice sounded spiked with loneliness, and so Flannery felt a quick rush of love for him, though she knew she was being foolish, a valentine jackass extraordinaire.

"*Uh.* Lunch? Oh. Sure!" Flannery was in pure cavewoman mode, her monosyllabic reply a false reflection of her SAT score.

"Great. Oh *God.* I can't believe I just said that even-if-you're-in-a-hurry bit. I sound like a sociopath, right?" He made his voice deep and starched, a *Masterpiece Theatre* voice-over: "He met his victims on the Columbia campus, luring them with dropped books. It is entirely unclear why any lovely young woman would have exchanged even three words with him."

Flannery smiled down at the pavement and wondered why her once-firm brain was softening into an unrepentant compliment whore, why it swirled mental violets and roses around the word *lovely.* He thought she was lovely! He found her pretty, captivating, dear! Or . . . did he? God, usage was everything! How she feared the colloquial, the reductive British *lovely,* which she thought meant quite satisfactory. *Thank you for those lovely mashed potatoes.* But she was thrilled, regardless, her bright uptown joy highlighted by the fact that she was not at school, a random gray day unfolding, but on a NYC street with a British boy who was grumbling about lunch options.

"In this blighted landscape of cran-apple muffins and *pan au chocolat,* of mango flaxseed smoothies and turkey sandwiches dressed with local organic field greens"—with a grand, sarcastic hand flourish, he indicated the clogged traffic on Broadway—"quite obviously from the verdant fields of upper Manhattan, what I'd really like is a tureen of hot applesauce and a generous serving of leg of mutton stew."

"That sounds so *good.*" Thrilled, sure, but worried that she was already turning into that daffy girl who agreed with any old thing a good-looking guy said, a once-brave adventurer happy to be shipwrecked on Patriarchy Island, Flannery quickly added: "Except I'm a vegan."

"A vegan?" Heath chuckled, and cut his eyes to the side.

But then the sky opened up, the surprise of ice globes pelting down, and all along the street came the harsh blooms of black umbrellas shooting open, of people canopying their newspapers over their heads or shielding their faces with backpacks, and Flannery knew this as the hot breath of Miss Sweeney on her neck, because her thoughts about Miss Sweeney weren't even secondary now. She certainly wasn't feeling the valiant despair of a person combing a college campus for a missing teacher. She was standing outside the gates of Columbia with Heath Smith, marveling at her bizarre good fortune.

"Good God," Heath said, flipping up the collar of his leather jacket. "This hail is as big as pearl onions! This wuthering day is a certain omen of pearl onion Armageddon."

Wuthering. Flannery's sunken heart rose again, her heart flew up and up, and Miss Sweeney's red-pen voice said: *Your heart flew up, Flannery? Is your heart a muscular blood-kite?* Well, Flannery's heart really was a muscular blood-kite by this point, and the hail felt like magical crystal rocks striking her body. At any given second a pink and purple Pegasus might come thundering down Broadway. Because: *wuthering*. In her most grandiose daydreams Flannery would never have envisioned going to lunch in Manhattan with a boy who used the word *wuthering*. Emily Brontë herself had to explain the word on page 4 of her masterpiece: "*'Wuthering' being a significant provincial adjective, descriptive of the atmospheric tumult to which its station is exposed in stormy weather.*"

Heath put his hand on Flannery's back—oh, she was glad to be coatless, to feel his whorled fingertips frying through her shirt, her cami, her bra strap, and then, skin—as they crossed Broadway like any lovers hustling along in the rain.

He pulled open the door of the first restaurant they passed, Nussbaum & Wu, and ordered cappuccinos and grilled cheese sandwiches—they ordered the same thing!—baby Swiss on rye, a non-vegan lunch to be sure. But Flannery consoled herself that cheese wasn't animal death, not even animal suffering, if the cow was raised on a family farm—Bessie and a silver bucket! A striped cat—fat from milk and mice—figure-eighting around the cow's legs while the kindly farmer on a wooden stool milked his favorite Guernsey. But the milk used to make the baby Swiss was probably from the dairy operation exposed in that documentary, the cows fatigued and miserable and penned in suffocating enclosures. Flannery vowed to eat more purely in the future while she enjoyed her sandwich, so greasy and glistening and delicious.

"This is crap," Heath said decisively, wiping his mouth with a paper napkin. "Cappuccino's not bad, though." He licked the milk foam from the cupid's bow of his top lip. Flannery felt her heart flutter, and she didn't even have to wait for Miss Swee-ney's red-pen voice, she knew it was a cliché. Still, there it was, a moth trapped in a valve.

"You can't really get a proper cheese sandwich in New York, can you? Like a slice of white cheddar and tomato on a roll? Is that rocket science?"

Flannery laughed. "What? Mine's so good."

Heath groaned. "The epicenter of innovative culinary de-lights, and here we are with our dismal sandwiches."

Here we are, thought Flannery, here we are: not floating off in some candied fantasyland, but sitting in the tangible world— the sharp corner of the chair against her leg and a regrettable half-moon of filth showing in her thumbnail as she ate her sandwich. She willed herself to consider Miss Sweeney, though Flannery herself was the very picture of delight trumping con-cern, leaning close to the boy to hear what he would say next.

"I should have never switched from tea." Heath sipped his cappuccino. "From my first sip of the fancy coffees, I was hooked. It's curtains for my pilgrim spirit. Now I could never sail off to America without a milk-frothed espresso drink; now I'd be the conquistador with a cappuccino to go, in search of a lost city to trash with disposable coffee cups. Also, did I tell you I plan to have my iPhone surgically grafted to my ear to enhance my American experience? Greetings, brain cancer."

Flannery grinned so enthusiastically at his dramatic dol-drums that she felt her top lip lodge over her gumline. Because who talked like this about coffee and cell phones? Even the way he said *cancer* made the word sound lush and vibrant as fresh spring flowers: "Con-*sah*." Cancer was an unbloomed yellow daffodil, not yet yolk yellow but tight and green, showing just a hint of eggy lip. Miss Sweeney appeared again, right there in Nussbaum & Wu, her voice slow, enunciated. *Flannery, is cancer a devastating killer, or is cancer an unfurled daffodil? Which came first, the chicken or the egg or the dreadful metaphor?*

Heath banged his knees on the booth when he stood. "Now I must relay a bit of fairly awkward news." He bowed at the waist. "I am making a trip to the gents' room. I shall return."

Flannery let loose with a string of hyena laughter as he walked away, and that was an unfortunate thing. But when he looked back and gave her a crooked half-smile, Flannery thought, *Manhattan is mine.* Everything at Nussbaum & Wu was beautiful and true: the bald man in his olive green trench coat playing Candy Crush on his cell phone and eating a brownie, the girl with storm-smeared eyeliner studying her organic chemistry book and drinking an orange smoothie, the warm, dark smell of brewing coffee, the perfectly angled rows of black-and-white cookies in the bakery case. O, brave new world indeed! She wanted to kneel down and kiss the sticky tile. If she were at school right now she'd be in gym class, learning archery. Archery! Katniss was yesterday's news. Today, Flannery was the girl who had taken a fast arrow to the heart.

"You need anything else?" A man with a bar towel slung over his shoulder and a bus tub of dirty dishes looked alarmed by Flannery's moony, nut-bar smile.

"I don't think so," Flannery said. She pointed to the general direction of the men's room: "But, well, I don't know for sure because um . . . my . . . he . . ."

The man sighed. "Your date is in the bathroom. I got it."

Her date! Nussbaum & Wu exploded with a confetti of fiery gold and silver hearts, the satisfying *pop pop . . . POP* of bottle rockets and the sizzle and flare of Roman candles. Because it occurred to Flannery that she *was* on her first date, and—check it off her list, people!—she would no longer be that person who had never gone on a date because she was currently ON A DATE. RIGHT NOW.

"But there are other people in the world, alright, sweetheart?" The waiter nodded in the direction of the people in line and at a couple awkwardly holding their sandwiches and smoothies and scanning the room, doing the high school cafeteria boogie: *Hey there, folks. Any room at your table?*

But Flannery hardly wanted to abandon the table, so she cleared her throat and said: "Actually, we're getting ready to order some more things." She nodded, assuring herself. "Some different things." As the man ambled off, Flannery listened to his strained asthmatic breathing, to the ceramic kisses of dishes jostling in the tub. Life. Was. Awesome.

Flannery avoided the eyes of the table-seekers by rummaging through her backpack as if looking for some crucial missing item. She found her tube of raspberry lip stain, squeezed a dab on her index finger, and took a cautious look toward the men's room as she dotted in on her lips: Who wanted to be caught in a moment of vanity? She stuck her hand in her backpack and covertly unsnapped her compact and angled it toward her face. Nothing in her teeth, and her skin looked pretty clear, but oh, God, her eyebrows were catastrophic. There was nothing she could do about that now, so she snapped her compact shut, took a long, shuddering breath, and pulled out Miss Sweeney's copy of *Wuthering Heights*.

Because this was something people did, a normal societal-sanctioned activity to fill a moment of leisure: They read while they waited for the next thing to happen. They held a book—thoughts and dreams and wood pulp—the Tree of Life slaughtered so that people could enter into a new world. Unless you had an e-reader.

But she did not have that cozy feeling of holding a beloved book in her hands, and anyone looking at Flannery hogging a table at Nussbaum & Wu might wonder why she pressed the book to her chest and squeezed her eyes shut as if in desperate prayer before opening *Wuthering Heights* again and gasping, *"Oh, Jesus."* They might wonder why a frown gripped the smooth, seventeen-year-old skin between her astounding eyebrows, why her mouth formed a drooping oval of surprise as she alternated between reading and flipping back to stare at the cover image of Cathy locked in Heathcliff's rough embrace. The old cliché had morphed into a truism: You really couldn't judge a book by its cover. Because the narrative Flannery had read in the bathroom at Sacred Heart remained. The moors were still vanished. It was still Miss Sweeney's story.

How odd it was to travel to Manhattan on a Wednesday morning with no possessions, with no need to worry about losing my phone or purse. The great, unsung freedom of empty hands! The back of the cab was gorgeously empty too, and I didn't use the computer touchscreen to check the weather or traffic patterns, and I averted my eyes from the celebrity news that bannered across the bottom of the screen. I tried not to look at the time, I tried to blur my vision, but there it was: 10:37. I tried not to think about the parking lot of Saint Thomas More filling up.

At 116th and Broadway, I stepped out of the cab: Columbia! World of joy! World of minor and major torments! World of knowledge, of bright, terrible mistakes! I walked through the entrance flanked by the granite statues representing Science and Letters, and right away wished I were still a student. Embarrassingly enough, I was the sudden poster girl for Those Who Will Not Grow Up; if only I were still living in the Berber-carpeted basement of my parents' house in suburban Kansas City, the Portrait of the Malingering Millennial as a Young Professional would have been complete. I thought to go to Carman Hall, to wander inside like the Ghost of Duplicities Past. But one glance at the dorm and I envisioned Brandon—or was it a memory?—stretched out on our freshman twin bed, shirtless, his hands behind his head, his arms V-ed out, and his smile harsh and sarcastic: *Hey, Cait. Where have you been?* My cut-rate Dickensian impulses vanished; instead, a smothering grief started in my chest like asthma. So I decided to cut across campus and fortify myself by visiting Jayne Means. Jayne had been my advisor at Columbia, and her kindness and wisdom had guided me through freshmen year drama and beyond. Sure, you could argue that spending Ivy League money to teach high school—the yearly tuition more than your first-year teacher's salary—is not an ingenious fiscal decision. But there's only one place in the world where I would have met Jayne Means.

Before I knocked on her open office door, I paused and watched her at her desk. She was squinting owlishly at her computer screen. In fact, with her soft, modulated voice, her ruffled blonde-gray hair, her solemn mouth and soft brown eyes, Jayne Means had always reminded me of a barn owl.

Jayne Means looked up and hooted: "Caitlin!"

She came to me; we hugged in the doorway. Jayne smelled aggressively of dark coffee beans and aloe hand sanitizer, and I closed my eyes and allowed myself the comfort of her—O, Ms. Clean Beans, Ms. Jayne Means—and the comfort of her office. There was the same

Flannery O'Connor painting of a chicken hanging above her desk, the window that looked out onto the Harlem skyscrapers, and the dank, basemented smell of old books. But the coffee smell trumped the book smell. Along with her computer, she also had an espresso maker on her desk and a dorm refrigerator next to her filing cabinet.

"Come in, Cait! I'm so happy to see you!"

"I had the day off—Saint Somebody's day!—so I came to the city." My first lie of the day.

"Here!" Jayne Means moved a stack of books off her extra office chair. "Sit!" She pointed at me. "Love the coat, but take it off and stay a while!"

"Thanks. I got it on clearance at Boden, but it didn't look quite so army green and full and multi-zippered in the catalog. If I wear it with a pith helmet I'll resemble a dumpy Ernest Hemingway." She laughed so kindly that I laughed along with her, but I didn't take off my coat.

"What do you want to drink? Latte? Espresso? Cappuccino? My brother got me this sleek machine for Christmas." She patted the knobbed stainless-steel machine like a little puppy. "And now I'm my own barista. Yours, too. What'll it be?"

I hadn't remembered her as being so swirlingly energetic; she was clearly making good use of her gift.

"Espresso?"

"Espresso it is, Caitlin." She used a bean grinder, and it made that splitting-screeching sound.

Flannery's own trembling hands made Miss Sweeney's words quiver as she read. She thought of her grandmother, who had Parkinson's and complained that the hand tremors turned the joy of reading into an embarrassing chore: "Holding the damn newspaper is like shaking maracas," she'd said to Flannery over pastries in the sunny breakfast nook of her condo. Flannery guffawed as if a progressive, debilitating disease were the very pinnacle of humor. She picked at her cherry popover as she listened to the soft *tra tra tra-tra tra tra* of the *Saint Augustine Record* in her grandmother's hands.

Because that was how it went. Life could yank the rug from beneath your feet at any time, and so, Flannery thought, whatever was happening with Miss Sweeney's copy of *Wuthering Heights,* whatever magic carpet ride she was on, she would go with it; she would embrace the day.

Flannery? Are you having some PDA with the day in general— there it was in her head again, unbidden, the voice of Miss Sweeney—*or will you embrace Aladdin himself while you fly over the city on your aforementioned magic carpet ride? As in the old song: "Why don't you tell your dreams to me? Fantasy will set you free."*

Flannery looked out the window toward the Columbia campus up the block, where Miss Sweeney was right now, apparently, and thought how she should race back to campus to find her, and then she looked around Nussbaum & Wu for Heath, but Heath was not perusing the moving van and poetry-reading flyers on the community board, nor was he ogling the dessert case. *I'll just read a bit more until Heath gets back from the bathroom,* she promised herself, and vowed to read fast:

While I waited for my espresso I sat with my hands folded loosely in my lap, as if casually praying for the perfect cup. I looked up at the clock. It was almost eleven, which meant it was almost ten o'clock in Kansas: Brandon's funeral was just about to begin. I tried not to think about it, but Dear Reader, my brain had a mind of its own and offered up cinematic visions of the priest walking into the church—all professionally sad eyes and dramatically folded hands and white vestments—flanked by altar boys. The pallbearers came next, but I didn't know who Brandon's friends were now, so I imagined them as generically handsome JCPenney models wearing dress blues, hoisting the casket. Jayne Means's office filled with the smell of warm candle wax and the polished cherrywood of pews, but I didn't hear the sudden majesty of the pipe organ's first notes, and nobody was being raised up on eagle's wings. Instead, I was possessed by an impromptu earworm from Hell, a bouffant-ed girl group singing: *A tisket! A tasket! It's Brandon in that cas-ket!* I imagined Brandon's dad arriving late, surprisingly handsome in a borrowed dark suit and tie, and looking like any other proud, devastated father, except for the telltale baby steps of a man in ankle chains and the uniformed sheriff's deputy walking behind him.

Jayne Means handed me a small, warm, porcelain cup. I was so grateful to hold something warm, to be distracted from funereal visions, that I thought I might cry.

"Espresso, Caitlin! Espresso without the *x*! We are beyond expresso, beyond *x*! Caitlin, we are so cosmopolitan that we are sans *x*!"

Jayne Means, my fellow native Midwesterner! We had always laughed about how people from Kansas and Ohio dream up an imaginary *x* in the word *espresso*. Jayne Means thought I would enjoy teaching high school and encouraged me to get my teaching certificate and take a couple years off before I went to graduate school. I didn't hold a grudge about the crappy advice, and as I drank my joltingly delicious espresso, my Sans *X*, and as Jayne Means talked, I realized what I had missed that year at Sacred Heart High: smart adults.

But now it appeared that she was staring at me expectantly, and so I started to talk nonstop.

"Oh my God, this is wonderful! Yu-*um*! It's the best. I've never had one so good. Ever." And so forth. I tried to make my voice über-joyful, but anxiety arrived, unbidden, a fuzzy caterpillar inching around my brain, flipping switches with its deft antennae and pleading: *"Caitlin, please clear your throat excessively! It's not a weird thing to do at all! Do it! Do it now! And, hey, you're welcome for the sudden sweat soaking your palms, making your cup feel awfully slippery, for the general feeling that you need to leave the room before you blurt out every bizarre thought you've ever had! You're mighty welcome!"*

I had stopped taking my Nardil Monday night, the night before last, when I'd received an e-mail from Brandon's mom. I hadn't seen her in seven years but she obviously held a grudge. The subject line simply said: *Bad news.*

My own mother had left a cryptic phone message late Sunday night: *"Caitlin, can you call me? I need to let you know that, well . . . Life doesn't always turn out the way we want it to, or hope it will. Sometimes we are unprepared for our . . . journey."* I had attributed her trembling voice to menopausal looniness and chardonnay, and had not remotely considered returning her call.

Brandon's mom's e-mail didn't include a personal note; there was just a link to the *Kansas City Star.*

I clicked.

Dear Reader, my vision is perfect, but what I saw—Brandon's obituary—made me press my face so close to the screen that I could barely read at all, the letters jumbling into Zapf Dingbats as my mouth opened and closed in fish-like palpitations. Still, the words reached me and filled me all night long, and so of course I didn't take my medicine—I was disgusted by the very thought of being babied by pharmaceuticals. I was going to have my brain cosseted and comforted while Brandon rocketed into the unknowable? Who was I to live in a tolerable, pillowed bubble of amped-up serotonin, to live in a world that no longer contained Brandon? Who was I to seek relief? But I'd tucked the almost-full bottle into my pocket before I left for school that morning; I hadn't shed it with most of my other earthly possessions and wondered if I could survive the side effects of withdrawal I'd been enduring: the bundle of barbed wire unspooling in my stomach, the chills despite streams of sweat bucketing down my back . . .

As Jayne Means's office shrank into a miniature steam room, I rambled on and on about how I missed the city, how living in Connecticut was not that different from living in Kansas, and how I wanted to move back to the city like, yesterday, but the rent, *the rent!* I currently lived in a charming—white pine floors and bay window—studio apartment in a 1930s building, which of course would have been cost-prohibitive in Manhattan. But the coziness only made me lonelier: I should have rented a sterile one-bedroom in a stark new complex, a home that, in the parlance of real estate advertising from Sunday circulars, would "reflect the person I was, and the carefree lifestyle I enjoyed." I told Jayne Means that I hadn't sent off any applications to graduate school because I had been super-busy, but that I didn't think I would return to teach at Sacred Heart again. I finished my Sans *X*. I was trying to dominate the conversation so Jayne Means couldn't segue into the territory of *Hey, do you ever hear from* . . . She had been not just my freshman year advisor, but my confidante, too, when my mind had been a swirling mess. (Compared to the crystal clear discernment I enjoyed now, am I right?) I was grateful for her help and kindness, and we had kept up a friendship throughout my time at Columbia and after, too; we exchanged ironic holiday cards and the occasional e-mail.

"Cait?" Her voice sounded fiercely casual. "You doing okay?"

Now I raised my eyebrows and leaned toward her, as if about to reveal a personal horror, the big surprise. But no. I called upon my Midwestern gift of small talk: "I'm so glad to have the day off! God, I'm so not into Sacred Heart! But probably the main thing I don't like about teaching is the other teachers!"

Jayne Means nodded, empathetic.

"Most of them seem vaguely mean and sluggish, too; they just don't seem to be working very hard. But then again, a few of the teachers are ambitiously pretentious and entirely stupid—a charming combo—and bringing their A game each and every day."

She rewarded me with a bright, caffeinated giggle.

"The math teacher is actually smart, and also a really good teacher, but she can't be *just* a good teacher, she has to put some pseudo-feminist sheen on it: On the back of her van there's a pink bumper sticker that says: *I'M A WOMAN AND I USE MATH EVERY DAY!* I can't tell you how much I want to change that innocuous *a* in math to a jaunty *e*."

Jayne Means leaned in collegially. "The other teachers can be a problem here, too. The new hire? The Swiss poet? Beautiful, even with this sort of . . . statement hair." She moved one hand to her earlobe, the other to her shoulder, frowning. "A retro bi-level bob with a Susan Sontag stripe of silver bolting down the side—she dyes it like that—and she's a strident vegan. It's not like I'm eating veal parmesan for breakfast. And being a vegan is good for the planet, being a vegan is more than okay. However . . ."

Here she paused, a good person weighing the bitchy impulse to gossip against the high road of silent observation. Jayne Means! Her last name should have been *Kinds*. I thought to tell her how much she had meant to me, what an inspiring and brilliant teacher she was.

She wasn't a saint, though: "Something less than okay? Her stance on nonrecyclable feminine protection. At the last faculty party she got drunk and went through all the purses—I know!—and then proceeded to give an extemporaneous lecture about not using feminine protection manufactured by evil corporations."

I laughed for a long time! For too long, as I contemplated how laughter would not be possible without vowel sounds, and I was about to share this breakthrough theory with her, when Jayne Means said: "Where's *your* purse, by the way?" Her voice was an accusatory shotgun staccato.

I shocked myself with the next thing I said, familiar as I am with my own lying ways. It was the ease with which I called upon an actual blush, how I willed a physiological response as I coyly remarked: "I left it with a friend at the coffee shop." When I said the word *friend,* I hooked quick hand quotes around the word and offered up an ironical smile, so that even *I* imagined I had some dreamy special someone waiting for me at the Hungarian Pastry Shop, but it also made me feel awful. I was disrespecting Brandon again.

"Oh, Caitlin," she said. "Good for you!" Her voice was packed with relief, with tenderness. Flannery O'Connor's painted chicken seemed to look at me askance.

"Confession time: I'm doing Match.com myself. Do. Not. Ask. It's completely humiliating. Seriously, don't ask!"

"Oh, wow," I said, swelling my voice to an enthusiastic trill: "That's great!" I felt the blood rushing to my face, but this time it was real. I was blushing on behalf of Jayne Means. When she'd been my advisor, and I'd been in the thick of my romantic drama, I'd thought of her as a role model, a paradigm shifter, just Jayne Means and her ironic tabby cats, Single and Lady, and how she'd laughed at all the get-married-or-you-will-die-lonely books, at the awful "authors" on the covers flashing their bleached teeth and emerald-cut solitaires. And now: Match.com?

I couldn't bear to think of Jayne being on the typically delightful Match.com date, the guy giving himself an after-lunch root canal with the frilled toothpick from his BLT while boasting about his twin passions: couponing and water-skiing. I understood the awful impulse of adult dating: the desire to put a sticky note on your forehead that said *I AM LONELY*. I recognized the accompanying desire to have the sticky note ripped off by another person: Touch me. See me. It was why I'd come to see Jayne Means. But Jayne was above Internet dating. I'm sorry; she just was.

And I believed I was above it too. Not just because I'd been on a Match.com date with a guy who walked so haltingly that I suspected he had a prosthetic leg and felt a corresponding tenderness for him, for his tenacity in the face of trauma and grueling physical therapy—only to discover he had walked into the movie theater and sat down without once bending his left leg because he didn't want to disturb Captain Ahab, the ferret napping in the roomy calf pocket of his maroon cargo pants. Mostly though, every Match man had been merely pretentious or boring, or a stupefying combination of the two, and so, Dear Reader, I had empirical evidence that proved the white-hot alchemy of true love only happened once. The clichéd lightning zigzagging across the night sky would never again form the same dazzling pattern. The world would never offer up another Brandon Marzetti-Corcoran. Or perhaps I had simply been poisoned by Emily Brontë, by the idea of everlasting soul mates? Because when I read in his obituary that Brandon had a fiancée—Megan Reynolds, a name so banal it sounded like an accessory shop at a low-rent strip mall—I felt no jolt of romantic grief or even girly jealousy, because I knew he still loved me.

I had always been in his thoughts.

Whatever pale passion he felt for his *fiancée*—the cornball rom-com sound of the very word!—meant nothing to me. Also, I felt pretty confident that his fiancée would not make the kind of sacrifice I was prepared to make.

And so I was more than happy to respect Jayne's wishes and not ask about her quotidian online-dating misadventures, to cut the conversation away from romance, and continue with many inane homilies from the Church of Caitlin.

"Oh, and it's not just the teachers: The students, the Sacred Heart girls, are pretty bad. Their brains are so sloggy from sexy vampires and perfect dystopias that they can't tolerate a protagonist living in a fictional real world: Oxymoronville, I know. This week I taught *Wuthering Heights,* and they can't abide Heathcliff, because he's such a downer. I mean, he's a bit of downer, I grant you, especially in his later years—"

"—When he goes from troubled love interest to vengeful sociopath?"

I offered up a blast of nervous laughter, fearing she was drawing upon a recent Match.com dating experience, and stayed on topic: "Well, according to my Sacred Heart girls, Heathcliff needs Zoloft."

When I said the word *Zoloft,* my hand shot down to my front zippered coat pocket, where my Nardil was stashed. I'd started on heavy antidepressants my freshman year, after Jayne Means had suggested I make use of the university counseling service. The medicine had saved me from my circular ruminations and despair, and now I wished that Jayne Means could facilitate my salvation once again. Dear Reader, I wanted her to be more than a kind human, more than my Wednesday morning confessor; I wanted her not to be a postfeminist Match.com Christ figure, but Christ himself/herself, immaculately good-humored and possessed with X-ray vision. I suppose I longed for a dramatic rescue, as anyone does, for Jayne Means to say: "Hey there, Cait, is that a big old amber cylinder of SSRIs in your pocket, or are you just happy to see me?"

Jayne Means gulped her Sans *X*. "If Emily Brontë would have had access to Zoloft, I wonder if she would have created *Wuthering Heights* as we know it, or a novel with more measured emotions? I'm just thinking aloud here, Cait, I hardly subscribe to the whole 'artist as manic genius' school of thought. And we can only speculate on what her mental state was like when she wrote *Wuthering Heights*."

"With a Zoloft prescription, Emily would have wiled away her evenings in the parlor doing cross-stitch with Charlotte. And a Zoloft-ed Heathcliff would have gotten over Cathy. He'd be looking for a new love on Match.com: 'I enjoy fresh air, foxy ladies, and strolling moors.'"

Jayne Means smiled nervously. God, not only was I yapping about romance again, I was talking so *loudly*. I couldn't stop myself, though: "Because that's what my Sacred Hearters like, a stupidly happy ending! They aren't just disdainful of *Wuthering Heights*. They crave a saccharine, unrealistic resolution in each and every book. They hated the *The Bell Jar*; O, how they dreamt of a world where Sylvia Plath would have stuck her head in the oven before she sat down at a typewriter."

"That's depressing." Jayne Means sighed. "And pretty typical, I'm afraid. The girl-on-girl literary meanness sure starts early."

"Oh, and they didn't even want to read *The Diary of a Young Girl*, because they did the 'Whole Anne Frank Thing' in eighth grade, and I suppose it's tiresome to read something twice, what with all the quality cable programming. How can Anne Frank be expected to compete with the Kardashians? I logged on to Goodreads and read the reviews of several of my students who had dazzled me with their critical skills. Get this: Anne Frank was simply not up to par. You know, the life of an extraordinary girl in an extraordinary situation was apparently 'not terrible or anything, just full of self-indulgent prose that never really goes anywhere.' One pithy reviewer with the intelligent username SACREDHEARTHATESHOMEWORK37 gave a magnanimous two stars! With a caveat, though: *'I'm being super generous because it probably deserves just one star. Spoiler alert: OMG IT'S SO BORING!'* "

"A spoiler alert for Anne Frank's *Diary of a Boring Young Girl*." Jayne Means laughed, pushing her fingers through her hair. She said it a second time with a sigh, a sad refrain. "Spoiler alert." Then again, louder and proscriptive: "Spoiler alert, Caitlin. All teachers get discouraged. Emily Brontë wrote *Wuthering Heights* after she'd quit her teaching job in the middle of a school year. She was homesick, lonely, and I'm guessing completely depressed. It's not like teaching is fun every single day for anyone. But the good students can make it a little easier, and they usually make up about a fourth of the class, and, in my experience, there's usually a brilliant, quiet one in the bunch."

"Oh, sure . . . there are a few bright spots; I'm always rooting for the underdog. One of my students is going here next year. She's a terrific student—a wonderful, original writer."

Flannery gasped and lightly pounded her fist to her forehead. *"Oh, God,"* she whispered, *"God, God, God!"* She didn't care if the people at the next table turned to look at her: an odd young woman crying out to the Lord and quite possibly ditched by her date. (Heath was taking an awfully long time in the bathroom.) Because, forget all the sublime sentences she'd read in her lifetime: Miss Sweeney's last sentence was her new favorite.

Jayne shook her head. "I'm sure she got in to Columbia because she had someone like you to help her. I knew you'd be a superb teacher; I could see it."

Jayne Means! She was so lovely.

"I'm actually not a good teacher. It's all her. And once she's here she'll be fine; she'll find her people and be more than fine. But for now she's plagued by the mean girls at Sacred Heart, and so I've tried to explain that high school is a relatively short chapter, and yet the mean girls are like cockroaches, that they'll marry and spawn more mean girls, and what can you do but move on and live your great big life. But also? This poor girl is saddled with the name . . . wait for it . . . Flannery!"

So Miss Sweeney felt *sorry* for her, and if it was searing humiliation to see it there in black and white, Flannery also relished the pity.

Jayne Means struck her hands to her heart, a beat of dramatic anguish that made me laugh, and I could tell my laughter pleased her. "That's a lot of name to carry . . . Of course I automatically love her parents for their literary taste, but also for their bravado: *Flannery*."

"Weirdly, at conferences, they seemed sort of cold, sort of random, really, not at all worthy of such a nice daughter, but I guess she got it from somebody. I don't know. About anything, actually. Just being in such a suffocating environment has depleted me: the parents, the students, the teachers . . . it's the whole atmosphere. Girls who think I can't see their vicious eye-rolls, or the way they exclude the girls who aren't great at sports or whose parents aren't all friends, or just, you know, if there's something special about a girl, of course she's punished for that. It makes me livid. It just infects my brain that it's allowed to go on. It's so hard not to say: Isn't this a Christian school? As in the much-touted philosophies of Christ?"

My heart felt like it was skipping beats. I oh-so-casually pressed both my hands to my sternum, hoping this would help my heart return to its usual dub-*dub* dub-*dub*. Something changed in Jayne Means's face as she looked at me; her natural expression vanished, and she put on the excessively neutral smile of one who might be dealing with a deranged person. She had a good memory, and I had shared stories of my bullied years with my own psychotic Catholic school girls before and even after my morphing into—say it!—a modest beauty who had caught the eye and the deep true heart, Dear Reader, of the captain of the football team: Brandon Marzetti-Corcoran. I paused to remind myself that Brandon had not fallen in love with my pilgrim soul when it had been shrouded in an extra thirty pounds and I'd worn the full metal jacket of orthodontia: top and bottom braces and the palate-extender that made me lisp. Of course when I had lost the pounds and the metal, he'd found my insights and bad poetry exquisite! Unforgettable. O, Brandon: I even loved his quotidian faults.

"The counselor at Sacred Heart is this bland, dim lady who, when I talk to her about improving the social atmosphere, says things like: 'Well, you know girls.'"

"Girls!" Jayne Means snorted. "Surely they are a dangerous species, best observed from a safe distance."

"Exactly," I said. "That is precisely what I am talking about. People can change, or, if they can't change, then they should be called out for their bad behavior." Yes, I was being self-referential and I was getting loud. My lips trembled. "The whole system makes me mental! The joy an evil person takes from bringing misery to a good person. It's part of every system; I get it. Even if you're not an evil person, you can make someone miserable." I thought of Brandon walking down the street by himself in New York. My mouth was so dry that my tongue felt alien in it, a strip of balsa wood sprouting from the back of my throat. "But it makes a person want to opt out and find, you know, a new paradigm, a new grid, and move from the center to the side, to the periphery."

"*Ah . . .* Caitlin?"

Her owlish eyes had gone even wider, and glassy, and just as I was making a mental note to simmer down and stash my crazy-girl persona, hail *pinged!* on Jayne Means's window. I wanted to be outside as soon as I heard it; I wanted to be pelted with hail. I could accomplish nothing if I stayed cozied up to my old professor. Brandon was not here. *PING PING PING!* Jayne Means didn't even mention the weather; Jayne Means was not the sort of person to make an insipid weather-related comment.

"Caitlin? I don't want to sound reductive, or full of psychobabble." She spoke softly, rubbing the mottled skin between her eyebrows, which had formed an inverted *V* of concern. The hail shattered on. She was trying to choose her words with care. "But sometimes situations seem more . . . dire . . . when we aren't feeling great. Also, this is such an awkward question, but . . . are you currently seeing a therapist? And can we pause to acknowledge that I have just uttered the least Midwestern question in the English language?"

Dear Reader, I didn't especially care for Jayne Means quizzing me about my mental health care plan.

"I am in fact seeing a therapist. She's great!" I tried to affect breezy laughter, but my teeth chattered like a wind-up Halloween skeleton. My psychiatrist was a kind-enough, chatty woman who favored heavy pharmaceuticals and brisk exercise—"Try a kickboxing class at the Y, Caitlin!"—but sitting in her office with the marigold walls and ergonomic office furniture, I sometimes wondered if I wouldn't fare better with a circumspect, dark-eyed therapist, a soulful Gabriel Byrne or

Dylan McDermott to listen to my troubles and gaze at me there on the worn couch with a smoky, guarded intensity.

"And I don't mean to sound dramatic about Sacred Heart! Certainly nothing is new or different in the world. Mean people have always really, really bugged me!" Insects everywhere shuddered at my slandering verb, and my sudden hatred for Jayne Means was nonsensical, quick and clean: the crisp *sheer sheer* of sewing scissors. I thought of how I'd cried in my hands in her office once, the freshman year follies, and when I finally lifted my face, she'd taken the brown napkin from beneath her bagel, leaned in close—a sweet-and-sour cloud of coffee breath and Mentos—and blotted the mascara tears from my face. Now I fixed my face in a casual smile, took the tiniest, tea party sip of my espresso, and said: "Brandon's dead."

Brandon's dead. The ash gray sound of it, with a touch of overdone drama—the PBS and chamomile tea consonants of death—as it rolled out of my ugly mouth. I watched Jayne Means bring her hand to her heart, her careful coral manicure to her peacock-blue silk shirt. Of course she remembered his name. She was kind like that. But I wasn't. As she offered her words of solace, my brain turned into a bad dog; it chased down Jayne Means's Match.com account and wrestled it to the ground, howling. How hopefully ironic it would be! "I don't care for walks on the beach, or hiking in the mountains, but if you're looking to discuss the protagonist in contemporary Irish literature, I'm your girl." And in a bright burst of meanness, I recalled her unfortunate cap-sleeved T-shirt emblazoned with the slogan: THIS IS WHAT A FEMINIST LOOKS LIKE! Poor Jayne Means! I had pitied her when she'd worn it to class. She didn't know that T-shirt only worked if you were a supermodel or a new baby or an old man with a beer gut. I feared some mean girl would sneak a photo of Jayne Means and post it on Facebook beneath the words *UH, DUH*. Because Jayne Means, the middle-aged college professor, was exactly what everyone thought a feminist looked like.

Now she was the one nervous and rambling. "So you're probably having a lot of triggers for your unresolved guilt and grief, thinking that you are responsible in some way—which of course you are not, Caitlin—since Brandon joined the Army right after you broke things off."

"The Marines! Civilians often use the general term *army* for all branches of the military, which is very inaccurate, as there's a big difference, say, between being in the Marines or the Merchant Marines or the Navy or the Air Force." I paused to add one more word, one arch syllable to shame Jayne Means for not knowing more about the men and women who protected our country: "So."

As if my snottiness were born of injured knowledge, as if I were some sort of military expert or knew more about Brandon's day-to-day life than any stranger happening upon his obituary. I printed it out as soon as I'd read it, but really, there had been no need. The words had imprinted on my brain instantly; I'd memorized them wholly and perfectly, as if preparing for an oration contest and about to wow the crowd with my personal Gettysburg Address of shock and sadness.

"I apologize." Jayne made a circular wiping motion with both hands, as if trying to physically erase her words from the air. "The Marines. My point is, your sensitivity is heightened right now, but beyond that, our experiences shape us. Of course you don't have much tolerance for job BS, Caitlin. I know it sounds like reductive pamphlet-speak, but as you sit here you are a different person than you would be if Brandon hadn't been killed."

The hail shattered on. I considered the cruelty of her last five words before I spoke.

"If Brandon hadn't been killed," I said, each word a sharply studded knife tearing up my tongue and tonsils, syllable by syllable, "I would still feel precisely the same way about everything."

Dear Reader, how could that statement ever be true? It's what I thought, though.

Jayne Means gave an exhausted smile. "I'm a little worried about you, Cait. Actually, I'm more than a little worried."

I smiled brightly. "Oh, totally don't be! I'm just . . . it's nothing." I regretted ever telling her about Brandon, about anything at all, I regretted ever going to Manhattan; I regretted being an insufferable Midwestern show-off and going to Columbia instead of the University of Kansas. I hated myself and I hated Jayne Means, a woman who had never shown me anything but kindness. I wondered how I could have ever found her to be a paradigm shifter, and what, exactly, I'd admired about her existence. Was it her apartment that smelled unironically of cat urine? Her embarrassing, sloganed clothes? Her pathetic, lonely life?

"How long has it been since Brandon—"

"You know what? I just can't talk about this anymore." I stood and put my little Sans X cup on her desk. I was being rude, but I considered it an Act-of-Mercy Rudeness. How could I tell Jayne Means that Brandon's funeral was starting as we sat there talking? She seemed pretty weirded out already. "And I'm running really late to meet John." I had chosen a highly original name for my long-suffering, purse-toting boyfriend.

Jayne Means protested, of course. She stood and put her hand on my face—searing the bony, starfish memory of her spinster's hand into my cheek—and said, "Caitlin! I'm so glad you're seeing someone. That's probably a big help for you right now, or at least a pleasant distraction. I'd love to talk more—"

But I cut her off. I was livid with Jayne Means for not saying what I needed to hear, though I had no idea what that might be. I backed out of her office as I embraced my inner mean girl: "Hey, and the whole Match.com thing? Good luck with *that!*"

Jayne Means inhaled sharply. Her face was a cameo of caffeinated hurt.

The weather was my punishment, ice slapping my face as I race-walked through campus, my eyes trained on the gates. I tried to relax my vision, to become one with the hailstorm—just another lowly physical manifestation!—so Brandon would come back to me, so the rain and the hail could cleanse us of all that had gone wrong, so I could watch Brandon lift his face to the weather, cold raindrops tee-tering on the ends of his dark, doll-like eyelashes, and falling on the bridge of his nose and the carved planes of his face as he put his cold hands on my naked back and whispered, *"Caitlin."*

But wonder was vaporizing, leaving a wicked blaze of nausea in its wake as I headed to the gates of Columbia. I was trying to quell the roiling in my stomach, so I started to move very, very slowly, my eyes on the ground, which is how I noticed the flowers: a dozen red roses loosely wrapped in a cone of deli plastic, propped at the allegorical statue of Letters, the woman holding an open book.

I felt Brandon's warm breath on my neck as I reached down for the bouquet.

Caitlin.

You have always been in my thoughts.

Four

"Did you miss me terribly, Flannery?" Heath had returned from the bathroom and now stood next to the table, offering up a rakish, leading-man smile. "Does it indeed seem an eternity since you last gazed upon my devilishly handsome vi-*sage*?"

Flannery had a moment of overwhelmed confusion—similar, she thought, to the eleventh-hour cramming for the math section of the PSAT, her brain too fried to take in more stimuli. No, it was nothing like that, really, because calculus didn't make her hands shake; working equations didn't make it hard to swallow. Still, she managed to offer up a quick laugh before she turned away and looked out the window for Miss Sweeney, who might be walking past Nussbaum & Wu with the taxicab bouquet clutched to her heart.

"I'm actually quite stupid," he said. "Please do not give me any encouragement." He looked pleased, though, and as Flannery registered his pleasure, she blushed, astonished to realize that a world-class nerd like herself knew how to act on a date. (*Don't forget to laugh at his jokes, gals! Boys love to feel they're showing you a fun time!*) She took a drink of her cappuccino, a long slug, her hand still shaking so much that she clapped her other hand on the cup to steady it. Would Heath find it odd that she drank two-handed, with her neck stretched back, a parched baby bear? And how could she be enjoying herself–laughing it up, ho, ho!—with Miss Sweeney in the depths of anguish, a dead lover's breath on her neck? The cappuccino dregs stinging Flannery's recently filled molar were a bracing antidote to this new reality, which had just offered up another miracle; she had apparently morphed into the typically callow Sacred Heart Girl.

"Answer me this, Flannery." He sat down and scooted his chair closer to hers, a small, thrilling gesture.

Heath: so companionable, so exciting!

Miss Sweeney: so despondent, so vulnerable.

Flannery wished she could parse these two worlds and give her full attention to each one. She thought of Heathcliff's despair about Cathy's growing interest in Edgar Linton, his plaintive gaze at the calendar: "*The crosses are for the evenings you have spent with the Lintons, the dots for those spent with me.*" She wanted a tidy system to separate the anxiety and joy converging in her chest.

"Were you worried that I escaped through the bathroom window?"

Flannery shrugged, envisioning Heath shimmying out of the men's room window and landing headfirst in a Dumpster of sodden vegetables and furiously squeaking rats in the alley behind Nussbaum & Wu. But along with the stinking produce would probably be old bouquets, too—spent roses with brittle stems.

"I did leave the restaurant, you know."

"Well . . . where'd you go, Bernadette?" Flannery wished she hadn't blurted something so weird, but Heath seemed nonchalant.

"I stepped outside for a cigarette. And actually my name is not Bernadette, though it's quite an understandable mistake."

"It's just a book I read that I really liked—"

"No need whatsoever for the apologetic tone, Flannery. I do have quite a lot in common with Bernadette, she of the wondrous visions at Lourdes, the young saint known as the most spectacular of *the* incorruptibles. I would like to, henceforth, be referred to as such myself."

"Um . . . You know what it means, right?"

"The most astonishing of the righteous, yes?"

"Ah . . . not *quite*." Flannery tried to shrug in a way she hoped was equally humble and fetching. "Actually not at all. The incorruptibles are the saints whose bodies—allegedly—didn't decompose after they died. Whenever the need arose, they could, you know, hop up and go about their earthly business."

"Great Scott!" Heath clapped his hands to his head.

Flannery laughed at his old-timey exclamation. "It's totally true."

In the heart of her fun, Miss Sweeney's words came to her, not the irreverent mockery of her studied verbs and extraneous adjectives, but the fierce voice from yesterday's lecture: *I would go to New York City, and I would never ever come back.*

"Well, Flannery, that's the last time I hear a cool phrase and start using it randomly. In any case, my definition is better. I would still like to be referred to as the most spectacular of the incorruptibles."

Nussbaum & Wu was playing *The Essential Bob Dylan*, Heath's knee bobbing to "Mr. Tambourine Man," but the sugary melody felt all wrong. Flannery looked out the window and imagined Miss Sweeney rattling her bouquet and singing along, harshly and sarcastically: *Hey there, Flannery Fields, you can flirt with Heath all day, but in your jingle-jangle morning you should be following me.*

Heath cleared his throat dramatically. "Am I boring you?"

Flannery looked back at Heath: "Oh, no, I'm just—"

"God, I'm *joking*. You are free to look out the window. You're a dreamy girl and all. I get it."

He was making fun of her, sure, but Heath's voice was so luscious, the scant *t* in his *get*, that she felt confident he was the most spectacular of anyone, of anything.

"But did you know, Flannery, that it's actually quite possible for a corpse *not* to deteriorate? It has to do with the quality of the soil."

She decided to make fun of him too. "You're quite Gothic."

"Shame you're not a Goth girl, then." Heath smiled, crinkling the skin around his eyes. "And it's pure science. Soil with a high concentration of peat can keep the skin on the bone. You need not be a saint at all."

Flannery's own smile receded into a neutral, nervous grin, and her words devolved too: "Oh? That's . . . good. Not having to be a saint is good."

Because the sum total of her knowledge about soil analysis came from *Wuthering Heights,* from Heathcliff, who had unearthed Cathy's casket eighteen years after her death and found her face wholly unchanged. It was for the reader to decide if this was due to the rich peat in Haworth—known not only for producing the heralded flora and fauna of the moors, but also for its embalming quality—or the supernatural.

"You might in fact be the patron saint of reading." Heath tapped the cover of *Wuthering Heights* with his forefinger. "Because you were so lost in this that you didn't see me walk out the door, or look up while I paced like a livid zoo leopard in front of the windows here." He raised his arm to the windows, to the receded world beyond the café. "Because God forbid I should be allowed to smoke inside an eating establishment while I enjoy conversation with a lovely girl. I suppose the powers that be think pneumonia is highly preferable to cancer."

Flannery nodded, though it was true that pneumonia usually *was* better than cancer. She looked back out the window for Miss Sweeney, a gesture that seemed fraught with contrived concern—where oh where could she be?—even though she truly was worried: She was! And she still felt so unnerved by Heath's graveyard ruminations that she considered the demise of Heath himself: He would probably die early and needlessly of a preventable cancer; he would be that skinny guy in loose jeans with a hole in his throat and the electric kazoo *bzzzz bzzzz* of an artificial voice box. But a lovely girl could hold two opposing thoughts in her head at once: Flannery had heard that kissing a smoker was like licking an ashtray, and she thought of the green ceramic shell ashtray in her grandfather's Florida condo, how licking it would be like tasting a deliciously seared sea-candy, and how ash was inherently holy and sexy: Ash Wednesday ashes smeared on your forehead, the charcoal briquettes glowing in the belly of the barbecue grill, a seared marshmallow on your tongue, all that sweet sizzling before death.

"I suppose if I quit smoking I can join the smug, healthy American Militia of Nicotine Haters. But I recognize that fanaticism is the heart of evil, so I buy a pack every morning, Flannery, and I smoke whenever I feel like it." He sighed and looked out the rain-pegged window of Nussbaum & Wu, flaunting his beautiful profile, suddenly morose. "Fighting the power, that's me."

"That sounds like a plan," Flannery said.

What else was there to say? She imagined that her brain was growing, swelling and rising like yeasty gray bread dough. Miss Sweeney's laughter rang in Flannery's ears, the descending *ha ha ha! ha ha ha!* of cathedral bells, and one red-inked sentence ribboned through Flannery's mind in Gothic font: *Give us this day our daily brain!* But Flannery did think her mind was expanding, trying hard to catch up with the shape-shifting universe.

Heath put his palm on the window. "I believe it's letting up out there."

Oh, God, Miss Sweeney was lost to her delusions, and instead of saying, "My teacher is in danger. I'm going to look for her right now. Nice knowing you!" Flannery pined for the harsh weather to last so she could have a semi-legitimate reason to stay inside Nussbaum & Wu with Heath.

"Would you want to take a walk with me? I love to walk right after the rain stops." He tipped his head and put his hand to his heart. "May God strike me dead for my relentless idiocy because walking after the rain stops is such a highly original concept. Most people prefer to stroll in the crashing rain."

"You are rather devoid of idiocy." Flannery had hoped to

sound sardonic, but her voice emitted a robotic cadence: *Greetings, earthling. I do not come from this planet. You, good sir, are rather devoid of idiocy.*

Heath took out his wallet, and Flannery quickly, and with maximum awkwardness—*Oops, there goes the cappuccino cup! Thank God I drank every last drop like I was in the Sahara, heh heh*—lunged for her backpack to get out some cash for the tip, but he waved her efforts away. She stared at his hands as he placed a five on the table. Heath had surprisingly wide fingers; his knuckles looked knobbed and raw in spots, as if he'd been exposed to the elements for too long, and his nail beds looked red and warm, rimmed with infection. As they walked through the maze of tables of Nussbaum & Wu, the hardware on Heath's leather jacket gave off a metallic cicada *creak creak*: Who even knew insect sounds were sexy?

Well, he was certainly different from any boy Flannery had ever been romantically involved with, which, granted, was a small pool. (A baby pool, really, holding only Brian McNamara, whom she'd met at a Knights of Columbus breakfast while visiting her grandparents in Florida. At first, it had been thrilling when he'd kissed her in the parking lot of Saint Mary, Star of the Sea, but the Knights had served pancake-and-sausage roll-ups—pigs in a blanket, which sounded like the punch line to an awkward sex joke—and Brian had braces: The porcine, maple/metallic taste of Brian's warm mouth had put her off food for the rest of the day. Plus, Flannery had been able to see the statue of the Virgin Mary staring at her from the side yard—granite seashells strung through her carved, flowing mermaid hair and a peaceful, stone smile—which hadn't made the make-out session any sexier.) And though they weren't technically romantically involved, not yet, Heath was following along so closely behind her that Flannery felt confident that anyone at Nussbaum & Wu would think he was her boyfriend.

But somewhere in Kansas, Miss Sweeney's old boyfriend was being laid to rest, and Miss Sweeney was in Manhattan searching for him. Flannery imagined her teacher's sadness presenting like an autoimmune disease, the lump in her throat migrating to her connective tissue, joints, and brain before attacking her rationale.

And Flannery was in Manhattan, too, while her friends and non-friends were rushing through the halls of Sacred Heart, the chemical citrus smell of clean girls and the impending boredom and minor heartaches of the day; here she was with the door of Nussbaum & Wu being swung open for her by Heath Smith: "You first, M'lady."

Heath Smith was certainly a real flesh-and-blood boy, unlike the fictional one dreamed up by Emily Brontë, another lonely girl. But Flannery's brain zoomed away from the laws of space and time, all those snoozy, corporeal constraints, to indulge her fantasy life, to imagine that she was with some clever boy who claimed his name was Heath Smith, but was in fact Heathcliff himself, with his cruel-to-be-cruel sexiness and fierce vulnerability.

Flannery marveled at the potentialities of the fast-paced miracle of the day. She was not only in upper Manhattan with Heath, she had apparently entered into Miss Sweeney's own private *Wuthering Heights,* and Flannery was on the pages too, not just a few casual mentions, but as essential backstory. Miss

Sweeney was carrying the roses that Flannery had found in the taxi.

Oh. My. God. Have I Gone Intertextual?

Wherever she was in the real world, Miss Sweeney lingered in Flannery's brain, choking back laughter. *Well, Flannery, perhaps you'll be given the chance to express your textuality with Heath Smith.*

But Flannery was already so deep in this new world that she would not have been surprised to see that other boy on the sidewalk outside of Nussbaum & Wu: the doomed Brandon Marzetti-Corcoran lingering between this world and the next.

The wuthering elements had cleared off, and a pale wash of winter rainbow arched over the island of Manhattan as Flannery and Heath walked down the street, dodging a pack of children on Razor scooters, moms in their athletic clothes pushing fancy double strollers with plaid hoods, and a pool of vomit on the sidewalk that made a mother screech: "Darwin! Watch your step!"

Heath snickered. "Because not everyone believes in your theory of evolution, young man. Some people believe in Christ or the stars."

"That poor kid! People will always be mocking his name." But Flannery laughed too, even with the considerable weight of her own name. She took a quick look up and down Broadway, searching for her teacher among all the random pedestrians, and as she could think of no way to ease into her tale, she asked a blunt question, and she sounded as phony and bizarre as any B-movie adventure actress: "Hey, can I tell you something that's *completely* crazy?"

"You may. I assure you, nothing is too crazy for me. Truly."

Flannery looked up at Heath. He was a confident Brit, a citizen of the world, really, while she was a suburban mouse, a Connecticut mall mouse, when you got right down to it. Well, she was mostly just a girl seized by the sudden desire never to be away from the boy striding next to her.

Miss Sweeney's red pen was unrelenting: *"Seized by the sudden desire?" Well, that's a little TMI, Harlequin Hannah.*

It was hard to know where to begin.

The boy looked down at Flannery. "Out with it, you. What's the crazy thing you want to tell me?" When he rested his hand on her shoulder, she shivered.

"Oh, you're freezing cold, Flannery."

"That's not it."

Their eyes met, and they both looked studiously away, taking an overwrought interest in pigeons picking at a rain-sodden hotdog bun in the gutter. Flannery wondered if it was possible to die of embarrassment, if there was a gravestone in her immediate future, baroque letters carved in marble: RIP LITTLE MISS AWKWARD. But then Heath darted behind Flannery, and gently slid her backpack off her shoulders and down the length of her arms. He took off his leather jacket—the fluidity of his movement was pure ballet—and draped it around Flannery's shoulders.

Though she felt like passing out, Flannery managed to make conversation. "Oh, thanks, but I'm fine."

He ignored that and took Flannery's backpack so she could stick her arms into the sleeves. The jacket was warm, heated by the blood and bones and internal organs of another human, of the biological manifestation of whatever their souls were sharing, and she now knew that magic existed in the world, that magic might suddenly burst the routine of any old dismal day.

She tried to figure out just the right way to say it; she tried to channel Miss Sweeney's confident conversational style. "So anyway, this is going to sound crazy, like get-thee-to-a-mental-hospital bananas, so brace yourself—"

"You're pregnant, and the baby is mine? I get it, though we've never even kissed, you've conceived, just being in my über-manly presence." He pitched his voice to a fine Elvis timbre, muting his British accent with a Tennessee twang: "Everything will be fine; I'll make an honest woman of you, Flannery."

If he was trying to shock her, Flannery felt pretty sure she could best him.

"It's actually a little crazier than that."

Heath leaned in close: "The question is: Is it crazier than *that*?" He tilted his chin at the woman walking in front of them, who was wearing a gold crushed-velvet coat with striped orange-and-black sleeves and a snarling, emerald-eyed tiger embroidered across the back.

Heath leaned down and laugh-whispered in Flannery's ear, "Do we think she's a William Blake groupie? Is this pure homage?" Heath cleared his throat dramatically and whispered: "*Tiger, tiger, burning bright, in the forests of the night.*"

The poem and his mouth so close to her face made Flannery light-headed. *Oh, Miss Sweeney, forgive my incessant dallying. I am sorry for your anguish, but this is the best day ever.*

She whispered back: "*What immortal hand or eye, could frame thy fearful symmetry?*" Though her voice cracked, she managed to squeak out another verse. "*In what distant deeps or skies burnt the fire of thine eyes?*"

"Oh, no," he said. Heath shook his fist at the sky, as if cursing God. "You're smart, too."

Flannery acted like she hadn't heard what he'd said, but she could not escape the raw ascension of bliss that made her feel as if she were floating down Broadway like a Macy's balloon, a bloated Garfield, bobbing along and ruing nothing, living entirely for the moment.

Miss Sweeney guffawed in her brain: *Easy there, girl. Simmer down with the parade poetry.*

But it was too late for any kind of moderate joy, all the churches in Manhattan had already lost their iconography: The lost saints and marble angels and carved Christs had flown down from the altars and architecture, leaving their old haunts stripped plain as Quaker meeting houses. Now their marble bodies turned supple and fluid as they maypoled around Flannery and sang Heath's three words, a trinity of bliss: *You're smart, too.*

Yet there was nothing unique about the moment: Flannery felt the same as anyone who had ever fallen in love in an instant, all the living and the dead who had known the hard-earned magic of finding the one person in the city who was perfect for you, the person who found you interesting and heart-wrenchingly beautiful: You, little old you! And, hey. *You're smart, too.*

Of course it was the *too* that thrilled Flannery. Smart was nothing, smart was easy, smart was a big fat score on her SAT, her name on the 4.00 honor roll, her name ringing out at the school assembly for GeographyBeeNationalHonorSocietyNationalMeritScholar, and so what? Smart was old news, a yawn fest. People had praised and mocked the smart part for years.

What no one had never noticed was the *too*. The angels took note and sang an improvised version of "Take a Walk on the Wild Side": *Too too too too too too! Flannery Fields, you, you, you, with your heartbreaking beauty, are smart, too! Too! Too! Too!*

Flannery tried to stifle her zooming joy; she tried to resume some shred of equilibrium and take a stab at normal conversation. "So, anyway. If you still feel like hearing the craziness . . ."

"Hit me. I'm ready. I've actually never been more ready."

"So the reason I'm here, the reason that I'm skipping school—"

He made a bullhorn with his hand. "Attention NYPD: The girl I'm walking with is a truant. Cuff her immediately!"

"I know, right? But, um . . ." Flannery was a little breathless from the fast walking. Her name had never been called out at a sports assembly. "So my favorite teacher disappeared this morning, and I took the train to Manhattan based on some things that I've read . . . and a few things that she said in class yesterday . . . I know she's here. She's in trouble, and I'm trying to help her. I'm trying to find her."

To her relief, Heath didn't say: *You chose to enjoy grilled cheese and cappuccinos in the midst of this valiant pilgrimage?*

She raised her hand—"Though I know it seems sort of impossible"—and arced it through the air to acknowledge all the buildings, and billions of people, all the kitchens and closets, the maze of clubs and commerce . . .

Heath shrugged. "If nobody ever went looking for anyone, we'd all stay lost." He sighed, and Flannery wondered if he were contemplating his own driftlessness. "I think you're going to find your teacher. I don't think it's the *least* bit crazy. And I can help you if you like."

"Um, thanks." Oh my *God,* she thought, Heath Smith is going to help me! "I haven't actually gotten to the crazy part yet."

"That changes things up, I suppose."

"So in my English class we've been reading . . . *Wuthering Heights.*" In her peripheral vision, Flannery watched for his reaction.

Heath nodded, slowly, decisively, and with a smug half-smile, the, oh-yeah-seen-it-all-before gesture of a person for whom nothing could be truly surprising, said, "Do you perhaps attend an all-girls school, Flannery?"

"Yes. Why?"

"*Mmmhmm,*" he said decisively.

"What?"

"Well. Old *Wuthering Heights*? It's a bit of a girl's book, really."

"*What?* It's not! It's a novel for anybody! For everybody! It shows that love and obsession are perfectly gender neutral, like when Cathy says: '*I am Heathcliff!*' Nobody's specifically masculine or feminine in *Wuthering Heights* or in life, either. What makes us alike, or different, is our emotional connection to the world."

Despite the day's miraculous trajectory, Flannery found it surprisingly easy to revert to nerd-girl mode. "I hate that whole girl's book/boy's book thing anyway, it's so sexist and goofy and demeaning to everyone's intelligence, it's not like anyone's brain has a penis sticking out of it, or—"

"I should hope not!" Heath burst out laughing. "That sounds like it would take a very delicate surgery to correct."

Flannery, whose face was currently on fire, couldn't recall ever saying the word *penis* out loud before—it sounded fleshy and *hideous*—and NOW was the time she had thought to bust it out?

"Flannery, how does a dentist apologize during a root canal?"

Her flustered response was also the appropriate one: *"What? What?"*

"Sorry, it appears I have touched a nerve. I won't refer to *Wuthering Heights* as a girl's book ever again."

"Good, because seriously, it's really not a girl's book, or a Gothic prequel to *Twilight. Wuthering Heights* is about obsessiveness, delusions, and purity and evil . . . Wow, I'm just thinking out loud here but I think it's not about mourning the past, but how the finality of the past can drive you *insane.* You know, how wishing someone you love were Christ himself, so that they could rise again."

She mentally scolded herself—*Really? Really with the resurrection talk?*—for being instructional and creepy, or maybe just creepy. And the brain/penis joke! *What in the world is wrong with me, and can it be fixed? God. I deserve to be mocked. The Sacred Heart girls are perhaps not horrible, just discerning, on to something . . .*

But Heath merely nodded. He didn't seem at all freaked out! Then again, Flannery didn't detect the intense interest she'd hoped to spark—she was now apparently a glutton for magic moments. She noted the moody boredom in his expression, and thought of how Miss Sweeney had written on her paper about the complex narration in *Wuthering Heights: "Axe the meandering."*

"And anyway, my teacher, she really loves the book, and she's really smart, like scary smart, but also, you know—"

He nodded. "Troubled?"

"Yes. She's just . . . different. She's totally sarcastic, but in a refreshing way, mostly. And she wrote me this really crazy good recommendation letter that got me into Columbia."

"Congrats!" He touched her shoulder, and Flannery felt the heat of his hand radiate through the leather jacket, to her sweater and blouse, to her skin . . .

"Thanks." Ugh, but she sounded so smug with the Columbia talk! If only she could communicate via snail mail, a parchment-and-pen missive wherein she could labor over every word so as not to sound so monumentally stupid. "Anyway, Miss Sweeney didn't show up for school this morning, and the police came to school . . . and I remembered Miss Sweeney told me how Manhattan was a great place to get lost, how you can be surrounded but still have your anonymity."

He nodded. "That's what I'm here for."

Flannery waited for Heath to elaborate. When he didn't, she filled the silence, breathlessly: "Yesterday in class we discussed where Heathcliff might have gone when he dropped out of *Wuthering Heights*. I surmised that he would come here, to New York City."

"You're quite the surmiser, Flannery."

Flannery wished she'd used the phrase "I figured" instead of the woefully mockable "I surmised." And Miss Sweeney rang in too, a distillation of so many red-inked comments: *The better word is rarely the fancier word, Flannery.* Yet Heath was smiling at her as if he found her words dear, not grandiloquent. She blushed, not the standard flash fire of humiliation, but a soft burn of pleasure.

"Miss Sweeney thought Heathcliff would flee to Manhattan too. The book you found that had dropped out of my backpack? It's her copy."

"She's Caitlin Sweeney?"

Flannery nodded. "I found her book at school this morning." She hoped Heath was entertaining the image of her casually selecting the book from Miss Sweeney's classroom bookshelf, not rifling through a handbag in a bathroom. "I read it this morning at school, and I read a little more when we were at the restaurant and you were . . ." She placed two fingers to her mouth, in imitation of a smoker. "I had some time to dip into *Wuthering Heights*." How, exactly, should she say it? "It's different now, changed. The book is full of Miss Sweeney's thoughts."

"I do that all the time myself. I'm always buying books, which is a bit funny as I was never really one for school. But I can never sell my used books. Luckily, I only pay a dollar or so for them in the first place. Those guys with blankets of books spread on the sidewalk? They've curated my American education. So, granted my used books are especially used, but that's not the issue. The last time I took a stack to the Strand, the guy was like, 'Dude, you wrote more in the margins than the author wrote in the actual text, we cannot possibly sell these.'"

Flannery had a blissful moment daydreaming of Heath's marginalia as she walked along Broadway. Perhaps he would pencil a bold gray box around a passage that stumped or inflamed him and add corresponding question marks or exclamation points with a lighter hand, the ghostliest graphite there in the side margin. And his words, of course, his notes to himself about the text, or maybe not relevant to it at all. Maybe he used the margins like a diary?

Flannery thought about Lockwood, the hapless tenant at Wuthering Heights who happened upon Cathy's childhood Bible in her stack of books: "*A fly-leaf bore the inscription—*

'Catherine Earnshaw, her book.' . . . I shut it, and took up another and another, till I had examined all. Catherine's library was select, and its state of dilapidation proved it to have been well used, though not altogether for a legitimate purpose: scarcely one chapter had escaped a pen-and-ink commentary—at least the appearance of one—covering every morsel of blank that the printer had left. Some were detached sentences; other parts took the form of a regular diary, scrawled in an unformed, childish hand."

Was excessive marginalia a trait of the British?

But Miss Sweeney's narrative was not marginalia. Her words were the original typeset pages, transformed.

"Um. Not quite like that. The book is now *written* from her point of view. The margins are blank. It's the standard text, but Miss Sweeney is the narrator."

"And Miss Brontë's original tale?"

Flannery raised her hands. "That's the thing . . . It's not there."

Heath seemed unfazed, or maybe he simply didn't believe what she was saying. "Well, that's quite a twist, then. Talk about an abridged edition. You were correct Flannery. That *is* in fact officially crazy."

The fortunate people of New York were walking about drinking coffees and talking on cell phones and buying newspapers, ignorant of the particular miracle that was unfolding, the miracle of the book, of the boy. Flannery had not met his eye when explaining about Miss Sweeney's copy of *Wuthering Heights,* but now she looked up; his eyes were so deep and dark brown that Flannery felt like she could spend days trying to discern his irises from his pupils.

Miss Sweeney chuckled in her mind, and scribbled a quick note: *You'd like to discern his irises! My, that's some contemplative gardening.*

But there were also people on Broadway who looked haggard, the formerly fortunate, Flannery supposed, or worse: those who had never known good days. A man with a full Grizzly Adams beard and a downtrodden, layered look—a great many shirts but no coat—approached Flannery and Heath, wobbling a bit, pushing cans and plastic bags and a smiling Papa Smurf doll in a rusted metal trolley. "Sir! Can you help out a vet?"

As Heath pulled a crumpled-up bill from his pocket and offered it to the man, Flannery nearly swooned with delight, thinking: *For he is good, too.* But Heath had not actually put the money into the man's hand—he'd held the bill by a corner and grimaced as the man daintily plucked it away: *God bless, God bless.* The purity of her infatuation stayed strong, but Flannery felt emboldened by Heath's rather priggish donation. Because if he, too, acted questionably at times, perhaps he wouldn't judge her for going out to a leisurely lunch when he learned she had known all along that her beloved teacher was in peril.

"I don't mean for this next part to sound quite so 'crazy.'" Flannery even made the dreaded finger quotes. "The bouquet I had earlier? I left it at the statue, and she picked it up. I could literally look over my shoulder and see Miss Sweeney walking down the street with those red roses. And she's struggling with some . . . mental issues."

Heath stopped walking. "So you're reading about her day in the city? This very day? In *Wuthering Heights*?"

Flannery glanced down, hoping he wouldn't slap his fore-head and suddenly remember an important appointment—"Nice meeting you, though! Best of luck!"—and disappear down a side street. When she looked back up at him, Heath brought his hand to Flannery's face, and brushed a strand of hair out of her eyes.

He nodded at her backpack. "Let's have a look."

His hand. His hand. Flannery's great American novel, composed of her complex thoughts and jaunty wordplay, would contain only those two words, typed over and over until they blended and devolved into a new, unintelligible word: *Hishand Hishand Hishand*. Flannery opened her mouth to speak, but the ghost of Heath's fingertips on her cheek seemed to have cut her vocal chords.

Miss Sweeney rang in with her own marginalia scrolled beneath the text of Flannery's two-syllable magnum opus: *So . . . his phantom phalanges have spirited away your words?* She also doodled a quick pencil likeness of Edvard Munch's *The Scream*: the anguished man with his hands covering his ears, and the open, oblong mouth with a cartoon bubble, not seen in the original, that read: *O, unholy hyperbole!*

Heath raised his hand and fanned his fingers toward his chest. "Give me *Wuthering Heights*, Flannery."

Flannery unzipped her backpack and pulled out the book. She knew she was right; she knew she wasn't making this up, yet she still felt relieved when Heath read aloud: "Manhattan, my old Alpha and Omega."

Heath read a bit further, as if the sidewalk were a standing-room-only library, and let out a low whistle when he flipped the page. He ran his finger along the inner binding of the book, just as Flannery had done in the bathroom stall at Sacred Heart.

"I need to read more," Flannery said. "I need to see where she's going."

"I'd say."

Flannery thought he sounded sarcastic but nice. Nice enough. He handed her the book and raised his hand like a maître d', toward a small park that seemingly had popped up out of nowhere and intersected the uptown and downtown lanes of Broadway. Straus Park. Flannery made a mental note to research this later and find out who, exactly, this Straus fellow was, and why there was a funny little park named after him. But the girl who took pleasure in sitting with a mocha and Googling random bits of intrigue seemed awfully far away right now.

"Thank you," Flannery said again, this time with such bare sincerity that it was Heath's turn to look flustered. They took the crosswalk and cut over to Straus Park. One bench was occupied by a man holding a dachshund wearing a hot-pink rhinestone collar, but the other was not only open, it supplied reading material: a *New York Post* that some thoughtful recycler had carefully tucked between the slats on the bench.

A small, satisfied sound came from the back of Heath's throat as he dislodged the paper. "Ah, the *Post*. A guilty pleasure." He sat and shook a cigarette out of his pack, and Flannery considered again how all the health class information was factually incorrect, that smoking was in fact completely sexy, and besides, you could get cancer even if you didn't smoke, as everyone knew.

Heath lit a match—the gorgeous sulfur strike sounded magnificent—and Flannery sat on the bench next to him and opened Miss Sweeney's copy of *Wuthering Heights*. She read, completely engrossed, but also periodically floating out of her body to observe herself sitting on the bench with Heath, to watch the two of them reading together.

She thought about the prelude to everyday romance, the essentials of advertising: baiting yourself with smoky gel eyeliner and the CHI iron, with witty Twittering and *hot yoga for a hot bod,* with the Paleo diet to de-flab the wheat/dairy belly. And when one achieved an actual romance, things became even trickier. Sure, you could have the pleasure and status of being someone's sweetheart, but a girl had to work pretty hard for her flowers and Valentine chocolates. Flannery rarely listened to music at school; instead, she put in her earbuds and eavesdropped: Nobody wanted the Scarlet A in their medical records, or their psyche, so having a boyfriend involved making the essential, covert trip to Planned Parenthood before stopping at the mall to quickly purchase a random decoy item, for later: *Look Mom! I spent three hours at Sephora but found the perfect opalescent lip gloss! (And, no, you old goose! I do not have birth control pills in my purse!)* And if the tedious Science Fair of chemically separating the egg from the sperm wasn't enough fun, one could also count on enduring the relationship problems documented in women's magazines that made all of romance sound like a draining part-time job with no perks— working the always-slammed Target Starbucks that didn't have a tip cup. But reading with another person didn't require appointments, or any particular vigor, and it was something you could do throughout your life. Sure, Mrs. Schmidt, the cranky PE teacher at Sacred Heart, had made a similar observation about swimming laps, but Flannery knew what she was doing right now was superior to the American crawl stroke; Flannery knew she had shattered the chemical candy heart of romance and was feeling something real. Because reading next to someone that you loved or might love, depending? Well, it was breathtaking.

Five

Dear Reader, I cradled the bouquet to my chest. The roses were softening, their furled edges blackening from the freezing air, and I imagined them as delicious as whorled red-velvet cakes edged with dark chocolate. I wanted to eat them, petal by petal, even if they tasted of petroleum and fertilizer. I would devour the long stems, too, and let the thorns pierce my tongue and tonsils, a penitent's delight! I gasped out, *"Oh, my love,"* and then his name came out of my mouth, essential as breathing: *"Brandon Brandon Brandon Brandon."*

Because there he was, crossing Broadway. He had changed out of his fatigues.

Two girls in the pedestrian crosswalk looked over at him, their shared gaze fawning and unsubtle, because in his pea coat and dark jeans, Brandon was every inch a James Dean dreamboat, a trite and familiar description of faux nostalgia, but also God's truth. I lowered my face to the bouquet and breathed in before I took off running. I raced across Broadway, zigzagging around clusters of pedestrians, always keeping my eyes trained on the back of his head. I longed to scream out, *Brandon! I'm right here! Look back!* But I also didn't want to break the spell. I wanted to walk next to him, to flip my hair and say casually: *Hey, you.* I wanted to look fetching and composed and let my eyes tell the story of true love: *I have come for you. Things will be different now.*

Oh, the world! I wanted to be free of all my past mistakes, free of the physical constraints of the known world, the boring breath and blood of it all.

I trailed Brandon closely, only letting him get a storefront or two ahead as I walked past our old haunts. When I looked up at the awning of Nussbaum & Wu, I remembered my first walk through the neighborhood with Brandon. We had wondered if they were roommates, if Caroline Nussbaum and Jane Wu had dreamed up the restaurant as they lounged in their dorm room, rock-paper-scissoring it to see whose last name would appear first on the sign. But in that second when I lifted my face to the NUSSBAUM & WU sign, a slave to memory bliss, I lost Brandon in the crowd.

I blamed it on the children. Where had these unnerving hordes of children come from? They were pouring out of the bookstore down the block and distracting me with their inane chatter as they commandeered the sidewalk, carefully pedaling by on their neon bikes with training wheels, though their helmets and elbow- and knee-padding suggested kiddie daredevils maneuvering death-drop hairpin turns and BMX half-pipes. And then the moms swarmed, a shifting sea of black yoga pants and strollers with plaid bonnets—and I couldn't see Brandon, I couldn't see the back of his head, and I went up on my tiptoes, and that's when my vision shuffled, when upper Broadway whirled into color and movement, but no discernable shapes. I flattened my feet to the concrete and put my hands out like I was surfing. Of course I dropped my bouquet. How could I hang on to anything? I seemed to be spinning furiously and far past the point of nausea. I was on a new frontier. I opened my eyes wider, trying to steady myself, but my vision blurred further, so I closed them tight.

Dear Reader, how mercilessly the world shook me! I was on some hellish electric gerbil wheel locked inside the jaws of the zipper at the Lyon County Fair, being spun around and around while simultaneously being flung back and forth. My dizziness intensified as my larynx went rogue, as I keened *"Bran-duhn"* in a feral soprano that bore no resemblance to my workaday teacher's voice or to the blandly iconic tones of my suburban Midwest upbringing: *Hey, everybody doin' okay? Anybody need a smoothie or some chips?* Our Lady of the Malls had left the building.

And then it was over as abruptly as it had started, and I tripped across the sidewalk and clung to the wall of Nussbaum & Wu in case it happened again. Two businessmen in dark coats looked at the spilled bouquet on the sidewalk and then over at me with guarded concern: I was a rabid dog they pitied but were too wary to approach. Their bare-bones kindness strengthened me, and I shrugged—it's *no big deal!*—and offered them what I hoped was a winsome smile right before . . .

Dear Reader, I pause to apologize and ask you to please cloud your mind with refreshing images: Fresh laundry drying on a clothesline! A wedge of lime in sparkling water! Because I projectile vomited my espresso onto the sidewalk, my stomach buckling with each sharp heave.

When it stopped, I kept my stance—crouched over with my head hanging down, my hands at my ears, holding back my hair—and longed to cave into myself and disappear. Of course that's not what I wanted at all. I wanted Brandon to appear and place his gloved hand on my head and say *Caitlin.* I wiped at my mouth shamefully, and looked up to see a man inside Nussbaum & Wu carrying a bus tub, a white towel flipped over his shoulder, frowning and muttering, cursing, probably.

And so I stumbled away from the windows and affected a blithe smile as my fellow pedestrians cut a sharp circle around me. The public vomiting both shamed me—the elementary school nightmare brought to vivid life—and energized me, for I found myself in possession of the renewed vim and vigor of the post-barfer as I skittered around on the sidewalk and picked up my bouquet. I rearranged it the best I could, stuffing the salvaged petals back into the plastic cone, holding the bouquet to my chest, the awful scrunch of cellophane and the rubber-banded stems pressed to my sternum as I hurried down Broadway, watching for Brandon.

I was distracted by a woman standing on the corner, one hand holding open an NYC guide book, the other hand protectively cradling a multi-zippered nylon handbag, which was also tightly strapped across her chest.

Before exiting the Midwest to attend Columbia, I, too, had heard the horror stories: My cousin's best friend lives in an apartment building where a Rockette was MURDERED with an ICE PICK! MY neighbor's aunt was shot RIGHT IN THE EYEBALL by an INSANE drug addict when she wouldn't give up her danged purse, and so she had to get herself a GLASS EYE. REAL NICE SOUVENIR, RIGHT?

Tessie Tourist looked up at the street sign at 106th and Broadway and broke into a smile. Just ahead was Straus Park, a tiny, triangular oasis for weary walkers: a few benches and trash cans and some ornamental bushes that bisected Broadway. She crossed over to the park, sat on a bench, and wrapped her arms around her handbag—her Baggalini boyfriend!—and read her guidebook. Just looking at the bench made my right hand throb with all the old hurt, the creaky tenderness.

I had always felt safe in Manhattan. I had never been a victim of random anything. No, I personally orchestrated each bit of doom that came my way. The very bench on which Tessie Tourist perched had been my first urban downfall. I am afraid, Dear Reader, that I am being entirely literal.

It was the first Friday night of my freshman year: I was out late with Brandon and Nancy Ping, my assigned roommate at Carman Hall, and to our delight the Morningside Heights bars were pretty lax about carding. We were enjoying the sort of tipsy evening where one ruminates on theology in a bar booth. Nancy, like me, was a former straight-A Catholic schoolgirl, jaded and liberal, the mildest of believers, but Brandon was all in. And so the two of us sat across from Brandon, taunting him with the most inane biblical wisdom, those verses never cross-stitched and placed in oak frames: rules on menstrual impurity, barley cake composed of human dung, etc. Brandon enjoyed his Heineken, nodding affably and letting us ramble before he offered up his Godly defense: "You're both looking at it in pieces. Anything can sound stupid if you take apart each and every detail." He took a long swig of beer, and then drew a square on the tabletop with his index finger. "You've got to look at the whole picture, all at once." He slowly circled his finger around in the square, as if coloring it in.

From my peripheral vision, I saw Nancy watch his moving hand. "I see," she said softly.

"It's the same thing with Neil Young," Brandon explained.

"Who's Neil Young?" Nancy looked at me as if I might know. I did.

"Who's Neil Young?" Brandon wiped a fake tear of despair.

"Nancy? Do NOT get him started on his love for old-man music."

"Reading the Bible is like listening to Neil Young's masterpiece, *After the Gold Rush*." Brandon ran his hand through his gold-brown hair, which hung to his shoulders and smelled like me: He used my cherry bark shampoo. "You can criticize certain . . . well, artistic choices, I guess. But you just have to put your headphones on and take the trip. And, man, it's beautiful."

It was the sort of evening where a girl leaps up onto a park bench to serenade her awesome new roommate and her boyfriend, the sort of evening where she morphs into a retro disco doll and sings: *"Night fever, night fever!"* It was dark, but I could see Brandon watching me and laughing, and Nancy watching Brandon watch me, and when I struck a certain dance move—my hand moving diagonally in front of my body a la John Travolta in his glorious white suit—I lost my balance. My wedge heel sunk into a slat in the bench, and I pitched forward.

"Caitlin!" Brandon yelled, as if his voice could catch me. I was falling at a weird angle, my body plunging in a twisting motion.

I landed with my full weight on my right wrist, my hand pancaked backward. It didn't hurt right away but it felt so cold, as if my hand had been plunged into a freezer while the rest of my body sweated in a tank top and short skirt. When Brandon and Nancy yelled *"Don't look!"* in unison, I obeyed, and then there was a bit of mild good luck, some slacker guardian angel stopped hitting the snooze button and threw me a bone: An empty cab screeched to a stop right next to us. Except the cabdriver *did* look, and he gasped, *"Oh my sweet dear Jesus."* He got out of the cab and helped Brandon and Nancy get me off the ground and into the backseat. All the while, my hand felt alien to me, a bundle of broken-off icicles that had glommed onto my arm.

I rode in the backseat between them. Brandon had taken off his T-shirt and loosely blanketed it around my hand, and Nancy cradled her own hands into a supportive nest for it. She was shivering, and by the sound of her constant swallowing and raspy breathing, trying not to cry.

A nauseated sleepiness came over me, and I started to recede, but the air moving over my wrist and hand was as intense as bucketing ice water, and I said, "Please turn the air conditioning off." From either side of me came whispered rosaries of assurance: Brandon saying, *You're gonna be fine, Cait; you're gonna be fine, Cait;* and from Nancy a string of *It's okay we're almost at the hospital It's okay we're almost at the hospital.* But no one was doing what I asked, and so I wailed: *"God, please please please turn off the air conditioner!"* The driver pumped the gas, our bodies lurched forward, and icy, silvery pain tornadoed through my hand. Brandon—O, sweet angel of Heineken breath and aquamarine eyes glowing in the darkness—whimpered out the bad news: "Caitlin, the air-conditioning isn't on. It's really hot in here."

My hand was hidden under a pale green sheet at the hospital. A social worker with a clipboard and an appealing necklace—it looked like a string of cherrywood pearls—and a white-coated surgeon stood at the end of my hospital bed. The surgeon was briskly showing me X-rays on a portable light board. He pointed to the illuminated bones piercing my skin, the compound fractures of my hand.

"The poor kindergarten turkey," I said. Nancy and Brandon were on the right side of my railed bed. Brandon was still shirtless and had some blood on his chest; it was also on Nancy's balled-up hands and on her arms. A nice nurse on my left side checked the IV line in my good hand. The morphine was doing a sweet trick, tucking me deeper and deeper into peace. I stopped thinking *My parents are going to freak out so hard* as I drifted into a haze of happy warmth, for the nighttime city beyond my hospital window was a sea of bobbing lights, still incandescent with possibility.

"Before we take you in for surgery, we need to talk for a quick minute about *exactly* how this happened." The surgeon's mouth was a grim line.

"My wedge got wedged," I blurted, my noun-to-verb wordplay failing to impress. My eyes kept fluttering shut. Still, even injured and fighting off prescriptive sleep, I retained the spirit of any pretentious eighteen-year-old. "I can actually describe the feeling of falling . . . more than the falling itself."

"Okay, Caitlin." The surgeon nodded in a companionable way right before he asked both Brandon and Nancy to step out of the room so he could speak privately with me. But he was looking at Brandon when he asked.

"Why"—Brandon's voice was soft, and he held the surgeon's gaze— "would I need to do *that?*" He folded his arms over his bare chest.

The surgeon looked over at the social worker and raised his eyebrows—*Do your thing, good cop*—and so she did; she smiled at Brandon empathetically, as if she, too, had just been implicitly accused of shattering a hand. "I understand that you want to stay with your friend. But it's a standard part of our patient care protocol." The morphine kicked in harder, and the world gentled: The voices in my room sounded cushioned and tunneled, beyond my understanding. My pain fell away. I felt only the slow warmth of euphoria as I lay in bed, tucking my chin to my chest, folding in on myself, as if in possession of a sweet, delirious secret I wasn't quite ready to share. But just as I was going deeper, deeper still, Nancy's voice pierced my halcyon half-sleep: *"She really did fall. He didn't do it! He loves her."*

And then a quick cave of airy, opiate dreaming, and it was morning: my right hand full of pins and rods and metallic pain, and the room faintly scented with the coppery smell of blood. I tapped the fingers of my left hand on my mattress.

I would be fine. I could still type.

The IV hurt, though, the constant, plastic fatness of it in my vein.

Nancy was in the twin bed next to me, sleeping on top of the hospital sheets, her hair pulled back in a still-smooth ponytail. Her red sundress—patterned with whimsical inch-high Eiffel Towers—was now wrinkled and stained brown with dried blood, and her eye makeup was all helter-skelter, but she was still the sort of girl who looked beautiful in the morning. She woke with a quiet moan, acclimating herself to the hospital room, to life, before she looked over at me.

"Oh, Caitlin." She propped her head up on her hand. It would be a while before I could do that. "Are you okay?"

"I don't know, actually," I croaked.

"Brilliant question. Sorry."

"Where's—"

"They wouldn't let Brandon stay. The jerky doctor—did you notice his shoes? I was like, 2001 just called, and it wants those earth-toned Dansko clogs back—he was such an elitist; last night he cornered me and asked if all three of us went to Columbia, and when I told him we did but Brandon didn't, he was all like . . . hmmm. I could so tell he was insinuating that if you don't attend an Ivy League university, you're automatically a domestic abuser. It was insane, Caitlin. It was discrimination! And then he claimed the hospital only allows one 'guest' to spend the night, and smiled as he said it, like: 'If I'm talking to Miss Gullibility here, I'll say whatever I like, because I'm not only a good-looking sandy-haired surfer type, I'm also a doctor, so dude, I'll be making the rules.'" Nancy held her hands out and jiggled her shoulders, aligning her torso as if about to catch a wave. "I'm totally going to call later and check on these so-called rules."

Nancy Ping, my other soul mate! She was a fortunate child of the suburbs, an eighteen-year-old ready to call out a surfing doctor on any perceived bullshit, and a big-hearted girl too, trying to cheer me by mocking comfy footwear. Brandon wouldn't make fun of anyone's shoes, but he also lacked the confidence to follow up, to phone the hospital PR department for a grudge-fueled chat.

She reached for her phone on the nightstand. "Brandon asked me to call him as soon as you woke up." Her nails were painted a glossy magnolia pink, radiant as stained glass, and as she tapped on her phone I thought about how every single thing Nancy did was attractive. "He's waiting at home."

By home she meant our dorm room at Carman Hall, which she surely hadn't planned to share with her roommate's boyfriend, and the memory of Nancy's easy magnanimity made me cry seven years later as I walked down Broadway, a few easily dabbed tears that swelled into a snuffly crescendo of racking sobs. I bent my head and avoided eye contact, which nobody was exactly dying to make with me.

I felt so cold and sick when I raised my eyes at the corner of 101st and Broadway and looked down the block to my right. There it was, and I perked up, for O, it was a sign within a sign, a literal one; Brandon had led me directly to the Broadway Hotel and Hostel, for it had not been in my thoughts. I wanted to get out of the cold, though; I wanted to sit down. I looked at the hotel sign and imagined Joseph and Mary returning to the barn in Bethlehem when they were in mourning for Jesus, of how it must have felt for his earthly parents to return to his birthplace and remember that moment, personal and universal, when the world changed. Dear Reader, I was headed back to the barn in my own personal Bethlehem, an unimpressive structure made luminous by the past.

I strode into the lobby as purposefully as any thrifty tourist who had booked reservations online weeks in advance. The air was a warmed-over mélange of hamster cages and fried eggs, and I had to breathe through my mouth while I waited to check in.

The hipster desk clerk hassled me about not having a photo ID, but I did possess a tear-streaked face, as well as an impromptu sob story about my purse being stolen, which I embellished with dramatic, ragged sighs. He listened to my tale, nodding and bored: "I'm lucky—*I guess*—that my credit card was in my coat pocket because *I just can't believe I had my purse ripped out of my hands on the uptown C train.* Sigh. *And by a man carrying a rolled up* Wall Street Journal, *wearing a very nice suit—like Barneys nice.* Sigh. *He might have bought it at their half-off sale, I have NO way of knowing, but the sad thing—the resonant thing—was that my fellow passengers went right back to texting and reading magazines.*"

I told him that I'd previously stayed in a fantastic room with an en suite bathroom and tropical decor, and even a window seat, on my first trip to New York, back when I was an incoming freshman at Columbia. I'd enjoyed such a wonderful week! Could I have that room for the night? I'd written quite a nice review of the hotel on Yelp, and would happily do so again. The clerk listened to me ramble with a progressively stonier expression, quite possibly I was boring him to death, but between being a previous guest, an avid Internet reviewer, and a Columbia grad, I was allowed to pay for a room using my Visa card without a photo ID.

Dear Reader, melancholy victory was mine. A key! I had a key! Well, a key-card, to be precise. And I was allowed to check into my private room early. The thought of staying in a hostel room with three unknown roommates and a pair of rickety iron bunk beds did not particularly appeal. It had appealed even less when Brandon and I had stayed there seven years before, a week of sweltering August to kill before I—well, we—could move into Carman Hall.

As I walked to the elevator, the clerk called out: "Don't you need to contact anyone about your stolen purse?" I shook my head, but he pointed at the front desk phone anyway: ancient and beige, with a pig's tail cord—it was that sort of place. The elevator, which provided a bumpy ascension to the fourth floor, smelled aggressively of bleach and floral cleanser, and my room was a chemical garden as well. I laid the roses on the nightstand and sat on the edge of the bed. The polyester bedspread, patterned with palm fronds, might have symbolized peace, but I had to train my mind away from my Emerald City chorus of potential mattress concerns: paisley-shaped stains and bedbugs and stray hairs, oh my! I listened to the muffled whine of traffic, to the aggrieved German man in the next room ordering takeout: *Two cokes and General Tso's chicken! Yes! Yes! General Tso's chicken!* The memory of being there with Brandon made the room a thousand times bleaker, and I also felt no closer to him. I gulped back a few tears of self-pity. I unzipped my coat and saw that the bottle of Nardil in my front coat pocket looked like a popped-out cylindrical hernia. I would try to be strong and not take one; I would try to power though my nausea.

Flannery put her hand, fingers splayed, in *Wuthering Heights* to hold her place, and unzipped her backpack with her other hand.

"Taking a break, then?" Heath put the newspaper on his knees and leaned in closer to Flannery on the bench.

"I actually just want to Google something real quick."

"Allow me," Heath said, his voice gallant, exaggerated as he leaned forward and pulled his phone from his back pocket.

"Oh, thanks. Can you Google Nardil withdrawal? *N, A . . .*"

"No, I got it. Hmm." Heath frowned at his phone screen. "Heavens."

"Not good?"

"Dizziness, nausea, dry mouth, extreme vertigo, toxic delirium, manic reaction, acute anxiety, auditory hallucinations, precipitation of schizophrenia, vivid nightmares with agitation, frank psychosis—"

"Okay," Flannery said, her voice hitting the tin-can high note of a beginning flute player. "Got it."

As she opened *Wuthering Heights* again, Heath kept staring at his phone screen. With his voice packed with tenderness, he said: "The psychosis is one of the least common reactions."

I pulled open the drawer of the nightstand and found a regular treasure trove of detritus nested in the corners: a string of waxed dental floss, three dirty pennies, and a pile of small white shards . . . No, Dear Optimistic Reader, not doughnut crumbs, these were not coconut flakes, but alas: toenail clippings! Of course I also found the standard cherry-red Gideon's Bible, the beautiful story of Jesus dying for our sins, aka The Best Dramatic Narrative Ever. I flipped through the sticky pages and found a twisted Tootsie Roll wrapper bookmarking Pentecost Sunday. Sometimes Brandon and I had gone to Mass with my parents, and I remembered that the Gospel of the Pentecost made Brandon laugh out loud right in the pew despite his steadfast belief—he'd had a childhood dream of becoming a priest, born of his faith, yes, but also his desire to break his family cycle, to be nothing like his father.

And it was hard for me not to laugh too, because the Gospel of the Pentecost advised against sorcery and, wait for it . . . orgies.

Brandon sputtered out a few gasping laughs he could not stifle. He broke out in full-on church giggles, and who could blame him? He was still hysterical on the drive home. We sat in the backseat, his hand on my knee. "Really, those two words together? *Sorcery* and *orgies*? At church? All I could think of was Albus Dumbledore grooving around in a Speedo."

Even my parents had to laugh, but I saw my mother twisting at her necklace, either because we were driving through Brandon's neighborhood, Sunshine Range, where the guard dogs lunged at the chain-link fences, or because she'd overheard Brandon whisper-singing along to the radio, jumbling the lyrics to the jokey Right Said Fred song, his Kansas accent disappearing into a vamping British boast: "I'm too sexy for my church, too sexy for my church, so sexy it hurts."

Truth.

Yes, we were that couple in the backseat laughing, in love with happiness, in love with ourselves and, quite often, usually every day, too sexy for our church. So go ahead and pity us, Dear Reader, go ahead and be the somber omniscient mom looking down from the throne of your minivan, knowing that sorrow is looming, knowing that sorrow is going to arrive sooner than we imagine.

The rose smell intensified as the furnace cranked out a wave of heat, and the room was getting too warm, though not as warm as it had been that August with Brandon. The chunky window air conditioner whistled out the faintest cool streams, but to be fair to the electrical system at the Broadway Hotel and Hostel, there was a lot of sweat-inducing activity in the room. Brandon had driven me to NYC a week before classes began so that we could explore the city together. Yes, two eighteen-year-olds with a hotel room of our own: Of course we were too busy to spare a thought on the cleanliness factor of the room or to inquire about the crappy air-conditioning, or to send a wordy reply text to my increasingly vexed parents, who yearned for a travelogue: *Can't wait to hear about the big adventure! Caitlin, let us know you are alive! Caitlin, did you withdraw another two hundred dollars from an ATM yesterday?* I replied to each text with a smiley-face emoji, hoping my parents would admire my enigmatic response.

My mom and dad had been annoyed but accepting about the whole deal with Brandon taking me to New York. I suppose they pined to be like everyone else's parents, to do the drop-off routine: to walk around campus gaping awkwardly, to join ranks with the stricken suburban moms with their capri pants and Coach bags and all those sad dads trying to be cool in their multi-pocketed cargo shorts and band T-shirts, but no one cared about The Clash anymore, no one remembered The Replacements. The parents all looked on the edge of tears, except for the ones who were already there, rubbing the soft skin beneath their lower lashes, and perhaps reflecting upon their own dorm-room days and that evil bitch that was Time's Winged Chariot: Their next group-living experience would probably be a nursing home staffed by meth users. Or perhaps they were just worrying about their own children, who had been loved, who had been forbidden sugary sodas and violent video games and sent to an expensive university. And now they were here. But why the surprise? Had the parents not really believed this moment would arrive? Because as they struggled their children's possessions onto the narrow elevator at Carman Hall, their Botoxed or baggy faces looked equally astonished to remember that, yes, this was teenage communal living and it might include alcohol poisoning, date rape, or loneliness. So I had spared my parents that sorrow. Actually, Brandon had spared them that moment of wrenching realization, and had they ever *thought* to thank him?

Dear Reader, they had feared that I would not go to NYC, that I would squander my youthful promise for the captain of the football team: Brandon, O, Brandon, shall we plan a prom night conception? Do I dare dream of china patterns? A Barbie ball gown with a pearl white veil? So their parenting style zoomed from helicopter to laissez-faire. They were terrified that I would start wearing an elaborate diamond engagement ring purchased at the mall, that I would try to bamboozle them with suburban teenage theories about why it was better, less elitist for me to bypass an East Coast Ivy League University, and instead move to rural Kansas with Brandon and attend Dodge City Community College or Coffeyville Community College. He had received football scholarships from both schools, and I could help him decide whether to be a Dodge City Conquistador or a Coffeyville Red Raven! So, at home I'd pretty much run the show, and after I received my early admission letter to Columbia, my only responsibility had been to go to school and attend church once a week.

Now the room was getting far too warm. I put the Bible back in the drawer and wished there were a copy of Brandon's favorite book, *Lives of the Saints*. He had received a copy for his First Communion and, despite his dyslexia, become so enamored with the tales of martyrdom that he read and reread every hagiography until he could recite each one from memory. He also believed that real-life saints walked among us—not in the way of general benevolence—Hark! The good-hearted masses!—but in specific reembodiments. The receptionist at the orthodontist office had once viciously whisper-scolded two boys who had mocked a fat girl in faded Daisy Dukes: *"We can all see you being horrible, and nobody thinks it's funny. Your appointments for the day are canceled. Have your mommies call and reschedule."* Brandon had graciously come with me to get my retainers checked, and he already had his arm around me there on the vinyl couch in the waiting room, but he leaned in closer to whisper: *"That's so badass. That's so Joan of Arc."* Which was kind of a stupid thing to say, but then again, when the receptionist picked up the ringing phone and blandly purred, "Thaaaank you for calling Super Smiles," I could see a fine wisp of smoke rise up from behind her head.

But Brandon's life had not been all whimsy and orthodontic hagiography. His father was in federal prison in Oklahoma for the sale and distribution of methamphetamine and manslaughter. I had met him just once, senior year, when he came to town via the sheriff's office as a CI. Dear, Gentle Reader who does not watch crime shows, he was a criminal informant. The police were trying to bring down a decade-old drug operation, whose main players had met working as fry cooks at Sonic, a detail I adored—popcorn chicken and a side of meth with chili fries, please!—and who continued working there while they sold drugs. Stay in school, kids, stay in school.

I took a day off from school to go to the courthouse with Brandon. When his dad walked haltingly into the courtroom in handcuffs, ankle shackles, lace-less canvas shoes, and an orange prison jumpsuit, Brandon had swallowed hard and had to look down at the ground. I put my hand on his back.

The sheriff's deputy uncuffed Brandon's dad and led him to his seat. I watched the jurors watching Brandon's dad being sworn in: The pool was composed of the drab and middle-aged, except for jurors five and six, two young women in their early twenties. They kept looking out at the gallery, at Brandon, admiringly, at first: *Mmm-mmm!* But then, as they figured out he was a near clone of the criminal informant—the same aquamarine eyes and lion-colored hair—they pressed their lips into neutral smiles of suspicion: *Hmmmm.*

Sure, Brandon had to wipe away a few tears, but he wasn't a drug dealer trying to charm or sway with his forlorn foxiness. He hadn't seen his dad in two years, and he simply missed him.

After Brandon's dad was sworn in, the Latino bailiff poured him a glass of water. He gulped it down and saluted the bailiff. "Hit me again, amigo!"

Brandon groaned quietly. The judge buckled her glossed lips and ran her hand through her short, frosted hair.

The deputy escorted Brandon's dad out of the courtroom after he gave his testimony, which was chiefly concerned with people named Jimbo and Big Tammy and Crystal Light and included the hilarious vernacular of Drug World, where the letter of the day was *T*! The letter *T* was curiously prominent in the labeling and selling of methamphetamine: a T-Ball, a T-shirt, a T-Rex! But I also found out something not quite so funny about myself. Brandon and I followed his dad and the deputy out of the courtroom, our strides shortened, so that we would not outpace a man in ankle shackles and his keeper.

When Brandon asked if he could talk to his dad for a moment, the deputy nodded politely and stepped back a foot to give them a moment of semi-privacy. Brandon had finished off a six-pack that morning before we went to the courthouse—could you blame him?—and he thanked the deputy just a shade too effusively. I took a look at the people huddled in conversation or waiting on benches in the corridor: attorneys in dress clothes—possibly defendants in dress clothes hoping to impress?—law enforcement, and those who wore orange prison gear, or fast-food uniforms, or the perpetual casual Friday apparel of the downtrodden—sloganed T-shirts and sweatpants.

"Hey, Dad," Brandon said brightly. "Man! It is awesome to see you. And hey!" He put his arm around me. "This is Caitlin."

Brandon's dad looked at me for a long moment. I chattered away, filling the silence. The pièce de résistance of my nervous small talk? "Brandon has told me so much about you!"

He smiled at me, his gold front tooth especially bright and glinty in the dismal gray corridor. Though his hands were cuffed behind him, he dipped his head to the side, foppish as you please, and his voice sounded courtly, deferential. "My, my. You are a beautiful young lady. May I call you *Cait*, Caitlin? Don't say no. I'm gonna call you *Cait*, Cait."

The deputy sighed. His eyes looked so flat and expressionless that I panicked. I gave the deputy an ingratiating, gummy grin, trying to telegraph: *My inclusion in this particular trio before you is purely circumstantial, sir! Clearly, I am not like them!* Because my father was not a prisoner; *my* father was a dentist. Did the sheriff not notice my perfect teeth, my long curls glossed and shining with Aveda pomade? Did he not watch the high school scholars quiz bowls on public TV? Good God, man! I was the pretty one who knew the capital of Bulgaria! Oh, I was proud of Brandon, proud of his crappy house, his football playing, his good looks, his kindness, but I was desperate for the deputy to see that not only was Brandon's father NOT LIKE ME, that Brandon, too, was NOT LIKE ME.

Oh, Dear Reader, why was my first instinct betrayal?

And why was Brandon receding from me in this room? I longed to hear him say my name. I no longer even remembered the exact sound of his voice, but I remembered when I could hear it in my mind: the memory of a memory. But I could still close my eyes and feel his hands on my back; I could remember lying with him in the very bed I was sitting on now. I remembered stoned laughter and the raisin pie smell of pot smoke floating out from the room next door, and our stained sheets, and the polyester pillowcases that had given me a sweaty red rash of acne to start off my freshman year, and I remembered joy. Because before I met Brandon, it had seemed to me that a girl had two choices: The world could crack open and you could walk into it by yourself, a private kaleidoscope of colorful experience fractured by loneliness, or you could enjoy the cozy contentment of being loved, the security of being in a couple, and yet long for solitude and adventure. Can you guess who had the best of both worlds during that blissful week? Who smiled up at the popcorn ceiling after Brandon had fallen asleep?

Who was that smug, sated girl and how had she been so replaced?

But it wasn't so much that completed feeling I wanted back; I wanted Brandon, I wanted him, I wanted him, I wanted him.

And I would join him in whatever new world he was in; and he was looking for me, too, trying to reach me, as evidenced by the roses left for me at Columbia! My love for him, my longing for him was so pure that I knew we could be together again. But I had to get out of the room, because the roses on the nightstand weren't so sure of my single-hearted sweetness, and I didn't want to think about my past stupidity, my floral snobbery. Their petal mouths curved into a dozen petulant smiles: *Oh, NOW you think we're pretty! Now you like Brandon's roses!*

I jumped up and said STOP a dozen times, one word for each rose. Because I couldn't go back like that, I was racing toward a new, futuristic love with Brandon. My mouth was sandpaper, so I stopped in the bathroom, but the only plastic cup on the sink had a curly hair attached to the side. Felled by provincialism and thirst, I stopped at the front desk to buy a bottle of water on my way out of the Broadway Hotel and Hostel. The clerk sighed when he saw me—*Super, here's the sobbing freak with no photo ID*—but he divined my need. He handed me a bottle of water that I downed in about three gulps. I was heading to the front doors, dodging the backpackers who milled around the lobby in annoying, bulky clusters, when I glanced up at the clock. It was 12:45.

The funeral would be over now; Brandon, buried.

The world spun me again: The rocketing blindness of vertigo had returned. I crouched on the lobby floor and squatted there, a sudden goose amongst the tourists and dreamers. It seemed like I was breathing through a tube, and when I inhaled harder, it narrowed to a soda straw, then a coffee stirrer. As I spun and gasped for air in the shuttling darkness, a hand reached out to me, and I grabbed it and pulled it close to my chin, as if it were a kitten. I held on tight, and when the vertigo stopped I opened my eyes to a shuttling blur, and then, as my vision steadied, I saw a tattoo of a Gothic cross on an inner wrist. The proportion was weird, though: *Oh.* It was upside down.

When I looked up, a skinny guy whose face was pebbled with acne scars gently pulled me to my feet. His black T-shirt was bedazzled with a golden Celtic cross, inverted, and he was weighed down with a duffle bag, guitar case, and a filthy thin parka tied around his waist. I still felt dizzy, unmoored, and I crashed into him, and we did a stumbling, accidental dance together—One two three! One two three!—until I regained my equilibrium. The desk clerk was looking over: *Would the clown show never end?*

There were two young women waiting to check in, trading looks and snickering. One acted as if she were merely smoothing down her asymmetrical blonde bob, but then she flashed a quick pair of devil horns over her head. When the upside-down cross guy turned away from me, not responding to my mumbled thanks, I saw the slogan in golden Gothic font on the back of his T-shirt: I DENY YOU, JESUS CHRIST THE DECEIVER.

The girls at the front desk were cracking up, no longer bothering to be discreet. O, the bullies of the world, Dear Reader, we are never free of them, not really. It is just when you are already down, they get to you, they just *do*, and the awful girls made me miss Brandon more desperately, for he would understand that the tattooed guy had likely endured something terrible in the name of Christ. Brandon had gone to Catholic school since kindergarten, not a Jesuit-run school in a city, all about equality and life-changing, but an insular, elitist, parish school in suburban Kansas, five miles from his run-down neighborhood, and because Brandon was from an undesirable family and dyslexic and *blah blah blah* he was only treated decently once his football-playing skills emerged: *Hark! At last, a valuable commodity.* Once he said to me, "For such an awesome guy, Jesus really has a lot of A-holes who practically *worship* him." And then, as if rewarding me for remembering his humor, his goodness, I heard it, Brandon's voice, softly, next to my ear: *"Your Prince Charming is a devil-worshiper?"* His laughter was kind, though. Forgiving. *"Only you, Caitlin. Only you."*

Six

A light rain started again, so Flannery closed *Wuthering Heights* and tucked it close to her body, protecting the love story of Miss Sweeney and Brandon Marzetti-Corcoran inside Heath's borrowed leather jacket.

"And so the parky weather returns." Heath stood and offered Flannery his hand.

She took it as if she were a geriatric who needed assistance rising from a park bench, and oh, the briefest touch of their lifelines, of all those random events that had to occur for this moment to take place . . .

"How's she doing coming down off the Nardil?"

"Not great. She's close, though. She's in the lobby of the Broadway Hotel and Hostel." Flannery took out the book to check the address, feeling like a plucky girl detective from a '40s film noir. She pined for stacked heels, brick-red lipstick, and a slim pencil skirt to complete the picture: Whatever angel was orchestrating the day had committed a serious sin of omission in the wardrobe department.

"The Broadway Hotel and Hostel is at 101st and Broadway!"
She tucked the book close to her again, glad to be topping her
stupid uniform with Heath's dreamy leather jacket, which
made her feel like an '80s punk rock girl with her favorite Dead
Kennedys cassette in her Walkman, or a '50s motorcycle chick
with a switchblade and pack of Lucky Strikes in her pocket, a
syrupy song playing in her heart. *Each night I ask the stars up
above/Why must I be a teenager in love?*

"Poor woman. That place is a bit heavy on the hostel and light
on the hotel, if you know what I'm saying, Flannery. I stayed
there when I first arrived in New York. It looks loads better on
the Internet. Though I suppose anyplace with shared bath-
rooms cannot be mistaken for the Waldorf." He visored one
hand over his face as looked down at Flannery. "I'm sorry I
didn't bring an umbrella."

"Me too!" She hoped it didn't sound like she was faulting
him for not bringing an umbrella. She only meant that she,
too, was sorry *she* hadn't thought to bring an umbrella. Conversation: It was *hard*.

He stuck the newspaper beneath the rock on the park
bench, leaving it for the next reader. "Flannery, if the powers
that be went to the trouble to make this bit of park in upper
Manhattan, they should have gone all the way and built a shel-
ter of glass walls, a lucent way station in the middle of Broadway, where you could observe the world while also being
protected from it." He looked at Flannery. "What's the word
for it?"

"Um. Like, a glass house? An atrium?"

"Hmmm." He tapped is finger on his bottom lip. "No, not
that."

She thought of *Wuthering Heights,* of Heathcliff looking through the window of the Lintons' plush drawing room: *"A shower of glass-drops hanging in silver chains from the centre, and shimmering with little soft tapers."* His description for chandelier was more luminous than the word itself.

But what could top Heath Smith's description of the word he didn't know? Flannery wanted to stop time and live forever in this moment, in Emily Brontë's shower of glass drops, in the lucent way station of Heath Smith. But he was looking down at Flannery expectantly, waiting for the word.

"Gazebo?"

"Gazebo," Heath snorted meanly.

But Flannery was uninjured, still thinking of *Wuthering Heights,* how Emily Brontë had given such sonorous dialogue to the scarcely educated orphan from Liverpool, and of Heath's own words from earlier, "I've never been one for school." And then Heath Smith said something very nice: "Should we hurry down to the Broadway Hostel and Hotel and have a hunt for your elusive Caitlin Sweeney?"

Flannery leaned over and zipped the book in her backpack, her thoughts jumbling wildly: This British Boy! *Wuthering Heights* as narrated by Miss Sweeney! Lucent way stations! The Broadway Hotel and Hostel! She tried to clear her mind by physically shaking her head, imagining her soft gray cerebellum sloughing open and releasing confetti of confused neurons and synapses that sparkled and swirled in her snow-lit skull. But even as she envisioned this, Flannery heard Miss Sweeney's red-pen voice: *Perhaps Google "basic anatomy of the brain" before you indulge in these neural snow globe musings.*

But it was Miss Sweeney who was shocking her, revealing a

life with all the verve and passion and stormy regret of *Wuthering Heights* itself. Flannery longed to be a heroine, to rescue Miss Sweeney from the Nardil withdrawal and her doomed, delusional pilgrimage of living in some futuristic bubble with Brandon. And here she also fancied herself a sort of modern Saint Augustina, because yes, she truly wanted to help Miss Sweeney, but . . . not quite yet.

If Flannery walked into the lobby of the hotel at this very moment and found Miss Sweeney, the day's adventure would come to a quick close. *Good-bye, Heath.*

Perhaps she and Miss Sweeney would share a meal at Grand Central Station (that would be nice) and then take the train home. God no, thought Flannery. For life at home already seemed so far away, an extraneous, murky scene from a black-and-white movie. Or maybe Miss Sweeney would be horrified to see Flannery walking into the Broadway Hotel and Hostel; the rest of the school year would be fairly awkward if Miss Sweeney had Flannery arrested for stalking. But either way, her time with Heath would be over.

The thought of never seeing Heath again was already forming a knot in her throat: The world without him would be flatter than Kansas. As they cut from Straus Park back to Broadway, Flannery realized she would need to work hard in the next nine blocks to be memorable, in case she had to bid him farewell, in case this was the best day of her life, the day that would bolster her during those countless blue days of the future. And so Flannery mentally whispered the mantra that had formed in the margin of her thoughts when she'd taken her SAT last year—after three previous practice PSATs—knowing her future would be dictated by the results. *This time everything counts. This time everything counts. This time every-thing counts.*

"So, Heath, what *exactly* brings you to New York?"

Flannery noted how false and pathetic she sounded. To stray from conversation about poetry or grilled cheese sand-wiches was to risk smothering the itinerant magic of life. What tricky business it was, this trying to delicately impose an im-plicit promise of permanence.

"Well, well," Heath said. "You're a curious kitten, are you not?"

He draped his arm around her shoulders in a manner that she guessed was merely companionable, but her snow globe brain was not sending out the correct *Hey, no biggie!* message: Instead, her neurons flashed just one word, spelled out in four neon-pink letters and chanted like an overwrought cheer-leader: *Give me an L, O, V . . . E!*

Oh, God, thought Flannery: *Cheerleader love?*

"Are you asking me what specifically brings a lad of my courage, integrity, and devastating good looks to your fair city?"

She was not by nature a giggler; she either laughed loudly or didn't get the joke. But Flannery giggled along as Heath an-swered her question and O, the weight of his arm on her shoul-ders was the opposite of depression: not the old gray veil, but a warm bolt of orange-yellow sunshine. "Well, Flannery, I could ask the same of you, could I not? Flannery, are you leading me into temptation? Could the whole missing teacher fiasco in fact be a ruse? Will I wake in a dark alley and discover that more than one of my valuable inner organs have gone missing and my incisions have been sewn up with dental floss? Oh, sweet

Flannery, if it's mint dental floss my stitches will sting like the devil himself is flogging me. I'll have to tell the police: I was walking with a magical girl in possession of a most magical book." Heath pleaded with an imaginary officer: "Stay with me, Mate. Things get sticky here: The book was transformative. I'm not speaking of any deep personal experience possible whilst reading the novel, but the actual pages transforming into something else, a new story. If there are any new stories. In any case, my girl was searching for her missing teacher just as I shall now search for my left lung and my kidney."

The weather was clearing up again, a good thing, because Flannery's face burned so ferociously it seemed as if the last few droplets of rain falling on her head might sizzle like hot oil in a pan. She wondered if pinprick streams of smoke rose out of her pierced lobes and rued the fact that her ghostly pallor served as an honest barometer of her inner life. Still, how could anyone retain a semblance of emotional calm if they were living this day, walking down Broadway and against all odds had turned into someone's magical girl?

"Alright, I'll come right out with it. Darling, I've sailed to the new world to make my fortune."

Darling! Yes, he'd said it in a snarky way, but there it was, along with the weight of his arm on her shoulders . . . And yet, Miss Sweeney was not only missing and in distress, she was withdrawing from her antidepressant cold turkey, she was delusional and physically ill, and still happiness rose in Flannery's heart.

"So, you're doing, like, a gap year?"

"I suppose I am, Flannery. Though I've no plans to go to university, so it may be a gap life. And making your fortune in

Manhattan is a touch more difficult than I'd imagined. Now, are you in need of any other pertinent facts about me? What have we learned thus far?"

"You are on a gap year, which may be extended to a gap life, and your name is Heath Smith?"

"Flannery, you *are* a genius."

"Thanks for the news flash." She had meant to sound only sporty, lighthearted, and so the note of irritation in her voice took her by surprise.

"Snippy, snippy!" Heath scissored his hands in the air.

Snippy was not what she was aiming for. All those long days at Sacred Heart when she should have been at a charm school in the Swiss Alps, if such a thing still existed. "And you're, of course . . ." Flannery's lips had already met and formed the pressed curve precipitating the *B* sound, when she panicked: Maybe Heath wasn't even British, but Australian? Was he a New Zealander? Flannery's voice was an uncertain whisper: "You're British?"

"It's a terribly embarrassing thing to be, so I appreciate you asking so delicately. Yes, it's true." He winced, approximating Flannery's tenuous question. "I am indeed British. I'm from the North—Yorkshire, a two-horse village called Haworth. But originally, I was from a bit further out, in Liverpool . . ."

Of course Flannery knew the locale of her favorite novel, so she knew the moors were in Yorkshire! "Oh! Just like . . ." She bit her lip, her heart banging. Maybe Heath was just making fun of her by concocting a geographical trajectory that matched up with *Wuthering Heights*'s Heathcliff, the starving orphan found in Liverpool by Cathy Earnshaw's father, and taken back to Wuthering Heights—which, according to literary speculation, was closely based on a real house in the village of Haworth, where Emily Brontë had lived most of her short life. Now Haworth had an established Internet presence; all the posted photos implied that earnest tourists—dorky but dear— with floppy hats and easels and journals were now a permanent fixture on the Yorkshire moors.

"Liverpool and Haworth do seem to be . . . rather notable towns," Flannery said archly, trying to allude to the fact she was in on the joke, a skill honed but never perfected at Sacred Heart.

"I suppose."

He supposed? Well, Flannery subscribed to the Haworth Village Twitter feed, so if Heath actually hailed from Haworth, she *supposed* she could blow his mind by bringing him up to speed on the local news: Rose & Co. Apothecary, the pharmacy where Emily Brontë's wayward brother had once purchased his opium, was undergoing renovation, and the Sainsbury's in the neighboring town of Keighley—free from the inflated prices of Brontë tourism—had a terrific sale going on Galia melons and cantaloupe.

Flannery gave a sarcastic, in-the-know nod, or what she hoped might pass as one. "So. A notable town with some very notable residents."

"So I've heard . . . John, Paul, George, and . . . who's the other chap?"

"That would be Ringo, Heath." Flannery could hear the trace of exasperation in her voice, and she was about to tell him that she was obviously referencing the Brontës of Haworth, not the Beatles of Liverpool, when he said: "So your Miss Sweeney, she's in serious trouble, yes?"

Heath was trying to keep her on track. Oh, even a complete stranger to Miss Sweeney showed more concern than Flannery.

Stay focused, she scolded herself.

"Yes, Miss Sweeney keeps trying to connect—I don't know what other word to use—with Brandon, whom she clearly loved a lot. He moved to Manhattan with her when she started school at Columbia."

"*With a love like that, you know you should be glad,*" Heath whisper-sang, but not meanly. "That's a tricky deal, then."

"She's tortured by visions of him, and not taking her medicine, and having some of those lovely symptoms. But she has the bottle of Nardil right in her pocket, so maybe she'll start taking it again? Maybe she'll feel better?"

"My doctor said the moment you decide you have no need for your medication—your brain rocketing off with whatever handy rationalization it cooks up—is dangerous, because that's when you need it most, that's when your free-floating despair is about to double down."

The thought of Heath waking up—she imagined him lonely, in rumpled flannel pajamas—and shaking a pill out of a bottle made Flannery a bit teary. My God, it was easier to obsess over the blatant nastiness of the dreadful than to consider the hidden tenderness—Heath and Miss Sweeney with their prescriptions and stomachaches—of the good.

"So again, I'm turning into a regular American with my fancy coffees and my antidepressants. But we all need our serotonin lifted a bit." He nodded at the street sign. "One hundred and first and Broadway! Greetings, Broadway Hotel and Hostel, ready or not, Caitlin Sweeney, here we come!"

Flannery felt light-headed as they turned onto what looked to be a residential street, except for the hotel and an animal hospital, where a couple stood embracing as the golden retriever tethered to the woman's wrist looked politely away. When the couple pulled apart and turned to go in different directions, the hems of their long, dark coats swung out and kissed: O, Love was all around.

And then Heath was pulling open the first doors of the Broadway Hotel and Hostel—the caught air of the vestibule—and then the second set of doors, and they were in the lobby.

"The aggressive smell of rose-scented cleanser mixed with a bouquet of eau de cat shit," Heath said. "A fetching combo."

"Agreed," Flannery said, ruing that pat response as she looked over at the reception desk, which was decked out in glittering bronze and surrounded by tourists. She wished—*always this impossible wish!*—that she could live her life via the written word, an e-mail edited down to reflect her best self: a girl of inherent kindness given to witticisms and highly original commentary. If only! She steeled herself for the awkwardness of seeing Miss Sweeney among the Swedish tourists walking in the door—their platforms and Hello Kitty sweatpants a look that shouldn't work, but did. Flannery imagined herself conjuring surprise to lessen the social awkwardness of seeing Miss Sweeney in the lobby: "Why, here *you* are at the Broadway Hotel and Hostel too? Wow! It's a small world—but I wouldn't want to paint it! *Heh heh.* This is a friend of mine . . . Heath." She was confident Miss Sweeney would affect neutral politeness but not lose an opportunity to pull Flannery aside and whisper, "Is that his real name? Nicely played, Miss Brontë."

Flannery looked around, and Heath did too: the piled suit-cases in front of the elevator, the long bench that ran parallel to the reception desk and held two groups of friends—Japanese girls who were laughing and taking selfies with their arms around one another, and lipsticked American boys wearing heels with rolled-up skinny jeans and debating their evening wardrobe choices: *"The yellow cowboy shirt with the pearl buttons? Yes, yes! A hundred times yes! God, where was Ryan? Is his phone off? He must be coming on the next bus. Text Ryan!"*

Flannery had the buoyant feeling that happiness was atmospheric at the Broadway Hotel and Hostel. She felt light but full, as if she'd been stuffed with clouds. She imagined herself on the bench with her own cozy group of friends, the people Miss Sweeney assured Flannery she would meet at Columbia.

"Do we see your Miss Sweeney anywhere? Since I don't know who I'm looking for, it's putting me at a bit of a disadvantage."

"She could be anywhere in here, I guess. I'm sorry. I don't see her yet."

"No, it's completely alright, I assure you. Well, now we're at the hotel. So. Perhaps we should do what one does at a hotel?"

She laughed—all hearty hilarity!—but her laughter trailed off quickly, morphing into the giggle of a pensive wee mousie: *"HA! HA! HA! Heh heh . . . heh."*

"Heavens, Flannery, I meant we should check and see if they offer free Wi-Fi. Do get your mind out of the gutter."

The clerk was busy and aggrieved. Guests clustered around the front desk in various states of pique, waiting to check in to the Broadway Hotel and Hostel, or waiting for some tardy amenity: The woman with a clenched jaw, pajama pants, and a lavender IT'S ALL GOOD! sweatshirt helpfully reminded the clerk that she had been assured of a set of bath towels *over an hour and fifteen minutes ago.* And so Flannery and Heath were able to walk around, unencumbered, though they were not, as yet, official guests of the hotel.

Heath took her gently by her elbow, and though it felt like a nurse's affection, practical and desultory, well, it was still pretty much magic. Next to the lobby there was a community area where people sat working at computers, and a fireplace and a nubby beige couch where a couple kissed with Friday night enthusiasm, their mouths cupped on one another's like CPR. Flannery thought of the couple on the street, their embrace, and their coat hems touching as they turned away from one another. Love was best seen from a filtered distance, not in oily close-up.

Heath noticed Flannery looking at the smoochers, and he waggled his eyebrows at her, a gesture that would be creepy if he were creepy.

"Has your Miss Sweeney found a beau?"

Flannery laughed. "*That's* not her."

"Ah, well. Do *you* have a current beau?"

"What?" Flannery said, though of course she had heard him, and whether she was buying herself time to think of a witty retort or just prolonging personal humiliation, she couldn't quite say.

Heath put his hand on her back—it made her feel like weeping with nervous joy. "Flannery, I have simply asked if you have a current beau. A *yes* or *no* will suffice."

She couldn't help but imagine a velvet hair bow sailing on a calm river and chastised herself for living in the confines of her nerd-tastic mind, absorbed in homophones while real life happened all around.

"Well, I don't have a boyfriend at the moment." Her words sounded hollow. "Or at any moment, actually. I've never had a real boyfriend."

"You've mostly gone out with mannequins, then, as well as a few dashing lads from the wax museum?"

"Yes, I mostly canoodle with dashing wax. How about you?"

"How about *you*, Heath?" He mocked her in the syrupy, faux-concerned tone of a daytime talk show host. And she felt herself blush from his unexpected meanness, her face a deep fryer of hurt.

Heath looked down at the floor. "Sorry. But I'm quite through with love, I assure you, Flannery. You are safe with me even in this particular locale."

Great, thought Flannery. *Safety.* Had she only been imagining their romantic tension, however slight? She faked a smile, as if being unworthy to enchant Heath was a source of terrific relief, and envisioned the girl that had broken his heart as a typical Sacred Heart beauty: smugly entitled, smooth-skinned and excellent at field hockey. *Shit.*

Heath looked around the room, at the kissing couple, at the arguing backpackers—more Mount Shasta than Manhattan in their North Face gear and hiking boots—and back at the reception desk, which was clearing out: Life was indeed good, the complaining lady now held a short stack of grayish bath towels and was striding purposefully toward the elevators with a satisfied grimace.

It seemed like Heath was looking for somebody too.

"Interesting," Flannery said, as if coolly. "What has made you turn away from romantic ventures?"

"Boring story. Boy meets girl, boy loses girl. Boy mourns. Et cetera. There are only five basic plots."

Flannery nodded, excited. This was her domain! Love was pure mystery, but plot lines were structured, knowable.

She mentally crafted her reply before saying it aloud—no more weird blurting for Flannery! She cribbed a line from her own *Wuthering Heights* essay. "So. Obsessive love and the eventual obsessing over lost love are at the heart of this story. Everything else is exposition and eyeliner."

Heath widened his eyes. "Well, you could say that. I mean, I suppose."

Flannery cringed and felt her shoulders rise to her earlobes, the old God-I'm-Stupid shrug, and she remembered, too late, that Miss Sweeney hadn't been in love with that line either. How her red ink had burned! Even in memory her red handwriting looked as jagged as animated flames: *For that matter, Flannery, might everything else be mascara and metaphor? Lipsticks and limericks? Please clarify.*

"I suppose it's the oldest story in the book, Flannery: The one person of all the souls, the living and the dead, who could flip the switch of the world and, ta-da, the lights come on and every little thing—even the dust motes—sparkles away. And that person leaves, and the world is brimming with torments." Heath looked away.

"But if music or poetry teaches us anything, it is that our hearts were made to be broken." Flannery was almost hyperventilating. "It's everywhere, the ubiquitous quality of heartbreak, the immutable sadness of romance." Somewhere in the

Broadway Hotel and Hostel, and deep into her delusional pilgrimage, Miss Sweeney emerged from her quest for the fifth dimension to offer up a red-pen snicker: *Does the word* immutable *fall into the lexicon of words better read than said? I do wonder, Flannery.*

"Right. Should we explore the immutable sadness of romance? I kid, Flan."

Flan: a nickname! She had never felt more like delicious custard!

Heath hooked his thumb toward the reception desk. "But we really should get our room now that the front desk has cleared out a bit."

Flannery breathed in sharply. *Our* room? The facts of the morning connected in her brain, like the bright, linked ovals of DNA and RNA in her biology textbook.

- *Miss Sweeney goes missing*
- *Chapter one of Miss Sweeney's copy of* Wuthering Heights *read in Sacred Heart bathroom: surprise!*
- *Skip school*
- *Take train to NYC to search for Miss Sweeney*
- *Meet beautiful British boy with a dubious name; he agrees to help find Miss Sweeney*
- *Stand at reception desk at hotel*

"Well, if I got a room," Flannery said, chastely, emphasizing the singular pronoun, "I would be here when Miss Sweeney returns. I mean, she already has a room here. And I could leave my backpack in the room," she rationalized. "I don't need to be lugging around my calculus and econ textbooks." She chuckled and rubbed her lower back, as if being a good sport about excruciating pain.

Heath laughed. "Dear Lord, as a side job, do you yodel down the steep, rocky riverbank?

Flannery squinted. *What?*

"Because you are highly esteemed at calling bluffs. Flannery, I was obviously *joking about getting the room*. Not that I wouldn't want to. Get a room."

Flannery was the caller of bluffs! A girl yodeling from steep cliffs. She tried to mentally stow away Heath's words—*Not that I wouldn't want to. Get a room*—so that she could marvel at them, later, when life resumed its regular shape. For now there was nothing left to do but stroll over to the reception desk, shuck off her backpack, and ask the clerk: "Do you have any rooms just for the day, maybe just till afternoon? I don't know how much time we'll need."

The clerk appeared to be choking on a sudden laugh.

Heath glowered. "She doesn't mean it like that, Mate."

"You can't just pay for a block of time during the day," the clerk said, managing to sound both bored and lecherous. "You've got to check in and pay for a night's lodging." His hair looked dirty (though artfully arranged), but his skin had a scrubbed, post-facial glow. His shirt cuffs were turned back far enough to reveal his tattooed forearms. "We are not an hourly facility."

Heath leaned in over the desk. "You've made that clear."

Being mistaken for a person purchasing an hourly hotel room for sexual relations was an unfamiliar embarrassment, a mixed blessing edged with the thrilling weirdness of the day. Heath defending her honor wasn't bad either.

Flannery shrugged. "I won't be using the room at night. I'm looking for my teacher, actually." She smiled up at the desk clerk and curled in her shoulders, trying to appear smaller, deferential. "Her name is Caitlin Sweeney. She checked in not too long ago."

"I can't, for security reasons, confirm who is or who is not a guest at the Broadway Hotel and Hostel."

"Top-notch security at this institution, Flannery," Heath stage-whispered. "This poseur fancies himself Homeland Security."

"Thanks, anyway," Flannery told the clerk. "We'll just hang out in the lobby and wait for her."

"Yeah." The clerk yawned, his mouth stretched wide, and let out the faintest growl as he finished exhaling and drew his lips back together. "That's not a possibility. The lobby area is not for the general public. The lobby is for guests of the hotel only."

Heath brought his fist down on the reception desk: "Come on, Mate! You can't possibly be serious." He raised his hand to indicate the general commotion in the lobby and common area. "How can you possibly tell who is or isn't a paying guest?"

Flannery looked at Heath and imagined the two of them later that night, paying guests staring down at Broadway from a hotel room with gauzy white curtains pushed to the side.

Emboldened, Flannery nodded at the desk clerk. "You know what? A room for the night, then."

"Alright, well, we do have a vacancy. A private room. Luck be a lady." He snapped his wrist and flung imaginary dice across the counter. "Sooo, first I'll need to see your IDs."

Flannery felt a magnanimous sorrow for anyone following

the usual trajectory of his or her day. She dug her driver's license out of her wallet and handed it to the clerk. Her hand trembled, but just a little—the day!

"I don't happen to have my identification on me," Heath said. "And I'm not staying in the room, anyhow."

The clerk nodded in his fatigued, seen-it-all-before manner as he made a copy of Flannery's license.

"No ID, Heath?" Flannery smiled up at him. "When you chop me up and stuff my body in a dry-cleaning bag there will be no evidence you even existed."

The desk clerk abandoned his hipster composure and laughed in a companionable way.

Heath glared at him. "I'm always afraid I'll lose my passport if I carry it with me, and trust me, I didn't anticipate the odd magic of this day."

She looked up at him. "That makes two of us."

"Three of us, actually," the clerk said, stone-faced. "Your room comes to one hundred fifty-seven eighty-three."

"Wow," Flannery said under her breath.

But the clerk looked over Flannery's shoulder to a newly arrived mom and daughter duo. The mom looked sporty and hopeful in her Puma jacket and jeans, but the teen embodied any Sacred Hearter: a girl sullenly daydreaming about staying at a generic and familiar Hampton Inn, a girl with the confidence to be openly disdainful—her arms crossed over her chest, her lips pursed in the sourest kiss as she gazed around, assured of her superiority over her fellow travelers at the Broadway Hotel and Hostel. Flannery could imagine the backstory, the mom saying, Come on, Olivia/Emily/Hannah, we'll have fun, and Olivia/Emily/Hannah saying *FINE* to get her mom to zip it, and now here they were at the Broadway Hotel and Hostel, with the mother's smile looking a little tight now, and both of them fully cognizant that all those Yelp reviews were useless because you never quite understood how things were going to be until you opened the door.

Flannery handed over her parents' credit card, reserved for emergency purposes, and this was certainly one, although she couldn't imagine how to explain the bill to her parents or if she would even need to. The old ways were gone.

"*Mmmm*, no. This won't work." The clerk chuckled and tapped the card. "The name on this doesn't match your license. Curious. I wouldn't have guessed you were engaged in identity theft."

"Um, it's my mom's," Flannery said. Mortified, she dropped the card when he handed it back to her, and conked her head on the reception desk as she went to pick it up.

"Oopsie!" Heath reached for his wallet. "Do you need some cash?"

"Oh, no thanks!" She said it far, far too brightly, and though she didn't have enough cash to pay for the room, she didn't want to take Heath's money, and, O, her bravado was vaporizing and the mom and daughter duo were *totally* eavesdropping, and God, where was Miss Sweeney? But just as Flannery was being sucked into a vortex of blundering doom, the desk clerk showed some mercy, or perhaps he'd simply grown weary of dealing with them.

"Look, you two can stay for a while and wait for your teacher. Whatever."

Flannery whispered her thanks, but Heath was more exuberant: "Well, thank you for your change of heart, sir." He put his hand to his heart with lavish sarcasm. "Truly, your kindness knows no reckoning." Heath turned and pointed at the long banquette across from the reception desk. "I suppose we should wait a bit for her, now that we've got clearance. Our Miss Sweeney would probably appreciate it."

Flannery grasped onto the pronoun *our*, closing her eyes for a second and cherishing the cozy plural sound as she sat with Heath and opened *Wuthering Heights*.

Seven

Dear Reader, after my devil-worshiping Prince Charming walked away, I was all alone again, the damsel in distress. I was disappointed that Brandon's voice was free-floating, that he hadn't physically appeared again, but his voice was such a comfort that I wanted more of his words. And so I took a seat on the long banquette across from the reception desk. I unzipped the coat pocket closest to my heart and took out the Ziploc bag that shrouded my most precious possession. (Yes, aside from the Nardil and my credit card, it was my only possession. But in any circumstance it would have been my personal shroud of Turin, only better, not a mere sweat-stained image of Brandon's face but proof of the inner workings of his heart.)

Just the week before, after all our lost years, I'd received a random, rambling missive from Brandon written on a soft stack of cream-colored bar napkins and stuffed in a business-sized envelope from an establishment called Emmerson Bigguns in Urbandale, Iowa. I had to sound out the lofty moniker as I stood at my mailbox . . . *Wha* . . . Oh, *God*.

Perhaps a collective of ironic hipsters owned the bar and were simply offering up satirical commentary about restaurants staffed by young women wearing bra tops and Daisy Dukes—Helloooo, Hooters!— by lowering the bar, by plunging the bar into the lithosphere with the grossest possible name, a name that called to mind jackasses with backward baseball caps snickering and nodding *oh yeah,* as busty waitresses served up Buffalo chicken wings and Budweisers. Brandon's name, scrawled in unfamiliar handwriting and spelled incorrectly, was on the upper left-hand corner above the business logo.

I unzipped the Ziploc and took out the napkins. I arranged them in chronological order in three curved rows on the padded bench. (Perhaps it looked like I was setting up to do tarot card readings at the Broadway Hotel and Hostel, because the desk clerk looked over and raised one hand in consternation—*GOD! What now?*)

Was it condensation from a cold beer glass that had wrinkled the napkins and, here and there, smeared the blue ink? Did Brandon holding the pen too intensely give the napkins all their soft rips and tears?

Dear Caitlin, Did you know what the big rule of e-mail is? Something will go wrong and your words to one person will be read by every person in your contacts. I Googled you on my phone and I got your e-mail from Sacred Heart High School but I am sending this snail mail I THINK.

I read your syllabus online and I know I have the right Caitlin Sweeney. You are torturing your students with your favorite books. BTW having your home address on Google is prob a bad move unless you have a pitbull or are married.

But then your last name might be different, maybe or maybe not. I'm getting MARRIED this summer, My wife 2 be Megan who is very intelligent and beautiful is keeping her own last name and who can blame her for not wanting Marzetti-Corcoran. Never enough boxes for all the letters. She's a marine 2.

So you are a teacher? It seems like you could have stayed in Kansas for that. I thought you would do something more exciting.

I just asked Tyler the bartender if they have any envelopes. Ex-Marine. He's checking in the office right now. Also FREE SHOTS.

I am on last day of leave for my mom and Liesel's wedding. They got married in Iowa today, and I am at this bar across from the Holiday Inn and all because our Kansas governor is against Marriage Equality and also not big on poor kids having a decent school lunch what a total douche.

Long road from here to there and back again and if you are wondering here is how it happened. That last night I saw you I walked all over the city the next day.

FEELING THE SHOTS PRETTY HARD BECAUSE I DONT DRINK ANYMORE I'M INTO FUCKING YOGA DON'T LAUGH.

NYC is a good place to get lost or to fucking off yourself NOT THAT I DID. The crowded blocks are good until you look at all the faces and think I am not me I am not me. I am that fucking guy across the street I'm floating outside my fucking body. Or worse I have no mask now. I'm straight up the fucking crazy guy.

And I kept walking and in Times Square I saw the recruitment office and I walked in.

The guy working that day was a marine. There was a watercooler and I was so thirsty Caitlin. I drank like a camel.

Mom was SO PISSED it was fucking epic. She was all: DO NOT LET THAT STUPID RICH GIRL RUIN YOUR LIFE. Does the truth hurt?

My dad thought you were great that one time he met you but consider the source. Short story long I went to basic training at Parris Island in S.C. the whole time thinking is this me? Maybe Mom is right and maybe this is a terrible idea but 2 late for that now.

Mom was still SO MAD at me but she and Liesel came for graduation and afterward at the reception with all the other parents wearing American flag ties and necklaces and such Mom drinks way 2 much red wine and says I wish my son wasn't doing this and 9/11 was an inside job no really I've done the research. Good times.

And then I think I'm going to Germany but long story off to Kandahar instead. I meet Megan and she is an angel in my life but still sometimes I float outside my body like my arms aren't attached to my body and for no reason. Unlike with my knee, totally fucking fucked from fucking football.

The bartender is back with the envelope and a stamp. He's looking at my phone where I Googled your address and writing your address on the envelope. Now he is writing my name in the corner of the envelope. He keeps stopping and saying that is one fucking long name. He asks are you ready to send it and I say no not yet and he says Shakespeare fucking lives.

You have always been in my thoughts.

You were too smart for me but why did I never see you at home afterwards? Bad timing I guess or maybe you never visit your parents, those jerks. Do you still go to church? Not me I am a fucking atheist these days but having church wedding to keep the peace and also I still pray and also I want to see you one last time before I get married. This is a dare to myself to see how stupid I can be. How can I fuck up my life? I will write a letter to Caitlin. I will write a letter to lying Caitlin. But I don't mean that. Except kind of.

Flying KCI to JFK overnight layover before arriving in Kandahar on Wed. afternoon. Meet me at the gates of Columbia or at the big church or the phone store or the book store or wherever the hell you want. Do you remember that shitty hotel? But it was great too and do you remember how we loved each other then? I do. My man Tyler just asked if I was writing a fucking novel. THE END. B M-C

He seemed smitten with the word *fuck*, which I found juvenile and disappointing, the frat boy vernacular writ large. And he'd written nothing about Afghanistan, and I wondered about so many specific things, like had he ever seen any girls on skateboards? I knew that Afghani girls were forbidden to ride bicycles yet allowed to ride skateboards, and I imagined Brandon walking down the street, uniformed and smiling politely at little girls in layered dresses and head scarves executing their perfect pop shuvits and ollies.

Mostly I wondered about the Marines, the specifics of his day-to-day life. Did Brandon have friends? Were they close? Was he constantly terrified? Did he feel lonely and disconnected around civilians, as Marines so often did in books and documentaries? But that world was locked away, left off the bar napkins.

Dear Reader, he didn't write back with any further instructions about meeting in NYC. But that was okay. To know that he drunkenly dreamed of being in Manhattan with me would suffice until further notice. He was back in Afghanistan, and I would hear from him again soon, I knew, my confidence born of that magic phrase: *You have always been in my thoughts.* I knew in my heart Brandon would never marry this "beautiful and intelligent" Megan person if she even existed. (I wondered why he had omitted "kindhearted" from the trifecta of desirable womanly traits: Why couldn't angelic Megan be an NFL cheerleader, a Fulbright Scholar, *and* a kidney donor?)

I knew that Brandon and I were soul mates, and that we would find our way back to each other.

Nine days later I received the e-mail from his mother.

But the days in between receiving Brandon's bar napkins and that e-mail?

My body enshrined in a plank of gold light cutting through the blinds of my classroom windows. My weird neighbor walking her manic, slobbering Irish setter and calling out to me: *"I am bananas about your darling coat!"* A blizzarding, bright snow day of morning storms and afternoon sunshine. Buying groceries with my face tucked down and turned to hide my huge smile, and me not caring if it looked like I was flirting with my shoulder, such was the depth of my private joy.

All the unheralded minutia of my daily life was rendered dear as I imagined it from afar, from my new life with Brandon: Oh, you mean back then? Back when I had to figure out what that bomb-ticking sound in my car meant, back when I snuck glances at the clock during curriculum meetings and wished I had brought a bottle of water, back when I was lonely as an eighteenth-century poet, back when I waited in the drive-through lane for my cheeseburger and fries and laughed out loud, Dear Reader, because there was someone across the world who held me in their thoughts, someone who had loved me once, someone who loved me still.

Flannery ran her hand along the vinyl-topped banquette where they sat, where Miss Sweeney had laid out Brandon's napkins. Oh God, how weird and depressing to think of Miss Sweeney toting around a Ziploc bag full of napkins, how awful that she knew the brutal loneliness of post-Cathy Heathcliff: *"The entire world is a dreadful collection of memoranda that she did exist, and that I have lost her!"*

Dear Reader, now it was up to me to find him, and I would! Invigorated by Brandon's words, I carefully put the bar napkins back into the Ziploc, zipped my coat, and headed out of the Broadway Hotel and Hostel. I tried to keep my thoughts from what had happened in Kansas City that morning, the rituals that belonged to the old, known world: the priest in his white vestments, the uniformed Marines, the grim drive to the cemetery after the funeral, and then the sad-sack buffet in the church basement at Saint Thomas More. The urn of coffee and the packets of powdered creamer and sugar, the little towers of Styrofoam cups, the stacked Chinet plates and the Costco bottled water, and the grieving, who, in their goodness would stand in sad semicircles quietly admiring the cold cuts and sweets the Altar Society had laid out:

I've always liked those honey-baked hams.

Somebody did a nice job on those pecan brownies.

Brandon's mom was a vegan and she also didn't eat sugar. But of course it didn't matter if she ate a Dijon mustard sandwich or a few Wheat Thins because for the rest of her life, anything she put in her stomach would sit like scrap iron.

My cheer vaporized pretty quickly.

I headed back down Broadway, trudging along as my wily brain chemistry cooked up a new scenario to find Brandon. I would not remain enslaved to my previous peripheral vision theories; I was going to make brief, meaningful eye contact with every person I saw on the street. I would need to focus, to be able to quickly spot Brandon, no matter where he was on a crowded Manhattan street or what form he had taken.

I do not mean that I would plop down next to a squirrel on the sidewalk and gaze intently into his nut-brown eyes on the off chance that the great love of my life had morphed into an urban rodent. I simply knew that it was time to really LOOK for Brandon, to open my eyes wider, and this seventh-inning corneal stretch seemed crucial, and made perfect sense to me as I walked down Broadway, a romantic on a hero's journey. I was Huck Finn; I was Holden Caulfield; I was Sal Paradise roaming upper Manhattan until I stopped into Starbucks to get a latte and use the bathroom and . . . Oh, *great*.

Dear Reader, What do young, male adventurers NEVER, ever need to do when they are covering ground on a personal quest? Think it over for a bit—this is for the win—but perhaps the answer is obvious?

YOU ARE CORRECT! GO TO DUANE READE AND BUY A SMALL BOX OF PLAYTEX TAMPONS! All those literary dream boys would miss the freewheeling pleasure of skulking right back into Starbucks with their hand plastered over the tampon box—slightly too big for their coat pocket, an inch of Barbie-doll pink packaging showing against black wool—and then getting back in line for the ladies' room!

But here's what they would miss too: the transgender woman in front of me wearing a long, highlighted wig, leaning against the wall and texting away. I peeked and saw her sentences punctuated with the four-leaf-clover emoji, and wondered who was the recipient of her good wishes, and then worried that I'd said my thoughts out loud, because she turned around sharply, as if about to tell me to mind my own business, but then seemed to reconsider. Her eyebrows were so severely waxed that I winced; how hard it was to be a person in the world, to make your way through.

She went back to her texting, shouting in all caps, which made it easier for a rubber-necker to read: *OMG LINE FOR LADIES ROOM AT STARBUCKS IS A DAMN FREAKSHOW. MY TIMING IS EX-QUISITE.*

But then she turned around again.

"You okay, girl?" The bathroom door opened and she held out her hand. "You go on ahead."

They would miss that, too.

"Thanks," I croaked out, her sudden and lavish kindness nearly undoing me. I went into the Starbucks bathroom and cried, both from the generosity of a stranger and because I remembered how discovering I'd started my period in another public bathroom had once given me such a zenith of bliss—cooling, sublime hallelujah choirs rising in my heart, in my veins—that I experienced a bathroom stall epiphany at Bed, Bath & Beyond at the Great Plains Mall: I would never, ever try heroin.

It had just arrived in the Kansas City suburbs, and my friends Emily A. and Rebecca O. had gotten drunk and tried it, and reported back: minds decisively blown. But whatever, because nothing could match the distilled rush of joy I knew when I learned that I was not, in the classy vernacular of reality TV, 16 and Pregnant. My period was a week and a half late. Yep, the old drama. One night in early spring, Brandon and I "should have been a lot more careful"—a grammatically awkward phrase perhaps better suited to describing generic regret about shoddy precaution, like burning your hand while quickly draining spaghetti from a pot of boiling water or forgetting your trusty all-weather jacket on a wuthering day. (Euphemism for the win! Sorry.)

Yes, Dear Reader, I was a smart girl, but not *quite* a rocket scientist there in Brandon's truck parked on the dirt road beyond the baseball diamonds: popcorn trees offering up a clumped canopy of exploded white blossoms, the scent and rustle of wild lilac bramble, a fuchsia-orange sunset fading to pink, and Brandon's mouth at my ear, softly. "I should probably drive to Walgreens, Caitlin."

"O . . . *kay*," I whispered, enthralled to pure sensation: the cool, ridged vinyl of the truck seat, his calloused hands—he never wore gloves when he lifted weights—pausing politely on my rib cage while he waited for a more definitive reply. I tilted my head back and sighed out, "*Waaal*greens."

And . . . curtain!

Cut to the next month, Brandon and I sitting in his truck in the

Kwik Mart parking lot after school (school was almost out for the summer, but guess who wasn't envisioning her anxiety-ridden self poolside in a black bikini?). When I told him about the looming possibility, he took a long, hard drink of his Tropical Cooler Slurpee, and then nodded. "Okay. It's okay. *Shit*. I'm so sorry."

"Thanks. I mean, I guess. I was there too."

"You probably aren't, though."

"Oh?" We could both hear the relieved lilt in that syllable.

Brandon took another draw off his Slurpee, the chemically bright liquid rising, rising, turning his clear straw to Windex blue. I watched the slight bob of his Adam's apple in profile as he swallowed.

"Well . . . Caitlin. Usually people think that they're . . . pregnant . . . and then? They aren't. They really aren't." Brandon even sounded a bit like a doctor! Okay, in truth, like a doctor not yet seventeen and currently fulfilling his science requirement with a class known as Rocks for Jocks, geology as taught by the semi-alcoholic football coach at Holy Angels High School. But then he looked out the window and quietly said, "Usually."

It was my turn to suck down my Slurpee with vigor, the therapeutic crunch of tiny ice crystals in my throat as I swallowed. Brandon was my first, but his list was longer and possibly included both the beautiful but dim Emily C. and, more horrifyingly, the beautiful and also kind-of-smart Emily N. I tried not to think or care about the romantic tribulations of his past because I was Brandon's present; I was Brandon's future.

"Don't worry," he said. He stuck his drink in the cup holder and started drumming his fingers on the steering wheel. "Because you know what?"

He looked over at me, his blue-green eyes clear as the most pristine lake, and who wouldn't want to drown in new love? "If you are, everything will be fine, Caitlin." He amped up his steering wheel drumming to a heavy metal solo, a crescendo he ended by accidentally honking the horn, startling us both into nervous levity.

But when Brandon stopped laughing, he started planning. "We could get an apartment. You know those remodeled ones by the riverfront? I know you like hardwood floors, Caitlin. And our moms could take turns watching the baby while we're at school, and then the three of us could go off to college together and it would be fine. It would be great. So great! I mean, I love kids."

Dear Reader, how quickly my heart turned cold as Christmas. My inner dialogue was definitive: *That is never, ever going to happen.* I said it not only to comfort myself, but to mercifully quash the optimism of a potential zygote perking up its undeveloped earbuds: *There is no way in hell that scenario is going to take place. I will never let myself get trapped. Never, never, never.* But how could I tell Brandon that I was not the sort of person who had a baby in high school? Really, it was something he might have noticed on his own.

But three days later in the ladies' room at Bed, Bath & Beyond on a rainy Sunday afternoon, all agony vanished. I swung open the door and cut through the expensive heart of the store, buoyant as a moonwalker, such was my joy! Vacuum cleaners! Coffee machines! Machines to turn fresh fruit into dried-up fruit in plastic bags! All those miracles of housebound happiness were not for me, no thank you!

I headed to the bathroom accessories in the back corner, past the scales and towel holders and waste baskets and met my mom in the shower curtain section, where she pressured me to choose between taupe and lavender stripes or interlocking watercolor circles. But the shower curtain was for my bathroom, and so I made my own triumphant selection: a bold map of the world on clear vinyl! (At home, free of its appealing packaging, it would never entirely lose its toxic odor.) And now I had no touristy daydreams, no interest in those bright, colonized continents I used to gaze at while I shampooed my waist-length teenage hair; now I was purely an explorer—hapless but passionate—and I would not stop searching until I found Brandon.

I walked out of the Starbucks bathroom and made eye contact with the generous stranger—her Latisse lashes so impossibly long, so soft-looking—and waved good-bye. She was already hurrying into the bathroom, but she raised her hand—the silvery jingle of bracelets, the flash of garnet nail polish—and waved back, and as she had already clearly established who she represented on my journey—*uh, duh!*—I would not have been the least surprised to see the stigmata there on her wide palm.

And then, I was back on the street, walking and watching. Here and there confused winter birds studded the sky, or maybe they knew exactly what they were doing: Maybe they chose to stay and brave the NYC chill for the familiar pleasures of pecking gravel from window-boxes, of scouring the sidewalk for *pan au chocolat* crumbs. Two stylish college-aged girls were walking in front of me, one wearing a belted khaki trench coat, the other in a cardinal red swing coat. The trench-coated girl was telling a story that made the swing-coater laugh and say, "Right? Precisely!"

I was shivering, my lungs shuddering in and out, taking extra-curricular breaths in between my actual life-sustaining breaths. I followed the girls for blocks, wanting to ease under the umbrella of their friendship. I remembered how I had walked into Carman Hall and seen Nancy for the first time. I was late for check-in so she was already in our dorm room when I pulled open the door.

Nancy Ping: glossy black hair hanging to the middle of her back—a Pantene commercial come to life—and skin so flawless it looked like a canvas. An orange sundress and sparkly silver flip-flops brightened her already considerable beauty; she was her very own chrome filter. After the requisite small talk, we had given our brief bios: *"I'm from New Jersey,"* she said apologetically. *"Kansas,"* I said with even greater remorse, and we discussed the cafeteria plan and electrical outlets and all the while there was the mind-blowing subtext of meeting a stranger I would now sleep ten feet away from every night, but that was the autumn experience of lucky, privileged eighteen-year-olds.

Her parents came into the room, their arms full of Nancy's numerous belongings, and they seemed a tad alarmed that my own parents were not milling around too, while of course Nancy seemed chagrined that her mom and dad even existed. Her parents obviously loved her dearly, for they were either talking too loudly in their valiant efforts to appear super upbeat about the college drop-off, or too quietly, and swallowing with pronounced effort, the lumps in their throat threatening to bloat into goiters. I thought they seemed pleased with me, though, and I imagined their conversation in the car on the way home: *That Caitlin seems nice, doesn't she?* But bless them, for they didn't know the half of it. They didn't know I had a boyfriend stashed at the little coffee shop/bookstore downstairs eating his overpriced untoasted two-pack of blueberry Pop-Tarts with trembling hands.

We had been out late the night before at the Five Lanterns Inn. Brandon was sad that our week of private reverie was ending; he felt more nervous than I did about school starting. The beautiful bartender kept tilting her head and half-smiling at Brandon, her harlot's faux-shyness fooling nobody. She gave Brandon free shots and free, breathy advice: *"Try this: I added fresh, grated ginger, just for you. It's sooo good for allergies. This one is flavored with cranberry. Thanksgiving in a shot glass, am I right? I wish I had a plate of turkey and mashed potatoes just for you."*

I was all jealous umbrage, and Brandon and I had some predictable back-and-forth:

She's tantalizing you with the promise of a warm holiday dinner? It figures, actually. She's got grandma hands—the veins all popped up like blue snakes. And I'll bet rattlesnake grandma is thirty-five if she's a day.

Oh, Cait, why are you always so mean? She's only twenty-four.

Oh my God, Brandon, she told you how old she was when I was in the bathroom? Does she know that you are underage and that she could go to JAIL for serving you liquor?

Captain Caitlin, you are correct. You should make a citizen's arrest.

Et cetera.

But on the three-block walk to the old Broadway Hotel and Hostel, our home away from home—I had to guide him, my arm around his back, because he was stumbling, and he whispered, "*I love you I love you.*" I loved him, too, and Brandon had every right to be nervous about school starting as his lodging was a bit up in the air, depending on how cool my roommate would turn out to be.

Nancy Ping was very cool indeed. Dear Reader, she was the friend I had always wished for in high school, when I was waiting to find my people.

Flannery sucked in her breath. *It's me. I knew it was me. I'm the Dear Reader.* Miss Sweeney had named their mutual longing. In her peripheral vision Flannery saw Heath look over at her, but she kept reading.

Nancy was kind and smart and funny, more so than me; she was inured to group thinking and generous with her wardrobe. (I imagined the girls walking down the block in front of me with their coats switched—the swing coat would be a swing-blazer on the taller, trench-coated girl.) I also loved Nancy's parents a little, just from meeting them that day at the dorm. As we talked more, Nancy's mom grew increasingly sarcastic and fun, and though her dad was working the unfortunate middle-aged hipster look in his red Chuck Taylors and Yankee Hotel Foxtrot T-shirt, he was so sweet. He looked devastated when he appeared in the doorway lugging in the last box before he and Nancy's mom would drive back to New Jersey, the backseat of their car vast and empty as the moon. And that last box? It was filled with individual cups of organic applesauce.

"Dad!" Nancy whisper-shrieked, *"There's not room for all of that!"* She flung her arm at her desk, already piled with sulfate-free shampoos and body wash and prescriptions and Ziploc bags of makeup, chargers, her blow-dryer, and her Sonicare toothbrush and Waterpik.

"Well now, Eric," Nancy's mom scolded brightly, anger in her smile. "No wonder you were so keen on packing the car by yourself last night. You and that goddamn Costco are just full of surprises."

"There's plenty of room on my side of the room," I offered, which was true. I just had a purse, a backpack, a laptop, and two big suitcases—mine a Coach peony print, and Brandon's, an ancient blue Samsonite plastered with a faded, partly peeled-off bumper sticker of a sexy mermaid that now only said: SAILORS HAVE MORE FU.

"Put it there, partner," I said, bizarrely affecting the voice of an old-time gunslinger while I motioned for him to put the box between my twin bed and desk. But Mr. Ping smiled at me gratefully, and over the protests of Nancy and her mom, he unloaded all the applesauce.

I let them have their private good-byes. I met up with Brandon in the coffee shop downstairs. He was sitting at a table by the windows, a gloomy figure with an empty Pop-Tart wrapper there amongst the depleted parents refreshing themselves with Vitaminwater and Clif Bars.

He looked so lost that I did a Miss-America-coming-down-the-runway walk to his table, smiling hugely and flipping my hair before I stopped in front of him and did a single step-ball-change, accompanied by jazz hands. "Everything's *fantastic!*" Then I lowered my voice to a normal range and sat next to him. "You can totally stay. We'll be pretty cozy sleeping in a twin bed, so rule number one: No more drunken freight-train snoring. I got a total of negative three hours sleep last night."

"Your math seems a little off." Brandon squinted as if seeing me from some great distance. "She really said that it's okay for me to live in the dorm room with you both? You already talked about it and got it all worked out?"

Dear Reader, the memory of Brandon looking down at the table and nervously pressing the wrinkles out of the foil Pop-Tart wrapper made me feel as if I were swallowing razor blades but it also strengthened my resolve to find him, to join him. I kept searching for him as I trailed the pair of friends along Broadway. For the moment I had everything under control, and though I was still sick, I also felt the warmth of my good intentions: *I am coming for you, Brandon. You are not alone.*

Of course, I hadn't actually asked Nancy Ping if it was okay if my boyfriend lived in our dorm room—her parents had been in the room! Yet I sensed she would be okay with it and I imagined things would unfold gradually—one night turning into a week, turning into a month, and then into the entire fall semester and then the spring semester, too—a laid-back trajectory, so that I would never have to ask at all.

"Nancy—her name's 'Nancy' and she's totally cool—said it's fine, no big deal at all."

Brandon nodded. "Okay," he said quietly. "Well. That makes one thing that's working out, then."

Brandon had hoped to get a job as a taxi driver and then rent an apartment close to Columbia when he'd saved enough money. He loved to drive at home—sometimes he would get on the highway at night and drive just for relaxation—so driving a cab seemed a perfect fit. But when he had called the NYC Taxi & Limousine Commission—after being transferred from extension to extension—he'd finally spoken with a man who had seemed perplexed by his questions. One could not apply for a job as a NYC cabdriver, not really; driving a cab required investment money, good fortune, special schooling, and a prohibitive in-the-know aesthetic, as so many things in NYC did.

"Let's take a little walk, B."

"I'm not really feeling that great."

But I coaxed him up, and we were off, walking the main path bisecting the quad that made the Columbia campus look like a movie set, all stone benches and green lawns and postcard-friendly statues—*The Thinker! The Library Lion!*—and then we were on Amsterdam Avenue, a whole new world to explore.

We went to the Hungarian Pastry Shop and admired the careful petit fours and dense baklava, the glazed, Technicolor glow of the kiwis and mandarin oranges on the fruit tartlets. (Brandon rued having spent money on Pop-Tarts.) We split a small pizza at V & T, where we were served by the crankiest old man in the history of cranky old men: He repeatedly moved our water glasses away from the edge of the table as if we were unsteady toddlers. But it was the best pizza we'd ever tasted, and so I asked Brandon the eternal question: "You know when I'm eating at Pizza Hut again?"

Revived by the delicious food, he laughed easily. "I'm going to guess . . . the twelfth of never?"

"Put it on your calendar."

We hadn't planned a sightseeing excursion, but the Cathedral of Saint John the Divine was right across the street. We held hands and craned our necks, trying in vain to see the towering, ornate church in its entirety.

O, Dear Reader. Seized by the Holy Spirit, by my own good fortune, I was entirely innocent of the fractured future. All of life in that August moment was distilled possibility: baklava and black olive pizza and someone to love.

Brandon and I followed clutches of tourists up the steps and into the coolness of the cavernous church. There was a happy family right in front of us: The mom and dad were both sporting Oklahoma Sooners T-shirts, but the dad was also wearing a brand new Columbia University baseball hat. When he walked into the Cathedral, the dad looked at the ceiling and said, "Dang! You could put a lot of hay in this barn." The college-aged son smiled tolerantly, more than tolerantly, his eyes behind his hipster Buddy Holly glasses looked so loving. Brandon was watching the family, his expression unknowable. Was he mourning his dream life, the one where his father was not a prisoner but a regular, responsible dude walking around with him on the Dodge City Community College campus: meeting the football coach, touring the gym and the locker room, and making a quick trip to Walmart for a case of Pepsi to stash in his dorm room before going downtown for steak dinners with the freshman football players and their families?

I panicked. What had I taken from him?

"Wow! Can you believe how huge this church is?"

Brandon looked askance at my false brightness, but the Cathedral of Saint John the Divine truly is the national monument of American churches—expansive and ecumenical, and, according to the literature at the welcome booth, constantly being built and changed. We did not pay the suggested donation, as it was a mere suggestion, but I couldn't resist buying a black tote bag that said MEET ME AT THE CATHEDRAL. I hung the empty bag on my shoulder, relishing its lightness.

"Is this a Catholic church?" Brandon asked.

I pointed to the Human Rights Campaign poster, the iconic blue and yellow stripes. "I would guess not. I think it's Episcopal."

He nodded.

He was not the sort of triple *H*—homophobic, hulking, and handsome—ex-football player from Kansas that you may be envisioning, Dear Reader. His mom had met her partner, Liesel, when Brandon was fifteen. Brandon loved Liesel; he loved the gift of security and normalcy she brought to their lives. Because of his mom's previous stormy relationships with men, Brandon had seen a lot. He once told me: *"If we ever have a daughter, I want her to grow up and marry another woman, not a man. I want her to be safe."*

Liesel worked as a Head Start preschool teacher and brought home the majority of the bacon, albeit lean. Brandon's mom was a lushly beautiful drummer who had given birth to him her senior year of high school. She had met Brandon's dad at a Descendants concert in Omaha; her joke—which never drew more than the awkward chuckle—was that she knew him "briefly, but well." She played in a number of semi-successful punk bands around the Midwest, always with little Brandon in tow.

Dear Reader, lest this sound too bucolic—punk rock played in the cornfield, anti-establishment fun for a red-state child!—Brandon started drinking beer like chocolate milk when he was five, and his mother, never the brightest bulb, thought this was okay, because children drank red wine in Europe *like it was chocolate milk.* By the time I met Lisa, she had already fallen in love with Liesel and quit the bands and the men and the drugs and the various combos thereof; she did yoga and cooked complicated vegan dinners for Liesel and Brandon. Lisa also sold life-sized cloth dolls of her favorite musicians: PUNK SOFTEES. Though her website had lots of "traffic," she was puzzled by her overall lack of financial success and delighted by the odd, intermittent windfall: Once a German X fan had commissioned an Exene Cervenka Punk Softee for what seemed a staggering sum.

Can I say that her work habits were not stellar?

My senior year I would race out of school, get in Brandon's truck, and drive to his house. (*Mom, going to yearbook meeting, home for dinner!*) Lisa would sometimes be relaxing on the living-room couch next to whatever half-finished Punk Softee she was creating. An odd tableau: Brandon's mom drinking a Heineken and watching TV, as if on a chaste date with naked, sexless Joe Strummer, all fabric and stuffing and with one already embroidered eye next to a smooth blank of ivory cotton, as if he had been in a horrible, eye-obliterating accident. I would awkwardly sit next to Joe Strummer and Lisa on the couch and take in her beauty—her cheekbones could cut cheap steak—while making small talk, but I was the duplicitous face of suburban ambition, always thinking: *Turn off the TV and let's get cracking on that Punk Softee, sister!*

Still, if she was a bit lax about beer-drinking kindergartners and Punk Softee productivity, Lisa had always been adamant that Brandon attend Mass. So I thought that being in a church, the normalizing sanctuary of this childhood, might make Brandon happy, or at least give him a little serenity.

We looked at the tapestries along the perimeters of the Cathedral of Saint John the Divine and walked down the aisle of the sanctuary— wooden chairs for tourists and sightseers—and right up to cordoned-off seats closer to the altar, where I imagined the actual parishioners sat on Sundays.

Brandon looked up at the altar. *"I'm scared,"* he whispered, as if talking to Jesus himself. *"I don't think this is going to work."*

"Yes, it is," I said brightly. "It totally is." I cranked it up a notch, and apropos of nothing, added a shrill British accent. "Work it shall!"

It sort of had to. Brandon had already passed on the football scholarships. He had no alternate plan. I put my hand on the back of his neck, that muscular nest. "It totally is, B." To cheer him up, I licked his neck and ran my hand through his hair. As we had approached the altar, I had noticed a few roped-off areas along the sides of the church. I took Brandon's hand and led him to the first alcove, and after a quick look around—the security guards had their backs turned, and the tourists had their cameras aimed at statues and tapestries, not wayward teens—I pulled him behind the velvet rope, an ornamental warning, and into a short hallway with two closed doors and a bulletin board listing volunteer duties.

"Cait," Brandon hissed, *"we should not be back here."*

I pressed my shoulder blades to the smooth coolness of the stone wall and pulled Brandon close. Dear Reader, I kissed him in the Cathedral.

He protested of course. "Really, Cait? We are in a *church*."

I laughed and kissed him again, this time smack on the jugular. "Well, since we aren't Episcopalians, it's all good." Just as he was relenting, kissing me back harder, I opened my eyes and saw a young-looking security guard in a navy blue uniform open his mouth.

"Hey!"

Brandon sprung off me, a pouncing leopard in reverse.

"You two can't be back here!"

The security guard's voice was loud, menacing even, but he politely lowered his eyes as I adjusted my scoop neck T-shirt, which had gotten pulled a little low. He wasn't a pervert; he just wanted us out of there. "Don't ever think you're alone in the Cathedral. We have cameras everywhere. You can be arrested for being in these areas."

"Well, you'll have to forgive us our trespassing!" I was proud of my churchy wit, but the security guard appeared immune to my charms. He gave a disgusted little tongue click and shook his head.

Brandon glared at me, then turned to the guard. "Hey, man. We shouldn't have been back here. We saw the rope and everything. I'm really sorry."

But the guard was talking into his headset: "I'm with the couple. I'm walking them out."

He pointed to the back of the church. "Let's go. We aren't pressing charges. You can't do things like that in the city," he said, correctly identifying us as bumpkins. "Maybe back in the day, before 9/11, you could find a cozy spot, and everybody would look the other way, but now? Just know you can pretty much count on being arrested if you're somewhere you shouldn't be."

Curious tourists whispered and gaped as the guard led us down the side aisle. Brandon had his hands in his pockets and his head down, but I smiled proudly, as if leaving the podium after my valedictorian speech: *Thanks to each and every one of you! You all played such an important part in this! Best wishes, everyone! Best wishes!* Because I had almost gotten arrested inside a *church*. My God, it was all so excellent! Anything could happen to a person in New York City!

"You two need to use better judgment." The guard held open the door for us, and then pulled it closed before I could offer up my slavering faux-gratitude for his life coaching.

On the steps of the cathedral was a silver-haired man, a bit stooped, but still handsome in his security uniform. He was giving us a big "Ain't love grand" kind of smile, and I grinned back shyly: *Yes sir, it most certainly is.* He looked a little melancholy, though, perhaps mourning the pre-9/11 world where life was freer, where darting behind a forbidden area could lead to a miracle of sorts: Conception in the Cathedral! The guard winked at me as we passed, and called out to Brandon: "Good night, Sweet Romeo."

We could still hear him chuckling to himself when we were down the stairs.

"It was Juliet's idea," Brandon groused under his breath.

And then we walked back to our room at Carman Hall, where Nancy met Brandon, where Nancy possibly fell in love at first sight, and we had a bit of bliss. Saturday became Sunday, and then Monday came, and Nancy and I went to class, and Brandon watched Netflix, and Monday bled into Tuesday and Wednesday and Thursday, and Brandon became another roommate, and Nancy never mentioned his perpetual presence. We formed a cozy trio of companionship, watching *Top Chef* and *Project Runway* obsessively, always guessing who the winner would be. The three of us walked to Nussbaum & Wu for smoothies and to the Hungarian Pastry Shop for cookies and coffee, and to V & T for pizza. That first week at Columbia, all of Manhattan was shrunk down to our little neighborhood. The city below 110th Street seemed like pure whimsy—Wall Street? Times Square? The East Village?—and possibly nonexistent. On Thursday night I pressed five dollars into Nancy's hand and asked her if she would mind going out for a latte.

"It's prostitution in reverse!" Nancy said cheerfully, packing up her backpack, and I couldn't disagree, not really. The business of paying one roommate a nominal sum so you could have relations with your other, unofficial roommate was a delicate business indeed and, Dear

Reader, I would omit it altogether, except to let you know that dorm life is full of shady etiquette, so fasten your seat belt.

I digress, though. My first week at Columbia was rather exciting—for his inaugural lecture in Frontiers of Science, the professor had stripped to his underwear and sat in a folding chair holding a stuffed bunny rabbit while images of war and destruction played out on a screen behind him, all in the name of quantum physics. It was a science class my parents wouldn't have envisioned when they rolled their favorite hyphenated word around in their mouths like the most sublime raspberry lozenge, *pre-med*. *Caitlin is pre-med.* I never had the slightest inclination to be a doctor, but because I was a thoughtful girl and they got such a kick out of the idea of me going to medical school, and because they were paying the bills, I indulged them in their misty, watercolored My-Daughter-Is-Going-to-Be-a-DOCTOR fantasy world for far too long: *But, Dad, medical schools like for you to take a lot of writing classes. God, Mom, everyone knows that a broad base in the humanities is the key component of admissions.* When it was time to apply to medical school, and I had to drop the nuclear reality bomb about the English Lit major, the truth left my parents as furious and wounded as awkward, overindulged junior high kids who had spent years bragging about all their kick-ass gifts from Santa.

It was clear from the subdued atmosphere of my Intro to Women's and Gender Studies class—why were my privileged peers covertly checking their phones instead of discussing Audre Lord's open letter to Mary Daly?—that I was not going to be the most dullardly student admitted to the freshman class. Far from it, actually. My first week at Columbia was a short, sweet respite of Happily Ever After.

And then, that Friday night: three compound fractures in my right hand, my good hand.

I was back at class on Tuesday, maneuvering my laptop with my left hand—a toddler could have typed faster—but when I wrote with my left hand my notes were a feathery jumble: illegible.

Dear Reader, can I blame my subpar ambidexterity for the way things turned out?

A guy in my Women's and Gender Studies class took pity on me when I showed up with my hand in a fat, neon-orange cast. He zipped my books in my backpack for me and carried my backpack to Carman Hall, where I rushed him off with the quickest thanks, in case Brandon or Nancy were lurking in the lobby.

Later that night he e-mailed me his notes.

The next morning when I was leaving for my 8:30 Spanish class, there were flowers waiting for me at the front desk: a vase of violets the exact shade of the Virgin Mary's iconic blue robes, and soft, snow-white pearls of lily of the valley that rose up over the violets like airborne confection, delicate as love itself. The card attached to the white vase by a length of pale blue velvet ribbon read: *Caitlin, Hope your hand is feeling better. Such a drag to have that happen so early in the semester! Best, Miles.*

The elevator dinged, and I spun around nervously, but Nancy had already left for class, and Brandon was still sleeping. Still, I knew I had to ditch the bouquet. I pawed through the Chipotle trash in the wastebasket with my good hand and sunk it to the very bottom and then stuck a half-eaten burrito bowl over the pristine blooms. I ignored the drippy girl working the front desk: *Oh my God, are you really just throwing those away?* But the flowers stayed in my mind all day, and when I thought of the quiet blue and white palette of the violets and lily of the valley—the surprise of Easter flowers in autumn— my Judas heart flew up with the splashy joy of resurrection.

Oh, I was a hard-hearted consumer. The red roses that Brandon had always bought for me now seemed obvious and Midwestern in their cloying effort to be pretty and perfect, which of course described me as well.

In my memory fugue, I had trailed the friends for blocks and blocks; when they disappeared into a clothes shop along Broadway, I thought to follow them inside, but my heart wasn't into admiring the black lace shirt they were inspecting: The act of buying cute clothes belonged to a different, doomed era.

I was thinking I'd never walked so far south on Broadway but I was wrong because there was Zabar's across the street, and my stomach ached from the memory of Brandon standing underneath the orange-and-white awning eating a warm salt bagel with scallion cream cheese, because, too late, I wanted to nourish him forever. My mind looped with memories, and some kind of all-over softening was happening, my peripheral vision fading to cataract cloudiness and even the faces directly in front of me looked hazy, almost featureless.

But I was not living in a dull, Brandon-less tundra—he was with me. I just needed to find the path to him.

Brandon, Brandon, Brandon: I whispered it three times with each exhaled breath.

I had come upon Westsider Books, where merchandise was displayed unattended on the sidewalk, an honor system on Broadway. I grabbed the corner of a scarred table stacked with clearance books and felt a splinter lodge in my palm. The faded index card on top of a spindle of author postcards read "1.00" in weather-smeared ink. I browsed a bit, my vision sharpening again. There was an unfairly schoolmarmish, pinch-faced pen-and-ink of Emily Brontë that telegraphed: *Why, yes, my wild-hearted adventures were all on the page.* Dear Reader, are we surprised that in 1846 she published her brilliant and subversive book under a male-sounding pseudonym? Yet

Wuthering Heights survives without an accompanying author photo to inform the reader: Why, yes, I'm a smart, soulful young woman *and also*, hot! There was also a postcard of James Baldwin in a sweater vest, smoking a cigarette, holding my gaze, and one of Kurt Vonnegut—heavily mustached, holding an unfurling roll of typing paper. Oh, and there was F. Scott Fitzgerald in a tweed suit—with his large, sensitive eyes, I sensed something Brandon-esque about him. (Alas, perhaps only a hopeless sucker for the pretty boys would write a phrase like "with his large, sensitive eyes.") And then there was Carson McCullers with her fetching bob and feline smile next to a young and darkly lipsticked Flannery O'Connor.

I picked up the postcard and flipped it over: *Iowa City, February 1947.* Flannery O'Connor was wearing a hair scarf and a muskrat fur coat in the valentine heart of bright, cold Iowa—a day of snow and sunshine—and standing on the front steps of a house with a porch swing, the metal chains reflecting in the front window. Her gloved hand rested on an iron handrail, and she was smiling so naturally that I guessed the photographer must have been someone she liked, some long-forgotten Iowa City friend.

Dear Reader, I whispered your name.

And then the door of Westsider Books opened.

"Caitlin? Caitlin!"

I recognized that voice.

Eight

Flannery closed *Wuthering Heights* and stood too fast. The lobby of the Broadway Hotel and Hostel swayed, the tourists and the desk clerk and the front desk itself listed to the left. Was Miss Sweeney's vertigo catching?

"Steady yourself, girl!"

Heath's hand skimmed her knee when he stuck it out to help Flannery, and if she needed any kind of hypothesis to prove she was Pavlov's lovesick dog, here it was! The bodily contact automatically reddened her face and made her heart leap, as it had all morning long, whenever Heath touched her shoulder or paid her any old haphazard compliment.

"She's just walked into Westsider Books," Flannery said.

"Don't know the shop. But then I'm not a reading fanatic like yourself, am I? Let's have a look." He Googled *Westsider Books* on his phone, squinting a bit, and Flannery wondered if Heath was too clumsy for contacts or too vain for glasses, and all the while her brain persisted with the hand-knee energy. Flannery thought about how her knee pulsed as though it contained a beating heart, the *dub-bub* feeling migrating outward, like tree rings. And even though Miss Sweeney was struggling in the real world, she remained an authoritative, red-ink voice in Flannery's brain: *And these migrating tree rings are the result of Heath's hand brushing your kneecap? Have you considered writing a chapbook dedicated to the unsung romantic potentialities of the patella?*

"I just clicked on the Yelp reviews: Molly G. thought the proprietor was a real stuffed shirt, but Jennifer V. just loves the place."

"Is it very far?"

A shuttle bus of Italian tourists walked in, all backpacks and guidebooks and cell phones, their hopeful eyes taking in the Broadway Hotel and Hostel.

Heath shrugged. "It's not that far, relatively speaking. It's not Berlin, but no more cat-and-mouse rambling along Broadway, eh?"

He stood and swept his hand. "You first, my dear."

He followed Flannery out of the Broadway Hotel and Hostel, and hailed a cab at the corner. Flannery knew that riding with him in the backseat of a banged-up, parrot-yellow Chevrolet was going to be the dreamiest mode of transportation. After Heath gave the cabdriver the address, the driver admired his accent (*Join the club,* thought Flannery) and asked, "Where do you hail from, young man?" When Heath said England, the driver nodded. "I thought so. I was in Dublin many years ago. Wonderful people!"

"Indeed," Heath agreed heartily, without a touch of condescension.

The cab heater cranked heat so intense it made Flannery

feel as if her chapped lips and hands might crack and bleed, and she was most certainly sweating in Heath's leather jacket. But the vibration of her phone distracted her from the terror of B.O.: It was her mother, returning the text that Flannery had sent hours ago:

> Hope U feel better. Dad and I just went to THE MOST FAB seminar! The Tumult in the Clouds: Images of the Cork City to Liverpool emigration via the engineered famine in Yeats' An Irish Airman Foresees His Death.

Heath looked at Flannery's phone, his chin grazing her shoulder. "The engineered famine? How very festive."

Flannery had not-so-casually tilted her phone toward Heath, and she was delighted that he was curious enough about her life to sneak a glance.

"They're at an Irish Literature conference in Florida. They aren't professors or anything—they're both IT specialists. They just love books." She cringed, remembering her father finishing his latest craft project just minutes before leaving for the airport: a plain canvas shopping tote embroidered with the cover of *Portrait of the Artist as a Young Man*. Oh God, his wooden embroidery hoop, his looped skeins of bright, silky thread. "Irish Literature is their bag."

"Ah, thanks to Irish writers you have the house to yourself?" Heath did a little waist-up boogie there in the backseat of the cab; he raised the roof. "*Wooh!*"

Flannery loved how Heath assumed she would take full advantage of an empty house instead of reading, playing Words with Friends, and watching TV into the early morning hours, lonely and a little scared. She missed the sound of her father making sure the glass doors were securely locked by sliding the door open and shut, over and over. The click of the lock, the click of the lock, the click of the lock. Yes, he had OCD but it could masquerade as parental concern if Flannery let go of rational thought and let the *swoosh* and *click* sounds fold into a love song.

Her phone vibrated again, and she and Heath looked at the screen. He whispered her mom's text, and Flannery, boiling in his jacket, shivered: *"I know that I shall meet my fate somewhere among the clouds above; Those that I fight I do not hate. Those that I guard I do not love."*

The cab screeched to a stop. The driver raised his hands up in a Lord-have-mercy gesture toward the crosswalk and divined the thoughts of every breathing soul on Broadway: "Guy's riding a goddamn six-foot-high unicycle across Broadway? I love it!"

Flannery laughed as she looked out at the man peddling—a foot back, a foot forward, his arms out for balance as he waited for the light to turn—but Heath was not so amused. "Cheerful as the circus, isn't he?" His voice was quiet, so the cabdriver couldn't hear. "Look at his *shoes*."

Her face grew hot as she looked at the unicyclist's dirty tennis shoes on the pedals, one sole hanging loose, the other a tread of rubber tongue lapping below the pedal. Did Heath think she had been laughing at an impoverished unicyclist? That she was a jerk for not noticing the sole-flapping loneliness of another human?

Before Flannery could lobby for her pure-hearted intentions—it was just the novelty of the gigantic unicycle in traffic!—she received another text from her mother. This time Heath read more loudly, and though she'd just been shamed, she felt her heart flowering with love. Miss Sweeney offered up a quick scolding: *Your aorta and capillaries are blooming with wisteria and Wild Blue Veronica?* But Flannery only had ears for Heath:

"'*My country is Kiltartan's cross, My countrymen Kiltartan's poor, No likely end could bring them loss or leave them happier than before. Nor law, nor duty bade me fight. Nor public man, nor cheering clouds. A lonely impulse of delight drove to this tumult in the clouds; I balanced all, brought all to mind, The years to come seemed waste of breath, A waste of breath the years behind. In balance with his life, this death. Bye.*' The bye is from your mom, I would think. Not the poet."

Flannery snorted, and immediately rued that porcine sound. "Of course my mother texts a poem—"

"It's a great poem, actually."

"Oh, I know. But she doesn't think to ask me how my day is going. Just: 'Stanza, stanza, stanza. Bye.' Typical."

Uh-oh! She could hear the unappealing self-pity in her voice and moved quickly to correct it. "But obviously I have no right to complain about anything. I'm not starving in Darfur. I don't have the Taliban forbidding my education. I'm not a slave or a prisoner in a concentration camp. I'm not trapped in a Magdalene Laundry. I realize that I'm an entitled whiner. I get it."

Heath nodded his agreement, though he spoke with kindness: "Abused girls, current and past, dream of being Flannery Fields, that is true. But it still doesn't mean you're not going to feel like shite sometimes."

Flannery was too distracted by the lovely long *i* of the British-y swear word that transferred mere shit to *shite* to berate herself for her crybaby ways. Oh, she reveled in the Louis Armstrong thrill of it all: *You like tomato and I like tomahto/You like potato and I like potahto . . .*

But Heath turned away from her and looked out the window, distracted. Flannery looked out her window to the sidewalk and absorbed the aftermath of his mood swing, the unmoored, tense loneliness so familiar to Flannery and, she guessed, to the Irish airman: *"Those that I fight I do not hate; those that I guard I do not love."*

Her love of *Wuthering Heights* had led her on many a sugar-and-caffeine-fueled Wild Google Chase. With a homemade latte in hand and her desk littered with the foil shreds from unwrapped Hershey's kisses, she had perused scholarly and not-so-scholarly research about how all of *Wuthering Heights* was an allegory for British-Irish relations: The port city of Liverpool was a primary emigration destination for the starved Irish, and Liverpool was where Cathy's father, Mr. Earnshaw, found the orphaned Heathcliff: *"starving, and houseless, and as good as dumb . . ."*

There Flannery sat, on any given starlit Saturday night, staring at her laptop. (While a sporty gaggle of her Sacred Heart classmates had seasonal fun: cross-country skiing at midnight—their BPA-free water bottles filled with Maker's Mark and Diet Coke—or skinny-dipping in the saltwater pool in Sarah K's backyard.) Flannery's companions were the other lonely souls with a Wi-Fi connection sharing their Internet wanderings and curiosity about Emily Brontë's intentions: Was she alluding to the famine immigrants—most of whom spoke only

Gaelic—when she wrote about Heathcliff: *"A dirty, ragged, black-haired child; big enough both to walk and talk: indeed, its face looked older than Catherine's; yet when it was set on its feet, it only stared round, and repeated over and over some gibberish that nobody could understand."*

As the cab pulled up to Westsider Books, and Heath paid the driver—*"Keep the change, Mate"*—Flannery zipped her phone and *Wuthering Heights* into her backpack. He held open the door for her, a minor courtliness that made Flannery's stomach flip. And then they were back in the elements—the air too cold to be refreshing, and an unlovely gray sky, the clouds bloated and stagnant—before Heath pulled open another door for her and they entered a warm world.

A staircase bisected the store, and books were stacked on the edges of the carpeted stairs leading to a tight loft area. The smell of paper and dust and glue permeated Westsider Books, and the companionable silence of readers was broken only by a pleasant snippet of arguing about Thomas Pynchon between the man working the front counter and a customer with a grocery bag of books to sell. Flannery felt at home among fellow word geeks, eyes cast down at the open books in their hands as if deep in prayer: Here was a frowsy middle-aged woman in a beige-and-brown plaid coat, a coat so bulky that it made her appear as if she'd ensconced herself in an earth-toned sofa, yet she was reading Pablo Neruda, her lips moving in grief or ecstasy or a combination thereof. Her poetic radiance vanished when she barked into her cell phone: "Yes, I AM still at the bookshop! The cat won't croak if I'm five minutes late with the goddamn Meow Mix." And then there was an elderly man in a crushed-velvet blazer (the exact luscious green of Thompson seedless grapes) leaning heavily on a cane, but with three books tucked, spines out, beneath his free arm, a trifecta of bliss that awaited him once he'd made his slow journey home: John Irving, James Baldwin, and Edna O'Brien. That was enough companionship for anyone, really.

"Do we see Miss Sweeney amongst our bookish friends?"

Flannery peered down every tightly shelved aisle of the shop. "I don't see her."

"Hmmm. Maybe she's in the ladies' room? Assuming there is one."

"Maybe."

"It's a bit of a bookish maze in here." Heath raised his hand to indicate the stairs to the loft. "Perhaps Caitlin Sweeney will descend like an angel. Though I suppose one generally ascends like an angel and descends like a devil. Well. We'll keep an eye out." He turned to the fiction shelves.

Flannery looked up, imagining Miss Sweeney walking down the steps, waving, a starlet at her premiere. But all her curiosity and anxiety about Miss Sweeney was tempered by finding herself in a bookstore with Heath, an experience so sublime that Flannery could give up the corporeal world for this interlude with him, buffeted from the outside world by an army of book spines. Oh, how these moments surpassed all previous delights: the vanilla lattes and the smoked poblano enchiladas and the winter's hush of rising at dawn to see silver white snow had silently blanketed the world while she slept, and then crawling back under the covers for another hour of deep, dreamless sleep, the triple-layer birthday cake studded with Junior Mints, the jeweled freshness of a blue pool on a stifling, hazy August day . . .

And Miss Sweeney was there, if not physically, busy editing Flannery's thoughts. *Being with Heath at the bookstore is superior to, among a great many other things: "the jeweled freshness" of a blue pool? I fear this sounds like a majestic deodorant composed of crushed sapphires.*

Heath leaned down and ran his finger along a row of book spines. "*B* is for Brontë. Here are your girls."

Flannery delighted in the Brontës being thought of as *her girls*. She envisioned herself a Yorkshire girl drinking hot tea and reading with Emily and Charlotte and Anne in the Haworth parsonage while their doting minister father nagged them to sit closer to the fireplace, wanting to make sure his girls stayed warm.

Heath pulled a copy of *Jane Eyre* off the shelf, held it over his face, and pitched his voice: "Oh, Emily, you think you're the best writer in our family, don't you? Admit it, you verbose little hussy."

Flannery was still holding her copy of *Wuthering Heights*— would the Pynchon-loving proprietor of Westsider Books think she was shoplifting?—and she masked her face with it as Heath had. "I am the real writer in the family, Charlotte. How many people are madly devoted to *Jane Eyre*? I hasten to guess not as many as are devoted to *Wuthering Heights*." Flannery lowered the book and resumed her Connecticut voice: "Although *Jane Eyre* has its own merits."

"Maybe this argument really happened," Heath said. "The Brontës had a rather contentious relationship."

"No! I think they supported each other, and they had to fight the patriarchy—"

"The patriarchy? Those eternal BASTARDS!" Heath clawed

at his face in mock-anguish and shook his fists at the heavens. Flannery collapsed into giggles, which, she noted, a touch worried, was probably precisely what the patriarchy expected from her.

"They really did have to fight the patriarchy. They used gender-neutral names so people wouldn't write them off as silly little women from the sticks. They loved their life in Yorkshire, though, their literary domesticity and life at home with their father. Emily in particular hated to be away from home."

"Oh, Flannery." Heath shook his head and offered up a few sad chuckles. "You disappoint me. You truly think Emily Brontë was a mere Pollyanna touched by genius? How could she write so keenly about emotional anguish if she knew nothing of it?"

"But Emily—and Charlotte, and Anne—did know anguish. They lost their mother when they were young, and they had two older sisters who died of tuberculosis, which went untreated at their abusive boarding school. Loss was all around them."

"You may be correct, Flannery, I don't know too much about that."

"Truthfully, I'm no expert. What I'm telling you is straight out of the *Norton Anthology*."

"In any case, your girl did it, didn't she? *Wuthering Heights*. It isn't a short story, is it? And of course she didn't have a fancy laptop, did she, Flannery? So that's quite a lot of ink and quill-pen action—was it the Protestant work ethic or a touch of mania? But let's cut to the chase. Emily's male characters? A bit over the top, am I right? Linton is a bit too much of a goody-goody, right? And Heathcliff? What an evil fellow. Or is he merely misunderstood?"

Flannery tried to keep her facial expression neutral, but her eyes widened.

"I thought you said *Wuthering Heights* was a girls' book. You seem to know a lot about it."

"I'm a genius." He winked—an odd, old man gesture: "You seem very happy in this store."

"Oh, I love bookstores." Oh, no. Did she have to sound so joyful? She chirped: "But I'm so worried about Miss Sweeney." Why did her voice sound false? She really *was* worried about Miss Sweeney!

Heath nodded in response to the growing gravity of Miss Sweeney's situation. He turned back to the fiction bookshelf and ran his finger along the *C*'s. "You know what? I imagine that someday I will be in a bookstore, someplace, and I will see your name on the spine of a book, and I will say, 'My goodness, I once met Flannery Fields, and she was a very nice girl indeed.' Is that what you are going to Columbia for in the fall? To be a writer?"

The sweet pleasure of Heath divining her dream heated Flannery's skin so intensely that it felt like her face might be crackling, caramelizing with pleasure. She fanned her face with *Wuthering Heights* and heard the caught laugh in Miss Sweeney's voice: *Infatuation has turned you to crème brûlée? Dial back the flame on that word torch, Flannery.*

Of course she was acting bizarre, just like any other person who dreamed of being a writer. Wanting to be a writer! It was so completely embarrassing, so . . . so self-aggrandizing, just . . . gross: *I'm a special snowflake and I'd like to share my pristinely original thoughts, via carefully crafted sentences, with the whole wide world!* Flannery imagined there were worse aspirations: The desire to be a writer probably ranked above dreaming about—*Someday! Somehow! If I work really, really hard!*—selling drugs to depressed tweens, but, really, not by that much.

"Yes, well, I guess that being a writer is something that I've considered, you know, vaguely, but it's not something I would actually pursue." Flannery crossed her arms over her chest, so that *Wuthering Heights* was right in front of her heart. But Heath smiled so kindly that she couldn't keep up the ruse. "I know it's stupid, and I know I should want to do something better, something that helps people."

"Has a writer never helped you? Has a book never helped you figure out your life while you were living it? What will your book be about?"

"I do have an idea, but it's probably just so incredibly stupid . . . but, okay. To begin with, it's all based on a true story. The setting is Kentucky."

"A fine start. Bluegrass and bourbon. Pretty horses and fast women."

"How do you *know* these things?"

"There's this newfangled invention called reading, Flannery. You might trouble yourself to look into it."

Flannery laughed, a little breathless from just thinking about her idea, which she truthfully considered an excellent one. "Anyhow, the time period is in the past, it's not in the way, way back, you know, it's not in 1712. It's the 1940s in the land of bluegrass and bourbon, specifically in Appalachia. There is a community of people who have blue skin. No, really. Their skin looks very, very blue. Google it, Heath: the Blue People of Kentucky. It's a minor blood disorder that gives them their blue-hued skin. They're perfectly healthy. But of course, it isolates them."

"They quite literally have the blues. Is that what you are saying to me?"

"Exactly, and so to avoid being bullied or harassed or worse, they go deeper and deeper into the Appalachian woods to live their lives, and they never make contact with outsiders. And then one blue girl walks out of the wilderness: She goes to a clinic with her brother, and though the country doctor working there has heard rumors about the Blue People of Kentucky, he has never actually encountered one. The doctor is shocked, but more importantly, kind and curious, and he figures out that the blue cast of their skin is caused by a recessive gene passed down through a small population intermarrying, and the cure is pure paradox: It's a common drug called 'methylene blue,' and one injection cures the blood disorder. So of course it makes me imagine how it felt for the Blue People of Kentucky to emerge from the forest. Would it be freedom or heartbreak? And it also reminds me of"—Flannery tapped the cover of *Wuthering Heights*—"Cathy and Heathcliff. Would they have been happier if they stayed blue, if they went deeper and deeper into the forest together? They could have lived out their lives in remotest Appalachia—the metaphorical American moors; they could have lived, you know—"

"Happily ever after?" Heath arched his eyebrow. "Rainbows and bloody balloons and watercolor sunsets?"

Flannery met his gaze. Why had she told him her idea? Oh, God. "Well, any potential plot sounds stupid when you attach the phrase 'rainbows and bloody balloons and watercolor sunsets.'"

Heath looked down at his feet. "True enough, Flannery, true enough. I apologize. Your book idea sounds wonderful. It's just making me a bit sad . . . for personal reasons."

"Oh," Flannery said quietly. "Okay. Is it because—"

"They're called 'personal reasons' because they're personal, Flannery." Heath smiled. "But your Blue Period is coming to an end. You, Flannery Fields, are the girl leaving the Appalachian woods. Say farewell to Kentucky—take your last sip of bourbon and ride off into the sunset on your racehorse. And listen, I really do like your idea quite a lot. I'm not just BS-ing you, Flannery. And I get where you're going with it: The methylene blue is the apple in the Garden of Eden, am I right?" But he didn't wait for her reply. "The blue girl that walked to the doctor's office and set everything in motion can't go back and live in the forest. She's just like Eve with her big crunchy bite, or Cathy with her impetuous, wandering heart. But really, couldn't Heathcliff just give her a break? Couldn't he have found a new girl? Couldn't everyone grow old and chuckle about their teenage antics? And original sin for all humanity because . . . of a bite of fruit? And the image of the long-haired girl in the Garden holding the waxed Red Delicious in front of her face? When you consider the agricultural geography, you know that Eve would have actually been holding a pomegranate—lovely ruby seeds and pith with inedible skin so tough you need a knife to slice into it, thus rendering Eve's symbolic bite nonsensical."

Flannery nodded. "Wow. You really have spent a lot of your gap year reading."

Heath nodded. "Just whatever I buy off the blankets on the street. It's pretty hit or miss. Lots of motivational books—if I want to find out who, exactly, is the thoughtless bastard who moved my cheese, or how to live my life with intention, I'm well set."

"I see," Flannery said archly, still smarting a bit from the "rainbow and balloons" comment. "Alright. Well, you've really broken down both *Wuthering Heights* and the Creation story for me with your mansplaining."

"Flannery! I already apologized. Don't be a grudgy goose." He punched her arm gently. "And I hate to ask, as it doesn't sound like a terrific compliment, but what is mansplaining?"

"When a man explains something to a woman, assuming she knows less than he does."

"So: not *quite* a compliment, but in the direct vicinity thereof."

Flannery laughed, warming to him again, and she was still eager, frantic, really, to talk about her novel. "You know in my book, I also plan to draw a subtle and ironic though meaningful—*I hope*—parallel to 'De Daumier-Smith's Blue Period,' this amazing short story by J. D. Salinger, who of course wrote . . ."

Flannery raised her hand and flicked her wrist with a flourish and held it there in midair like a game show hostess indicating a fabulous prize; she smiled and nodded, as if enjoying the covetous *oohs* and the *ahs* of the studio audience. But Heath was silent.

Flannery dropped her hand and laughed, thinking how easy it was for a common fact to slip your mind. "The title of J. D. Salinger's seminal novel? I'll give you a little hint." She echoed Miss Sweeney's words, how she'd introduced the book to the class before their first discussion. "It's not the Bible, and it's not the Koran, but people either love it or hate it."

"I'm quite sure I have no idea, Flannery."

"The first famous young-adult novel?"

"I already said—"

"Catcher in the Rye!"

But Heath didn't have the face-palm OhmyGodofcourse! moment. He shrugged. "Never heard of it, as I previously said, Flannery. Is it a takeoff of 'Coming through the Rye,' the Burns poem?"

"What?" Sure, she knew the poem from freshman lit—Miss Piccone's literary crush on Robert Burns had prompted many assignments. But she was mostly surprised that Heath knew an obscure poem from over two hundred years ago and not the famous book published in the 1950s, and that he sang a few stanzas under his breath: *Can a body meet a body coming through the rye? Can a body kiss a body need a body cry?*

Heath pulled another book from the shelf. "What's this? God, not another title thief! Everybody's ripping off Scotland's favorite son. This fellow John Steinbeck stole his title from the Burns poem, 'To a Mouse.'"

Flannery laughed. "John Steinbeck, great American novelist and title thief!"

"What's this about then, this *Of Mice and Men*?" He thumbed through a few pages.

"You've never read *Of Mice and Men*?"

He mistook her surprise for snobbery and pitched his voice in horrifying imitation of hers. "'You've never read *Of Mice and Men*?' Oh, how many famous books have escaped the eyes and heart of poor Heath Smith? What a shame. What a shame for Heath to be so hopelessly stupid, what a sorry shame it is."

"I'm sorry," she stammered. "I didn't mean it like that. It's just that . . . it's assigned a lot in school, so I just assumed . . .

It's probably only assigned in American schools . . ." Flannery stopped her rambling apology and tried, instead, to summarize *Of Mice and Men* for Heath, but her words sounded watery and rambling, unworthy.

Still, Heath shuddered. "Even a heartless bastard like myself couldn't keep reading something so sad."

Flannery nodded, still flustered. "It is sad," she said absently.

"I bet I know a book we both have read." Heath found a slim volume on the shelves and pulled it out with a satisfied: "Here we are!" He held "Bartleby, the Scrivener: A Story of Wall Street" so Flannery could see the cover. "Now, this one I've read, Flannery. But if someone asked me if I'd like to read about old Bartleby again, I'd have to look them straight in the eye and say . . ."

Heath and Flannery said it in unison: "*I would prefer not to.*"

It was the lamest of literary jokes, a lame subset of jokes in the first place, yet Flannery felt the tension between them dissipate and she knew the joy of instant connection—Instant Karma knocking her off her feet!—a geeky bliss that suggested their cerebellums had just joined, gray matter to gray matter. Flannery imagined a nerd baby flying out of a book wearing over-sized horn-rimmed glasses and yelling "MAMA," a definitive Immaculate Conception that would make Flannery Madonna of the nerds.

Yet in these fast seconds of fanciful happiness, Flannery felt a pang of shame: Miss Sweeney had not been in her thoughts at all. She looked at Heath in profile, his finger moving along the book spines, and shivered, desire and dread converging as she held up Miss Sweeney's copy of *Wuthering Heights*. "This is the book I need to read."

"Of course. I'm sorry; we've gotten a bit off track." He swept his hand to the carpeted stairs, where Flannery perched on one side of the third step like a cat, her back stretched straight and her legs drawn close.

"Just let me pay," Heath said. "And I'll join you."

"Oh?" Flannery looked up. "What are you buying?"

He held out a book with blue peacock feathers on the cover, *The Complete Stories of Flannery O'Connor*. "I'm quite keen on her first name."

Flannery's heart fluttered: *Hope is the thing with feathers.*

Miss Sweeney's red-ink words scrolled away in Flannery's mind: *That's Dickinson, not Brontë, Dear Reader. Know your Emilys.*

Flannery opened *Wuthering Heights* and read.

Nine

Dear Reader, so there I was, a Flannery O'Connor postcard in my hand, hearing that familiar voice: It seemed like a minor miracle for the two of us to be in the same exact spot in all of Manhattan, but it was a misfired miracle, for I had not conjured Brandon, but his nemesis, Miles McPherson, with his small rectangular glasses, and, beneath his unbuttoned jacket, a Charlie Brown sweater—wavy merino wool with a big zigzag across the chest—hipster Brooklyn all the way. It was the same sweater he'd worn in his photo from the cover of the *New York Times Book Review*. My mouth dropped open from the surprise, and I felt like I might vomit up my Starbucks. Since I hadn't eaten any solid food—since when?—my stomach was basically a coffee urn.

"Oh, hey, Miles," I said casually, though I hadn't seen him since my Columbia days. I put the postcard back on the spindle.

"You cut your hair."

Miles looked so sad standing there in the entrance of Westsider Books, his left arm holding the door open, the cold air streaming in. I could see the man at the cash register watching us. I assumed we would quickly find out if he was the owner and responsible for the heating bill, or if he just worked there.

"I guess I did." I touched the ends of my long bob, as if surprised. It wasn't like I'd gone full-on Sinead. I just hadn't wanted to be the person who grew old with princess curls streaming down her back.

"It's still nice. I remember the first time I saw you in Gender Studies. You were sitting next to the window, and the sun was hitting your hair, and it was all lit up—red and gold and chestnut brown and blonde, a rainbow of dark fire tones."

Dear Reader, Good God, *who* talked like that? Miles McPherson.

"Oh, I—"

"Mr. McPherson?" The man at the cash register sounded cheerful. "Would you mind pulling the door shut?"

Owner.

"Sorry!" Miles called out, still looking at me. He pushed the door back even farther so I could walk in.

I brushed past Miles as I entered Westsider Books; my hand started to hurt, that old metallic ache. A rod still aligned my middle finger.

"Also, your eyelashes were pure black, and I wondered how you had your fire-hair and black eyelashes."

God. Like he didn't know. "Mascara."

"As I found out later. The silver tube in my bathroom."

Now, along with the jarring memory of my betrayal of Brandon, I felt the onset of a migraine: blinking zebra stripes obscuring the vision in my left eye.

"So what are you doing in the city, Caitlin? Are you living here now?"

"I live in Connecticut." I took a deep breath. The store smelled of moldy books and winter coats packed too long in mothballs. Was Brandon in here? Was he watching, furious? Or was this part of a still-unfolding plan? Did Brandon now have the power to punish me by arranging a coincidental meeting with Miles that I would find excruciating?

"Oh? Connecticut?" Miles blanched as if I'd told him I'd just been released from prison. No, he would have found the fact I'd been to prison interesting, whereas Connecticut, which Miles surely perceived as the zenith of provincial blandness, only disappointed. "I wasn't sure what happened, if you moved back to Kansas after graduation, or what."

Right! I was confident that he'd Googled me at least once or twice and knew very well that I was on the faculty at Sacred Heart High, but I humored him. I looked around Westsider Books as if I, too, weren't sure what had happened since I'd finished college, but thought that perhaps this magical shop held the answer. Stacks of books towered next to the jammed bookshelves, and here and there I spotted their authors, come to life, not merely disembodied voices communicating their experience of love and despair and grief and wonder through sentences: These were living, breathing humans.

In the back was a dark-haired man in a plaid shirt, the resident tabby cat figure-eighting around his feet until he reached down and picked it up: Jack Kerouac snuggling the feline. There was a bearded guy in a corny J.Crew safari trench coat who caught my eye and looked away, shy. Oh, okay: *That* was why the women liked Hemingway.

I looked back at Miles. I met his gaze; we were the same exact height. "Well, I know what *you've* been up to. Congratulations on your book."

Miles nodded, and breezily thanked me, as if my thanks were his due—ah, the old arrogance. "Now I'm working on trying to finish my next one. But. The twins aren't the best sleepers, so I'm just averaging like four or five hours of sleep each night myself. Did you know that I'm married and have twins?"

I nodded. I had a subscription to *New York* magazine, and had read the feature article on his literary life, and so was duly informed that Miles had married the summer after he'd graduated from Columbia, to "a woman I had known only a month, but who looked like a Disney Princess and swore like a sailor." I thought that an awfully curious phrase, as Miles had grown up wealthy on the Upper East Side, and to my knowledge, didn't know anyone who served in the Navy. There was a photo of his wife, Gwendolyn McPherson (née Adams-Wilson), a self-described "feminist stay-at-home mom" holding their twins, Pearl and Buck. Dear Reader, my Midwestern childhood had included many trips to Disney World, and while his wife certainly looked lovely enough to wait tables at *any* second-tier Disney theme restaurant in Orlando, she could have never strolled the grounds of the Magic Kingdom and been mistaken for royalty. Miles and his wife had moved to Iowa City for the writing program and had returned to NYC with his novel published to acclaim and brisk sales. *The Sorrows of Young Tate* was hailed as a "masterful post-ironic journey of American Manhood."

"I'm so happy for all your good fortune."

Miles snickered; he was a smart guy.

But even my insincere good wishes seemed like a betrayal of Brandon, and slammed me with nausea. The blinking in my left eye was pronounced—the zebra stripes fattening, morphing into electric rectangles. I casually put up my hand to shield the eye. Still, I could make out Sylvia Plath in the poetry section—her matte red lipstick and pearls, winter white coat over an angora sweater and pencil skirt—standing across the aisle from my fellow Kansan, Langston Hughes, in polished wing tips, with his immaculate gray wool suit. Both poets looked so elegant in their furious griefs, all *daddy you bastard* and the dream deferred.

"Caitlin? Hey. Is your eye bothering you?"

I had the terrible memory of how kind Miles had been when I'd shattered my hand: Oh, the carrying of books, the sending of flowers. Of course I had warmed to him. The first time Nancy saw me walking with Miles on campus, she looked annoyed: We (Nancy, Brandon, and I) were meeting for lunch at V & T, and I was running late. The second time was at the library, where Miles was telling me a story about his brother Evan, who was in rehab, and how his mother cried whenever she got off the phone with him. I was engrossed in his tale when Nancy walked past, giving me the wariest grin. I managed to wave, but I had my head tilted close to Miles, amazed at the equalizing power of meth. Who were the madmen behind America's best marketing campaign? *Try Meth! It's not just for poor Midwesterners working at fast-food restaurants!* Who knew meth could mess you up even if your dad managed a hedge fund and your mom was the principal cellist in the New York Philharmonic?

The third time Nancy saw Miles—Dear Reader, cue the biblical symbolism of betrayal, the cock crowing in the distance!—would break Nancy's soft freshman heart, and mine, too.

"Miles McPherson?" A crazy woman (I know: glass houses, but at least I wasn't wearing a long, matted raccoon tail clipped to the back of my coat and a knit Christmas tree hat) approached Miles and struck up a determined conversation about *The Sorrows of Young Tate.*

He gave me an apologetic look as she continued to corner him, and I remembered his politeness, but little else. Miles seemed vague, somehow, undefined: How could Miles ever have competed with Brandon? How could I even, now, mention them in the same sentence? Oh, I was such a fool, because the moment that I held the vase of violets that Miles had sent me, I'd walked right out of my personal Garden of Eden.

Alright, so the Garden of Eden had been a dorm room shared with Nancy and with Brandon, who spent most of his morning and early afternoon slumped on a twin bed, watching movies on my laptop, pausing to get up, stretch like an indulged cat, drink a Heineken if there was one left from the previous night's six-pack (not usually), and eat a handful of Wheat Thins. He had to be careful, as he wasn't an official roommate, and we shared a bathroom with our suitemates, Amanda from Louisville and Leah from Des Moines. I assumed they were geniuses, to make it to Columbia from their backwater states: Yes, Dear Reader, fanciful thinking for someone from Kansas. One morning my first week at school, Amanda had lightly knocked on the door from the bathroom side. It was so odd to answer the *bathroom* door instead of the door to the hallway. Also, I was the only one in the room, another rarity.

She was in a fluffy white bathrobe, asking could she borrow my CHI iron? Hers had conked out.

"Oh, of course! I probably left it plugged in anyway."

Amanda laughed. "You always do! I'm like Fire Marshall Bob, switching it off every morning. I knew it was yours. I figured it wasn't Nancy's!"

I touched the ends of my long, fake-straight hair, feeling self-conscious about my natural frizz and curls, and also vaguely uncomfortable to be reminded of Nancy's naturally straight black hair, a gift of her Chinese ancestors. The most casual observation about race or ethnicity gave me Midwestern nervousness.

Amanda thanked me and pulled the door half-shut before she opened it again. "Where's Anne Frank?"

"What?"

"You know of what I speak." She made her voice tragically throaty, as if narrating a History Channel documentary. "The hidden room-mate."

I had no words.

"Leah and I hear someone pissing like a racehorse in the middle of the night; it's not a girly stream. Also, *pret-ty* sure you and Nancy don't leave the toilet seat up." Amanda was still laughing when she closed the bathroom door.

Dear Reader, I sat on my bed and fumed for a full five minutes. Sure, I was surprised because I thought we had been so careful, so quiet, and yet obviously our suitemates knew Brandon was living on the other side of the bathroom door. Mostly I couldn't believe Amanda's casual anti-Semitism. Because, really, equating a boyfriend crashing at the dorm with Anne Frank's situation? It was beyond callous: It was sickening.

After my thoughts had stewed into a frenzy, I yanked open the bathroom door and proceeded to bitch Amanda out while she calmly flat-ironed her hair in the mirror. But when I was done ranting, she gave it right back to me.

"Hey, Caitlin? First of all, I am not making a joke out of Anne Frank. I think *you* are making a joke out of her: turning her into a handy-dandy poignant symbol of injustice. Also? It's totally reductive to think that Anne Frank wouldn't have had a sense of humor, to think she was something other than a regular girl, smart and funny, with a crooked smile and a side barrette, who liked to write in her diary, who had something terrible happen to her because people went about their day, la de da, probably issuing a lot of platitudes: Let's not rock the boat! Let's not make a mountain out of a molehill! And the majority of people looked the other way and let something crazy-terrible happen. But don't make Anne Frank into the manic pixie dream girl of suffering. She was just a random Jewish girl like me, but she was like you, too, my crinkly-haired Catholic sister. *Ouch!*"

A dramatic end to her soliloquy: Amanda had burned her forehead with the CHI iron. I was peeved about being called out for my bland, unjustified Midwestern self-righteousness, but she was doing such a horrible job straightening the back of her hair that I went ahead and did it for her—my good hand using the iron, my casted hand sectioning her hair—while we hotly debated the meaning of the CHI acronym: *Cultural Hatred Industry? Conquer Humidity Intensely?* Amanda also wondered if there was a hashtag for a Catholic trying to school her suitemate, whom she hadn't known was a Jew, on Anne Frank and anti-Semitism.

The crazy lady was jabbering away, still hanging on to Miles. She had her hand on his coat sleeve; grime showed under her thick yellow fingernails, which were of differing, jagged lengths and flecked with the distant remains of sparkly blue nail polish. Miles was a neat freak so I had to smile when he looked down at her DIY manicure in such close proximity to his own scrubbed hand.

He noticed me smiling and smiled back, and I remembered how I had once felt about him. Dear Reader, I didn't understand the trajectory of romance, of life. Brandon had been my first love and when we'd moved to New York together I thought he would be my only love. Oh, but my wild heart had briefly given way to Miles, it had, and I hadn't understood that romance was mostly a whimsical game of charades, that you could switch partners to experience the mysterious and the unique over and over—*Your phrases are pure magic! I love it when you tease out my hidden meaning*—but that a pattern would form, nonetheless, and you would soon grow bored with your partner's quirky allegiance to Rockabilly or *Middlemarch* or KFC hot wings.

The first time Miles kissed me, we were standing in a deserted hallway in John Jay Hall: a new mouth on mine, his body so close I could feel his heart beating through his T-shirt. October had come in like a lion, cool air and already the crunch of leaves. We pulled apart, lowered our eyes, and kissed again, pressing our jacketless bodies together a little harder. Miles was basically the same size as me, perhaps a little thinner, while Brandon was much taller, and muscular—comparatively, it was all so interesting. Miles seemed so pleased to be kissing me, to be lightly rubbing my thumb that jutted out of my orange cast, and oh the deep, shameful truth: It wasn't so much kissing Miles that felt exciting, but the act of betrayal itself.

When I got back to the dorm room, Nancy was stretched out on her bed, playing Scrabble on her iPhone.

"Hey. Where's Brandon?"

"Taking a walk. What's going on?"

"Nothing," I snapped.

Nancy laughed. "Okay."

"Sorry."

Nancy smiled at me and went back to her game. She was a very pleasant person to live with.

I looked at the cafeteria menu taped to the wall, checking out the evening's dismal entrees. Nancy and I were pretty much wasting our meal plan and loading up our credit cards with takeout, because it seemed sad for Brandon to eat alone and sadder still to smuggle food from the cafeteria for him, as if he were an adorable, forbidden puppy we were sheltering from the storm.

Nancy stared into her phone. "A *Q* and an *X*, so a potential high score. But no vowels, so how can I possibly make a word?"

"It's feast or famine," I agreed, for I, too, was an iPhone Scrabbler. "The vowels are always a problem."

I held my hurt hand in front of me like an apple and brushed my lips over the rough cast. "So, you know that guy Miles?"

Nancy frowned, still looking at the phone, trying to solve the vowel conundrum. "The short guy with the swoopy hair?"

"He's not that short! And he's pretty charming, actually. He could be George Clooney's son. He's got that smile, that whole easy, self-deprecating vibe."

"You think?"

"Nancy, come on. You seriously don't see any resemblance between Miles and George Clooney?"

"They both have arms and legs."

"Well, apparently, the multi-limbed Miles has developed"—I added a syrupy twang to my next words—"fe-aylings for me."

"What?" Nancy looked up from her phone, grimacing. "Gross. How do you know?"

Well. The gross was a little off-putting. I leaned back on my bed and laid my head on my pillow, which smelled of floral hair gels and Chanel Chance perfume and Brandon. My hand injury and personal drama prevented me from going to the Laundromat in a timely fashion. I rolled over so I was facing the wall—it was so hard to get comfortable, the surgical rods aligning my fingers radiating a frozen, metallic pain—and carefully bolstered my comforter around my hurt hand.

"Miles told me. Pretty directly."

"Oh my God. Cait!" Nancy tossed her iPhone on her bed; she walked—it was all of three steps and really more of a leap—over and sat on the edge of my bed. "Does he not know about Brandon?"

"Oh, he knows. I told him my boyfriend from home was living

in my dorm room. He finds it unthinkably bizarre, you know, that Brandon wouldn't have gone to college himself; that he's just hanging around here. The good news? Miles has pronounced you a saint for putting up with the whole situation."

"He's never even *met* me. *Uggh.* Why would he frame my life as a situation to 'put up with,' or condescend to me by pronouncing my sainthood?"

"So says Our Lady of Dormitory Endurance and Kindness!"

"Well, he sounds like a complete asshole."

I turned to look at her. "Nancy, you're a saint that speaks the language of the people. No lofty Latin or holy hosannas for you!"

"How is it his business? Brandon is *awesome*. And he's not hanging around doing nothing. He takes long walks around the city, and he thinks about things, he has so many unusual perspectives, and he likes to talk—"

"I kissed him. Miles. I kissed Miles."

"Caitlin?" Her hurt-bird voice sounded full of wonder, for she had not known I could be such a jerk.

I turned back to the wall and punished myself by thinking of a good person who never did anything stupid or unkind, a high school friend, Kelson Garcia: She was spending a gap year with Jesuit Core, working with homeless families in Miami. I envisioned Kelson walking down the beach, wearing a white eyelet sundress and a crown of daisies while I drifted on the ocean, a passenger on a barge of sludge, flies buzzing around my filthy face.

"Why would you ever kiss someone that . . . wasn't Brandon?" Nancy shielded her eyes with her hands, as if it was all too much, and pulled her hair back into a ponytail, securing it with one of the black rubber bands she wore on her wrist like a bracelet. "Are you going to tell him?"

"God, no!"

I couldn't judge Nancy's silence: Did she think I was kind for sparing Brandon's feelings, or a liar—via the old sin of omission—on top of being a cheater?

"It's just all getting . . . kind of old. He hasn't found a job. He's using my debit card to buy food and, of course, beer."

I waved my hand to indicate all the Heineken bottles, which, despite his lax schedule, Brandon couldn't find time to recycle. Afternoon sunlight rectangling in through the dorm window illuminated the bottles: They sparkled in the metal trash can like candy-green sea glass. But not really. Not quite.

Nancy shrunk back, horrified that I would allude to something so pedestrian as a cache of beer bottles or my alarming debit card activity. But earlier that week I had picked up her copy of *The Second Sex* and was absently reading a page when I saw a series of ghostly *B*'s in the margin, a few swollen, circular hearts.

"I just don't get it! Why would you kiss *Miles*?"

"I don't know, exactly. The kiss itself was a bit mediocre."

Nancy snorted. "Shocking."

"Really?" I thought Miles was sort of fetching.

"That guy? He's just like any ambitious, entitled guy I went to high school with. I know his deal just by looking at him."

"That might be a touch reductive."

"Trust me, Caitlin. Miles? Every other guy you meet here, or maybe for the rest your life, will be his emotional, intellectual doppelgänger."

"Oh, thank you," I whispered, as if overcome by gratitude. "Thank you ever so much, Dr. Phil."

Nancy was sitting cross-legged on the edge of my bed and nervously jiggling her foot, creating a vibration that made my hand hurt. I touched her knee, and she stopped.

"Oh. Sorry."

"It's okay. It's just with Brandon, I'm always driving the bus, you know?"

She didn't. She looked at me as puzzled as if I were wearing a New York City Transit Authority shirt.

I stared at the wall again, taking comfort in the swirled pattern of the ecru paint, and began a self-serving soliloquy:

"In high school, you know, we were a thing. I was the super-smart girl, which, trust me, is *a lot* easier to be in Kansas than here—and he was gorgeous, the captain of the football team, and everyone was like: *Those two?* And I lived in the leafy suburb of McMansions with granite countertops, reverse-osmosis water filters, and Merry Maids and Chem-Lawn service, and he lived in a meth-y neighborhood with super-junky houses, the front yards full of jacked-up Camaros—primer gray, and always waiting for that elusive paint job—and ancient plastic toys and staked pit bulls and . . . Oh my God, Nancy. Just saying this out loud makes me realize how I was so invested in the hokey idea of it all, my self-aggrandizing idea of romance." I lowered my voice and added in the dramatic cadence of a miniseries voice-over: "He was poor, but handsome, with modest intellectual skills. She was upper, upper-middle class, and bitchy, and possessed an uncanny ability to pencil in the correct ovals on *all* manner of achievement tests."

Nancy forced a chuckle, though it was saturated with disgust: *"Heh."*

"But now, being with Brandon here . . . I'm just seeing how much *work* it all is."

"Caitlin!" Nancy gasped.

And I didn't stop there.

"I love Brandon but I don't know . . . will he just live with me forever and never do anything? Do I have to be responsible for both of us, forever and ever, Amen? I mean, it's not like I don't wish things could be easier for him. His dyslexia is so bad that he can't really enjoy a book, and he transposes letters whenever he writes. He's just not like us. The only thing he's ever excelled at is playing football, but he's not good enough to play for a four-year school, not even a hokey little Catholic university in Kansas. He got scholarships from two community colleges but he passed; he passed on playing football to come to Columbia with me."

"That's amazing. Brandon loves you so much. He *sacrificed* something for you, Caitlin."

"I guess. But then again, it's not like Notre Dame was calling."

"Well, *God.*"

"I know I'm being harsh. But to be honest, the present tense is kind of a drag. I need some distance from him. I do."

"But Caitlin, how's that going to work when you're sharing half a room with someone? With someone who loves you? He *loves* you."

"I want to go out with Miles."

Nancy sucked in her breath.

"He's someone I wouldn't have to worry about; he has his own thing going on; in fact he's quite self-involved. But I'm stuck. What would Brandon do if I broke up with him? He has no place to go. God, I can't let him sleep in the park. He doesn't even have the money to get himself home. I would have to—my parents would have to—fund the break-up."

After saying something so nakedly crappy, I tried to joke: "Love and capitalism, am I right, ladies?"

But Nancy didn't laugh. She was silent, and in the silence, I heard the softest metallic *click.*

When I turned over and looked at Nancy—tears in her eyes, her quivering mouth—she looked at the door. "He was here!"

Dear Reader, it was my turn to gasp. *"Brandon?"*

Nancy nodded. "He was outside, by the door. It was open just an inch or two. I thought maybe he had his headphones on. But then he shut the door."

I covered my eyes with my casted hand. My mind floated back to my high school youth group: The youth minister's exuberance bordered on mania, and of course she was a "Love the sinner, Hate the sin" homophobe, to boot. When challenged on any biblical truth, she would turn especially nutty, and claim that the fact that Jesus had once walked on earth was enough proof that we high school kids should stick to all archaic rules: *"He was here!* Do you not *get* it? *Dadgummit!* Do I have to explain it to you again and again? He walked among us! He was here!"

Like the chorus of a pop song, *I knew, I knew, I knew* that Brandon had heard me say terrible things, and that life as I had known it—just fifteen minutes before—had ended.

Dear Reader, while I had been lost in the pangs of dorm-room horror, Westsider Books had kept on hopping. Miles was still holding court. A hipster dude had joined the crazy lady and was quizzing Miles about a geographic inconsistency in his novel, and asking if he knew Alyssa something or other from the Iowa Writers' Workshop. My sole relief was that the migraine in my eye had faded to a buzzy gray whorl.

I heard a great deal about Alyssa. Alyssa was a fiction writer, but she had done the poetry program, not fiction, because she didn't want to get bogged down with craft or plot. Alyssa just wanted to concentrate on, like, the purity of *words*. The crazy lady said she *got it*; she loved words too. And the proprietor of Westsider Books looked on, smiling, at the impromptu salon.

And then, Dear Reader, I saw her. My vision turned from blinking to blurred, as if I were viewing her through a camera lens Vaselined for an aging starlet. Emily Brontë descending the staircase, holding an armful of books. Her coat was root-beer-brown crushed velvet, and a pencil secured the loose bun at the nape of her neck. I thought she would be with her sisters, but she walked alone. I had just a few seconds, but I had a chance. I wanted to tell Ms. Brontë what she had meant to me, a hand crashing through the window, wanting connection. It was my hand, and Emily Brontë held it. I wanted to say that she wrote about the soul-crushing aftermath of romantic love perfectly, to tell her that my class was studying *Wuthering Heights*, writing speculative essays about where Heathcliff had gone when he dropped out of the narrative.

But he came back. Heathcliff came back: Vengeful and heartsick, yes, but he came back.

I couldn't help myself. I put my hand out and touched her velvet sleeve as she passed by. Emily Brontë gave me a shy smile and a cursory, "Hi!" She didn't stop to chat. Miles raised his head and looked over at me, the smallest frown gripping the skin between his eyebrows. The touch of crushed velvet was the briefest succulence. I rubbed my fingers over my chapped lips, trying to memorize the texture of Emily Brontë's gorgeous coat when, unbelievably, the hipster dude put his arm around Miles, whipped out his phone, and took a selfie, as if Miles were Jay Z or Taylor Swift, not a lucky young writer. Miles and the improbable book groupie distracted me so that I lost sight of Emily Brontë in the bookstore. I walked to the door and saw her there on the sidewalk. As she looked though the glass at me, her previous reticence vanished and she recited a stanza of her own poetry. Dear Reader, though I had always mocked situation-specific Facebook memes and the pointed poetry on inspirational greeting cards, her words, forming in my heart as she moved her lips, were exactly what I needed to hear at that moment: *"Little mourned I for the parted gladness / For the vacant nest and silent song / Hope was there, and laughed me out of sadness / Whispering: winter will not be long."*

I put my hand on the glass door and watched her turn away and disappear into the crowd, and then I pulled the handle and walked out of Westsider Books. No, Dear Reader, I wasn't going to stalk Emily Brontë on Broadway; I needed, more than ever, to look for Brandon.

Of course Miles followed me out, jogging to catch up. "Sorry, Caitlin. But I'm so grateful—astounded, really—that people have responded so generously to my book that I want to spend a little time with each person who has read it."

I had heard Miles say these exact words to Terry Gross last week, employing an NPR-friendly aw-shucks voice. I was running my tongue over my teeth, trying to come up with a little moisture. My mouth was so very dry, but I managed to mumble, "Cool. Great seeing you. Take care."

He kept pace as I walked down Broadway, reaching over to touch my left hand, its silvery white hash mark scars. Brandon had been with me when I'd broken my hand. Miles had stayed at the hospital with me when I'd had the rods removed eight weeks later. How quickly the world had moved then, how fluid life had been, when I did not yet know that some choices were irrevocable.

Miles seemed alarmed: "Caitlin! Can you tell me what's wrong?"

Tears slid into the corners of my mouth. *Ah,* I thought, *I'm crying.*

"I'm just in a hurry," I said briskly. I was licking my tears, relishing the warm water.

"But what is *wrong*?"

Poor Miles! We'd stayed together, off and on, until I'd finally broken things off for good our third year at Columbia. My parents had been bummed. They had met him twice and *loved* him; his parents had tolerated me with a certain This-too-shall-pass-or-so-we-hope wariness. (Yes, Dear Reader, the old switcheroo: When Miles's parents had discussed covenants at Gay Head or the improbable buoyancy of the salads at Chez Panisse, or any old thing foreign to my social milieu, I would think: *I am Brandon!*)

And now, as we walked along Broadway, Miles found himself in a rather awkward segue. He had to shed the swagger of the successful person sticking it to the woman who had failed to love him properly in the past and move into a new territory of pure concern, of kindness.

He walked with me for a few more blocks, making gentle small talk. I couldn't stop crying. God, I was dying to get away from him. I felt antsy, my body serving up a new delicacy, Ants Two Ways: the plain old jumbled feeling of anxiety, plus I was pretty sure thousands of ants were crawling on my hands: a moving mosaic, their tiny, feathery legs going this way, this way . . . no THAT WAY. And if Brandon saw me walking companionably with Miles it would ruin everything.

"Miles, listen, I've got to run."

"Hey! Cait? Where are you going?"

"I need to check my e-mail." As soon as I said it, the words felt true. I did want to check my e-mail, and then, Oh God, I was desperate to check my e-mail.

"But I don't have my phone with me."

"Just use mine," he said, digging into his jacket pocket.

"No." I held my hands to my face as if to protect myself from all the wretched decisions I'd ever made. *"Got to go,"* I sobbed. I took off running across the street, the screeching brakes and predictably furious honking of the uptown traffic, and made it safely to the other side of Broadway to the grumbling of fellow pedestrians. *Damn, you trying to get yourself killed?* But there it was in the distance, the great glass ship, magnificent as any Oz: the Apple Store.

I took one last look across at Miles. He was standing where I'd left him, his hands in his pockets. Soon he would be home to his cursing Disney princess and his twins, but for now he was watching me. How sad he looked, for the grudging space where Miles had kept me in his heart would surely be empty now—The vacant nest! The silent song!—because the conceited, fun young woman he'd once loved was now so changed. Dear Reader, he did not know that those we have lost return to us in different forms.

Ten

Flannery closed Miss Sweeney's copy of *Wuthering Heights* and looked up at Heath. He was standing, his elbow on the staircase, absorbed in *The Complete Stories of Flannery O'Connor* that he'd just purchased.

"We really have to get to the Apple Store," Flannery told him. "Miss Sweeney's on her way. We can catch up with her this time."

Heath nodded. "Let's go, Flan. Can I stick my book in your bag?"

"Sure." Flannery unzipped her backpack, slipped *Wuthering Heights* inside, and held the pack out to Heath. As they stepped out, Heath handed the bookseller at the front desk a Sharpie. "Thanks for the loan, Mate."

"Well, no problem whatsoever," the shopkeeper said, his voice cheery and fulsome, though Flannery had noted his terse words on the phone earlier: O, all the world loved an Englishman.

And then they were back outside, the bustle of Broadway,

Heath checking his phone for the address of the closest Apple Store. "Do you think I might receive a credit on my bill for Googling the Apple Store on my Apple phone?" He tapped his phone screen. "Ah, just as I thought. The store is down the street a bit."

They took off walking, and the traffic moved so slowly that Flannery and Heath outpaced the cars on Broadway. Frustrated drivers rolled down their windows, a teeming multitude of driver's ed teachers from Hell: *"Pull up closer to the curb, asshole. Stop your goddamn texting and learn to drive!"*

Heath pulled out a cigarette and gave Flannery an apologetic shrug. "Do you mind?"

"Of course not! It's perfectly fine!" Flannery couldn't help being such an exuberant proponent of smoking: Oh, the strike of the match in the cold air, and Heath bringing the cigarette to his mouth . . .

"So the other Flannery?" Heath draped his arm around her shoulders. "Flannery O'Connor?"

"Yes. Her. What?" It was hard to walk and think straight with her upper body caved in his arm, and he smelled *so* dizzyingly good—smoke and pine needles and copper and paper and the faint black licorice undertone of nicotine—that Flannery wanted to reach up and bite his shoulder. She really did. Oh God, she wanted Flannery O'Connor to stray from the Southern Gothic and write a short story about a girl in Manhattan who was simultaneously falling in love and discovering her latent vampire impulses . . .

She heard the voice of Miss Sweeney: *You would like Flannery O'Connor to rise from the dead, only to sit at some lonely kitchen table in Georgia with a lined tablet and a pencil and write a teenage vampire love story for you? Does this seem like a judicious way for the resurrected Flannery O'Connor to spend her miraculous corporeal hours?*

"Now I'm admiring your parents not just for giving you such a lovely name, but such a wonderfully bookish one as well. She's quite a writer, it seems, just from the short bit I had a chance to read. Tell me, do you have brothers and sisters at home? Sweet Baby William Blake? A frightfully moody preteen Mary Shelley?"

"No, it's just me. One and done, as my parents like to say. How about you?"

"I'm adopted. One brother and one sister." Heath pulled his arm from her shoulder and pointed at the stoplight. "This is our cross street. Here we are." He pointed at the glass Apple Store across Broadway.

"You must miss them, living so far away. Have they been here to visit?"

"They don't have the faintest idea where I am." Heath nodded, as if assuring himself of this sad fact. "It's complicated."

"Everything is," Flannery said, companionable, empathetic.

He spoke slowly, and with a touch of condescension: "No. I assure you, it really, really is quite complicated." And with that he exhaled a plume of smoke over his shoulder and stubbed the cigarette out under his shoe. "Shall we?"

He held the door open for her, and they walked into the gleaming, glass Apple Store just like any other young couple in possession of an iPad with a cracked screen or a credit card at the ready for a new laptop. But as Heath rubbed the back of his neck and glowered at the sleek computers on long, low tables, a sales associate in a blue polo gave him the side-eye and tentatively approached Flannery.

"Oh, we're just looking, but thanks." Because they *were* just looking: an exercise in overstatement, given her sidetracked zeal to locate Miss Sweeney.

Tourists on the street snapped photos through the glass, which gave Flannery the rudderless feeling of being outside and inside at the same time, and Heath's discomfort escalated; he was now muttering to himself as he looked up at the curved glass ceiling. Other customers looked up too, and as Flannery joined them, stretching her neck back, she thought of Emily Brontë's thorn trees at Wuthering Heights: *"all stretching their limbs one way, as if craving alms of the sun."*

She snuck a look at Heath's raised face: What if Heath wasn't just being flip about coming from Liverpool, then Haworth? She thought about his family story: the adoption, the one sister and brother, and not being in touch with them when he was so far from home . . .

"God, this place!" Heath kept looking up at the glassed-off sky. "It's like an elaborate trick, right. Look up at the heavens! But look only while you're waiting in the queue for your computer to be fixed. Otherwise, let's all hook ourselves up to these little machines and see the sky on your retina screen—it will be loads clearer."

A few roving Apple employees traded coded, neutral expressions: *Yeah, we've heard it all before.* And an older woman in business clothes and sensible low heels gave Flannery a droll eye-roll, as if to telegraph: You must be having fun with *him*. But Flannery was in fact having the most miraculous day of her life: It was a ruthless thing to admit, as Miss Sweeney was probably having the worst day of her life, but it was also true, even in this moment with Heath ranting, diluting the magic.

"Whether you're a shepherd in Andorra or working at City Hall in Biloxi, you will be sucked into the artificial world. Wi-Fi will find you, eventually."

Flannery gave a smile of supplication to the Apple employee closest to her, letting her know that everything was completely fine, that Heath was merely an unusually animated shopper.

"We will not all sleep, Flannery, not today anyway, but we will all be changed."

She nodded. "Probably so."

He lifted his hands, an irritated, palms-up gesture, as if to say: *Really? Is that all you've got to say on this crucial topic?*

So Flannery tried again. "Yes, well, I mean, we'll all be changed, because it's like a nouveau greenhouse in here, an enclosed environment for growth, but instead of tomatoes or hydrangea, Apple is nurturing ideas and words and glass and metal. And they're definitely not sleeping."

Heath grimaced. *"What?"*

Well, Flannery herself didn't quite understand what she'd just said, but Heath's Luddite monologuing was fairly irritating. "Actually, Heath, for people with disabilities, access to computers has been life-changing." Why had her voice suddenly taken on the sunny tone of a peppy public service announcement? "My neighbor, Finn is his name, has autism, and his iPad changed his life."

But Heath seemed not to care about Finn, or that men and women, brilliant introverts, she guessed, had concocted machines to help people live more fulfilling lives, machines that could help a teacher who had gone off her meds find her way back home, for instance. He loped around by the iPhone display, speaking loudly and more manically. "You know, your teacher leaving like she did—no wallet, no phone, no laptop? I salute her. I really do. It's a brave thing to go against the grain, or the screen, I suppose. I almost hope we don't find her. If she makes it to her deluded fifth dimension, I'll bloody cheer for her. Caitlin Sweeney goes off the grid entirely! Free-floating despair for the win!"

"Free-floating despair for the win?"

Heath would cheer if Miss Sweeney had . . . gone off the grid entirely? He would cheer if Miss Sweeney had . . . the word formed in her head, but she would not allow herself to think it. She swept it away by staring at Heath, by wondering how the mercurial whiplash of his words could take her from ecstasy to a premonition of grief within the space of a few minutes. Sure, his itinerant kindness felt like a drug, but perhaps his harsh words about Miss Sweeney's plight revealed his true character; perhaps he had just presented his essential self in the Apple Store.

Wuthering Heights was right there in her mind, Cathy scolding her sister-in-law for her burgeoning romantic interest in Heathcliff: "*It is deplorable ignorance of his character, child, and nothing else, which makes that dream enter your head. Pray, don't imagine that he conceals depths of benevolence . . . he's a fierce, pitiless, wolfish man.*"

Flannery needed Miss Sweeney right now; she perhaps had never needed her more, for who else would be able to help her discern this day? She walked away from Heath and into the heart of the busy Apple Store, threading her way through the rows of computers, looking for Miss Sweeney in earnest now: a zooming second of hope when she saw a woman hugging a taller man—mulberry black fingernails and the sleeves of her black-and-white houndstooth jacket on his back—until they pulled apart, and Flannery saw the face of a lovely stranger. And a familiar laugh speeded Flannery's heart, but when she turned to look, the woman was a girlish sixty-year-old with gray braids and a fringed suede jacket. Oh, she was moving fast as she searched, her breath growing ragged as she took the stairs to the lower level. When Flannery was halfway down the steps, she heard a slight jangle from the buckles on Heath's leather jacket.

"Flannery? Flan?"

She kept going, but Heath moved even faster, taking the spiral stairs two at a time, jostling an already-annoyed couple arguing about a warranty; he passed Flannery and waited for her at the bottom of the stairs. But she stayed on the last step, so that they were now eye-to-eye. "I'm just going to take a quick look around for her down here, Heath. In case she happens to be on the lower level of the Apple Store, and not, say, in the fifth dimension."

Heath winced and ran his hand through his hair. "Flannery, I'm sorry. I really, really am. Sometimes I get a bit ahead of myself. And look, I don't want Miss Sweeney to blast off to the fifth dimension. Of course I don't. Sometimes I say the stupidest things."

She nodded in agreement. But he looked so miserable standing there in his checked shirt with his hands jammed into his front pockets. Heath might not be concealing depths of benevolence, but he was nice, mostly. She dropped her brusque tone: "It's okay. I say stupid things all the time. Everybody does."

"I'm not sure if I can help you find her." He rubbed his palm down his face and looked out the windows. "I'm as lost as your own Miss Sweeney."

Flannery lowered her eyes, reverent. What other response was there when someone had just husked themselves in the brightness of the Apple Store, revealing the soft center of their hurt?

"You're helping me just by being here." Flannery meant to sound only logical, a no-nonsense proponent of the buddy system, but her voice pitched and cracked on the *here*.

"Are you hungry?"

"No, not at *all*." She said it forcefully, as if it would be absurd to enjoy some food with Heath while Miss Sweeney was delusional and wandering the city. But it was pretty difficult to be righteous with Heath standing so close to her. "I mean, maybe. A little. I am kind of hungry, yeah."

Heath smiled. "That's all the answers at once."

His voice sounded so . . . husky, so sweetly nicotined, and just as she thought those words, the red-pen voice of Miss Sweeney entered her mind: *So he's a sled dog enjoying a sugared Marlboro Light?*

"I have the metabolism of a hummingbird, Flannery. I'm forever starving, and I know a lovely place to eat just around the corner. Could we just go off-book for a bit and get some supper?"

Heath reached for her hand, and when she hesitated, he said: "Come on. You can read more when we get there." And so with her own heart speeding to a hummingbird thrum, she took his hand and quickly looked around the lower level for Miss Sweeney (which even to herself seemed perfunctory, as she was already envisioning sitting at another table for two with Heath) before heading upstairs and walking outside: Manhattan in the magic hour before nightfall, darkening dusk settling over the city.

They walked up Broadway to the next crosswalk, amid all the real New Yorkers who were getting off work—carrying their to-go dinners in planet-killing Styrofoam—and talking on their cell phones, their voices frantic, heartfelt: *"Did you find your keys?" "Is Mona home yet?"* Every single soul seemed lost; all were resplendent in their hidden tenderness. Heath held her hand tighter. "You'll love this place, Flannery. They do quite a nice shepherd's pie if you're in the mood for something savory."

Heath led her down a few blocks to a street lined with brownstones before he stopped at a glass door in the middle of a windowless brick building. Shamrocks and snowflakes decorated the glass door: O'KELLEYS EST. 1844, stenciled in Kelly green.

Heath reached for the door handle.

"Hey, wait. Is this a bar?" She winced at her Pollyanna ways.

Heath laughed. "If you're expecting a den of iniquity, I am afraid you'll be terribly disappointed. You'll see nobody doing Jell-O shots off various body parts at O'Kelleys, nor do they have wet T-shirt contests."

Heath pulled the worn handle—the string of silver bells on the door shivering against the glass—and Flannery stepped into pine paneling and the smell of warmed-over roast beef, an illuminated HAMM'S sign behind the bar, and a female bartender of a certain age with darkly penciled eyebrows and a fluffy mohair sweater, all pastel shades of green and pink that made Flannery think of swirled saltwater taffy.

She looked at Flannery and then gave Heath a broad wink. "Did you kidnap this poor girl?"

"Indeed I did, Eileen." He reached over the bar, and they hugged. "That's why, as her cruel captor, I'll be feeding her your shepherd's pie and cappuccino. For two, please."

Eileen didn't look at Flannery but addressed her elliptically, as she filled two glasses with soda water from a spigot behind the bar. "Oh, of course, your Mr. Heathcliff doesn't like plain water; he's got to have his bubbles, doesn't he? And His Nibs can't have a nice hot coffee from the pot, he has to have his hand-crafted cappuccino with a light dusting of cinnamon." She pushed the water across the bar at Heath. "There's a nice booth open, best grab it before some pensive effing alcoholic with a Moleskine occupies it for the rest of the night."

"A lot of writers come here," Heath told Flannery.

"Oh, cool," Flannery said, her voice lilting with pleasure. It was so thrilling to be at a bar!

Eileen was now working on another order, using tongs to pull a pickled egg out of the murky depths of a glass gallon jar and mumbling to herself: "Why do people order these abominations?"

"Why does she call you 'Heath*cliff*'?"

Heath shrugged. "Why not?"

"I'll sling your proverbial hash in a bit," Eileen called over.

Overcome with gratitude to find herself tucked inside another new world in the new world, Flannery smiled at her. "Thank you. Thank *you*."

Miss Sweeney snarked, adding a quick: *That last gratuitous "thank you" brought to you by the department of redundancy department.*

Eileen looked at Flannery and sighed, as if greatly disappointed, before she scolded Heath. "Christ eating a cracker, Heathcliff, you've got yourself a Catholic school girl with pristine manners, haven't you? I tell you this, and you listen well: You are going to Hell in a handbasket made of thorned rose branches."

Two men sitting at the bar laughed and clinked beer mugs; it was all a little nerve-wracking, so Flannery was more than glad when Heathcliff picked up their waters from the bar. She followed him as he made his way through O'Kelleys, cutting across the improvised dance floor—a dozen feet of floor space created by a few tables shoved to the wall next to the jukebox— where a lone, drunken man in snakeskin cowboy boots swayed to Neutral Milk Hotel. Heath and Flannery mazed around the pool table and old-school foosball table, and finally made their way to the red vinyl booth in the back.

Heath slid into the same side of the booth as Flannery and proceeded to slam his soda water. From her peripheral vision, Flannery watched his Adam's apple bob with each gulp.

She took a drink of soda water too, the bubbles fizzing like pure hydrogen peroxide in her throat as a powerhouse soprano belted out: *"This is dedicated to the one I love."*

Heath clapped his hand to his forehead. "Oh, Dear Lord, they have the Shirelles on the jukebox. I was just complaining about the high-tech world and not giving America credit for its two finest exports, the motorcar and Motown. As I'm not in possession of a vintage Mustang convertible, would you care to have a dance with me, Flannery?"

Dancing? Flannery could see another couple in the next booth, two guys in plaid shirts, kissing. They looked bulky as lumberjacks but kissed so delicately—not the standard smash-mouthed PDA—that Flannery felt happy for them, for every-one! Oh, Manhattan, she thought, you are the city of love! But she still felt nervous about dancing.

The Shirelles agreed, filling O'Kelleys with their smoke-and-honey vocals, and Heath was inspired too, urgent even. "Come *on*," he pleaded, and she took his hand and allowed herself to be led out of the booth.

"Wait, I'm already pretty hot." As she took off Heath's jacket, she immediately rued the double meaning and double entendre of that quick sentence—both a self-aggrandizing and delusional proclamation about her appearance, and also, more alarmingly, it sounded as if she were referencing some bar-room barometer of sexual excitement. She put Heath's jacket on the side of the booth with her backpack.

Heath turned to the plaid-shirt kissers, who were taking a break from the action. "Keep an eye on things, Mates?" They nodded languorously at the jacket and backpack and sipped their cranberry-colored cocktails.

Heath walked Flannery over to the little makeshift dance floor next to the jukebox. He put one hand on the side of her waist, and held out his other hand. She instinctively knew to clasp his hand and put her other hand on his shoulder. It's the evolution of the species, Flannery thought. Our hands know where to go.

Miss Sweeney's red pen was gentle: *Easy there, Charlene Darwin.*

Heath moved his feet. Flannery moved hers in time, two baby steps up, two to the side: This was dancing.

Flannery felt like she might levitate, but had no choice but to live in the perfection of the moment. Heath reached down, his chin stubble scraping her temple, and put his mouth to her ear, his warm breath like supersonic CPR, overstimulating her heart. "Why are you looking for her?"

Flannery, dazed from the slow dancing and the proximity of Heath's mouth, closed her eyes and listened to the Shirelles sing out the sweet ache of love—several seconds of bliss—before she answered.

"Miss Sweeney is . . . nice." Well, that sounded stupid, but forming words while Heath had his large hand on her waist was so puzzling: a far-off dream of conjugating Latin verbs underwater. "She helps me with my writing, but also with my life. She thinks I'll be happy here. Her theory is that I'll find my people here in Manhattan. Truthfully? I don't have that many friends now."

"Join the club, Flannery. Your teacher sounds lovely."

"She is. She makes books come to life, which I know sounds massively stupid." O, the beautiful weight of his hand, her forehead brushing against the softness of his worn shirt, her eyes fluttering shut, the dreamy half-darkness of the dance floor. "Not just *Wuthering Heights,* either. All the books: When we read *The Diary of Young Girl*—it wasn't like reading it in junior high, where the horror of her ending overshadows every page—Miss Sweeney focused on her prose, on Anne Frank's beautiful, lively writing."

"I've never heard of Anne Frank, Flannery. Another name for my reading list."

The Shirelles sang out: "*Tell all the stars above, this is dedicated to the one I love.*"

His body was so close to hers, and she kept swaying to the

Shirelles, but . . . How could Heath not have heard of Anne Frank? How was that even possible? Didn't everyone, all across the world, know who Anne Frank was?

"Heath?"

"Yes?"

She raised her face.

"What is it, Flannery?"

Could he be a lost saint of the moors, cheating death and passing through the ages in his corporeal perfection?

Had he joined the most spectacular of the incorruptibles?

It's you, she thought. *It's you. Is it you?*

If Miss Sweeney had been leading her all along, if her revised edition of *Wuthering Heights* had been not just a diary, but a heartfelt travelogue written specifically for Flannery, then it was also entirely possible that Heath Smith, the brokenhearted boy on gap year, was Heathcliff himself, taking his leave from *Wuthering Heights.* And it wasn't that he'd escaped the inevitable transformation from vibrant human to empty-eyed anatomy class skeleton. He had appeared living and breathing, wholly resurrected, though he had only ever existed on the pages of *Wuthering Heights.*

Flannery knew it sounded hardcore crazy, a literary resurrection that perhaps took a greater suspension of disbelief than the heralded religious one, and who would believe it, who would open their mind and heart, and make themselves so vulnerable to the spirit world that lay just beyond the cover?

He looked in Flannery's eyes, and his face moved closer to hers, closer, closer still, until she couldn't focus, and then came the shock of his mouth covering her own.

Heath's front teeth clicked Flannery's, and they pulled apart and then kissed again. Her brain slowed, distilling her thoughts into pure sensation. There was no more: *Could it really be you?* There was just the taste of his chapped lips, his plush tongue: ethereal salt and cigarettes.

Flannery felt tears prick her eyes. Flannery loved him, and she also loved every person in O'Kelleys, and the Blue People of Kentucky, and every last girl at Sacred Heart, and all the lost souls of Manhattan, and every person in the universe, and she loved each lonely galaxy and far-flung constellation and comet, and she most certainly loved the Shirelles for providing their transcendent soundtrack for her first kiss with Heath.

Silence: The Shirelles stopped singing. The world quieted. Free-floating despair was a memory of a memory and then forgotten altogether. Life outside this moment blurred at the edges before it fell away, leaving no ache for permanence, no ache for an ephemeral moment to announce itself—*This is a miracle! Take note!*—and be smelted into a hallowed gold bar of remembrance. There was only:

Mouth

Warmth

Purity

And then

"GET A . . . ROOM!"

Flannery and Heath pulled apart, and as that phrase and its meaning registered in her mind, she smoothed down her hair and licked her lips and looked around at the amused, gaping faces at O'Kelley's. She wondered what social response was required of her at this particular moment in life.

Heath certainly knew.

He raised his hands in the air, fingers splayed in the universal "A guy just can't win" gesture.

Who had yelled? The skinny dude at the bar receiving high fives seemed a likely suspect. And the first nasty guitar riff of AC/DC's "You Shook Me All Night Long" was now playing on the jukebox; soon the infamous sex romp lyrics would start.

Eileen sang along—*"She had the sightless eyes telling me no lies/knocking me out with those American thighs"*—as she carried their food on a round tray, following Flannery and Heathcliff, who shirked their way back to their booth.

"Here you go, lovebirds." Cinnamon-sprinkled hearts were swirled into the milk foam of their cappuccinos, and the starburst slits in the top crusts of their shepherd's pies oozed golden gravy.

"Cutlery?" She pulled forks and spoons from her apron pockets and clanged them down on the table. "Napkins?" She reached across the table and tapped the silver napkin dispenser with her burgundy fingernail. "Protection?" She produced a small green package, and laid it next to Heath's shepherd's pie like an after-dinner mint.

"God!" Heath gasped. *"Eileen!"*

Flannery was delighted to see Heath's olive skin flush. Sure, she was blushing, too, but that was the norm, especially when dinner was served with a side order of Trojan.

Eileen put her hands on her hip. "Is there a problem, sir?"

"We won't be needing that." Flustered, he yanked a napkin out of the dispenser and covered up the condom package.

Flannery joked: "You've made a nice little blanket for it." She was warmly rewarded with Eileen's phlegmy cackle.

Flannery hardly knew herself. Who was this girl tossing out lighthearted bon mots about birth control?

Heath sighed in mock despair. "God knows the last thing I need is you lot pairing up against me."

Eileen put her hand on Flannery's head and gave her a gentle shake, as if she were a puppy. "I like this girl. She's alright." She slid her hand down to Flannery's chin and turned her face so that Flannery was looking up at her. "Look at you. You've got the whole world ahead of you, don't you?" Up close, Flannery could see Eileen's reasoning behind her heavy-handed eye shadow application: the scar-slashed crescent of skin between her right eyelid and brow.

"*What a dream,*" she whispered to Flannery. "*What a dream it would be to be you, right now.*"

Had anyone ever looked at her so lovingly? That Flannery felt so seen, so beloved—and by a near stranger—seemed nearly as miraculous as kissing a boy in Manhattan on a wintry Thursday evening, and not just any boy: Heathcliff himself. But Eileen's sudden and spectacular kindness was also a bracing antidote to the haze of dream-world, and filled Flannery with guilty panic. Here she was dancing at O'Kelleys while Miss Sweeney wandered the city in despair; here she was marveling at literary time travel as a true possibility, though *literary time travel* sounded so goofy and grandiose that it shamed her further.

When Eileen pulled her hand away, Flannery was sorry to lose the feeling of a rough, warm hand cradling her chin but she unzipped her backpack and pulled out Miss Sweeney's copy of *Wuthering Heights*. "I need to read," she told Heath. "I really need to read."

Eileen was walking away with her tray tucked under her

arm, but she'd heard Flannery. "That's the problem with a smart girl, isn't it?" She looked over her shoulder and winked at Heath. "She'll have the *need*, but the need will be to read."

"Alrighty, then, Eileen," Heath called out. "Thank you for serving us such hearty portions of awkward."

Flannery opened the book. "I'm just going to—"

"It's what I do, Heathcliff," Eileen yelled back. "I serve up the delectable awkward."

"Indeed," Heath muttered happily and attacked his dinner. He stabbed his fork into the crust of his shepherd's pie, and a delicious, savory-smelling steam rose up, lamb and potatoes and peas and rosemary.

"Go ahead and read, Flannery. You should keep reading."

But she already was.

Eleven

I pulled the door open to the Apple Store, the glass ship in the city of dreams, and I could feel the movement, the swift currents of waves rocking the floorboards. I was in New York City, yes, but I was back in Kansas, too: I could feel the vibration of Brandon's truck engine as we flew along the back roads, gravel crunching beneath the tires. No, I was not a nouveau Dorothy wanting to click my heels three times and go home, far from it. I loved Manhattan and I wanted to live there again, with Brandon. I only wanted another night at the Tallgrass preserve, to hear the cicadas and the call of the Eastern Phoebe, to lie next to Brandon on a cool slab of rock. Oh, but the glass ship ramped up my vertigo, and I stumbled over to a long table of computers and held on tight. I hurtled backward and the new buzzing in my ears was a plague of locusts descending, and my joints felt like they were connected by cold iron bars.

"Hi. Can I help you?"

I kept my eyes squeezed closed until my vision stopped shuttling around.

"Um. Miss? Is everything going . . . okay for you?"

Oh, you *bet*, I thought. I opened my eyes to an Apple employee in her bright blue polo shirt, giving me a smile of professional friendliness. But her eyes told a different story: Apparently I was now a scary person capable of weirding out a nice, normal gal. Other shoppers were giving me plenty of elbow room as well, observing my table-clinging from a polite distance.

"Can I use a computer?" No, that didn't sound quite right. "I want to try some out. I'm in the market . . ." But I couldn't quite piece together that last sentence. I thought of the flea market where Brandon's mom sold her big soft dolls, her Punk Softees, and where you could buy earrings for a dollar, but also Eames chairs and organic smoothies and bongs and Christian homeschool materials: Bible verse stickers, felt boards with Jesus and the saints, and the inspirational spelling book *D Is for Disciple!* Oh, how I wanted to be in that market on a sunny spring day, to bring his mom a blackberry ginger juice and revel in her warm smile of thanks, to see Brandon high-five his mom after she sold a one-of-a-kind treasure from her booth, Henry Rollins or Iggy Pop going home with some elderly, happy hipster.

The Apple employee was smiling expectantly, but I had no idea what else to say to her. I squinted at her, stumped, my mouth half-open: *D is for Dumbass!*

"Feel free to use a computer." She chuckled and swept her bony white hand in the air, a seagull taking flight. "Take your pick."

On a shiny silver laptop that looked smooth and sweet and compact, a foil-wrapped chocolate bar of a computer, I logged into my Gmail account and found six new e-mails: three from Sacred Heart, one from the police department, and one from Zappos. And then I started scrolling back, looking for my last e-mail from Brandon, the one I'd never deleted. It was now more than six years old, and I didn't know if a statute of limitations for gazing at old e-mail existed, but I kept scrolling. I had 18,000 unread e-mails—the Gap was very keen to get in touch with me—so I had to go back and back.

The last time I'd actually seen Brandon had been at Carman Hall. After overhearing my disgusting, world-changing words to Nancy, aka the backstabbing *I want to go out with Miles* monologue, Brandon had disappeared. I had lain awake the first night, wondering if he would call or text—he couldn't get back into Carman without Nancy or me, since he didn't have a dorm ID. But morning came, and The Day After The Drama passed, and my Brandon-less life commenced: Yes, I felt flayed by the harsh twists and turns of life, and was prone to protracted crying jags, but I figured Brandon had gotten himself back home. Oh, and I was also hanging out with Miles.

Nancy was not as worried about Brandon as I thought she would be, and so I assumed her obvious little crush was just the old passing fancy. We started exploring the city together—two girls on the go! One Saturday morning walking with our coffee in Central Park, we saw two children—a little boy in a white oxford shirt and navy blue shorts and a little girl in a white dress with a navy sash—vogueing gamely for their mother, who was taking their photo. Their father yelled encouragement: "Smile, Chandler! Smile, Lily!" The nanny fake-smiled as she waited by a stroller some twenty feet away. The mom—all honey-blonde blown-out hair and gym arms and dark-rinse skinny jeans—kept yelling, "Smile, silly Lily! Smile, Chandler! I'm looking for your very best smile! I want the best of the best, buddy!"

Chandler and silly Lily were posing in front of a large gray rock, and from our vantage point on the sidewalk, Nancy and I could see a big old rat behind the rock. Dear Reader, of course we *Oh my God-ed* and convulsed with laughter, and I regret to report we took out our phones and walked closer so we could take the *Rich Kids and the Rat* photo. The parents kept up with their "Smile!" routine, not knowing that hantavirus loomed right around the jagged granite corner, not knowing they were giving two college girls the laugh of their lives. The rat swished his fat posterior back and forth; he had found a discarded spool of pink cotton candy and lowered his head to eat. O, how our hearts sang! How grateful Nancy and I were to the sweet-toothed litterbug who had furthered our joy with a sloppily discarded cotton candy. But from where I stood I couldn't fit the rich kids and the rat in the frame, so I aimed my phone directly at the rat. He (or she) frantically gorged, and when he lifted his head, a puff of pink cotton candy lodged on his little rodent head, the briefest bouffant. I got the photo. Buddy, I got the best of the best.

Nancy and I couldn't speak for a good ten minutes, and later our abdominal muscles ached from laughing so deliriously: *Did we just see George Washington Rat about to forge Central Park West in his powdered pink wig? No! The rat was just on his way to Rodent Wigstock.* Dear Reader, we agreed that the wigged transformation of the rat was just the sort of physical miracle—our personal loaves and fishes—that we would not witness again in our lifetimes.

The next Friday, Nancy left me a note saying that she had gone to her parents' house for the weekend. Miles and I went for sushi and to hear Junot Díaz read on campus, and I felt awfully pleased with myself, pleased that this was how I now I spent my Saturday nights, my sweet, broadening horizons! Still, it felt a little weird to head home at 9:30 on a weekend night, even with company.

Miles and I went back to my dorm room, since Nancy was in New Jersey. We were walking down the hallway at Carman, laughing about how Miles's roommate, Phillip, was a perpetual presence, due to his agoraphobia, and wasn't that just the best luck ever?

I unlocked the door; I flipped on the light.

"Oh my God, Caitlin?" Nancy pulled her comforter over her face and moaned: "Caitlin, I'm so sorry."

Dear Reader, there are some moments so otherworldly that it is best to run, to run away and to make no excuses for your exit: Flee the scene. Do not stand and blink; do not make your mouth a perfect oval and emit a banshee wail of sorrowful surprise.

Brandon propped up on his elbows, squinting from the sudden light. He smiled at me—his dimples showed—and said brightly: "Hey there, Caitlin!" I had the horrible memory of once placing a Skittle in Brandon's dimple to see if it would stay (it had): a personal science fair of new love.

Nancy started to cry.

Copper-colored stars showered into my vision: Yes, I was seeing stars, as if I were a cartoon Southern belle—Why, oh *my* stars— instead of a shocked college student. Brandon! How I had missed him! If not for the incongruency, I would have told him I loved him right then and there, and if not for our three hearts, which would re- main fiercely broken, Nancy and Brandon and I could have been the hapless, slutty stars of an MTV reality show about hooking up with roommates. All we needed to complete the unfortunate tableau was an empty Captain Morgan bottle next to Nancy's twin bed and a hot- pink string bikini top dangling from a phallic bedpost. Instead, there was Nancy's bra on the floor—pale lilac trimmed with white lace— horrifying as a severed head.

I put my casted hand over my eyes.

From beneath the covers came a noise from Nancy, halfway be- tween a groan and a whimper, and I regretted that we would never be able to laugh about this together, to indulge our word-girl fun: *From beneath the covers, Nancy grimpered. She grimly grimpered!*

Miles commented, "Awkward!" and politely looked away. Perhaps because Miles had gone to boarding school, these dormitory dramas were entirely familiar to him. In any case, he navigated the awkwardness with mastery. He stepped back into the hallway and offered up a casual: "Sorry, guys! Carry on."

Miles: the only person on the scene without a crucial bit of information.

"Carry on? Well, aye, aye, Captain. At your service, sir!" Brandon stood, and gave him a salute. "Also, what a great jacket that is, would you call that color *puce*?"

Brandon himself was wearing no clothes at all, so Miles couldn't slam his fashion sense. In truth, I had noticed earlier that his jacket, possibly a blazer, looked a bit odd—wide-wale corduroy in a faded shade of gray with a lavender undertone. Brandon was correct: puce. Well, Miles had the confidence to wear any jacket he'd picked up at a thrift store for five dollars. (And he always bought his jeans at Barneys.) But right at that moment, Miles looked extremely unsure of himself.

Brandon was not a fighter by nature, but it seemed like that might be about to change.

I gripped the baggy sleeve of Miles's puce jacket and whisper-hissed, "Let's *go*."

"Leaving so soon, Caitlin?" Hearing Brandon say my name was pure punishment. "You got some big, big plans with Tiny Tim?" I could see a stripe of muscle pulsing in Miles's jawline as we started down the hall. He *was* on the short side. By now Nancy was fully sobbing underneath the covers. No more grimpering for her. *You deserve it,* I thought.

But really, she didn't.

Miles whispered. "Wait. Is that *him*?" He walked faster when I nodded. I banged my good hand on the elevator button but we were stuck, waiting. Oh God! We should have taken the stairs at the other end of the hall, but we obviously couldn't walk past my room again. And just as I was regretting yet another life decision, I heard a loud *thunk,* and then Miles's voice, stripped of all irony: *"Owwww!"*

And then came another *thunk,* and another, and Miles doubled over just as the elevator dinged, but he managed to scramble inside after me. There were two girls getting out, alarmed at the way Miles was whining and holding his back.

I looked down the hall. It was the last time I would see Brandon alive.

He had stepped back into my dorm room, but his head was poking around the corner, watching me. Dear Reader, what had I done, and could it possibly be undone? He held out one hand, palms up, and I would spend years discerning if that gesture meant: *What do I care, Caitlin? Enjoy your life with the puce blazer dude,* or *O, come back to me.* My vision of the hallway narrowed as the elevator doors moaned and started to pull together, a gray frame shrinking the picture into a vertical slice before that world disappeared altogether.

From inside the elevator I heard one of the girls say: "What is *up* with all the . . . Oh my God, is it *applesauce?*"

I slept in Miles's twin bed that night, fully clothed. Phillip the agoraphobic was just eight feet away, so Miles and I had to whisper. He had taken eight ibuprofen and sounded a little loopy. "I feel like I've been branded."

Brandoned, I thought.

"The pain is incredible. It feels like I have circles of fire on my back. You wouldn't believe it."

I didn't say: *Shattering my hand can hardly be expected to compare to the agony caused by being struck in the back by three individually sized containers of organic applesauce.* Instead, I made a soothing sound: *Hhmm.*

"At first I thought I'd been shot. I thought he had a *gun.*"

It occurred to me that Miles had never shot skeet—he'd never heard the satisfying shatter of the clay pigeon after the shotgun kicked and bruised his shoulder; certainly he had never gone hunting. Though I was mostly a vegetarian and delighted to be away from the Midwestern camo and beer culture, apparently my ingrained ideas of proper masculinity still enslaved me. I found myself disgusted that Miles would mistake pureed apples for gunfire.

I envisioned Nancy's dad stacking the organic applesauce next to my bed, and wondered if my old life had just vaporized.

It had.

Nancy moved into a single room on the eighth floor of Carman. We successfully avoided one another for the rest of freshman year, except once when I stepped into the elevator and it was just the two of us. Nancy immediately put her phone to her ear and faked a call: *"I'll be there in five minutes."* She proceeded to tell the empty air how sorry she was for running late until we reached the lobby and went our separate ways.

"He's got quite an arm," Miles whispered. "I will give him that. And incredible aim."

I closed my eyes and saw a football torpedo out of Brandon's hand and arc across the Kansas sky: higher, higher still, sailing above the cottonwood trees before it descended between the goal posts. "I know."

Victory at the Apple Store: I had finally found my last e-mail from Brandon. It had arrived the week after the applesauce incident. I had not heard from him in the interim, and, sad to say, I had not been particularly worried about Brandon.

I was out to dinner with Miles at a restaurant called Massawa. He was shocked, forlorn, even, that I'd never eaten Ethiopian food, and eager to show me what I'd been missing. When I took the first bite of my entree—the spiced pumpkin and beef such a sublime blend, such a perfect bite—that it seemed I had been waiting my whole life for time to pass so that I could live in this moment, to be eating Duba B'siga in Manhattan, with someone named Miles.

But then Miles offered up a condescending *"I told you it was good,"* as if I were a stodgy culinary xenophobe pining for a Big Mac and had to be cajoled into trying something new. I felt so vexed that when my phone dinged, alerting me to a new e-mail, I took my phone out of my jacket pocket. I tapped the mail icon, and there it was, an e-mail from Brandon. The subject line was empty.

I clicked.

I would very much like to write that I raced to the bathroom of Massawa all those years ago and vomited up my Duba B'siga, such was my distress. And in fairness to myself—for who else would I rather see treated justly?—my hands did tremble as I looked at my phone. But I cleaned my plate that night.

Seven years later, in the vast brightness of the Apple Store, and fully knowing what I would find, it took more courage than it had when I was sitting across the table from Miles in Massawa, but I did it.

I clicked, and each word was a gut-wrenching punch, so that right there, in the supremely bright Apple Store, I knew the howling grief of Heathcliff: *"The murdered do haunt their murderers, I believe. I know that ghosts have wandered on earth. Be with me always—take any form—drive me mad! Only do not leave me in this abyss, where I cannot find you."*

"Doin' okay?"

I looked up. The Apple employee smiled at me; she had the glowingly over-bleached teeth of my Sacred Heart students, an emerald nose ring, and short, wheat-colored hair.

"This new Airbook is *tight.* And it's a good deal, too. Do you *so* love it?"

I nodded, my brain all abuzz with *"The murdered do haunt their murderers."*

"Wish my employee discount was a little more rad. I want one myself."

I started to sob, but my belated sensitivity only made my fellow pilgrims in the Apple Store uncomfortable: A mother started talking in a loud singsong voice to her little girl, "Look Nora! This iPad has that Caillou app you like." Two teenage girls shared a glance of empathy tinged with disgust: *Wow, check her out, kinda sad but way to be a freak at the Apple Store.*

While the poor Apple employee fumbled for something to say ("Um, are you . . . Oh, hey . . . *Uh,* I think we have a box of Kleenex at the Genius Bar . . . located directly at the back of the store . . .") I pulled my coat tighter around me and walked out of that magnificent glass ship.

Now the sky was dark, and when I saw a cab coming down the street, I raised my hand, and it stopped, all lucky, fluid motions. I was still sobbing when I opened the door and slid into the backseat.

The cabdriver turned around to look at me.

"Hello? Are you okay?"

I nodded. "Can you take me uptown?"

"What's the address?

"Can we just drive for a little bit ,and then I'll decide?"

"Will you be able to pay for it?"

"What?"

The second time he asked with pique: "Will you be able to pay for it?"

Yes, I told him. Dear Reader, I was ready.

Twelve

"We have to leave now, and we have to go fast." Her thumb on the spine, she held out the pages so Heath could read.

"Oh?" His shepherd's pie was nearly gone, just a few spring green peas and cubed potatoes glistening in the greasy gravy. He prepared to fork another bite as Flannery pointed at a page. "This part, Heath! Just read this part!" She put her index finger on Brandon's e-mail as she handed Heath the book. "Start with 'the murdered do haunt their murderers.'"

"Alright then, Missus." Heath raised his eyebrows at her bossiness and read. Flannery watched his face turn from neutral to distressed, his mouth hooking to one side.

"Jesus," he whispered. "She's ready?"

"Right?" Flannery took the book from him. "We have to go."

The scrappy guitars of the Ramones filled O'Kelleys with the battle cry of the disenchanted: *I wanna be sedated*. The plaid-shirted couple danced—a sort of pogo-hopping, along with some ironic air guitar; they kissed and laughed as Flannery took one last, longing look back. Heath was holding the door for her.

"Dining and dashing are we?" Eileen had a bar cloth slung over her shoulder and she held two pints of dark beer. "A very classy move, Heathcliff, and a surefire way to impress your date."

"I'll settle up later, Eileen." Heath gave her a quick, apologetic shrug. "We've got to fly."

"You're fine, love."

"Thanks," Flannery called back to her, and walked out of the warmth of the bar.

"Oh God, Heath, it got dark while we were inside. We stayed too long."

"We're fine."

But he was already walk-running to Broadway, where he flagged a cab. They scrambled into the backseat and sat close together, their thighs touching.

"We'll give you the proper address in a minute, Mate," Heath told the cabdriver. "For now, just get us uptown, please." He turned to Flannery and lowered his voice: "That deodorizer he's got hanging from the rearview mirror? It's like a cherry orchard in here. Pretty sure it's where Chekhov got his inspiration."

Here, Heath's blanket-reading knowledge surpassed her Sacred Heart curriculum; Flannery hadn't read *The Cherry Orchard*. "I don't know the book."

"It's a play, actually. Or am I mansplaining again?"

She guessed that Heath was only acting carefree to keep her calm, but they had already indulged too much time on personal delight. Flannery pushed the book at him. "Read the next part out loud." She added a plaintive "Please."

Heath cleared his throat, mumbled "*I shall be telling this with a sigh,*" and began:

The cab headed uptown, and I decided on my destination: The Cathedral of Saint John the Divine.

Heath stopped reading and told the cabdriver: "The Cathedral of Saint John the Divine, please."

"Okay, that's good," Flannery said, reassuring herself. "We know where she's going, or where she is. Go on. Go!"

And so Heath read:

"The Cathedral is close by Columbia," I instructed the driver. "It's on—"

"I know where the Cathedral is!"

The cabdriver was insulted, as if I had mistaken him for a tourist. "I have been there many times, of course."

An ID clipped to the plastic partition separating the front and back seats displayed his photograph and his name, which boasted eleven consonants and seemed impossible to pronounce. I scolded myself for my Midwestern phonetic bigotry: Good God, would I never be able to leave Kansas?

I closed my eyes and thought about the Tallgrass nature preserve, the call of the Eastern Phoebe, and making love to Brandon on a slab of cool rock. I started to cry again. The cab was stopped at a red light. The driver slid open the partition: "Here! Take this." He tossed a bottle of Dasani water onto the backseat and slid the partition shut.

I drank half the bottle at once, lavish coldness sluicing down my throat, and then remembered I should save some.

"Whatever it is that is bothering you, you will triumph over it."

He used a scolding tone, but his words were so caring. Dear Reader, by this point I was beyond all pep talks. I was ready.

"Life is long. There are many second chances, as you will see . . ."

"Okay," I said amiably, mentally insulating myself from his ongoing missive of optimism.

When he pulled up to the Cathedral, I thanked him for his kindness. I slicked my credit card through the reader and added a big tip.

"The time when life seems most distressing is in fact the time of personal growth—"

I slammed the cab door shut and went hobbling along the pavement, and then a second wind sent me sprinting up the steps like a crazed contestant on an ecclesiastical game show—impassioned and righteous—as I followed other visitors into the Cathedral. The guard manning the door warned us that closing time would be in thirty minutes.

The memory of visiting the Cathedral with Brandon in much happier circumstances didn't fill me with grief, because I was on a new path. I looked up, as one does in a cavernous church. Dear Reader, vertigo shook me, but gently and just for a second. I looked down and walked over to rows of wooden chairs. The main worship space closer to the altar was cordoned off; reserved, I supposed, for genuine parishioners who baked casseroles and served punch and sheet cake after baptisms. I sat on a wooden chair. I looked at the altar.

Heath paused. He brought the book to his forehead, lost in thought.

"Keep reading," Flannery pleaded. "Or I can."

"No, I just want to say quickly: Caitlin Sweeney? She's so extreme, isn't she? You, Flannery, can't let yourself get swept up in all this kind of drama when you are at Columbia. You've got to stay focused. If you find a nice group of friends, you'll be fine. To be a writer, you can't put yourself through this kind of college drama or you'll have no energy left to write. And don't make the mistake of piling all your hopes and dreams on one person. This one true soul mate business is total nonsense. It simply doesn't work."

"Okay! Sage advice. Thanks."

"Listen, I'm not just chattering to hear the melodious sound of my own lips flapping. I actually know what I'm talking about; you can trust me on that. Don't be too extreme about things. Enjoy a little moderation . . ."

"Thank you, Heath. Now can you get back to the book, *please*?"

Squinting, he held the book closer to his face.

Flannery rapped on the cab's partition. "Sir? Sir? Is there a light in here?"

"What do you need?" the driver asked.

"No, we're fine." Heath switched his phone to flashlight mode, a handy cone of sunshine in the darkness, and continued reading.

A group of girls sitting in front of me—popular high school types who had gone rogue from their school group—were laughing and taking selfies. I put the water bottle on the chair next to me, took my bottle of Nardil from my pocket, and shook out two pills. I swallowed them with a small sip of water, but they stuck in my throat like little bricks. I drank more water.

I gazed around at the security guards patrolling the aisles and noted tired-looking families with their backpacks and travel guides, and I saw an actual priest or a woman dressed as such. I downed three more pills, but my stomach started to heave. I wrapped my arms around myself and crouched down, waiting for the nausea to pass. Dear Reader, a bit of humor: I popped back up at the exact second the girls in front of me posed for yet another iPad selfie. I looked over their shoulders at the photograph—laughing, beautiful girls with bright wool coats and glossy hair—and saw myself in the very corner, a suicide photo-bomber and ghastly-looking, to boot: The last vestiges of my morning mascara had smeared into sloppy half-moons beneath my eyes.

I took four more Nardil, and Brandon reached over and put his hand on my knee.

Heath stopped reading. "God. Flannery?"

She was silent, staring ahead at the back of the cabdriver's head.

He reached across the seat and squeezed her hand.

"Thanks," Flannery said, her voice high and hoarse. "Keep reading."

"Brandon," I whispered. "You're here."

"Hey, you," he said shyly, smiling down at the Cathedral floor before he tilted his head and looked at me.

"Brandon. I'm so, so sorry for everything."

"Don't worry about any of that." He kissed my temple. "I'm sorry too. Mostly I'm just so happy to see you."

A cellist was warming up, perhaps for a wedding, and the music filled me. Brandon let out a sigh of contentment, and I detected the smell of chilled red roses. There was no more water, so I chewed up my next batch of Nardils, a generous handful, enjoying the chalky crunch, so reminiscent of a childhood candy—Pez, perhaps?

I closed my eyes, and there was the soapy smell of warmth.

I saw a shoe: astronaut silver and cobalt blue and black, with thick, safe, silver treads enclosed in a thin layer of black rubber. I kept my eyes shut, the luxury of sleep, of letting go, after my frenetic journey.

A little boy was sitting in a metal folding chair, one leg tucked under, and one leg swinging back and forth, his silver tread flashing. Oh, I thought, it's *you*. I didn't actually know him. My junior year at Columbia I lived in an apartment with no washer and dryer, and so I frequented the Laundromat. One night I was doing laundry and watching TV, the loneliness of a Sunday night pierced with the anxiety of CNN reporting on Afghanistan—helmeted soldiers, the quake and boom of gunfire in a land that looked entirely yellow and gold, baked by sun—Oh, where was the remote control?

A woman around my age had walked in with her little boy. Her metal trolley, lined with a wrinkled trash bag, was piled high with laundry. She put a twenty in the metal bill-changer and out came a cache of quarters, loud as a drum machine. She put her quarters in a Ziploc bag. The little boy, on a different mission, ran across the Laundromat to the empty table in front of the TV. He flipped his Incredible Hulk backpack onto the table, as if to call dibs, and then went racing to the vending machine, his little face tense and focused as he ran his finger along the glassed-in rows. And then he raised his fist in the air: *Yes!* "Mama!" He hopped from foot to foot. "Mama!"

"Hold *on*, hold on," his mother said, her voice slow and fatigued. She was pulling her laundry—sheets and pillowcases, a Teenage Mutant Ninja Turtles towel, striped shirts, and jeans—from the trolley, but she stopped and walked over to the vending machine.

"Skittles, Mama! Can I get the Skittles? Please!"

"No, baby, those are so hard on your teeth. Get the cheese crackers—you like those too."

"The Skittles aren't hard on my teeth. Skittles make my teeth feel *great*."

He kept campaigning until the mother shut him down with a firm: "*Stop*. You aren't getting the Skittles. Period, end of story."

His lips trembled. He held his arms stiffly to his sides and stared down at the linoleum. The mother sighed; she put quarters into the machine and punched the buttons.

The little boy plunged his hand into the hollow area beyond the metal flap and let out a joyful sound. He hugged his mother's leg. "Thank you, Mama!" He ran back to the table with his Skittles and sat down. He looked up at the Afghanistan footage. "Mama?"

"I'm *coming*," she said. She walked down the row of washers, to the remote control, which was attached to the wall, and changed the channel to Nickelodeon.

"*SpongeBob*! Thank you! Thank you!" The little boy ripped open his Skittles and sorted them in color-coded circles on the table.

The mother stood behind his chair, watching. "You're doing a good job getting all those colors together. Getting them all organized."

He arranged the Skittles into red, green, yellow, orange, and purple blooms, concentric and cheerful.

She put her hand on her little boy's head. "You enjoy your Skittles and your *SpongeBob*."

He looked at the TV, pulled one leg up, and started to carefully eat his Skittles in a pattern, one from each pile. He was going to make them last. His face was radiant; his leg swung back and forth.

The mother went back to her laundry. She checked her phone as she sorted her clothes. When *SpongeBob* broke for a commercial, the little boy turned around to make sure she was there. She crossed her eyes and stuck her tongue out, and the little boy laughed and popped an orange Skittle into his mouth, and for the first time in my life I thought: *I could do that.*

It was pure arrogance, as I knew nothing about how to take care of anyone, let alone an actual child. I'd never had the slightest desire for a cat or a dog, and as a child I'd once stuck my Pet Rock facedown in my underwear drawer because I didn't like the expectant gaze of his googly, glued-on eyes. Yet in the warm, bleach-clean world of the Laundromat, the words repeated in my brain, unbidden, urgent: *I could do that.*

Never mind that my pregnancy scares—one with Brandon, and one a few years back with the nice guy who'd cut my custom blinds at Home Depot (Dear Reader, don't judge)—both had ended with the transcendent peace denied to so many of my friends, and that the sheer randomness of life accounted for the fact that I had gratefully stashed tampons in the pocket of my purse and resumed my regular days, while they had scheduled the grim appointments. Never mind that I deeply pitied the two people I knew with children: my cousin Emily, who had gotten pregnant her freshman year in college, and my friend Brogan, who gave birth to twins the summer after our senior year in high school. Their lives of drudgery and bleak routine allowed no time to gorge on Doritos and daydream, to walk into an afternoon movie, just because. My beautiful cousin nursed her skinny baby— who flailed his arms without warning and looked like a bizarre little dinosaur about to take flight—all day on the couch before changing into her "dress-up" sweatpants for a quick trip to the grocery store. And Brogan's twins had once had the stomach flu and head lice AT THE SAME TIME, and her apartment was a tornado of toys and random plates of halved grapes and crackers, of neon-bright, tyrannical preschool notes—*no gluten, no nuts, no dairy in the snacks, please*— beneath La Leche League magnets on the refrigerator, which also served as an art gallery: every inch crammed with taped-up drawings of crayoned lines and dots and squashed circles. I could only pray that Emily and Brogan wouldn't fall into the trap of searching for self/societal respect via mama-centric bumper stickers that espoused various viewpoints but shared the same *I'm awesome and my beliefs are awesome* aesthetic: MOTHERHOOD: IT'S A PROUD PROFESSION! EVERY MOTHER IS A WORKING MOTHER! A MOTHER'S PLACE IS IN THE HOUSE . . . *AND IN THE SENATE!* Oh. Snap?

Any thought of children I'd ever had was accompanied by the mantra: I will never let myself get trapped. I will never let myself get trapped.

Dear Reader, I was right.

But there at the Laundromat, my old ideas vaporized, and I thought: *I could do that!*

The little boy laughed at *SpongeBob* and chewed his Skittles. The mother finished loading all the clothes into washers and now had a moment to enjoy a game on her phone. Her finger swiped at the screen, but now and again she paused to watch her son watch TV. He was smiling—old SpongeBob was quite a character—and eating in a rainbow pattern, one color at a time.

I could give a child their Skittles victory.

The mother noticed me admiring her son and gave me a shy smile. For me, at that moment, she was not just the Holy Mother, but also the archangel Gabriel heralding miraculous news: *I could make someone happy.*

Back and forth the little black-and-silver shoe went, hitting the rusty leg of the folding chair, the sweetest metronome—*click, click, click*—as the Cathedral closed in around my body. I shut my eyes and New York City pigeons and the Eastern Phoebe of the Tallgrass preserve and music and city lights and traffic and the faces of my students, especially your face, my Dearest Reader, formed a final collage.

But perhaps this is a disappointing close for one so enamored with the splendid drama of Emily Brontë? Perhaps we both assumed my ending would burn incandescent, mirroring the glorious fever dream of *Wuthering Heights*, Cathy in all her Goth glory: *"Heaven did not seem to be my home; and I broke my heart with weeping to come back to earth; and the angels were so angry that they flung me out into the middle of the heath on the top of Wuthering Heights; where I woke sobbing for joy."*

But not so much. Yes, Brandon was next to me, and Neil Young, accompanied by cello and birdsong, sang about a silver spaceship flying up to the haze of the sun, but mostly it was the little shoe swinging from sharp close-up to blurry slow motion, soft, softer still, a memento of love. Brandon put his arms around me, and I rested my head on his shoulder, and as I entered into peace, I allowed the words from Brandon's e-mail to print across my mind in all caps, just as he had typed it years ago.

CAITLIN I JOINED THE MARINES. IF I GET MY FUCKING HEAD BLOWN OFF IT WILL BE ALL YOUR FAULT.

Dear Reader, we were teenagers.

Thirteen

Heath touched her shoulder. "Flannery, I'm so sor—"

The cab was stuck at a red light, but she was already open-ing the cab door and running up Amsterdam Avenue, her backpack thumping with each footfall. What was Heath in the midst of saying? Oh my God, was he offering her . . . no, no, *no.* But the word appeared in her mind in the cursive watercolor font of the grocery store sympathy-card section: *Condolences*? Flannery whispered, *"Please God please God"* to the rhythm of her feet striking the pavement. Amped up on shock and adrenaline and shame—while Miss Sweeney despaired at the Cathedral, her brain chemicals betraying her by sentimental-izing some stupid shoe into a guidepost, a rubber-soled sooth-sayer, Flannery had been kissing at O'Kelleys—she ran so fast that, by the time she reached the Cathedral, she could hardly breathe.

Two police cars and an ambulance were parked out front, and the gossipy buzz of people gathered on the sidewalk—their faces raised, perplexed—terrorized Flannery further as she raced up the steps. A security officer called out: "Miss, the Cathedral is closed for the evening." But Flannery bolted past and raced straight to the two uniformed NYPD officers—a middle-aged female and a younger male—guarding the entrance.

"Please, please, may I go inside just for a moment? This is an actual emergency."

"Miss, no one is allowed inside right now as the security guard *just* told you." The male officer raised his hand, indicating the long flight of steps. "You need to exit the area."

"But you don't understand," Flannery panted. "You just don't . . ."

The female officer said: "You're okay. Take a breath, hon."

"My teacher's inside, just right inside, just sitting inside the Cathedral right now."

The officers nodded slowly, and in unison, as they looked at Flannery.

"Oh, please! Oh my God! You have to let me in! She's in such terrible trouble." It took her a second to realize—the sound echoed in her ears—that she was screaming.

The officer put his hand on Flannery's shoulder. "It's okay," he said. Flannery heard the cautionary tone embedded in his voice and knew she needed to pull herself together. And so she smiled, the evolutionary response of the good girl, though smiling made absolutely zero sense in this particular situation. "I can show you. Because it's all in the book. Just one second, please." Flannery held one finger in the air and offered up another shrill "*Please!*" before she squatted down and rummaged in her backpack for Miss Sweeney's copy of *Wuthering Heights*. "Just a second, please!" Her voice carried the repetitive anguish of a pet store parrot: *"Just a second please! Just a second please!"* She searched through each zippered compartment. "Just . . . !"

But the book was gone.

She looked up at the officer and opened her mouth to speak, but she coughed instead—a harsh, violent bark—and began to sob.

The police officers exchanged glances. The female officer squatted next to Flannery and spoke softly: "If you've misplaced a book, you'll probably find it later. Don't worry." Her voice sounded both compassionate and loaded with purposeful casualness: "Let's you and I take a walk for a moment, shall we?"

"Oh, no. I can't leave." Flannery shuddered. "I have to help her."

"I get it." She stood and then reached down to help Flannery up, a hand gently under her elbow. "I understand what you're saying. But let's just take the quickest little walk."

As the officer led her down the Cathedral steps, Flannery kept looking over her shoulder, all her synapses firing, wondering if she should just turn back, if she should storm the Cathedral. And then—his absence realized suddenly, a new tornado of knives in her gut: *Heath?*

Her brain swirled in midnight carnival mode, jumbled sirens and strobing lights and sharply cold air and concocted comfort: *Heath will find me. I shouldn't have jumped out of the cab so quickly. He's probably so worried. So worried and searching!*

Flannery looked for him, but found only strangers with an air of giddy expectation, as if waiting for a bejeweled unicorn to gallop down the Cathedral steps. *Miss Sweeney, Miss Swee-ney.* She thought back to her AP Biology class, where they had just finished up a unit on the brain. During the class discussion about the length of time a person could survive without oxygen to the brain, her teacher had given the stereotypical example of a chicken with its head cut off still dashing around the farm yard in a herky-jerky manner: The brain stem, in its innocence, could still function for about sixty seconds, unaware that it was sending neural messages into the ether.

The police officer walked Flannery across the street to the Hungarian Pastry Shop. "Let's go inside," she said brightly. "I really, really like this place. It is yum*my*."

Flannery wanted to shout, OH MY GOD STOP ACTING LIKE NOTHING IS WRONG! But what she actually wanted was for the officer to do a *better* job acting like nothing was wrong.

The café was a crowded haven of light and warmth, of petit fours and baklava and bright sugar cookies. Finding a seat seemed impossible, so they stood by the front windows; the police officer carefully positioned herself so that she was the one with the window view. She took a hand-held tape recorder, a pen, and a doll-sized notebook out of her jacket pocket. As she flipped open the notebook, Flannery noticed the CVS sticker on the back: $1.79. It was just a regular little spiral notebook, nothing special or official at all.

The officer clicked on her tape recorder and briskly asked Flannery's name and phone number and age and home address before she resumed her forced naturalness: "Okay, Flannery. Got it. By the way, that's a pretty cool name. I like *F* names. My oldest daughter's name is Felicia."

Flannery wondered how the officer's preference for *F* names was relevant in an emergency situation. "Thanks?"

"So . . . the young woman who was inside the Cathedral? Can you tell me her name?"

Flannery nodded. "Yeah." But she stood silently in the bustling Hungarian Pastry Shop, stress causing her mind to retreat into a known pattern. The officer's dark eyes were lined with a silvery lavender pencil, and she'd fringed her lashes with deep violet mascara. *Her irises are highlighted by the precise purple shades of irises*, Flannery thought. She waited for Miss Sweeney's voice to intrude, but when she didn't offer up a quick corrective to Flannery's Springtime-at-Sephora description, she panicked. What had the officer just said about Miss Sweeney being inside the Cathedral?

"The name of the young woman? Your teacher?"

"Wait." She flipped up her flattened palms as if she and the officer had just switched roles, and now Flannery was in charge and directing traffic to stop, to *hold the hell up!* "Miss Sweeney really was *there*?" Her voice rose, and cracked. "She was in the Cathedral, and you didn't let me see her?"

The officer spoke with the calm cadence of someone discussing lunch options. "We're both just trying to get things figured out here. That's just what we're doing. We're not doing anything but that. So, what's Miss Sweeney's first—"

"Caitlin! Her name is Caitlin Sweeney. Is she okay?"

"I'll let you know everything as soon as I find out."

Dear God, lie to me if you need to, just tell me she's fine.

"How did you know to look for her at the Cathedral? Had you talked to her earlier in the day?"

"It was all in the book. In *Wuthering Heights*."

"Well, o*kay*." The officer nodded a tad too enthusiastically, as if now concerned that Flannery wasn't merely despondent but mentally ill.

"So you say the book—*Wuthering Heights*—was helping you locate your teacher?"

"It's pretty hard to explain. I wish I had the book." Flannery heard the caught edge of tears hovering in her voice.

The officer squinted, tilted her head, and murmured, "*Mmm hmm.*" Perhaps she was taking a moment to sort it out, even to help Flannery develop a logical narrative. "So, you were—"

"And Heath has been helping me too. But now we've gotten separated. Not like, you know, romantically." Flannery shrugged. "Well, sort of."

The officer put her pen to her doll's notebook. "Who's Heath?"

"A friend."

The officer was staring at Flannery. "What's his last name?"

"Heath?" Flannery blinked repeatedly and buckled her mouth back and forth, all the odd facial tricks and tics to ward off tears. She would not deny it; she would not deny him. "His last name is 'Earnshaw.'"

The officer sighed. "You've been spending the day with Heath Earnshaw? With Heathcliff Earnshaw?" She clenched her mouth on one side and tapped her pen on her notebook, exasperated, looking like she wanted to scold Flannery for being such a smartass, but how could she be anything but kind to the distraught girl in front of her? "The dreamy bad boy from *Wuthering Heights* is the one who is helping you look for your teacher?"

Flannery nodded, imagining Heath taking the Cathedral

stairs two at a time, searching for her. Would he be shouting out her name—her real name this time—and holding out Miss Sweeney's copy of *Wuthering Heights*?

"Yes, Heathcliff *has* been helping me. You know, just in the way that characters from books help you."

It was a bit of a Judas kiss, but now Flannery was desperate to get back to the Cathedral, to see if Heath had come back for her.

"You know how it is." Flannery smiled at the officer, as if confiding in a fellow *Wuthering Heights* fanatic, and maybe she was. "Certain characters seem to reach out from the page to offer you their hand and show you how they've triumphed over their own sorrows and difficulties."

It was a phrase both so incongruent with Heathcliff's experience in *Wuthering Heights,* and so ripe with clichéd crap that she listened for the scorching red-pen voice of Miss Sweeney, but Flannery's mind was quiet.

The officer answered her cell phone ("*Sorry,*" she mouthed to Flannery and gave her a companionable eye-roll) and spoke softly: "Okay. Alright . . . well. *Uh-huh.* Hang on, will you?" She muted her phone and asked Flannery if she had transportation to get home.

"I'm actually meeting my parents in thirty minutes." The Eloise books from her childhood gave her the knowledge to add "At the Plaza Hotel."

"Make your parents buy you the lobster mac 'n cheese." She handed Flannery a business card embossed with a police badge. "I'll be in touch." But she stalled a bit: "You feeling okay now?"

Along with her iris eyes, she wore festive carmine-red

lipstick, and Flannery envisioned her applying it carefully in the rearview mirror of her squad car, blotting it with a tissue, a Kleenex kiss.

"I'm fine, thanks! Thanks for your help." Flannery walked over to the pastry case and drummed her fingers on her chin as if confounded by an excruciating cookie choice—humble chocolate chip or lime basil shortbread? The officer put her phone to her ear, took one last forlorn glance at Flannery— who avoided her gaze by staring directly into the pastry case, as if hypnotized by the lure of sugar and wheat and her wolfish appetite—and walked out the door.

Finally. Flannery waited at the counter and counted to twenty before she went outside, hoping to put some space between herself and the officer. The ambulance was just pulling away from the Cathedral, the flashing lights a new and terrible starlight, aggressive and insistent. The cold air stung her eyes and open mouth as she watched the ambulance, as her thoughts flurried in a circular pattern of terror and good wishes. *Hurry!! Oh God, please! Get her to the hospital as fast as you can! Save her! You can do it! Hurry!*

She needed to tell Heath what was happening, and so Flannery automatically tore through her backpack looking for her phone. When she found it—*Yes! She wasn't losing everything! She wasn't going completely crazy!*—it took her a second, her index finger hovering over the screen, to remember that of course she didn't have Heath's number.

And then the flashing lights of the ambulance went dark at the intersection. Flannery's entire being buzzed, as if she were being electrocuted with dread: silver Christmas tinsel unspooling in her veins, lightning strikes zigzagging through her limbs. Because the problem with knowing a novel so dearly that passages came to you unbidden—normally a whimsical pleasure, a reward for your close reading—presented itself to Flannery as she watched the quiet ambulance. The words of a devastated Heathcliff were in her heart as Flannery stared at the illuminated rear window and saw the profile of a paramedic sitting all too still: "*'Did she die like a saint? Come, give me a true history of the event. How did—?' He endeavored to pronounce the name, but could not manage it; and compressing his mouth he held a silent combat with his inward agony.*"

Dry-mouthed and breathing harshly, yet giving herself an inner pep talk, Flannery walked across the street to the Cathedral: *Miss Sweeney could be fine. She might be fine. She's probably fine. She's just sleeping, and they didn't want to disturb her with the lights and sirens and such!*

God, where was Heath? As she climbed the Cathedral steps, Flannery's mind bloomed with an OCD daisy chain of prayer: *Please bring her back to me; please bring him back to me; please bring her back to me; please bring him back to me.* She swanned her neck back as far as it would go and stared up at the Cathedral of Saint John the Divine. Though no one was asking her to choose, she thought to strike a nonsense deal with the devil or the literary gods or Jesus or any icon or entity able to shimmy through the ambulance doors and save Miss Sweeney: *I will give up Heath.*

Flannery would give him up in return for Miss Sweeney; she would. *Please bring her back to me; please bring her back to me.* Flannery envisioned the rest of the school year at Sacred Heart: Miss Sweeney would continue to be her teacher, and Flannery would continue to endure the mockery of the popular girls—a problem which now seemed so minimal that she hardly recognized the old, angsty Flannery, who had taken the minutia of the day to heart. Oh, how Flannery longed to be sitting in AP Lit class studying the roses and the crosses in the crown molding and looking forward to zipping out at lunch for a caramel Frappuccino. How she wanted to glance out the window and see Miss Sweeney running late, rushing though the parking lot with her hair wet at the ends and tapping on lip gloss with her finger and then smashing her lips together purposefully: *Okay, day. Let's do this thing.* Of course Flannery was sorry to lose Heath; she believed she would never know the sublime communion of dance floor kissing again. Yet to save Miss Sweeney? *See ya.*

But as she sat on a cold Cathedral step and looked up at the dark sky, romantic sorrow came to her in the quotidian old way of shock chased by heartache. *What? What? I will never see him again in this lifetime? He'll never come back to me?* But I still have his jacket, Flannery thought, her absolute correctness about this fact the briefest tactile reassurance. She touched the jagged metal teeth of the zipper finger and the silky, well-worn lining of the inner cuffs. *Heath.* It seemed a given that Flannery would never meet anyone like him again.

And she was certain that she wouldn't meet anyone like Miss Sweeney again. Flannery imagined Miss Sweeney wide awake and bantering with the attentive paramedic; Flannery pictured him as good-looking and affable and totally charmed by Miss Sweeney's quick wit. *Caitlin Sweeney,* he would think, you are just . . . *wow.* Their burgeoning ambulatory romance would be a done deal before they reached the hospital.

The doctors would adjust Miss Sweeney's medicine; her

equilibrium would return, and with it the realization that *of course* she hadn't been Brandon's murderer—God, the weight of that for Miss Sweeney!—and that Brandon was not ghosting around Manhattan but definitively dead and gone, God rest his soul. She would stop feeling so terrorized by nostalgia and regret, and remember that romantic mayhem was an essential component of a well-lived life, that is, a life touched by *Wuthering Heights.*

Flannery envisioned Miss Sweeney sitting in the Hungarian Pastry Shop with the paramedic, coffee cups and shared sweets on the table between them. Miss Sweeney would be alternating between laughing with her new love and frowning at the real-estate section of the *Times*. But who could put a price on the life she and her handsome paramedic would enjoy in the City of Dreams? *Oh, Miss Sweeney, say hello to Manhattan happiness, your sequel will be superior to the original.*

But now the night was cold, the night was dark, and Heath was nowhere to be found.

Flannery stood and walked down the Cathedral steps. Dizzy, she bent from her waist, her backpack thunking her in the head as she kept imagining the dreamscape coffee shop scenario; she would concentrate on that because the potential reality was too dire to contemplate. Besides, anything could still happen! Heath might reappear, prayed for or not, and the day could assume its bizarre trajectory with the implicit promise of any adventure story: twists and turns, why, of course, but everything will turn out just fine in the end!

From the dark street, the Hungarian Pastry Shop looked swarming and luminous as a Christmas Day migraine. Flannery wasn't sure where to go, so she went back inside. Should she buy a brownie? An éclair? Did anything matter? She felt grateful for the proximity of other bodies, for the boisterous girls waiting in line behind her, who reeked of lavender body spray and were passionately debating song lyrics: "No, it's not *'All the other girls are stars, you are the Northern Lights'*; it's *'I saw you standing at the bar, you looked hot in nasty tights.'*"

Flannery ordered water and a petit four, stumbling over the *petit*; she took Spanish not French—was the second *t* silent, and how, she wondered, could silent consonants matter if Miss Sweeney was no longer in the world. *But she is,* she told herself brightly, *I know she is.* She stared at the top, pearlized layer of the petit four and deciphered an upper-case *H* swirled into a dark chocolate fleur-de-lis. *Heath.* Flannery rolled her tongue around in her mouth and licked her lips, hoping she could still taste him.

"Next!" The woman working the register waved Flannery away and beckoned the laughing girls to zip it and order, all in one swift back-and-forth motion, her multi-ringed fingers and silver nail polish glittering.

Flannery looked around for somewhere to sit. The rows of wooden tables were packed together so tightly and the air felt so overheated and humid that she wished for some airy, sprawling mall restaurant; she wanted to jettison the quaint. Her brain kept sending out aftershocks. *Miss Sweeney. Miss Sweeney. Miss Sweeney.* The voice in her head, ready to call Flannery out for her desire to "jettison the quaint," remained silent.

But she didn't have to wallflower around hoping someone would offer her a chair, because right away two girls waved at her with an openhearted friendliness so foreign to her girl-world experience that it startled Flannery more than if they had flipped her off.

"Here! Come sit with us! We have an extra chair. Go for it. It's always so crowded in here, right?"

Flannery nodded. She guessed that it was. "Oh, thanks."

She slid the backpack off her shoulder and took a seat. She drank and drank; she drained the glass, and still her mouth felt dry.

Please bring her back to me.

The girls smiled at Flannery as if her thirst was unexceptional. One had on a North Face jacket and jeans, her long, sand-blonde hair secured into a hasty ponytail, low and loose. But the girl sitting next to her wore a celery-green vintage cocktail dress, and her thick, dark hair was coiled into a chignon. Dark lipstick and a generous and impeccable application of cat eyeliner furthered her 1940s starlet look, and the brown mink stole hanging over the back of her chair sent it right over the top.

She noticed Flannery looking and ran her hand over the fur. "It's fake! Don't call PETA!"

Her friend laughed. "She's already been hassled once today. Somebody in a passing car SCREECHED: *Only stupid animals wear fur!*"

"Which would have been embarrassing enough on its own." She made eye contact with Flannery, including her in the conversation. "But I misheard it. I thought they said, *Only stupid animals wear fear,* so I was like, *well, Megan and I need to walk in a more confident manner because we are apparently getting heckled for our* strides, *of all things.* I'm Jolene, by the way, and this is Megan." She touched her friend's arm.

Flannery nodded and swallowed. It was challenging to hold back tears with Miss Sweeney in an ambulance, Heath missing, and two random girls being so nice to her.

She swallowed again. "I'm Flannery."

The boy at the next table, who had looked to be asleep, jerked upright. His hair was buzzed, and he wore geek-chic glasses, but right now his most pronounced feature was an intense grimace. "*Flannery*? Oh my God, how awful. I feel your pain. I feel your pain on a cellular level." He folded his arms on the table and rested his head.

Megan shook her head. "Don't listen to him!"

Flannery opened her mouth to say something, but her throat felt so tight and swollen from this constant vigilance to hold back her tears that she offered up a tight, trembling smile instead.

Jolene nodded and addressed the boy: "You shouldn't have stayed up all night watching *Dr. Who*. That's why you're so crabby. Sterling told me when he woke up this morning you were *still* watching in some kind of trance." She turned back to Flannery. "I *love* your name."

Megan nodded. "Me too. I never knew a single Flannery until I came to Columbia and you're the *third* one I've met."

Three Flannerys?

She felt her freak factor plummet, the smallest spike of happiness in her heart, but God, how could that be? "Oh, I don't actually go here," she said quietly. "I'll start in the fall. But, you know, not yet." Her voice pitched, then thickened: "I just came for the day."

Jolene nodded. "I was kind of wondering, because of your skirt! I recognize the plaid." She lowered her voice: "Connecticut Catholic girls. We are legion."

Flannery smoothed her skirt, feeling both exposed and accepted.

Megan shuddered. "Are you going to do a secret handshake next?"

She smiled broadly at Jolene and Flannery. "You are some creepy ladies."

"I know! Flannery, you will be so happy to never wear pleats or plaid again. I burned all my skirts from Saint Theresa's, but unfortunately the memories are burned in my brain, so it was merely freaking symbolic. Still, it helped to see all that plaid go up in flames."

"Okay," Flannery squeaked. "Cool." But if she'd never gone to Sacred Heart, she would never have worn this skirt; and she would also never have met Miss Sweeney. To burn it was unthinkable.

"She wrote an essay about the epic skirt bonfire," Megan stage-whispered to Flannery. "It was all *kinds* of awesome."

Jolene shrugged modestly. "It was just okay. But I have a really good professor who helped me revise it."

"You're so lucky," Megan said. "I can't believe I'm stuck with David Johnston and you get Jayne Means."

Flannery sucked in her breath when she heard the name of the professor whom Miss Sweeney had written about so lovingly, the professor she had gone to see this very morning.

"Jayne gave the best lecture about Emily Dickinson last week, and this week we studied Emily Brontë—who arranges a syllabus like that, by first name? God, she's brilliant. Anyway, Jayne claims that *Wuthering Heights* is a feminist book, because of Catherine's HE is ME monologue: You know, how we, men and women, are all, at heart, genderless— gender free?—because we are equally crazy, loving, brutal, wild-hearted, whatever. And Heathcliff? Jayne puts him in historical perspective: He's not just the cartoon harsh guy, but someone trapped in his particular circumstance, and who, in another place and time, might have been completely different."

Flannery had just taken a bite of her petit four; the bright icing shattered in her mouth like stained glass.

From inside her backpack her cell phone buzzed. Flannery took it out and saw a 212 area code. She took the police officer's card out of her jacket pocket. The numbers matched.

Not yet, she thought. She pushed the *decline call* button on her phone. *I do not have to answer. No one can make me answer.* Because if Flannery simply declined to hear any bad news, Miss Sweeney could stay alive and whole and vibrant—even if it meant she was currently hallucinating her dead boyfriend and wandering the streets of NYC. Because to be alive, Flannery thought, to keep the story going, that was the thing . . .

Megan pulled her ponytail around and stroked it like a fluffy blonde kitten snuggling on her clavicle. "God, *Wuthering Heights.* Quite the fever dream."

Jolene nodded. "It's magic."

Megan sighed. "Oh, but of course I had to get David Johnston. He wears wide-wale corduroy trousers that actually make an audible—I swear—*whistling* sound when he walks. He also uses air quotes ironically."

Jolene sympathized: "Ugh."

"It's even more annoying than using air quotes literally." Megan looked at both Jolene *and* Flannery, including her in their freshman musings: "Would there be such a thing as figurative air quotes?"

Flannery's phone buzzed again. Oh God, how she wanted to answer it!

But she envisioned the paramedic giving Miss Sweeney mouth-to-mouth resuscitation, each buzz from Flannery's phone a breath forced into Miss Sweeney's lungs. She couldn't risk it; she had to keep Miss Sweeney alive.

The boy slumped at the table raised his head again. "Figurative Air Quotes! Best. Band. Name. Ever. Called it!" As if struck by narcolepsy, he put his head right back down.

Megan and Jolene laughed, and even Flannery managed a laugh, though her insides felt so shredded that she didn't understand how her body had produced a carefree sound.

Encouraged by the girls' mirth, the boy jolted back up. He looked right at Flannery. "I have a question. I shall be asking this with a sigh, Flannery."

Flannery nodded gamely. "Okay."

"Is your middle name O'Connor?"

Flannery always wrote "Olivia" in the middle name blank on her school forms, but now in the overly bright Hungarian Pastry Shop, with a police officer calling to tell her something joyful or horrible, did her embarrassing literary name even matter? Still, Flannery answered him a bit ruefully: "It is. My name is Flannery O'Connor Fields."

"That. Is. Tragic. I fiercely hate your parents on your behalf. I offer you my boundless empathy. Boundless."

Jolene and Megan protested, saying that it was an incredible honor to be named after Flannery O'Connor.

Flannery shook her head. "It's awful. It's just so . . . fake."

He clapped his hands and shouted *YES.* A sensitive woman working on her laptop at the next table took a slug of coffee and made a great show of putting in her earbuds.

The boy lowered his voice. "Fake Flannery O'Connor and the Figurative Air Quotes! *That* is the best band name ever. Called it. Done. *Finis.* We shall not know the likes of it again."

The buzz of the phone, the buzz of the phone; the officer trying and trying. Could a person choose not to be the recipient of bad news? Could a body simply live in flux?

"And just so you know, Flannery?" The boy tapped the table with his index finger as if frantic to get her fullest attention. "I think parents who give their children literary names should be sent to the guillotine. It's like wearing a name tag that says, 'HELLO, MY NAME IS REFERENTIAL,' and my parents are pretentious and have cursed me with a name I will never be able to live up to. And God forbid I try to be a writer myself." He reached across the table and held out his hand. "Flannery O'Connor Fields, allow me to introduce myself. I am Langston Hughes Hoffman."

"Really?" Flannery shook his hand.

Megan smiled. "He really is."

"You *do* feel my pain."

"Please, you are named after great writers! I mean, my name, 'Megan'? 'Megan' is *tragic*."

"Oh my God," Jolene said. "Is anyone here really going to compete with me in the worst name contest? Spoiler: You will not win."

Jolene drummed the table. "The winner is . . . Jolene Herrara Johnson. How many Puerto Ricans have the name *Jolene*? No need to get out pencil and paper for this equation, though, put away your calculators and abandon your abacus, because the number is one—"

"Abandon your *abacus*," Langston Hughes Hoffman marveled. "Second best band name ever."

Flannery thought of the colorful wooden beads on her old abacus, the possibility of joy: the officer's voice on the phone sounding pleasant, chipper, even! *Hon? Your teacher is recovering at the hospital. She'll be going home tomorrow. Hope you're having a fun night at the Plaza. Don't forget the lobster mac 'n cheese!*

And so Flannery half-listened to the table conversation while she continued to puzzle out a new narrative for Miss Sweeney...

"My mom falls in love with a dude from Mississippi—my dad—and agrees to name her first child Jolene, because his mother, my grandmother, is vice president of the Dolly Parton fan club? Yes, I'm named after her famous song, and song names are the worst."

Flannery smiled at Jolene, and wondered if the officer was calling to say it was a different woman in the Cathedral, that it wasn't Caitlin Sweeney at all. It was a complete stranger, and furthermore, the stranger had survived.

Langston Hughes Hoffman weighed in: "Author names are worse than song names. But the new trend of food names might be even worse. In years to come the students sitting here will be named Apple, Fig, and Pluot."

Perhaps a thrilling missive from Miss Sweeney awaited her, perhaps clicking open her Gmail account would be nirvana. *F: I forgot to get a substitute when I went to the ophthalmologist this morning and Sacred Heart called out a search party. Embarrassing. On the attendance sheet it said you were absent after first hour. Everything okay? Miss S.*

Megan gave Langston a hearty, ironic thumbs-up. "Dibs on Pluot. Look for it on my baby announcement in twenty years. No, really, I like the synthesis of the plum and the apricot: Pluot." She tried out an alternate pronunciation: "Plu*ot*."

Flannery's phone buzzed again, a repetitive dirge in her hand. Even sitting with such welcoming and fun people she felt completely walled off. She now not only knew where Heathcliff had gone when he'd dropped out of the narrative of *Wuthering Heights,* she knew why he'd left. It wasn't just that he'd eavesdropped on Cathy's prudent and cruel plans to marry the rich neighbor; Heathcliff had gone away because he couldn't bear to lose the optimistic (if delusional) hope that Cathy wouldn't marry Edgar Linton after all. Living away, he could escape the certainty of their nuptials. Heathcliff could daydream Cathy's last-minute change of heart; his mind's eye could send her running out of the parsonage in her lace dress, her ribbon-bound wedding bouquet of wildflowers loosening as she ran, heather and bluebells falling on the moors.

Heathcliff wanted to linger in the ellipses of fading possibility; to believe that Cathy was waiting for him in Wuthering Heights in her lace dress, her candlelit face at the window, forever looking out for him in the darkness . . .

Megan yawned. "We should probably take off soon. Flannery, are you staying around here?"

"Today was kind of a last-minute trip. I . . . wasn't able to get a hotel room." She thought back to the Broadway Hotel and Hostel where she'd stood at the reception desk with Heath, and where Miss Sweeney had reminisced in the haze of her

Nardil withdrawal, toenail clippings in the nightstand and the Gideon's Bible in her hand. Flannery thought about the Gospel of the Pentecost, not the verse about sorcery and orgies that had sent the young Caitlin Sweeney and Brandon Marzetti-Corcoran into hysterics, but the haunting lament of Christ: "I have much more to tell you, but you cannot bear it now."

Flannery switched off her phone.

Jolene looked at Megan, who telegraphed her agreement with a nod.

"You can come back to the dorm and stay with us."

Megan smiled at Flannery. "My cousin was just visiting, and so we already have an air mattress in the room. It leaves a good six inches of floor space for us all to move around, but you could take a look at Carman, and see how you like dorm life."

"No one *likes* dorm life," Langston said. He tilted his head at Megan and Jolene. "But these two are pretty fun."

"Okay," Flannery squeaked out. "That's so awesome of you guys. I could be a serial killer. It's really so nice of you to share your room with me."

Langston laughed. "Truthfully? You're not really giving off a serial killer vibe."

When Flannery put her phone into her backpack, she saw Heath's purchase from Westsider Books: *The Complete Stories of Flannery O'Connor*. She took it out and stared at the cover, her brain absorbing the incongruence of seeing the word *O'Connor* crossed out and *Fields* written in: *The Complete Stories of Flannery Fields*.

Heath. Heath with his borrowed marker at the bookshop.

Flannery clutched the story collection to her heart. She would continue looking for him when she moved to the city, especially on winter days when she wore his jacket. And whenever she wondered if Heath, the most spectacular of the incorruptibles, had been a mere delusion, the fever dream of a stressed-out *Wuthering Heights* fangirl, Flannery consoled herself with the indelible proof—paper and leather—of their day together.

She tucked the book back into her backpack, walked out of the Hungarian Pastry Shop, and set off for Carman Hall with her new friends. But the vibration of her cell phone was a pulse of lonely anxiety Flannery would carry with her the rest of her life, the happy ending she couldn't quite pull off: *Why did I take the journey if I couldn't save her?*

Flannery's sorrow was a loosening knot; she felt like she might completely come undone, but she was also buoyed by walking along with Jolene and Megan to her left and Langston to her right, and by those who trailed behind: Brandon Marzetti-Corcoran and Caitlin Sweeney, and the other Flannery O'Connor and the other Langston Hughes, and Miss Emily Brontë, and all the other souls who had given of themselves, who had shown their love in person, or on the page.

Flannery looked across at the Cathedral of Saint John the Divine, towering like a holy dinosaur standing sentry, hunkering protectively over Flannery and her friends as they walked back to the dorm.

And then came a red-inked missive, either conjured by her own longing or by the supernatural power of love that allows the vanished to live on in our hearts and souls. *Flannery: Did you really look up and see an extinct animal given to contorting his oversized body on your behalf? Were my lessons about mean-ing, sense, and clarity all in vain?*

And so Flannery tried it a new way.

In the shadow of the great Cathedral, Flannery walked home with her people.

Acknowledgments

Heartfelt thanks to Lisa Bankoff for her faith in *Dear Reader*, and for all her creativity and dedication.

It is a writer's dream to have Amy Einhorn, Caroline Bleeke, and Sarah Dotts Barley edit their book. I am deeply grateful to each of you.

Thank you to my fantastic writing group—Judy Bauer, Laura Moriarty, and Lucia Orth—for their true camaraderie and careful reading. My sister Jane was an early and encouraging reader of *Dear Reader*, too.

For kindness and inspiration, my thanks to Sara Eckel, Andrea Hoag, Stefanie Olson, and Sharon Zehr.

And a world of thanks to Laura Kirk—with whom I shared a few NYC apartments, and dreams, back in the day—for all the years of friendship.

Thank you to my parents, Pat and Mike O'Connell, storytellers extraordinaire, and to my oldest friends, my brother, Patrick, and my sister, Jane.

Thank you to my openhearted children, Juliana, Zach, and Veronica. You've given me the world.

And lastly, thank you to my husband, Steve Hill, who gave me my own Manhattan love story.